HOUSE SHUDDERS

AN ANTHOLOGY OF HAUNTED HOUSE STORIES

EDITED BY
Martin H. Greenberg
&
Charles G. Waugh

DAW BOOKS, INC.
DONALD A. WOLLHEIM, PUBLISHER

1633 Broadway, New York, NY 10019

DAW Book Collectors No. 721.

First Printing, September, 1987

1 2 3 4 5 6 7 8 9

PRINTED IN THE U.S.A.

BEWARE OF THE HAUNTS!

As the sun goes down and the light grows dim, the creatures of night begin to rise, stalking the darkness to seek out new victims for horror's dread realm. So light a candle to guide you through winding halls and down creaky stairs into the secret depths of eerily evil dwellings, such masterful creations as:

Bram Stoker's "The Judge's House"—He came in search of a quiet place to study, and found he'd signed an unbreakable lease for a true haven of horror. . . .

David H. Keller's "The Thing in the Cellar"—From the time he could first crawl, Tommy had fled as far from his parents' cellar as he could go. But surely now he was old enough to put childish fears aside . . . or was he?

Charles L. Grant's "The Children, They Laugh So Sweetly"—A new start, a new house, a new job, that was all he needed . . . until the ghosts of his own past found their way home to his new address!

HOUSE
SHUDDERS

ACKNOWLEDGMENTS

Contents

INTRODUCTION

"Horror and the Hearth of Darkness"

The Haunting became one of my favorite movies when, out of fear, my date jumped onto my lap. This sudden emotional arousal is an important reason for the popularity of horror stories. There's not much physiological diffence among states of arousal, so interpreting a feeling as "fear," "joy," or "anger" depends on our assessment of what we think we should be feeling. When a person sees a horror picture alone, he attributes arousal to the film, and decides he is frightened. With a pleasant companion, however, a person might decide the feelings result from attraction, and act accordingly. Indeed, in many ways, manipulating feeling labels is easier than changing intensity levels. Social scientists call such mislabeling the Ovid-Horowitz phenomenon. (Ovid was a Roman poet who advised young men to keep fast chariots outside the Colosseum when taking dates to gladiatorial events and Horowitz was a nineteenth-century social scientist who suggested the principle.)

Does this mean scary movies are a better buy? No. Horror books don't always have as strong an immediate impact as movies, but they are cheaper and can be read out loud, told around campfires, or mailed off with eight-by-ten glossies and can easily haunt your dreams.

Besides, scaring ourselves is as much fun as allowing someone else to scare us. Adaptation Level theory suggests we all seek optimum levels of stimulation. Too much, and we cut down—taking vacations or less demanding jobs. Too little, and we seek increases—with new hobbies or adventurous stories. James Tiptree's famous Ph.D. dissertation illustrates this point. New objects were investigated by animals familiar with their environments, but avoided by those in unfamiliar situations. Presumably, the former wanted more excitement. The latter wanted less. Optimum stimulation levels for individuals vary widely, of course, as introverts and extraverts demonstrate. But, at times, all of us need more excitement than we receive.

Horror stories even offer therapy for personal upsets, assuming awful things haven't happened to us directly.

In uneasy times, such stories may provide a rationale for our feelings. For example, negative rumors flourish not in earthquake epicenters, but in surrounding areas. Those experiencing terrible damage have reason for their fears. Those escaping serious damage feel frightened and wonder if their discomfort is legitimate. To them, rumors justify terror by suggesting potentially worse things waiting. Thus upset remains, but upset over upset is diminished. Horror stories may serve a similar function.

Horror stories may also reduce anxiety by comparison. For example, in this book terrifying, seemingly unstoppable creatures slobber and squish in the night. After reading about protagonists encountering them, our problems may seem smaller. We begin to realize things are not so bad that they couldn't be worse. Personal stress declines.

Do we guarantee horror stories as a universal panacea? Obviously not. Yet we think the seventeen tales in this book worth several nights' time. They may do some good. They probably won't harm. And reading them is certainly better than other leisure activities people seem determined to engage in these days.

As our title, *House Shudders,* indicates, this book is specifically devoted to tales of domestic terror—a sort of hearth of darkness.

Usually a ghost is thought responsible for the terror—though sometimes other agents are discovered. Thousands of stories and hundreds of movies fit this category. Just think of some of the great ones: *The Turn of the Screw,* novel by Henry James (1898), filmed in 1961 (*The Innocents*) and 1974; *The Ghost Breaker,* play by Paul Dickey and Charles W. Goddard, filmed in 1915, 1922, 1940 (*The Ghost Breakers*), and 1953 (as *Scared Stiff*); *Uneasy Freehold* (aka: *The Uninvited*), novel by

Dorothy Macardle (1941), filmed in 1944 *(The Uninvited);*
The Haunting of Hill House, novel by Shirley Jackson
(1959), filmed in 1963 (*The Haunting*); and *Hell House,*
novel by Richard Matheson (1971), filmed in 1973 (*The*
Legend of Hell House.)

Why is *domestic* terror so popular? There is unity of
setting to provide dramatic strength and ease of staging,
if a play is involved. Familiar settings are also easier to
write about, tend to interest big audiences, and maintain
suspension of disbelief when fantastic elements appear.
For who of us has not been frightened by a creak in the
house, late at night, when home alone? And homes do
seem the most logical location for ghosts, since most
people live and die in them.

Yet, despite the popularity and number of these tales,
just four variations exist. The *bogus story* reveals the
terror to be something natural, such as a madman or
criminal. (Since our volume collects fantastic horror, this
type has been excluded.) The *traditional story* depicts the
terror as something fantastic (not currently known to
exist) and supernatural (unexplainable by natural laws).
Ghosts are most common, but other beings would include werewolves, vampires, zombies, and so forth. The
Janus story, usually emphasizing a psychological approach,
leaves the nature of the terror unresolved. In *The Turn*
of the Screw, for example, are there really ghosts, or
is the governess just overly imaginative? Is the explanation natural or fantastic? We may choose an interpreta-
tion, but we never really know, for the author does not
say. Finally, the *science fictional story* depicts the terror
as something fantastic (not currently known to exist), but
natural (explainable, or believed to be explainable, by
natural laws). Obvious examples are aliens, robots, mu-
tants, death rays, and new poisons. But it is also possible
to argue, as Bulwer-Lytton does, that if ghosts exist and
the same could be said for other traditional monsters),
they must be explainable by natural laws. While a Sumerian
would have thought a holographic image supernatural,
we, who have more knowledge, know it is not.

Examples of Janus, traditional, and science fictional
stories are all included in this anthology, and trying to
label stories might be an interesting game. (Careful of
Lovecraft's story though, an understanding of his Cthulhu

Mythos is needed to get it right.) In choosing stories, our primary concern (given scariness), however, has been memorability. Images of yellow wallpaper, rose-covered vines, Bel Aire plumbers, and jumping cats all haunt our minds, and if you read on, they'll soon do the same to you.

EDWARD BULWER-LYTTON

The House and the Brain

A friend of mine, who is a man of letters and a philosopher, said to me one day, as if between jest and earnest, "Fancy! since we last met, I have discovered a haunted house in the midst of London."

"Really haunted?—and by what? ghosts?"

"Well, I can't answer that question: all I know is this—six weeks ago my wife and I were in search of a furnished apartment. Passing a quiet street, we saw on the window of one of the houses a bill, 'Apartments Furnished.' The situation suited us; we entered the house—liked the rooms—engaged them by the week—and left them the third day. No power on earth could have reconciled my wife to stay longer; and I don't wonder at it."

"What did you see?"

"Excuse me—I have no desire to be ridiculed as a superstitious dreamer—nor, on the other hand, could I ask you to accept on my affirmation what you would hold to be incredible without the evidence of your own senses. Let me only say this, it was not so much what we saw or heard (in which you might fairly suppose that we were the dupes of our own excited fancy, or the victims of imposture in others) that drove us away, as it was an undefinable terror which seized both of us whenever we passed by the door of a certain unfurnished room, in which we neither saw nor heard anything. And the strangest marvel of all was, that for once in my life I agreed with my wife, silly woman though she be—and allowed, after the third night, that it was impossible to stay a fourth in that house. Accordingly, on the fourth morning

13

I summoned the woman who kept the house and attended on us, and told her that the rooms did not quite suit us, and we would not stay out our week. She said, dryly, 'I know why: you have stayed longer than any other lodger. Few ever stayed a second night; none before you a third. But I take it they have been very kind to you.'

" 'They—who?' I asked, affecting to smile.

" 'Why, they who haunt the house, whoever they are. I don't mind them; I remember them many years ago, when I lived in this house, not as a servant; but I know they will be the death of me some day. I don't care—I'm old, and must die soon anyhow; and then I shall be with them, and in this house still.' The woman spoke with so dreary a calmness, that really it was a sort of awe that prevented my conversing with her further. I paid for my week, and too happy were my wife and I to get off so cheaply."

"You excite my curiosity," said I; "nothing I should like better than to sleep in a haunted house. Pray give me the address of the one which you left so ignominiously."

My friend gave me the address; and when we parted, I walked straight toward the house thus indicated.

It is situated on the north side of Oxford Street (in a dull but respectable thoroughfare). I found the house shut up—no bill at the window, and no response to my knock. As I was turning away, a beer-boy, collecting pewter pots at the neighboring areas, said to me, "Do you want anyone at that house, sir?"

"Yes, I heard it was to be let."

"Let!—why, the woman who kept it is dead—has been dead these three weeks, and no one can be found to stay there, though Mr. J—— offered ever so much. He offered Mother, who chars for him, £1 a week just to open and shut the windows, and she would not."

"Would not!—and why "

"The house is haunted: and the old woman who kept it was found dead in her bed, with her eyes wide open. They say the devil strangled her."

"Pooh!—you speak of Mr. J——. Is he the owner of the house?"

"Yes."

"Where does he live?"

"In G—— Street. No. —."

"What is he—in any business?"

"No, sir—nothing particular; a single gentleman."

I gave the pot-boy the gratuity earned by his liberal information, and proceeded to Mr. J——, in G—— Street, which was close by the street that boasted the haunted house. I was lucky enough to find Mr. J—— at home, an elderly man, with intelligent countenance and prepossessing manners.

I communicated my name and my business frankly. I said I heard the house was considered to be haunted—that I had a strong desire to examine a house with so equivocal a reputation—that I should be greatly obliged if he would allow me to hire it, though only for a night. I was willing to pay for that privilege whether he might be inclined to ask. "Sir," said Mr. J——, with great courtesy, "the house is at your service, for as short or as long a time as you please. Rent is out of the question—the obligation will be on my side should you be able to discover the cause of the strange phenomena which at present deprive it of all value. I cannot let it, for I cannot even get a servant to keep it in order to answer the door. Unluckily the house is haunted, if I may use that expression, not only by night, but by day; though at night the disturbances are of a more unpleasant and sometimes of a more alarming character. The poor old woman who died in it three weeks ago was a pauper whom I took out of a workhouse, for in her childhood she had been known to some of my family, and had once been in such good circumstances that she had rented that house of my uncle. She was a woman of superior education and strong mind, and was the only person I could ever induce to remain in the house. Indeed, since her death, which was sudden, and the coroner's inquest, which gave it a notoriety in the neighborhood, I have so despaired of finding any person to take charge of the house, much more a tenant, that I would willingly let it rent-free for a year to any one who would pay its rates and taxes."

"How long is it since the house acquired this sinister character?"

"That I can scarcely tell you, but very many years since. The old woman I spoke of said it was haunted when she rented it between thirty and forty years ago.

The fact is, that my life has been spent in the East Indies, and in the civil service of the Company. I returned to England last year, on inheriting the fortune of an uncle, among whose possessions was the house in question. I found it shut up and uninhabited. I was told that it was haunted, that no one would inhabit it. I smiled at what seemed to me so idle a story. I spent some money in repairing it—added to its old-fashioned furniture a few modern articles—advertised it, and obtained a lodger for a year. He was a colonel retired on half-pay. He came in with his family, a son and a daughter, and four or five servants: they all left the house the next day; and, although each of them declared that he had seen something different from that which had scared the others, a something still was equally terrible to all. I really could not in conscience sue, nor even blame, the colonel for breach of agreement. Then I put in the old woman I have spoken of, and she was empowered to let the house in apartments. I never had one lodger who stayed more than three days. I do not tell you their stories—to no two lodgers have there been exactly the same phenomena repeated. It is better that you should judge for yourself, than enter the house with an imagination influenced by previous narratives; only be prepared to see and to hear something or other, and take whatever precautions you yourself please."

"Have you never had a curiosity yourself to pass a night in that house?"

"Yes. I passed not a night, but three hours in broad daylight alone in that house. My curiosity is not satisfied but it is quenched. I have no desire to renew the experiment. You cannot complain, you see, sir, that I am not sufficiently candid; and unless your interest be exceedingly eager and your nerves unusually strong, I honestly add, that I advise you not to pass a night in the house."

"My interest *is* exceedingly keen," said I, "and though only a coward will boast of his nerves in situations wholly unfamiliar to him, yet my nerves have been seasoned in such variety of danger that I have the right to rely on them—even in a haunted house."

Mr. J—— said very little more; he took the keys of the house out of his bureau, gave them to me—and, thank-

ing him cordially for his frankness, and his urbane con-
cession to my wish, I carried off my prize.

Impatient for the experiment, as soon as I reached
home, I summoned my confidential servant—a young
man of gay spirits, fearless temper, and as free from
superstitious prejudices as any one I could think of.

"F——," said I, "you remember in Germany how
disappointed we were at not finding a ghost in that old
castle, which was said to be haunted by a headless apparition? Well, I have heard of a house in London which, I
have reason to hope, is decidedly haunted. I mean to
sleep there to-night From what I hear, there is no doubt
that something will allow itself to be seen or to be heard—
something, perhaps, excessively horrible. Do you think if
I take you with me, I may rely on your presence of mind,
whatever may happen?"

"Oh, sir! pray trust me," answered F——, grinning
with delight.

"Very well; then here are the keys of the house—this
is the address. Go now—select for me any bedroom you
please; and since the house has not been inhabited for
weeks, make up a good fire—air the bed well—see, of
course, that there are candles as well as fuel. Take with
you my revolver and my dagger—so much for my
weapons—arm yourself equally well; and if we are not a
match for a dozen ghosts, we shall be but a sorry couple
of Englishmen."

I was engaged for the rest of the day on business so
urgent that I had not leisure to think much on the nocturnal adventure to which I had plighted my honor. I dined
alone, and very late, and while dining, read, as is my
habit. I selected one of the volumes of Macaulay's *Essays*.
I thought to myself that I would take the book with me;
there was so much of the healthfulness in the style, and
practical life in the subjects, that it would serve as an
antidote against the influence of superstitious fancy.

Accordingly, about half-past nine, I put the book into
my pocket, and strolled leisurely toward the haunted
house. I took with me a favorite dog—an exceedingly
sharp, bold and vigilant bull-terrier—a dog fond of prowling about strange ghostly corners and passages at night in
search of rats—a dog of dogs for a ghost.

It was a summer night, but chilly, the sky somewhat

gloomy and overcast. Still there was a moon—faint and sickly, but still a moon—and if the clouds permitted, after midnight it would be brighter.

I reached the house, knocked, and my servant opened with a cheerful smile.

"All right, sir, and very comfortable."

"Oh!" said I, rather disappointed; "have you not seen nor heard anything remarkable?"

"Well, sir, I must own I have heard something queer."

"What—what?"

"The sound of feet pattering behind me; and once or twice small noises like whispers close at my ear—nothing more."

"You are not at all frightened?"

"I! not a bit of it, sir," and the man's bold look reassured me on one point—viz., that happen what might, he would not desert me.

We were in the hall, the street-door closed, and my attention was now drawn to my dog. He had at first run in eagerly enough, but had sneaked back to the door, and was scratching and whining to get out. After patting him on the head, and encouraging him gently, the dog seemed to reconcile himself to the situation, and followed me and F—— through the house, but keeping close at my heels instead of hurrying inquisitively in advance, which was his usual and normal habit in all strange places. We first visited the subterranean apartments, the kitchen and other offices, and especially the cellars, in which last there were two or three bottles of wine still left in a bin, covered with cobwebs, and evidently, by their appearance, undisturbed for many years. It was clear that the ghosts were not wine-bibbers. For the rest we discovered nothing of interest. There was a gloomy little backyard with very high walls. The stones of this yard were very damp; and what with the damp, and what with the dust and smoke-grime on the pavement, our feet left a slight impression where we passed.

And now appeared the first strange phenomenon witnessed by myself in this strange abode. I saw, just before me, the print of a foot suddenly form itself, as it were. I stopped, caught hold of my servant, and pointed to it. In advance of that footprint as suddenly dropped another. We both saw it. I advanced quickly to the place; the

footprint kept advancing before me, a small footprint—
the foot of a child; the impression was too faint thoroughly to distinguish the shape, but it seemed to us both
that it was the print of a naked foot. This phenomenon
ceased when we arrived at the opposite wall, nor did it
repeat itself on returning. We remounted the stairs, and
entered the rooms on the ground floor, a dining-parlor, a
small back parlor, and a still smaller third room that had
been probably appropriated to a footman—all still as
death. We then visited the drawing-rooms, which seemed
fresh and new. In the front room I seated myself in an
armchair. F—— placed on the table the candlestick with
which he had lighted us. I told him to shut the door. As
he turned to do so, a chair opposite to me moved from
the wall quickly and noiselessly, and dropped itself about
a yard from my own chair, immediately fronting it.

"Why, this is better than the turning tables," said I,
with a half-laugh; and as I laughed, my dog put back his
head and howled.

F——, coming back, had not observed the movement
of the chair. He employed himself now in stilling the
dog. I continued to gaze on the chair, and fancied I saw
on it a pale blue misty outline of a human figure, but an
outline so indistinct that I could only distrust my own
vision. The dog now was quiet.

"Put back that chair opposite me," said I to F——;
"put it back to the wall."

F—— obeyed. "Was that you, sir?" said he, turning
abruptly.

"I!—what?"

"Why, something struck me. I felt it sharply on the
shoulder—just here."

"No," said I. "But we have jugglers present, and though
we may not discover their tricks, we shall catch *them*
before they frighten *us*."

We did not stay long in the drawing-rooms—in fact,
they felt so damp and so chilly that I was glad to get to
the fire upstairs. We locked the doors of the drawing-
rooms—a precaution which, I should observe, we had
taken with all the rooms we had searched below. The
bedroom my servant had selected for me was the best on
the floor—a large one, with two windows fronting the
street. The four-posted bed, which took up no inconsider-

able space, was opposite to the fire, which burnt clear
and bright; a door in the wall to the left, between the bed
and the window, communicated with the room which my
servant appropriated to himself. This last was a small
room with a sofa-bed, and had no communication with
the landing-place—no other door but that which con-
ducted to the bedroom I was to occupy. On either side of
my fireplace was a cupboard, without locks, flush with
the wall and covered with the same dull-brown paper.
We examined these cupboards—only hooks to suspend
female dresses—nothing else; we sounded the walls—
evidently solid—the outer walls of the building. Having
finished the survey of these apartments, warmed myself a
few moments, and lighted my cigar, I then, still accompanied by F——, went forth to complete my reconnoiter.
In the landing-place there was another door; it was closed
firmly. "Sir," said my servant, in surprise, "I unlocked
this door with all the others when I first came; it cannot
have got locked from the inside, for——"

Before he had finished his sentence, the door, which
neither of us then was touching, opened quietly of itself.
We looked at each other a single instant. The same
thought seized both—some human agency might be detected here. I rushed in first, my servant followed. A
small blank dreary room without furniture—few empty
boxes and hampers in a corner—a small window—the
shutters closed—not even a fireplace—no other door than
that by which we had entered—no carpet on the floor,
and the floor seemed very old, uneven, worm-eaten,
mended here and there, as was shown by the whiter
patches on the wood; but no living being, and no visible
place in which a living being could have hidden. As we
stood gazing round, the door by which we had entered
closed as quietly as it had before opened: we were
imprisoned.

For the first time I felt a creep of undefinable horror.
Not so my servant. "Why, they don't think to trap us,
sir; I could break the trumpery door with a kick of my
foot."

"Try first if it will open to your hand," said I, shaking
off the vague apprehension that had seized me, "while I
unclose the shutters and see what is without."

I unbarred the shutters—the window looked on the

little backyard I have before described; there was no ledge without—nothing to break the sheer descent of the wall. No man getting out of that window would have found any footing till he had fallen on the stones below.

F——, meanwhile, was vainly attempting to open the door. He now turned round to me and asked my permission to use force. And I should here state, in justice to the servant, that, far from evincing any superstitious terrors, his nerve, composure, and even gaiety amidst circumstances so extraordinary, compelled my admiration, and made me congratulate myself on having secured a companion in every way fitted to the occasion. I willingly gave him the permission he required. But though he was a remarkably strong man, his force was as idle as his milder efforts; the door did not even shake to his stoutest kick. Breathless and panting, he desisted. I then tried the door myself, equally in vain. As I ceased from the effort, again that creep of horror came over me; but this time it was more cold and stubborn. I felt as if some strange and ghastly exhalation were rising up from the chinks of that rugged floor, and filling the atmosphere with a venomous influence hostile to human life. The door now very slowly and quietly opened as of its own accord. We precipitated ourselves into the landing-place. We both saw a large pale light—as large as the human figure but shapeless and unsubstantial—move before us, and ascend the stairs that led from the landing into the attics. I followed the light, and my servant followed me. It entered, to the right of the landing, a small garret, of which the door stood open. I entered in the same instant. The light then collapsed into a small globule, exceeding brilliant and vivid; rested a moment on a bed in the corner, quivered, and vanished.

We approached the bed and examined it—a half-tester, such as is commonly found in attics devoted to servants. On the drawers that stood near it we perceived an old faded silk kerchief, with the needle still left in a rent half repaired. The kerchief was covered with dust; probably it had belonged to the old woman who had last died in that house, and this might have been her sleeping room. I had sufficient curiosity to open the drawers: there were a few odds and ends of female dress, and two letters tied round with a narrow ribbon of faded yellow. I took the liberty to possess myself of the letters. We found nothing else in the room worth noticing—nor did the light reappear; but we distinctly heard, as we turned to go, a pattering footfall on the floor—just before us. We went through the other attics (in all four), the footfall still preceding us. Nothing to be seen—nothing but the footfall heard. I had the letters in my hand: just as I was descending the stairs I distinctly felt my wrist seized, and a faint soft effort made to draw the letters from my clasp. I only held them the more tightly, and the effort ceased.

We regained the bedchamber appropriated to myself, and I then remarked that my dog had not followed us when we had left it. He was thrusting himself close to the fire, and trembling. I was impatient to examine the letters; and while I read them, my servant opened a little box in which he had deposited the weapons I had ordered him to bring; took them out, placed them on a table close at my bed-head, and then occupied himself in soothing the dog, who, however, seemed to heed him very little.

The letters were short—they were dated; the dates exactly thirty-five years ago. They were evidently from a lover to his mistress, or a husband to some young wife. Not only the terms of expression, but a distinct reference to a former voyage, indicated the writer to have been a seafarer. The spelling and handwriting were those of a man imperfectly educated, but still the language itself was forcible. In the expressions of endearment there was a kind of rough wild love; but here and there were dark and unintelligible hints at some secret not of love—some secret that seemed of crime. "We ought to love each other," was one of the sentences I remember, "for how every one else would execrate us if all was known." Again: "Don't let any one be in the same room with you at night—you talk in your sleep." And again: "What's done can't be undone; and I tell you there's nothing against us unless the dead could come to life." Here there was underlined in a better handwriting (a female's), "They do!" At the end of the letter latest in date the same female hand had written these words: "Lost at sea the 4th of June, the same day as——."

I put down the letters, and began to muse over their contents.

Fearing, however, that the train of thought into which I fell might unsteady my nerves, I fully determined to keep my mind in a fit state to cope with whatever of marvelous the advancing night might bring forth. I roused myself—laid the letters on the table—stirred up the fire, which was still bright and cheering—and opened my volume of Macaulay. I read quietly enough till about half-past eleven. I then threw myself dressed upon the bed, and told my servant he might retire to his own room, but must keep himself awake. I bade him leave open the door between the two rooms. Thus alone, I kept two candles burning on the table by my bed-head. I placed my watch beside the weapons, and calmly resumed my Macaulay. Opposite to me the fire burned clear; and on the hearthrug, seemingly asleep, lay the dog. In about twenty minutes I felt an exceedingly cold air pass by my cheek, like a sudden draught. I fancied the door to my right, communicating with the landing-place, must have got open; but no—it was closed. I then turned my glance to my left, and saw the flame of the candles violently swayed as by a wind. At the same moment the watch beside the revolver softly slid from the table—softly, softly—no visible hand—it was gone. I sprang up, seizing the revolver with the one hand, the dagger with the other: I was not willing that my weapons should share the fate of the watch. Thus armed, I looked round the floor—no sign of the watch. Three slow, loud, distinct knocks were now heard at the bed-head; my servant called out, "Is that you, sir?"

"No; be on your guard."

The dog now roused himself and sat on his haunches, his ears moving quickly backward and forward. He kept his eyes fixed on me with a look so strange that he concentered all my attention on himself. Slowly he rose up, all his hair bristling, and stood perfectly rigid, and with the same wild stare. I had no time, however, to examine the dog. Presently my servant emerged from his room; and if ever I saw horror in the human face, it was then. I should not have recognized him had we met in the street, so altered was every lineament. He passed by me quickly, saying in a whisper that seemed scarcely to come from his lips, "Run—run! It is after me!" He gained the door to the landing, pulled it open, and rushed

forth. I followed him into the landing involuntarily, calling him to stop; but, without heeding me, he bounded
down the stairs, clinging to the balusters, and taking
several steps at a time. I heard, where I stood, the
street-door open—heard it again clap to. I was left alone
in the haunted house.

It was but for a moment that I remained undecided
whether or not to follow my servant; pride and curiosity
alike forbade so dastardly a flight. I re-entered my room,
closing the door after me, and proceeded cautiously into
the interior chamber. I encountered nothing to justify my
servant's terror. I again carefully examined the walls, to
see if there were any concealed door. I could find no
trace of one—not even a seam in the dull-brown paper
with which the room was hung. How, then, had the
THING, whatever it was, which had so scared him, obtained ingress except through my own chamber?

I returned to my room, shut and locked the door that
opened upon the interior one, and stood on the hearth,
expectant and prepared. I now perceived that the dog
had slunk into an angle of the wall, and was pressing
himself close against it, as if literally striving to force his
way into it. I approached the animal and spoke to it; the
poor brute was evidently beside itself with terror. It
showed all its teeth, the slaver dropping from its jaws,
and would certainly have bitten me if I had touched it. It
did not seem to recognize me. Whoever has seen at the
Zoological Gardens a rabbit fascinated by a serpent,
cowering in a corner, may form some idea of the anguish
which the dog exhibited. Finding all efforts to soothe the
animal in vain, and fearing that his bite might be as
venomous in that state as in the madness of hydrophobia,
I left him alone, placed my weapons on the table beside
the fire, seated myself, and recommenced my Macaulay.

Perhaps, in order not to appear seeking credit for a
courage, or rather a coolness, which the reader may
conceive I exaggerate, I may be pardoned if I pause to
indulge in one or two egotistical remarks.

As I hold presence of mind, or what is called courage,
to be precisely proportioned to familiarity with the circumstances that lead to it, so I should say that I had been
long sufficiently familiar with all experiments that apper-
tain to the Marvelous. I had witnessed many very ex-

traordinary phenomena in various parts of the world—phenomena that would be either totally disbelieved if I stated them, or ascribed to supernatural agencies. Now, my theory is that the Supernatural is the Impossible, and that what is called supernatural is only a something in the laws of nature of which we have been hitherto ignorant. Therefore, if a ghost rise before me, I have not the right to say, "So, then, the supernatural is possible," but rather, "So, then, the apparition of a ghost is, contrary to received opinion, within the laws of nature—*i.e.*, not supernatural."

Now, in all that I had hitherto witnessed, and indeed in all the wonders which the amateurs of mystery in our age record as facts, a material living agency is always required. On the continent you will find still magicians who assert that they can raise spirits. Assume for the moment that they assert truly, still the living material form of the magician is present; and he is the material agency by which, from some constitutional peculiarities, certain strange phenomena are represented to your natural senses.

Accept, again, as truthful, the tales of spirit Manifestation in America—musical or other sounds—writings on paper, produced by no discernible hand—articles of furniture moved without apparent human agency—or the actual sight and touch of hands, to which no bodies seem to belong—still there must be found the MEDIUM or living being, with constitutional peculiarities capable of obtaining these signs. In fine, in all such marvels, supposing even that there is no imposture, there must be a human being like ourselves by whom, or through whom, the effects presented to human beings are produced. It is so with the now familiar phenomena of mesmerism or electro-biology; the mind of the person operated on is affected through a material living agent. Nor, supposing it true that a mesmerized patient can respond to the will or passes of a mesmerizer a hundred miles distant, is the response less occasioned by a material fluid—call it Electric, call it Odic, call it what you will—which has the power of traversing space and passing obstacles, that the material effect is communicated from one to the other. Hence all that I had hitherto witnessed, or expected to witness, in this strange house, I believed to be occasioned through some agency or medium as mortal as myself: and this idea necessarily prevented the awe with which those who regard as supernatural things that are not within the ordinary operations of nature might have been impressed by the adventures of that memorable night.

As, then, it was my conjecture that all that was presented, or would be presented to my senses, must originate in some human being gifted by constitution with the power so to present them, and having some motive so to do, I felt an interest in my theory which, in its way, was rather philosophical than superstitious. And I can sincerely say that I was in as tranquil a temper for observation as any practical experimentalist could be awaiting the effect of some rare, though perhaps perilous, chemical combination. Of course, the more I kept my mind detached from fancy, the more the temper fitted for observation would be obtained; and I therefore riveted eye and thought on the strong daylight sense in the page of my Macaulay.

I now became aware that something interposed between the page and the light—the page was overshadowed: I looked up, and I saw what I shall find it very difficult, perhaps impossible, to describe.

It was a Darkness shaping itself forth from the air in very undefined outline. I cannot say it was of a human form, and yet it had more resemblance to a human form, or rather shadow, than to anything else. As it stood, wholly apart and distinct from the air and the light around it, its dimensions seemed gigantic, the summit nearly touching the ceiling. When I gazed, a feeling of intense cold seized me. An iceberg before me could not more have chilled me; nor could the cold of an iceberg have been more purely physical. I feel convinced that it was not the cold caused by fear. As I continued to gaze, I thought—but this I cannot say with precision—that I distinguished two eyes looking down on me from the height. One moment I fancied that I distinguished them clearly, the next they seemed gone; but still two rays of a pale-blue light frequently shot through the darkness, as from the height on which I half believed, half doubted, that I had encountered the eyes.

I strove to speak—my voice utterly failed me; I could

only think to myself, "Is this fear? it is *not* fear!" I strove
to rise—in vain; I felt as if weighed down by an irresist-
ible force. Indeed, my impression was that of an immense and overwhelming power opposed to any volition—
that sense of utter inadequacy to cope with a force beyond
man's, which may feel *physically* in a storm at sea, in a
conflagration, or when confronting some terrible wild
beast, or rather, perhaps, the shark of the ocean, I felt
morally. Opposed to my will was another will, as far
superior to its strength as storm, fire, and shark are
superior in material force to the force of man.

And now, as this impression grew on me—now came,
at last, horror—horror to a degree that no words can
convey. Still I retained pride, if not courage; and in my
own mind I said, "This is horror, but it is not fear; unless
I fear I cannot be harmed; my reason rejects this thing, it
is an illusion—I do not fear." With a violent effort I
succeeded at last in stretching out my hand toward the
weapon on the table; as I did so, on the arm and shoulder I received a strange shock, and my arm fell to my
side powerless. And now, to add to my horror, the light
began slowly to wane from the candles; they were not, as
it were, extinguished, but their flame seemed very gradually withdrawn; it was the same with the fire—the light
was extracted from the fuel; in a few minutes the room
was in utter darkness.

The dread that came over me, to be thus in the dark
with that dark Thing, whose power was so intensely felt,
brought a reaction of nerve. In fact, terror had reached
that climax, that either my senses must have deserted
me, or I must have burst through the spell. I did burst
through it. I found voice, though the voice was a shriek.
I remember that I broke forth with words like these—"I
do not fear, my soul does not fear"; and at the same time
I found the strength to rise. Still in that profound gloom I
rushed to one of the windows—tore aside the curtain—
flung open the shutters; my first thought was—LIGHT.
And when I saw the moon high, clear, and calm, I felt a
joy that almost compensated for the previous terror.
There was the moon, there was also the light from the
gas-lamps in the deserted slumberous street. I turned to
look back into the room; the moon penetrated its shadow
very palely and partially—but still there was light. The

dark Thing, whatever it might be, was gone—except that
I could yet see a dim shadow, which seemed the shadow
of that shade, against the opposite wall.

My eye now rested on the table, and from under the
table (which was without cloth or cover—an old mahogany round table) there rose a hand, visible as far as the
wrist. It was a hand, seemingly, as much of flesh and
blood as my own, but the hand of an aged person—lean,
wrinkled, small, too—a woman's hand. That hand very
softly closed on the two letters that lay on the table: hand
and letters both vanished. There then came the same
three loud measured knocks I heard at the bed-head
before this extraordinary drama had commenced.

As those sounds slowly ceased, I felt the whole room
vibrate sensibly; and at the far end there rose, as from
the floor, sparks or globules like bubbles of light, many-
colored—green, yellow, fire-red, azure. Up and down, to
and fro, hither, thither, as tiny Will-o'-the-Wisps the
sparks moved slow or swift, each at his own caprice. A
chair (as in the drawing-room below) was now advanced
from the wall without apparent agency, and placed at the
opposite side of the table. Suddenly as forth from the
chair, there grew a shape—a woman's shape. It was
distinct as a shape of life—ghastly as a shape of death.
The face was that of youth, with a strange mournful
beauty: the throat and shoulders were bare, the rest of
the form in a loose robe of cloudy white. It began sleek-
ing its long yellow hair, which fell over its shoulders; its
eyes were not turned toward me, but to the door; it
seemed listening, watching, waiting. The shadow of the
shade in the background grew darker; and again I thought
I beheld the eyes gleaming out from the summit of the
shadow—eyes fixed upon that shape.

As if from the door, though it did not open, there grew
out another shape, equally distinct, equally ghastly—a
man's shape—a young man's. It was in the dress of the
last century, or rather in a likeness of such dress (for
both the male shape and the female, though defined,
were evidently unsubstantial, impalpable—simulacra—
phantasms); and there was something incongruous, grotesque, yet fearful, in the contrast between the elaborate
finery, the courtly precision of that old-fashioned garb,
with its ruffles and lace and buckles, and the corpse-like

aspect and ghost-like stillness of the flitting wearer. Just as the male shape approached the female, the dark shadow started from the wall, all three for a moment wrapped in darkness. When the pale light returned, the two phantoms were as in the grasp of the shadow that towered between them; and there was a bloodstain on the breast of the female; and the phantom male was leaning on its phantom sword, and blood seemed trickling fast from the ruffles, from the lace; and the darkness of the intermediate Shadow swallowed them up—they were gone. And again the bubbles of light shot, and sailed, and undulated, growing thicker and thicker and more wildly confused in their movements.

The closet door to the right of the fireplace now opened, and from the aperture there came the form of an aged woman. In her hand she held letters—the very letters over which I had seen *the* Hand close; and behind her I heard a footstep. She turned round as if to listen, and then she opened the letters and seemed to read; and over her shoulder I saw a livid face, the face as of a man long drowned—bloated, bleached, seaweed tangled in its dripping hair; and at her feet lay a form as of a corpse, and beside the corpse there cowered a child, a miserable squalid child, with famine in its cheeks and fear in its eyes. And as I looked in the old woman's face, the wrinkles and lines vanished and it became a face of youth—hard-eyed, stony, but still youth; and the Shadow darted forth, and darkened over these phantoms as it had darkened over the last.

Nothing now was left but the Shadow, and on that my eyes were intently fixed, till again eyes grew out of the Shadow—malignant, serpent eyes. And the bubbles of light again rose and fell, and in their disorder, irregular, turbulent maze, mingled with the wan moonlight. And now from these globules themselves, as from the shell of an egg, monstrous things burst out; the air grew filled with them, larvæ so bloodless and so hideous that I can in no way describe them except to remind the reader of the swarming life which the solar microscope brings before his eyes in a drop of water—things transparent, supple, agile, chasing each other, devouring each other—forms like nought ever beheld by the naked eye. As the shapes were without symmetry, so their movements were without order. In their very vagrancies there was no sport; they came round me and round, thicker and faster and swifter, swarming over my head, crawling over my right arm, which was outstretched in involuntary command against all evil beings. Sometimes I felt myself touched, but not by them; invisible hands touched me. Once I felt the clutch as of cold soft fingers at my throat. I was still equally conscious that if I gave way to fear I should be in bodily peril; and I concentrated all my faculties in the single focus of resisting, stubborn will. And I turned my sight from the Shadow—above all, from those strange serpent eyes—eyes that had now become distinctly visible. For there, though in nought else round me, I was aware that there was a WILL, and a will of intense, creative, working evil, which might crush down my own.

The pale atmosphere in the room began now to redden as if in the air of some near conflagration. The larvæ grew lurid as things that live in fire. Again the room vibrated; again were heard the three measured knocks; and again all things were swallowed up in the darkness of the dark Shadow, as if out of that darkness all had come, into that darkness all returned.

As the gloom receded, the shadow was wholly gone. Slowly as it had been withdrawn, the flame grew again into the candles on the table, again into the fuel in the grate. The whole room came once more calmly, healthfully into sight.

The two doors were still closed, the door communicating with the servant's room was still locked. In the corner of the wall into which he had so convulsively niched himself, lay the dog. I called to him—no movement; I approached—the animal was dead; his eyes protruded; his tongue out of his mouth; the froth gathered round his jaws. I took him in my arms; I brought him to the fire, I felt acute grief for the loss of my poor favorite—acute self-reproach; I accused myself of his death; I imagined he had died of fright. But what was my surprise on finding that his neck was actually broken. Had this been done in the dark?—must it not have been by a hand human as mine?—must there not have been a human agency all the while in that room? Good cause to suspect it. I cannot tell. I cannot do more than state the fact fairly; the reader may draw his own inference.

Another surprising circumstance—my watch was restored to the table from which it had been so mysteriously withdrawn; but it had stopped at the very moment it was so withdrawn; nor, despite all the skill of the watchmaker, has it ever gone since—that is, it will go in a strange erratic way for a few hours, and then come to a dead stop—it is worthless.

Nothing more chanced for the rest of the night. Nor, indeed, had I long to wait before the dawn broke. Nor till it was broad daylight did I quit the haunted house. Before I did so, I revisited the little blind room in which my servant and myself had been for a time imprisoned. I had a strong impression—for which I could not account—that from that room had originated the mechanism of the phenomena—if I may use the term—which had been experienced in my chamber. And though I entered it now in the clear day, with the sun peering through the filmy window, I still felt, as I stood on its floor, the creep of the horror which I had first there experienced the night before, and which had been so aggravated by what had passed in my own chamber. I could not indeed bear to stay more than half a minute within those walls. I descended the stairs, and again I heard the footfall before me; and when I opened the street door, I thought I could distinguish a very low laugh. I gained my own home, expecting to find my runaway servant there. But he had not presented himself; nor did I hear more of him for three days, when I received a letter from him, dated from Liverpool to this effect:

"Honored Sir—I humbly entreat your pardon, though I can scarcely hope that you will think I deserve it, unless—which Heaven forbid—you saw what I did. I feel that it will be years before I can recover myself: and as to being fit for service, it is out of the question. I am therefore going to my brother-in-law at Melbourne. The ship sails tomorrow. Perhaps the long voyage may set me up. I do nothing now but start and tremble, and fancy IT is behind me. I humbly beg you, honored sir, to order my clothes, and whatever wages are due to me, to be sent to my mother's, at Walworth. John knows her address."

The letter ended with additional apologies, somewhat incoherent, and explanatory details as to effects that had been under the writer's charge.

This flight may perhaps warrant a suspicion that the man wished to go to Australia, and had been somehow or other fraudulently mixed up with the events of the night. I say nothing in refutation of that conjecture; rather, I suggest it is as one that would seem to many persons the most probable solution of improbable occurrences. My belief in my own theory remained unshaken. I returned in the evening to the house, to bring away in a hack cab the things I had left there, with my poor dog's body. In this task I was not disturbed, nor did any incident worth note befall me, except that still, on ascending and descending the stairs, I heard the same footfall in advance. On leaving the house, I went to Mr. J——'s. He was at home. I returned him the keys, told him that my curiosity was sufficiently gratified, and was about to relate quickly what had passed, when he stopped me, and said, though with much politeness, that he had no longer any interest in a mystery which none had ever solved.

I determined at least to tell him of the two letters I had read, as well as of the extraordinary manner in which they had disappeared, and I then inquired if he thought they had been addressed to the woman who had died in the house, and if there were anything in her early history which could possibly confirm the dark suspicions to which the letters gave rise. Mr. J—— seemed startled, and, after musing a few moments, answered, "I am but little acquainted with the woman's earlier history, except, as I before told you, that her family were known to mine. But you revive some vague reminiscences to her prejudice. I will make inquiries, and inform you of their result. Still, even if we could admit the popular superstition that a person who had been either the perpetrator or the victim of dark crimes in life could revisit, as a restless spirit, the scene in which those crimes had been committed, I should observe that the house was infested by strange sights and sounds before the old woman died— you smile—what would you say?"

"I would say this, that I am convinced, if we could get

to the bottom of these mysteries, we should find a living human agency.'

"What! you believe it is all an imposture? for what object?"

"Not an imposture in the ordinary sense of the word. If suddenly I were to sink into a deep sleep, from which you could not awake me, but in that sleep could answer questions with an accuracy which I could not pretend to when awake—tell you what money you had in your pocket—nay, describe your very thoughts—it is not necessarily an imposture, any more than it is necessarily supernatural. I should be, unconsciously to myself, under a mesmeric influence, conveyed to me from a distance by a human being who had acquired power over me by previous *rapport*."

"But if a mesmerizer could so affect another living being, can you suppose that a mesmerizer could also affect inanimate objects: move chairs—open and shut doors?"

"Or impress our senses with the belief in such effects— we never having seen *en rapport* with the person acting on us? No. What is commonly called mesmerism could not do this; but there may be a power akin to mesmerism, and superior to it—the power that in the old days was called Magic. That such a power may extend to all inanimate objects of matter I do not say; but if so, it would not be against nature—it would be only a rare power in nature which might be given to constitutions with certain peculiarities, and cultivated by practice to an extraordinary degree. That such a power might extend over the dead—that is, over certain thoughts and memories that the dead may still retain—and compel, not that which ought properly to be called the SOUL, and which is far beyond human reach, but rather a phantom of what has been most earth-stained on earth, to make itself apparent to our senses—is a very ancient though obsolete theory, upon which I will hazard no opinion. But I do not conceive the power would be supernatural. Let me illustrate what I mean from an experiment which Paracelsus describes as not difficult, and which the author of the *Curiosities of Literature* cites as credible: a flower perishes; you burn it. Whatever were the elements of that flower while it lived are gone, dispersed, you know not wither;

you can never discover nor recollect them. But you can, by chemistry, out of the burnt dust of that flower, raise a spectrum of the flower, just as it seemed in life. It may be the same with the human being. The soul has as much escaped you as the essence or elements of the flower. Still you may make a spectrum of it.

"And this phantom, though in the popular superstition it is held to be the soul of the departed, must not be confounded with the true soul; it is but eidolon of the dead form. Hence, like the best attested stories of ghosts or spirits, the thing that most strikes us in the absence of what we hold to be soul; that is, of superior emancipated intelligence. There apparitions come for little or no object—they seldom speak when they do come; if they speak, they utter no ideas above those of an ordinary person on earth. American spirit-seers have published volumes of communications in prose and verse, which they assert to be given in the names of the most illustrious dead—Shakespeare, Bacon—heaven knows whom. Those communications, taking the best, are certainly not a whit of higher order than would be communications from living persons of fair talent and education; they are wondrously inferior to what Bacon, Shakespeare, and Plato said and wrote when on earth. Nor, what is more noticeable, do they ever contain an idea that was not on the earth before. Wonderful, therefore, as such phenomena may be (granting them to be truthful), I see much that philosophy may question, nothing that it is incumbent on philosophy to deny, viz., nothing supernatural. They are but ideas conveyed somehow to other (we have not yet discovered the means) from one mortal brain to another. Whether, in so doing, tables walk of their own accord, or fiend-like shapes appear in a magic circle, or bodyless hands rise and remove material objects, or a Thing of Darkness, such as presented itself to me, freeze our blood—still am I persuaded that these are but agencies conveyed, as if by electric wires, to my own brain from the brain of another. In some constitutions there is a natural chemistry, and these constitutions may produce chemic wonders—in others a natural fluid, call it electricity, and these may produce electric wonders.

"But the wonders differ from Normal Science in this— they are alike objectless, purposeless, puerile, frivolous.

They lead on to no grand results; and therefore the world does not heed, and true sages have not cultivated them. But sure I am, that of all I saw or heard, a man, human as myself, was the remote originator; and I believe unconsciously to himself as to the exact effects produced, for this reason: no two persons, you say, have ever told you that they experienced exactly the same thing. Well, observe, no two persons ever experience exactly the same dream. If this were an ordinary imposture, the machinery would be arranged for results that would but little vary; if it were a supernatural agency permitted by the Almighty, it would surely be for some definite end. These phenomena belong to neither class; my persuasion is, that they originate in some brain now far distant; and that that brain had no distinct volition in anything that occurred; that what does occur reflects but its devious, motley, ever-shifting, half-formed thoughts; in short, that it has been but the dreams of such a brain put into action and invested with a semi-substance. That this brain is of immense power, that it can set matter into movement, that it is malignant and destructive, I believe; some material force must have killed my dog; the same force might, for aught I know, have sufficed to kill myself, had I been as subjugated by terror as the dog—had my intellect or my spirit given me no countervailing resistance in my will."

"It killed your dog! That is fearful! Indeed it is strange that no animal can be induced to stay in that house; not even a cat. Rats and mice are never found in it."

"The instincts of the brute creation detect influences deadly to their existence. Man's reason has a sense less subtle, because it has a resisting power more supreme. But enough; do you comprehend my theory?"

"Yes, though imperfectly—and I accept any crochet (pardon the word), however odd, rather than embrace at once the notion of ghosts and hobgoblins we imbibed in our nurseries. Still, to my unfortunate house the evil is the same. What on earth can I do with the house?"

"I will tell you what I would do. I am convinced from my own internal feelings that the small unfurnished room at right angles to the door of the bedroom which I occupied, forms a starting point or receptacle for the influences which haunt the house; and I strongly advise you to have the walls opened, the floor removed—nay, the whole room pulled down. I observe that it is detached from the body of the house, built over the small backyard, and could be removed without injury to the rest of the building."

"And you think, if I did that—"

"You would cut off the telegraph wires. Try it. I am so persuaded that I am right, that I will pay half the expense if you will allow me to direct the operations."

"Nay, I am well able to afford the cost; for the rest, allow me to write to you."

About ten days afterward I received a letter from Mr. J——, telling me that he had visited the house since I had seen him; that he had found the two letters I had described replaced in the drawer from which I had taken them; that he had read them with misgivings like my own; that he had instituted a cautious inquiry about the woman to whom I rightly conjectured they had been written. It seemed that thirty-six years ago (a year before the date of the letters) she had married, against the wish of her relations, an American of very suspicious character, in fact, he was generally believed to have been a pirate. She herself was the daughter of very respectable tradespeople, and had served in the capacity of nursery governess before her marriage. She had a brother, a widower, who was considered wealthy, and who had one child of about six years old. A month after the marriage, the body of this brother was found in the Thames, near London Bridge; there seemed some marks of violence about his throat, but they were not deemed sufficient to warrant the inquest in any other verdict than that of "found drowned."

The American and his wife took charge of the little boy, the deceased brother having by his will left his sister the guardian of his only child—and in the event of the child's death, the sister inherited. The child died about six months afterward—it was supposed to have been neglected and ill-treated. The neighbors deposed to have heard it shriek at night. The surgeon who had examined it after death said that it was emaciated as if from want of nourishment, and the body was covered with livid bruises. It seemed that one winter night the child had sought to escape—crept out into the backyard—tried to scale the wall—fallen back exhausted, and been found at morning on the stones in a dying state. But though there was some evidence of cruelty, there was none of murder; and the aunt and her husband had sought to palliate cruelty by alleging the exceeding stubbornness and perversity of the child, who was declared to be half-witted. Be that as it may, at the orphan's death the aunt inherited her brother's fortune. Before the first wedded year was out the American quitted England abruptly, and never returned to it. He obtained a cruising vessel, which was lost in the Atlantic two years afterward. The widow was left in affluence; but reverses of various kinds had befallen her; a bank broke—an investment failed—she went into a small business and became insolvent—then she entered into service, sinking lower and lower, from housekeeper down to maid-of-all work—never long retaining a place, though nothing decided against her character was ever alleged. She was considered sober, honest, and peculiarly quiet in her ways; still nothing prospered with her. And so she had dropped into the workhouse, from which Mr. J—— had taken her, to be placed in charge of the very house which she had rented as mistress in the first year of her wedded life.

Mr. J—— added that he had passed an hour alone in the unfurnished room which I had urged him to destroy, and that his impressions of dread while there were so great, though he had neither heard nor seen anything, that he was eager to have the walls bared and the floor removed as I had suggested. He had engaged persons for the work, and would commence any day I would name.

The day was accordingly fixed. I repaired to the haunted house—he went into the blind dreary room, took up the skirting, and then the floors. Under the rafters, covered with rubbish, was found a trap-door, quite large enough to admit a man. It was closely nailed down, with clamps and rivets of iron. On removing these we descended into a room below, the existence of which had never been suspected. In this room there had been a window and a flue, but they had been bricked over, evidently for many years. By the help of candles we examined this place; it still retained some mouldering furniture—three chairs, an oak settle, a table—all of the fashion of about eighty years ago. There was a chest of drawers against the wall,

in which we found, half-rotted away, old-fashioned articles of a man's dress, such as might have been worn
eighty or a hundred years ago by a gentleman of some
rank—costly steel buckles and buttons, like those yet
worn in court-dresses, a handsome court sword—in a
waistcoat which had once been rich with gold-lace, but
which was now blackened and foul with damp, we found
five guineas, a few silver coins, and an ivory ticket,
probably for some place of entertainment long since passed
away. But our main discovery was in a kind of iron safe
fixed to the wall, the lock of which it cost us much
trouble to get picked.

In this safe were three shelves, and two small drawers.
Ranged on the shelves were several small bottles of crystal, hermetically stopped. They contained colorless vola-
tile essences, of the nature of which I shall only say that
they were not poisons—phosphor and ammonia entered
into some of them. There were also some very curious
glass tubes, and a small pointed rod of iron, with a large
lump of rock-crystal, and another of amber—also a lode-
stone of great power.

In one of the drawers we found a miniature portrait set
in gold, and retaining the freshness of its colors most
remarkably, considering the length of time it had probably been there. The portrait was that of a man who might
be somewhat advanced in middle life, perhaps forty-
seven or forty-eight.

It was a remarkable face—a most impressive face. If
you could fancy some mighty serpent transformed into a
man, preserving in the human lineaments the old serpent
type, you would have a better idea of that countenance
than long descriptions can convey: the width and flatness
of frontal—the tapering elegance of contour disguising
the strength of the deadly jaw—the long, large, terrible
eye, glittering and green as the emerald—and withal a
certain ruthless calm, as if from the consciousness of an
immense power.

Mechanically I turned round the miniature to examine
the back of it, and on the back was engraved a pentacle;
in the middle of the pentacle a ladder, and the third step
of the ladder was formed by the date 1765. Examining
still more minutely, I detected a spring; this, on being
pressed, opened the back of the miniature as a lid.

Withinside the lid were engraved, "Marianna to thee—be faithful in life and in death to ——." Here follows a name that I will not mention, but it was not unfamiliar to me. I had heard it spoken of by old men in my childhood as the name borne by a dazzling charlatan who had made a great sensation in London for a year or so, and had fled the country on the charge of a double murder within his own house—that of his mistress and his rival. I said nothing of this to Mr. J——, to whom reluctantly I resigned the miniature.

We had found no difficulty in opening the first drawer within the iron safe; we found great difficulty in opening the second: it was not locked, but it resisted all efforts, till we inserted in the clinks the edge of a chisel. When we had thus drawn it forth we found a very singular apparatus in the nicest order. Upon a small thin book, or rather tablet, was placed a saucer of crystal: this saucer was filled with a clear liquid—on that liquid floated a kind of compass, with a needle shifting rapidly round; but instead of the usual points of a compass were seven strange characters, not very unlike those used by astrologers to denote the planets.

A peculiar, but not strong nor displeasing odor came from this drawer, which was lined with a wood that we afterward discovered to be hazel. Whatever the cause of this odor, it produced a material effect on the nerves. We all felt it, even the two workmen who were in the room—a creeping tingling sensation from the tips of the fingers to the roots of the hair. Impatient to examine the tablet, I removed the saucer. As I did so the needle of the compass went round and round with exceeding swiftness, and I felt a shock that ran through my whole frame, so that I dropped the saucer on the floor. The liquid was spilt— the saucer was broken—the compass rolled to the end of the room—and at that instant the walls shook to and fro, as if a giant had swayed and rocked them.

The two workmen were so frightened that they ran up the ladder by which we had descended from the trapdoor; but seeing that nothing more happened, they were easily induced to return.

Meanwhile I had opened the tablet: it was bound in plain red leather, with a silver clasp; it contained but one sheet of thick vellum, and on that sheet were inscribed within a double pentacle, words in old monkish Latin, which are literally to be translated thus: "On all that it can reach within these walls—sentient or inanimate, living or dead—as moves the needle, so work my will! Accursed be the house, and restless be the dwellers therein."

We found no more. Mr. J—— burnt the tablet and its anathema. He razed to the foundations the part of the building containing the secret room with the chamber over it. He had then the courage to inhabit the house himself for a month, and a quieter, better-conditioned house could not be found in all London. Subsequently he let it to advantage, and his tenant has made no complaints.

CHARLOTTE PERKINS GILMAN

The Yellow Wallpaper

It is very seldom that mere ordinary people like John and myself secure ancestral halls for the summer.

A colonial mansion, a hereditary estate, I would say a haunted house, and reach the height of romantic felicity— but that would be asking too much of fate!

Still I will proudly declare that there is something queer about it.

Else, why should it be let so cheaply? And why have stood so long untenanted.

John laughs at me, of course, but one expects that in marriage.

John is practical in the extreme. He has no patience with faith, an intense horror of superstition, and he scoffs openly at any talk of things not to be felt and seen and put down in figures.

John is a physician, and *perhaps*—(I would not say it to a living soul, of course, but this is dead paper and a great relief to my mind)—*perhaps* that is one reason I do not get well faster.

You see he does not believe I am sick!

And what can one do?

If a physician of high standing, and one's own husband, assures friends and relatives that there is really nothing the matter with one but temporary nervous depression—a slight hysterical tendency—what is one to do?

My brother is also a physician, and also of high standing, and he says the same thing.

So I take phosphates or phosphites—whichever it is,

and tonics, and journeys, and air, and exercise, and am absolutely forbidden to "work" until I am well again.

Personally, I disagree with their idea.

Personally, I believe that congenial work, with excitement and change, would do me good.

But what is one to do?

I did write for a while in spite of them: but it *does* exhaust me a good deal—having to be so sly about it, or else meet with heavy opposition.

I sometimes fancy that in my condition if I had less opposition and more society and stimulus—but John says the very worst thing I can do is to think about my condition, and I confess it always makes me feel bad.

So I will let it alone and talk about the house.

The most beautiful place! It is quite alone, standing well back from the road, quite three miles from the village. It makes me think of English places that you read about, for there are hedges and walls and gates that lock, and lots of separate little houses for the gardeners and people.

There is a *delicious* garden! I never saw such a garden—large and shady, full of box-bordered paths, and lined with long grape-covered arbors with seats under them.

There were greenhouses, too, but they are all broken now.

There was some legal trouble, I believe, something about the heirs and coheirs; anyhow, the place has been empty for years.

That spoils my ghostliness, I am afraid, but I don't care—there is something strange about the house—I can feel it.

I even said so to John one moonlight evening but he said what I felt was a *draught*, and shut the window.

I get unreasonably angry with John sometimes. I'm sure I never used to be so sensitive. I think it is due to this nervous condition.

But John says if I feel so, I shall neglect proper self-control; so I take pains to control myself—before him, at least, and that makes me very tired.

I don't like our room a bit. I wanted one downstairs that opened on the piazza and had roses all over the window, and such pretty old-fashioned chintz hangings! but John would not hear of it.

He said there was only one window and not room for two beds, and no near room for him if he took another.

He is very careful and loving, and hardly lets me stir without special direction.

I have a schedule prescription for each hour in the day; he takes all care from me, and so I feel basely ungrateful not to value it more.

He said we came here solely on my account, that I was to have perfect rest and all the air I could get. "Your exercise depends on your strength, my dear," said he, "and your food somewhat on your appetite; but air you can absorb all the time." So we took the nursery at the top of the house.

It is a big, airy room, the whole floor nearly, with windows that look all ways, and air and sunshine galore. It was nursery first and then playroom and gymnasium. I should judge; for the windows are barred for little children, and there are rings and things in the walls.

The paint and paper look as if a boy's school had used it. It is stripped off—the paper—in great patches all around the head of my bed, about as far as I can reach, and in a great place on the other side of the room low down. I never saw a worse paper in my life.

One of those sprawling flamboyant patterns committing every artistic sin.

It is dull enough to confuse the eye in following, pronounced enough to constantly irritate and provoke study, and when you follow the lame uncertain curves for a little distance they suddenly commit suicide—plunge off at outrageous angles, destroy themselves in unheard of contradictions.

The color is repellent, almost revolting; a smoldering unclean yellow, strangely faded by the slow-turning sunlight.

It was a dull yet livid orange in some places, a sickly sulphur tint in others.

No wonder the children hated it! I should hate it myself if I had to live in this room long.

There comes John, and I must put this away—he hates to have me write a word.

We have been here two weeks, and I haven't felt like writing before, since that first day.

I am sitting by the window now, up in this atrocious nursery, and there is nothing to hinder my writing as much as I please, save lack of strength

John is away all day, and even some nights when his cases are serious.

I am glad my case is not serious!

But these nervous troubles are dreadfully depressing.

John does not know how much I really suffer. He knows there is no *reason* to suffer, and that satisfies him.

Of course it is only nervousness. It does weigh on me so not to do my duty in any way!

I meant to be such a help to John, such a real rest and comfort, and here I am a comparative burden already!

Nobody would believe what an effort it is to do what little I am able—to dress and entertain, and order things.

It is fortunate Mary is so good with the baby. Such a dear baby!

And yet I *cannot* be with him, it makes me so nervous.

I suppose John never was nervous in his life. He laughs at me so about this wallpaper!

At first he meant to repaper the room, but afterward he said that I was letting it get the better of me, and that nothing was worse for a nervous patient than to give way to such fancies.

He said that after the wallpaper was changed it would be the heavy bedstead, and then the barred windows, and then that gate at the head of the stairs, and so on.

"You know the place is doing you good," he said, "and really, dear, I don't care to renovate the house just for three months' rental."

"Then do let us go downstairs," I said, "there are such pretty rooms there."

Then he took me in his arms and called me a blessed little goose, and said he would go down to the cellar, if I wished, and have it whitewashed into the bargain.

But he is right enough about the beds and windows and things.

It is an airy and comfortable room as any one need wish, and, of course, I would not be so silly as to make him uncomfortable just for a whim.

I'm really getting quite fond of the big room, all but that horrid paper.

Out of one window I can see the garden, those mysterious deepshaded arbors, the riotous old-fashioned flowers, and bushes and gnarly trees.

Out of another I get a lovely view of the bay and a little private wharf belonging to the estate. There is a beautiful shaded lane that runs down there from the house. I always fancy I see people walking in these numerous paths and arbors, but John has cautioned me not to give way to fancy in the least. He says that with my imaginative power and habit of story-making, a nervous weakness like mine is sure to lead to all manner of excited fancies, and that I ought to use my will and good sense to check the tendency. So I try.

I think sometimes that if I were only well enough to write a little it would relieve the press of ideas and rest me.

But I find I get pretty tired when I try.

It is so discouraging not to have any advice and companionship about my work. When I get really well, John says we will ask Cousin Henry and Julia down for a long visit; but he says he would as soon put fireworks in my pillowcase as to let me have those stimulating people about now.

I wish I could get well faster.

But I must not think about that. This paper looks to me as if it *knew* what a vicious influence it had!

There is a recurrent spot where the pattern lolls like a broken neck and two bulbous eyes stare at you upside down.

I get positively angry with the impertinence of it and the everlastingness. Up and down and sideways they crawl, and those absurd, unblinking eyes are everywhere. There is one place where two breadths didn't match, and the eyes go all up and down the line, one a little higher than the other.

I never saw so much expression in an inanimate thing before, and we all know how much expression they have! I used to lie awake as a child and get more entertainment and terror out of blank walls and plain furniture than most children could find in a toy-store.

I remember what a kindly wink the knobs of our big, old bureau used to have, and there was one chair that always seemed like a strong friend.

I used to feel that if any of the other things looked too fierce I could always hop into the chair and be safe.

The furniture in this room is no worse than inharmonious, however, for we had to bring it all from downstairs. I suppose when this was used as a playroom they had to take the nursery things out, and no wonder! I never saw such ravages as the children have made here.

The wallpaper, as I said before, is torn off in spots, and it sticketh closer than a brother—they must have had perseverance as well as hatred.

Then the floor is scratched and gouged and splintered, the plaster itself is dug out here and there, and this great heavy bed which is all we found in the room, looks as if it had been through the wars.

But I don't mind it a bit—only the paper.

There comes John's sister. Such a dear girl as she is, and so careful of me! I must not let her find me writing.

She is a perfect and enthusiastic housekeeper, and hopes for no better profession. I verily believe she thinks it is the writing which made me sick!

But I can write when she is out, and see her a long way off from these windows.

There is one that commands the road, a lovely shaded winding road, and one that just looks off over the country. A lovely country, too, full of great elms and velvet meadows.

This wallpaper has a kind of sub-pattern in a different shade, a particularly irritating one, for you can only see it in certain lights, and not clearly then.

But in the places where it isn't faded and where the sun is just so—I can see a strange, provoking, formless sort of figure, that seems to skulk about that silly and conspicuous front design.

There's sister on the stairs!

Well, the fourth of July is over! The people are all gone and I am tired out. John thought it might do me good to see a little company, so we just had mother and Nellie and the children down for a week.

Of course I didn't do a thing. Jennie sees to everything now.

But it tired me all the same.

John says if I don't pick up faster he shall send me to Weir Mitchell in the fall.

But I don't want to go there at all. I had a friend who was in his hands once, and she says he is just like John and my brother, only more so!

Besides, it is such an undertaking to go so far.

I don't feel as if it was worthwhile to turn my hand over for anything, and I'm getting dreadfully fretful and querulous.

I cry at nothing, and cry most of the time.

Of course I don't when John is here, or anybody else, but when I am alone.

And I am alone a good deal just now. John is kept in town very often by serious cases, and Jennie is good and lets me alone when I want her to.

So I walk a little in the garden or down that lovely lane, sit on the porch under the roses, and lie down up here a good deal.

I'm getting really fond of the room in spite of the wallpaper. Perhaps *because* of the wallpaper.

It dwells in my mind so!

I lie here on this great immovable bed—it is nailed down, I believe—and follow that pattern about by the hour. It is as good as gymnastics, I assure you. I start, we'll say, at the bottom, down in the corner over there where it has not been touched, and I determine for the thousandth time that I *will* follow that pointless pattern to some sort of a conclusion.

I know a little of the principle of design, and I know this thing was not arranged on any laws of radiation, or alternation, or repetition, or symmetry, or anything else that I never heard of.

It is repeated, of course, by the breadths, but not otherwise.

Looked at in one way each breadth stands alone, the bloated curves and flourishes—a kind of "debased Romanesque" with *delirium tremens*—go waddling up and down in isolated columns of fatuity.

But, on the other hand, they connect diagonally, and the sprawling outlines run off in great slanting waves of optic horror, like a lot of wallowing seaweeds in full chase.

The whole thing goes horizontally, too, at least it seems

so, and I exhaust myself in trying to distinguish the order of its going in that direction.

They have used a horizontal breadth for a frieze, and that adds wonderfully to the confusion.

There is one end of the room where it is almost intact, and there, when the crosslights fade and the low sun shines directly upon it, I can almost fancy radiation after all—the interminable grotesques seem to form around a common center and rush off in headlong plunges of equal distraction.

It makes me tired to follow it. I will take a nap I guess.

I don't know why I should write this.

I don't want to.

I don't feel able.

And I know John would think it absurd. But I *must* say what I feel and think in some way—it is such a relief!

But the effort is getting to be greater than the relief.

Half the time now I am awfully lazy and lie down ever so much.

John says I mustn't lose my strength, and has me take cod liver oil and lots of tonics and things, to stay nothing of ale and wine and rare meat.

Dear John! He loves me very dearly, and hates to have me sick. I tried to have a real earnest reasonable talk with him the other day, and tell him how I wish he would let me go and make a visit to Cousin Henry and Julia.

But he said I wasn't able to go, nor able to stand it after I got there; and I did not make out a very good case for myself, for I was crying before I had finished.

It is getting to be a great effort for me to think straight. Just this nervous weakness I suppose.

And dear John gathered me up in his arms, and just carried me upstairs and laid me on the bed, and sat by me and read to me till it tired my head.

He said I was his darling and his comfort and all he had, and that I must take care of myself for his sake, and keep well.

He says no one but myself can help me out of it, that I must use my will and self-control and not let any silly fancies run away with me.

There's one comfort, the baby is well and happy, and does not have to occupy this nursery with the horrid wallpaper.

If we had not used it, that blessed child would have! What a fortunate escape! Why, I wouldn't have a child of mine, an impressionable little thing live in such a room for worlds.

I never thought of it before, but it is lucky that John kept me here after all. I can stand it so much easier than a baby, you see.

Of course I never mention it to them any more—I am too wise—but I keep watch of it all the same.

There are things in that paper that nobody knows but me, or ever will.

Behind that outside pattern the dim shapes get clearer every day.

It is always the same shape, only numerous.

And it is like a woman stooping down and creeping about behind that pattern. I don't like it a bit. I wonder—I begin to think—I wish John would take me away from here!

It is so hard to talk with John about my case, because he is so wise, and because he loves me so.

But I tried it last night.

It was moonlight. The moon shines in all around just as the sun does.

I hate to see it sometimes, it creeps so slowly, and always comes in by one window or another.

John was asleep and I hated to wake him, so I kept still and watched the moonlight on the undulating wallpaper till I felt creepy.

The faint figure behind seemed to shake the pattern, just as if she wanted to get out.

I got up softly and went to feel and see if the paper *did* move, and when I came back John was awake.

"What is it, little girl?" he said. "Don't go walking about like that—you'll get cold."

I thought it was a good time to talk, so I told him that I really was not gaining here, and that I wished he would take me away.

"Why darling!" said he, "our lease will be up in three weeks, and I can't see how to leave before.

"The repairs are not done at home, and I cannot possibly leave town just now. Of course if you were in any danger, I could and would, but you really are better dear, whether you see it or not. I am a doctor, dear, and

I know. You are gaining flesh and color, your appetite is better, I feel really much easier about you."

"I don't weigh a bit more," said I, "nor as much; and
my appetite may be better in the evening when you are
here, but it is worse in the morning when you are away!"

"Bless her little heart!" said he with a big hug, "she
shall be as sick as she pleases! But now let's improve the
shining hours by going to sleep, and talk about it in the
morning!"

"And you won't go away?" I asked gloomily.

"Why, how can I, dear? It is only three weeks more
and then we will take a nice little trip of a few days while
Jennie is getting the house ready. Really, dear, you are
better!"

"Better in body perhaps—" I began, and stopped short,
for he sat up straight and looked at me with such a stern,
reproachful look that I could not say another word.

"My darling," said he, "I beg of you, for my sake and
for our child's sake, as well as for your own, that you will
never for one instant let that idea enter your mind! There
is nothing so dangerous, so fascinating, to a temperament
like yours. It is a false and foolish fancy. Can you not
trust me as a physician when I tell you so?"

So of course I said no more on that score, and we went
to sleep before long. He thought I was asleep first, but I
wasn't and lay there for hours trying to decide whether
that front pattern and the back pattern really did move
together or separately.

On a pattern like this, by daylight, there is a lack of
sequence, a defiance of law, that is a constant irritant to
a normal mind.

The color is hideous enough, and unreliable enough,
and infuriating enough, but the pattern is torturing.

You think you have mastered it, but just as you get well
underway in following, it turns a back-somersault and
there you are. It slaps you in the face, knocks you down,
and tramples upon you. It is like a bad dream.

The outside pattern is a florid arabesque, reminding
one of a fungus. If you can imagine a toadstool in joints,
an interminable string of toadstools, budding and sprout-
ing in endless convolutions—why, that is something like
it.

That is, sometimes!

There is one marked peculiarity about this paper, a thing nobody seems to notice but myself, and that is that it changes as the light changes.

When the sun shoots in through the east window—I always watch for that first long, straight ray—it changes so quickly that I never can quite believe it.

That is why I watch it always.

By moonlight—the moon shines in all night when there is a moon—I wouldn't know it was the same paper.

At night in any kind of light, in twilight, candle light, lamplight, and worst of all by moonlight, it becomes bars! The outside pattern I mean, and the woman behind it is as plain as can be.

I didn't realize for a long time what the thing was that showed behind, that dim sub-pattern, but now I am quite sure it is a woman.

By daylight she is subdued, quiet. I fancy it is the pattern that keeps her so still. It is so puzzling. It keeps me quiet by the hour.

I lie down so much now. John says it is good for me, and to sleep all I can.

Indeed he started the habit by making me lie down for an hour after each meal.

It is a very bad habit I am convinced, for you see I don't sleep.

And that cultivated deceit, for I don't tell them I'm awake—O no!

The fact is I am getting a little afraid of John.

He seems very queer sometimes, and even Jennie has an inexplicable look.

It strikes me occasionally, just as a scientific hypothesis—that perhaps it is the paper!

I have watched John when he did not know I was looking, and come into the room suddenly on the most innocent excuses, and I've caught him several times *looking at the paper!* And Jennie too. I caught Jennie with her hand on it once.

She didn't know I was in the room, and when I asked her in a quiet, a very quiet voice, with the most re-strained manner possible, what she was doing with the paper—she turned around as if she had been caught stealing, and looked quite angry—asked me why I should frighten her so!

Then she said that the paper stained everything it touched, that she had found yellow smooches on all my clothes and John's, and she wished we would be more careful!

Did not that sound innocent? But I know she was studying that pattern, and I am determined that nobody shall find it out but myself!

Life is very much more exciting now than it used to be. You see I have something more to expect, to look forward to, to watch. I really do eat better, and am more quiet than I was.

John is so pleased to see me improve! He laughed a little the other day, and said I seemed to be flourishing in spite of my wallpaper.

I turned it off with a laugh. I had no intention of telling him it was *because* of the wallpaper—he would make fun of me. He might even want to take me away.

I don't want to leave now until I have found out. There is a week more, and I think that will be enough.

I'm feeling ever so much better! I don't sleep much at night, for it is so interesting to watch developments; but I sleep a good deal in the daytime.

In the daytime it is tiresome and perplexing.

There are always new shoots on the fungus, and new shades of yellow all over it. I cannot keep count of them, though I have tried conscientiously.

It is the strangest yellow, that wallpaper! It makes me think of all the yellow things I ever saw—not beautiful ones like buttercups, but old foul, bad yellow things.

But there is something else about that paper—the smell! I noticed it the moment we came into the room, but with so much air and sun it was not bad. Now we have had a week of fog and rain, and whether the windows are open or not, the smell is here.

It creeps all over the house.

I find it hovering in the dining room, skulking in the parlor, hiding in the hall, lying in wait for me on the stairs.

It gets into my hair.

Even when I go to ride, if I turn my head suddenly and surprise it—there is that smell!

Such a peculiar odor, too! I have spent hours in trying to analyze it, to find what it smelled like.

It is not bad—at first, and very gentle, but quite the subtlest, most enduring odor I ever met.

In this damp weather it is awful, I wake up in the night and find it hanging over me.

It used to disturb me at first. I thought seriously of burning the house—to reach the smell.

But now I am used to it. The only thing I can think of that it is like is the *color* of the paper! A yellow smell.

There is a very funny mark on this wall, low down, near the mopboard. A streak that runs round the room. It goes behind every piece of furniture, except the bed, a long, straight, even *smooch*, as if it had been rubbed over and over.

I wonder how it was done and who did it, and what they did it for. Round and round and round—round and round and round—it makes me dizzy!

I really have discovered something at last.

Through watching so much at night, when it changes so, I have finally found out.

The front pattern *does* move—and no wonder! The woman behind shakes it!

Sometimes I think there are a great many women behind, and sometimes only one, and she crawls around fast, and her crawling shakes it all over.

Then in the very bright spots she keeps still, and in the very shady spots she just takes hold of the bars and shakes them hard.

And she is all the time trying to climb through. But nobody could climb through that pattern—it strangles so; I think that is why it has so many heads.

They get through, and then the pattern strangles them off and turns them upside down, and makes their eyes white!

If those heads were covered or taken off it would not be half so bad.

I think that women gets out in the daytime!

And I'll tell you why—privately—I've seen her!

I can see her out of every one of my windows!

It is the same woman, I know, for she is always creeping, and most women do not creep by daylight.

I see her on the long road under the trees, creeping along, and when a carriage comes she hides under the blackberry vines.

I don't blame her a bit. It must be very humiliating to be caught creeping by daylight!

I always lock the door when I creep by daylight. I can't do it at night, for I know John would suspect something at once.

And John is so queer now, that I don't want to irritate him. I wish he would take another room! Besides, I don't want anybody to get that woman out at night but myself.

I often wonder if I could see her out of all the windows at once.

But, turn as fast as I can, I can only see out of one at one time.

And though I always see her, she *may* be able to creep faster than I can turn!

I have watched her sometimes away off in the open country, creeping as fast as a cloud shadow in a high wind.

If only that top pattern could be gotten off from the under one! I mean to try it, little by little.

I have found out another funny thing, but I shan't tell it this time! It does not do to trust people too much.

There are only two more days to get this paper off, and I believe John is beginning to notice. I don't like the look in his eyes.

And I heard him ask Jennie a lot of professional questions about me. She had a very good report to give.

She said I slept a good deal in the daytime.

John knows I don't sleep very well at night, for all I'm so quiet!

He asked me all sorts of questions, too, and pretended to be very loving and kind.

As if I couldn't see through him!

Still, I don't wonder he acts so, sleeping under this paper for three months.

It only interests me, but I feel sure John and Jennie are secretly affected by it.

*   *   *

Hurrah! This is the last day, but it is enough. John had to stay in town overnight, and won't be out until this evening.

Jennie wanted to sleep with me—the sly thing! but I told her I should undoubtedly rest better for a night all alone.

That was clever, for really I wasn't alone a bit! As soon as it was moonlight and that poor thing began to crawl and shake the pattern, I got up and ran to help her.

I pulled and she shook, I shook and she pulled, and before morning we had peeled off yards of that paper.

A strip about as high as my head and half around the room.

And then when the sun came and that awful pattern began to laugh at me, I declared I would finish it today!

We go away tomorrow, and they are moving all my furniture down again to leave things as they were before.

Jennie looked at the wall in amazement but I told her merrily that I did it out of pure spite at the vicious thing.

She laughed and said she wouldn't mind doing it herself, but I must not get tired.

How she betrayed herself that time!

But I am here, and no person touches this paper but me—not *alive!*

She tried to get me out of the room—it was too patent! But I said it was so quiet and empty and clean now that I believed I would lie down again and sleep all I could; and not to wake me even for dinner—I would call when I woke.

So now she is gone, and the servants are gone, and the things are gone, and there is nothing left but that great bedstead nailed down, with the canvas mattress we found on it.

We shall sleep downstairs tonight, and take the boat home tomorrow.

I quite enjoy the room, now it is bare again.

How those children did tear about there!

This bedstead is fairly gnawed!

But I must get to work.

I have locked the door and thrown the key down into the front path.

I don't want to go out, and I don't want to have anybody come in, till John comes.

I want to astonish him.

I've got a rope up here that even Jennie did not find. If that woman does get out, and tries to get away, I can tie her!

But I forgot I could not reach far without anything to stand on!

This bed will *not* move!

I tried to lift and push it until I was lame, and then I got so angry I bit off a little piece at one corner—but it hurt my teeth.

Then I peeled off all the paper I could reach standing on the floor. It sticks horribly and the pattern just enjoys it! All those strangled heads and bulbous eyes and waddling fungus growths just shriek with derision!

I am getting angry enough to do something desperate. To jump out of the window would be admirable exercise, but the bars are too strong even to try.

Besides I wouldn't do it. Of course not. I know well enough that a step like that is improper and might be misconstrued.

I don't like to *look* out of the windows even—there are so many of those creeping women and they creep so fast.

I wonder if they all come out of that wallpaper as I did?

But I am securely fastened now by my well-hidden rope—you don't get *me* out in the road there!

I suppose I shall have to get back behind the pattern when it comes night, and that is hard!

It is so pleasant to be out in this great room and creep around as I please!

I don't want to go outside. I won't, even if Jennie asks me to.

For outside you have to creep on the ground, and everything is green instead of yellow.

But here I can creep smoothly on the floor, and my shoulder just fits in that long smooch around the wall, so I cannot lose my way.

Why there's John at the door!

It is no use, young man, you can't open it!

How he does call and pound!

Now he's crying for an axe.

It would be a shame to break down that beautiful door!

"John dear!" said I in the gentlest voice, "the key is down by the front steps, under a plantain leaf!"

That silenced him for a few moments.

Then he said—very quietly indeed, "Open the door, my darling!"

"I can't," said I. "The key is down by the front door under a plantain leaf!"

And then I said it again, several times, very gently and slowly, and said it so often that he had to go and see, and he got it of course, and came in. He stopped short by the door.

"What is the matter?" he cried. "For God's sake, what are you doing!"

I kept on creeping just the same, but I looked at him over my shoulder.

"I've got out at last," said I, "in spite of you and Jane. And I've pulled off most of the paper, so you can't put me back!"

Now why should that man have fainted? But he did, and right across my path by the wall, so that I had to creep over him every time!

BRAM STOKER

The Judge's House

When the time for his examination drew near Malcolm Malcolmson made up his mind to go somewhere to read by himself. He feared the attraction of the seaside, and also he feared completely rural isolation, for of old he knew its charms, and so he determined to find some unpretentious little town where there would be nothing to distract him. He refrained from asking suggestions from any of his friends, for he argued that each would recommend some place of which he had knowledge, and where he had already acquaintances. As Malcolmson wished to avoid friends he had no wish to encumber himself with the attention of friends' friends, and so he determined to look out for a place for himself. He packed a portmanteau with some clothes and all the books he required, and then took a ticket for the first name on the local timetable which he did not know.

When at the end of three hours' journey he alighted at Benchurch, he felt satisfied that he had so far obliterated his tracks as to be sure of having a peaceful opportunity of pursuing his studies. He went straight to the one inn which the sleepy little place contained, and put up for the night. Benchurch was a market town, and once in three weeks was crowded to excess, but for the remainder of the twenty-one days it was as attractive as a desert. Malcomlson looked around the day after his arrival to try to find quarters more isolated than even so quiet an inn as The Good Traveller afforded. There was only one place which took his fancy, and it certainly satisfied his wildest ideas regarding quiet; in fact, quiet was not the proper word to apply to it—desolation was the only term conveying any suitable idea of its isolation. It was an old rambling, heavy-built house of the Jacobean style, with heavy gables and windows, unusually small, and set higher than was customary in such houses, and was surrounded with a high brick wall massively built. Indeed, on examination, it looked more like a fortified house than an ordinary dwelling. But all these things pleased Malcolmson. "Here," he thought, "is the very spot I have been looking for, and if I can only get an opportunity of using it I shall be happy." His joy was increased when he realized beyond doubt that it was not at present inhabited.

From the post office he got the name of the agent, who was rarely surprised at the application to rent a part of the old house. Mr. Carnford, the local lawyer and agent, was a genial old gentleman, and frankly confessed his delight at anyone being willing to live in the house.

"To tell you the truth," said he, "I should be only too happy, on behalf of the owners, to let anyone have the house rent-free for a term of years if only to accustom the people here to see it inhabited. It has been so long empty that some kind of absurd prejudice has grown up about it, and this can be best put down by its occupation— if only," he added, with a sly glance at Malcolmson, "by a scholar like yourself, who wants its quiet for a time."

Malcolmson thought it needless to ask the agent about the "absurd prejudice"; he knew he would get more information, if he should require it, on that subject from other quarters. He paid his three months' rent got a receipt, and the name of an old woman who would probably undertake to "do" for him, and came away with the keys in his pocket. He then went to the landlady of the inn, who was a cheerful and most kindly person, and asked her advice as to such stores and provisions as he would be likely to require. She threw up her hands in amazement when he told her where he was going to settle himself.

"Not in the Judge's House!" she said, and grew pale as she spoke. He explained the locality of the house, saying that he did not know its name. When he had finished she answered:

"Aye, sure enough—sure enough the very place! It is the Judge's House sure enough." He asked her to tell

him about the place, why so called, and what there was
against it. She told him that it was so called locally
because it had been many years before—how long she
could not say, as she was herself from another part of the
country, but she thought it must have been a hundred
years or more—the abode of a judge who was held in
great terror on account of his harsh sentences and his
hostility to prisoners at Assizes. As to what there was
against the house itself she could to tell. She had often
asked, but no one could inform her; but there was a
general feeling that there was *something,* and for her own
part she would not take all the money in Drinkwater's
Bank and stay in the house an hour by herself. Then she
apologized to Malcolmson for her disturbing talk.

"It is too bad of me, sir, and you—and a young gentleman, too—if you will pardon me saying it, going to live
there all alone. If you were my boy—and you'll excuse
me for saying it—you wouldn't sleep there a night, not if
I had to go there myself and pull the big alarm bell that's
on the roof!" The good creature was so manifestly in
earnest, and was so kindly in her intentions, that Malcolmson, although amused, was touched. He told her
kindly how much he appreciated her interest in him, and
added:

"But, my dear Mrs. Witham, indeed you need not be
concerned about me! A man who is reading for the
Mathematical Tripos has too much to think of to be
disturbed by any of these mysterious 'somethings,' and his
work is of too exact and prosaic a kind to allow of his
having any corner in his mind for mysteries of any kind.
Harmonical Progression, Permutations and Combinations,
and Elliptic Functions have sufficient mysteries for me!"
Mrs. Witham kindly understood to see after his commis-
sions, and he went himself to look for the old woman
who had been recommended to him. When he returned
to the Judge's House with her, after an interval of a
couple of hours, he found Mrs. Witham herself waiting
with several men and boys carrying parcels, and an up-
holsterer's man with a bed in a cart, for she said, though
tables and chairs might be all very well, a bed that hadn't
been aired for maybe fifty years was not proper for
young bones to lie on. She was curious to see the inside
of the house; and though manifestly so afraid of the

"somethings" that at the slightest sound she clutched on to Malcolmson, whom she never left for a moment, went over the whole place.

After his examination of the house, Malcolmson decided to take up his abode in the great dining room, which was big enough to serve for all his requirements; and Mrs. Witham, with the aid of the charwoman, Mrs. Dempster, proceeded to arrange matters. When the hampers were brought in and unpacked, Malcolmson saw that with much kind forethought she had sent from her own kitchen sufficient provisions to last for a few days. Before going she expressed all sorts of kind wishes; and at the door turned and said:

"And perhaps, sir, as the room is big and draughty, it might be well to have one of those big screens put round your bed at night—though, truth to tell, I would die myself if I were to be shut in with all kinds of—of 'things,' that put their heads round the sides, or over the top, and look on me!" The image which she had called up was too much for her nerves, and she fled incontinently.

Mrs. Dempster sniffed in a superior manner as the landlady disappeared, and remarked that for her own part she wasn't afraid of all the bogies in the kingdom.

"I'll tell you what it is, sir," she said, "bogies is all kinds and sorts of things—except bogies! Rats and mice, and beetles; and creaky doors, and loose slates, and broken panes, and stiff drawer handles, that stay out when you pull them and then fall down in the middle of the night. Look at the wainscot of the room! It is old—hundreds of years old! Do you think there's no rats and beetles there! And do you imagine, sir, that you won't see none of them? Rats is bogies, I tell you, and bogies is rats; and don't you get to think anything else!"

"Mrs. Dempster," said Malcolmson gravely, making her a polite bow, "you know more than a Senior Wrangler! and let me say, that, as a mark of esteem for your indubitable soundness of head and heart, I shall, when I go, give you possession of this house, and let you stay here by yourself for the last two months of my tenancy, for four weeks will serve my purpose."

"Thank you kindly, sir!" she answered, "but I couldn't sleep away from home a night. I am in Greenhow's Charity, and if I slept a night away from my rooms I

should lose all I have got to live on. The rules is very
strict; and there's too many watching for a vacancy for
me to run any risks in the matter. Only for that, sir, I'd
gladly come here and attend on you altogether during
your stay."

"My good woman," said Malcolmson hastily, "I have
come here on purpose to obtain solitude; and believe me
that I am grateful to the late Greenhow for having so
organized his admirable charity—whatever it is—that I
am perforce denied the opportunity of suffering from
such a form of temptation! Saint Anthony himself could
not be more rigid on the point!"

The old woman laughed harshly. "Ah, young gentle-
men," she said, "you don't fear for naught; and belike
you'll get all the solitude you want here." She set to
work with her cleaning; and by nightfall, when Malcolmson
returned from his walk—he always had one of his books
to study as he walked—he found the room swept and
tidied, a fire burning in the old hearth, the lamp lit, and
the table spread for supper with Mrs. Witham's excellent
fare. "This is comfort, indeed," he said, as he rubbed his
hands.

When he had finished his supper, and lifted the tray to
the other end of the great oak dining-table, he got out his
books again, put fresh wood on the fire, trimmed his
lamp, and set himself down to a spell of real hard work.
He went on without pause till about eleven o'clock, when
he knocked off for a bit to fix his fire and lamp, and to
make himself a cup of tea. He had always been a tea-
drinker, and during his college life he sat late at work
and had taken tea late. The rest was a great luxury to
him, and he enjoyed it with a sense of delicious, volup-
tuous ease. The renewed fire leaped and sparkled and
threw quaint shadows through the great old room; and as
he sipped his hot tea he reveled in the sense of isolation
from his kind. Then it was that he began to notice for
the first time what a noise the rats were making.

"Surely," he thought, "they cannot have been at it all
the time I was reading. Had they been, I must have
noticed it!" Presently, when the noise increased, he satisfied himself that it was really new. It was evident that at
first the rats had been frightened at the presence of a
stranger, and the light of fire and lamp; but that as the

time went on they had grown bolder and were now disporting themselves as was their wont.

How busy they were; and hark to the strange noises! Up and down behind the old wainscot, over the ceiling and under the floor they raced, and gnawed, and scratched! Malcolmson smiled to himself as he recalled to mind the saying of Mrs. Dempster, "Bogies is rats, and rats is bogies!" The tea began to have its effect of intellectual and nervous stimulus, he saw with joy another long spell of work to be done before the night was past, and in the sense of security which it gave him, he allowed himself the luxury of a good look around the room. He took his lamp in one hand, and went all around, wondering that so quaint and beautiful an old house had been so long neglected. The carving of the oak on the panels of the wainscot was fine, and on and round the doors and windows it was beautiful and of rare merit. There were some old pictures on the walls, but they were coated so thick with dust and dirt that he could not distinguish any detail of them, though he held his lamp as high as he could over his head. Here and there as he went round he saw some crack or hole blocked for a moment by the face of a rat with its bright eyes glittering in the light, but in an instant it was gone, and a squeak and a scamper followed. The thing that most struck him, however, was the rope of the great alarm bell on the roof, which hung down in a far corner of the room on the right-hand side of the fireplace. He pulled up close to the hearth a great high-backed carved oak chair, and sat down to his last cup of tea. When this was done he made up the fire, and went back to his work, sitting at the corner of the table, having the fire to his left. For a little while the rats disturbed him somewhat with their perpetual scampering, but he got accustomed to the noise as one does to the ticking of a clock or to the roar of moving water; and he became so immersed in his work that everything in the world except the problem which he was trying to solve, passed away from him.

He suddenly looked up, his problem was still unsolved, and there was in the air that sense of the hour before the dawn, which is so dread to doubtful life. The noise of the rats had ceased. Indeed it seemed to him that it must have ceased but lately and it was the sudden cessation which had disturbed him. The fire had fallen low, but still it threw out a deep red glow. As he looked he started in spite of his *sang froid*.

There on the great high-backed carved oak chair by the right side of the fireplace sat an enormous rat, steadily glaring at him with baleful eyes. He made a motion to it as though to hunt it away, but it did not stir. Then he made the motion of throwing something. Still it did not stir, but showed its great white teeth angrily, and its cruel eyes shone in the lamplight with an added vindictiveness.

Malcolmson felt amazed, and seizing the poker from the hearth ran at it to kill it. Before, however, he could strike it, the rat, with a squeak that sounded like the concentration of hate, jumped on the floor, and, running up the rope of the alarm bell, disappeared in the darkness beyond the range of the green-shaded lamp. Instantly, strange to say, the noisy scampering of the rats in the wainscot began again.

By this time Malcolmson's mind was quite off the problem; and as a shrill cock-crow outside told him of the approach of morning, he went to bed and to sleep.

He slept so soundly that he was not even awakened by Mrs. Dempster coming in to make up his room. It was only when she had tidied up the place and got his breakfast ready and tapped on the screen which closed in his bed that he woke. He was a little tired still after his night's hard work, but a strong cup of tea soon freshened him up, and, taking his book, he went out for his morning walk, bringing with him a few sandwiches lest he should not care to return till dinnertime. He found quiet walk between high elms some way outside the town, and here he spent the greater part of the day studying his Laplace. On his return he looked in to see Mrs. Witham and to thank her for her kindness. When she saw him coming through the diamond-paned bay window of her sanctum she came out to meet him and asked him in. She looked at him searchingly and shook her head as she said:

"You must not overdo it, sir. You are paler this morning than you should be. Too late hours and too hard work on the brain isn't good for any man! But tell me, sir, how did you pass the night? Well, I hope? But, my heart!

sir, I was glad when Mrs. Dempster told me this morning that you were all right and sleeping when she went in."

"Oh, I was all right," he answered smiling, "the 'some-things' didn't worry me, as yet. Only the rats; and they had a circus, I tell you, all over the place. There was one wicked-looking old devil that sat up on my own chair by the fire and wouldn't go till I took the poker to him, and then he ran up the rope of the alarm bell and got to somewhere up the wall or ceiling—I couldn't see where, it was so dark."

"Mercy on us," said Mrs. Witham, "an old devil, and sitting on a chair by the fireside! Take care, sir! Take care! There's many a true word spoken in jest."

"How do you mean? 'Pon my word I don't understand."

"An old devil! The old devil, perhaps. There! sir, you needn't laugh," for Malcolmson had broken into a hearty peal. "You young folks thinks it easy to laugh at things that makes older ones shudder. Never mind, sir! Never mind! Please God, you'll laugh all the time. It's what I wish you myself!" and the good lady beamed all over in sympathy with his enjoyment, her fears gone for a moment.

"Oh, forgive me!" said Malcolmson presently. "Don't think me rude; but the idea was too much for me—that the old devil himself was on the chair last night." And at the thought he laughed again. Then he went home to dinner.

This evening the scampering of the rats began earlier; indeed it had been going on before his arrival, and only ceased whilst his presence by its freshness disturbed them. After dinner he saw by the fire for a while and had a smoke; and then, having cleared his table, began to work as before. Tonight the rats disturbed him more than they had done on the previous night. How they scampered up and down and under and over! How they squeaked, and scratched, and gnawed! How they, getting bolder by degrees, came to the mouths of their holes and to the chinks and cracks and crannies in the wainscoting till their eyes shone like tiny lamps as the firelight rose and fell. But to him, now doubtless accustomed to them, their eyes were not wicked; only their playfulness touched him. Sometimes the boldest of them made sallies on the floor or along the moldings of the wainscot. Now and again as they disturbed him Malcolmson made a sound to frighten them, smiting the table with his hand or giving a fierce "Hsh, hssh," so that they fled straight away to their holes.

And so the early part of the night wore on; and despite the noise Malcolmson got more and more immersed in his work.

All at once he stopped, as on the previous night, being overcome by a sudden sense of silence. There was not the faintest sound of gnaw, or scratch, or squeak. The silence was as of the grave. He remembered the odd occurrence of the previous night and instinctively he looked at the chair standing close by the fireside. And then a very odd sensation thrilled through him.

There, on the great old high-backed carved oak chair beside the fireplace sat the same enormous rat, steadily glaring at him with baleful eyes.

Instinctively he took the nearest thing to his hand, a book of logarithms, and flung it at it. The book was badly aimed and the rat did not stir, so again the poker performance of the previous night was repeated; and again the rat, being closely pursued, fled up the rope of the alarm bell. Strangely too, the departure of this rat was instantly followed by the renewal of the noise made by the general rat community. On this occasion, as on the previous one, Malcolmson could not see at what part of the room the rat disappeared, for the green shade of his lamp left the upper part of the room in darkness, and the fire had burned low.

On looking at his watch he found it was close on midnight and, not sorry for the *divertissement,* he made up his fire and made himself his nightly pot of tea. He had got through a good spell of work and thought himself entitled to a cigarette, and so he sat on the great carved oak chair before the fire and enjoyed it. Whilst smoking he began to think that he would like to know where the rat disappeared to, for he had certain ideas for the morrow not entirely disconnected with a rat-trap. Accordingly he lit another lamp and placed it so that it would shine well into the right-hand corner of the wall by the fireplace. Then he got all the books he had with him, and placed them handy to throw at the vermin. Finally he lifted the rope of the alarm bell and placed the end of it on the table, fixing the extreme end under the lamp. As he handled it he could not help noticing how pliable it was, especially for so strong a rope, and one not in use. "You could hang a man with it," he thought to himself. When his preparations were made he looked around, and said complacently:

"There now, my friend, I think we shall learn something of you this time." He began his work again, and though as before somewhat disturbed at first by the noise of the rat, soon lost himself in his propositions and problems.

Again he was called to his immediate surroundings suddenly. This time it might not have been the sudden silence only which took his attention; there was a slight movement of the rope, and the lamp moved. Without stirring, he looked to see if his pile of books was within range, and then cast his eye along the rope. As he looked he saw the great rat drop from the rope on the oak armchair and sit there glaring at him. He raised a book in his right hand, and taking careful aim, flung it at the rat. The latter, with a quick movement, sprang aside and dodged the missile. He then took another book, and a third, and flung them one after another at the rat, but each time unsuccessfully. At last he stood with a book poised in his hand to throw, the rat squeaked and seemed afraid. This made Malcolmson more than ever eager to strike, and the book flew and struck the rat a resounding blow. It gave a terrifying squeak, and turning on his pursuer a look of terrifying malevolence, ran up the chair-back and made a great jump to the rope of the alarm bell and ran up it like lightning. The lamp rocked under the sudden strain, but it was a heavy one and did not topple over. Malcolmson kept his eyes on the rat, and saw it by the light of the second lamp to a molding of the wainscot and disappear through a hole in one of the great pictures which hung on the wall, obscured and invisible through its coating of dirty and dust.

"I shall look up my friend's habitation in the morning," said the student, as he went over to collect his books. "The third picture from the fireplace; I shall not forget." He picked up the books one by one, commenting on them as he lifted them. "*Comic Sections* he does not mind, nor *Cycloidal Oscillations*, nor the *Principia*, nor *Quarternions*, nor *Thermo-dynamics*. Now for the book that fetched him!" Malcolmson took it up and looked at it. As he did so he started, and a sudden pallor over-spread his face. He looked round uneasily and shivered slightly, as he murmured to himself:

"The Bible my mother gave me! What an odd coincidence." He sat down to work again, and the rats in the wainscot renewed their gambols. They did not disturb him, however; somehow their presence gave him a sense of companionship. But he could not attend to his work, and after striving to master the subject on which he was engaged gave it up in despair, and went to bed as the first streak of dawn stole in through the eastern window.

He slept heavily but uneasily, and dreamed much; and when Mrs. Dempster woke him late in the morning he seemed ill at ease, and for a few minutes did not seem to realize exactly where he was. His first request rather surprised the servant.

"Mrs. Dempster, when I am out today I wish you would get the steps and dust or wash those pictures—specially that one the third from the fireplace—I want to see what they are."

Late in the afternoon Malcolmson worked at his books in the shaded walk, and the cheerfulness of the previous day came back to him as the day wore on, and he found that his reading was progressing well. He had worked out to a satisfactory conclusion all the problems which had as yet baffled him, and it was in a state of jubilation that he paid a visit to Mrs. Witham at The Good Traveler. He found a stranger in the cozy sitting-room with the land-lady, who was introduced to him as Dr. Thornhill. She was not quite at ease, and this, combined with the doc-tor's plunging at once into series of questions, made Malcolmson come to the conclusion that his presence was not an accident, so without preliminary he said:

"Dr. Thornhill, I shall with pleasure answer you any question you may choose to ask me if you will answer me one question first."

The doctor seemed surprised, but he smiled and an-swered at once, "Done! What is it?"

"Did Mrs. Witham ask you to come here and see me and advise me?"

Dr. Thornhill for a moment was taken aback, and Mrs. Witham got fiery red and turned away; but the doctor was a frank and ready man, and he answered at once and openly:

"She did: but she didn't intend you to know it. I suppose it was my clumsy haste that made you suspect. She told me that she did not like the idea of your being in that house all by yourself and that she thought you took too much strong tea. In fact, she wants me to advise you if possible to give up the tea and the very late hours. I was a keen student in my time, so I suppose I may take the liberty of a college man and, without offense, advise you not quite as a stranger."

Malcolmson with a bright smile held out his hand. "Shake! as they say in America," he said. "I must thank you for your kindness and Mrs. Witham too, and your kindness deserves a return on my part. I promise to take no more strong tea—no tea at all till you let me—and I shall go to bed tonight at one o'clock at latest. Will that do?"

"Capital," said the doctor. "Now tell us all that you noticed in the old house," and so Malcolmson then and there told in minute detail all that had happened in the last two nights. He was interrupted every now and then by some exclamation from Mrs. Witham, till finally when he told of the episode of the Bible the landlady's pent-up emotions found vent in a shriek; and it was not till a stiff glass of brandy and water had been administered that she grew composed again. Dr. Thornhill listened with a face of growing gravity, and when the narrative was compete and Mrs. Witham had been restored he asked:

"The rat always went up the rope of the alarm bell?"

"Always."

"I suppose you know," said the doctor after a pause, "what the rope is?"

"No!"

"It is," said the doctor slowly, "the very rope which the hangman used for all the victims of the Judge's judicial rancor!" Here he was interrupted by another scream from Mrs. Witham, and steps had to be taken for her recovery. Malcolmson having looked at his watch, and found that it was close to his dinner hour, had gone home before her complete recovery.

When Mrs. Witham was herself again she almost assailed the doctor with angry questions as to what he meant by putting such horrible ideas into the poor man's mind. "He has quite enough there already to upset him," she added. Dr. Thornhill replied:

"My dear madam, I had a distinct purpose in it! I wanted to draw his attention to the bell rope, and to fix it there. It may be that he is in a highly overwrought state, and has been studying too much, although I am bound to say that he seems as sound and healthy a young man, mentally and bodily, as ever I saw—but then the rats— and that suggestion of the devil." The doctor shook his head and went on. "I would have offered to go and stay the first night with him but that I felt sure it would have been a cause of offense. He may get in the night some strange fright or hallucination; and if he does I want him to pull that rope. All alone as he is will give us warning, and we may reach him in time to be of service. I shall be sitting up pretty late tonight and shall keep my ears open. Do not be alarmed if Benchurch gets a surprise before morning."

"Oh, Doctor, what do you mean? What do you mean?"

"I mean this, that possibly—nay, more probably—we shall hear the great alarm bell from the Judge's House tonight," and the doctor made about as effective an exit as could be thought of.

When Malcolmson arrived home he found that it was a little after his usual time, and Mrs. Dempster had gone away—the rules of Greenhow's Charity were not to be neglected. He was glad to see that the place was bright and tidy with a cheerful fire and a well-trimmed lamp. The evening was colder than might have been expected in April, and a heavy wind was blowing with such rapidity increasing strength that there was every promise of a storm during the night. For a few minutes after his entrance the noise of the rats ceased; but so soon as they became accustomed to his presence they began again. He was glad to hear them, for he felt once more the feeling of companionship in their noise, and his mind ran back to the strange fact that they only ceased to manifest themselves when that other—the great rat with the baleful eyes—came upon the scene. The reading-lamp only was lit and its green shade kept the ceiling and the upper part of the room in darkness, so that the cheerful light from the hearth spreading over the floor and shining on the white cloth laid over the end of the table was warm and cherry. Malcolmson sat down to his dinner with a good appetite and a buoyant spirit. After his dinner and a cigarette he sat steadily down to work, determined not to let anything disturb him, for he remembered his promise to the doctor, and made up his mind to make the best of the time at his disposal.

For an hour or so he worked all right, and then his thoughts began to wander from his books. The actual circumstances around him, the calls on his physical attention, and his nervous susceptibility were not to be denied. By this time the wind had become a gale, and the gale a storm. The old house, solid though it was, seemed to shake to its foundations, and the storm roared and raged through its many chimneys and its queer old gables, producing strange unearthly sounds in the empty rooms and corridors. Even the great alarm bell on the roof must have felt the force of the wind, for the rope rose and fell slightly, as though the bell were moved a little from time to time, and the limber rope fell on the oak floor with a hard and hollow sound.

As Malcolmson listened to it he thought to himself of the doctor's words, "It is the rope with the hangman used for the victims of the Judge's judicial rancor," and he went over to the corner of the fireplace and took it in his hand to look at it. There seemed a sort of deadly interest in it, and as he stood there he lost himself for a moment in speculation as to who these victims were, and the grim wish of the Judge to have such a ghastly relic ever under his eyes. As he stood there the swaying of the bell on the roof still lifted the rope now and again; but presently there came a new sensation—a sort of tremor in the rope, as though something was moving along it.

Looking up instinctively Malcolmson saw the great rat coming slowly down toward him, glaring at him steadily. He dropped the rope and started back with a muttered curse, and the rat turning ran up the rope again and disappeared, and at the same instant Malcolmson became conscious that the noise of the rats, which had ceased for a while, began again.

All this set him thinking, and it occurred to him that he had not investigated the lair of the rat or looked at the pictures, as he had intended. He lit the other lamp without the shade, and, holding it up, went and stood opposite the third picture from the fireplace on the right-hand side where he had seen the rat disappear on the previous night.

At the first glance he started back so suddenly that he almost dropped the lamp, and a deadly pallor overspread his face. His knees shook, and heavy drops of sweat came on his forehead, and he trembled like an aspen. But he was young and plucky, and pulled himself together, and after the pause of a few seconds stepped forward again, raised the lamp, and examined the picture which had been dusted and washed, and now stood out clearly.

It was of a judge dressed in his robes of scarlet and ermine. His face was strong and merciless, evil, crafty, and vindictive, with a sensual mouth, hooked nose of ruddy color, and shaped like the beak of a bird of prey. The rest of the face was of cadaverous color. The eyes were of peculiar brilliance and with a terribly malignant expression. As he looked at them, Malcolmson grew cold, for he saw there the very counterpart of the eyes of the great rat. The lamp almost fell from his hand, he saw the rat with its baleful eyes peering out through the hole in the corner of the picture, and noted the sudden cessation of the noise of the other rats. However, he pulled himself together and went on with the examination of the picture.

The Judge was seated in a great high-backed carved oak chair, on the right-hand side of a great stone fireplace where, in the corner, a rope hung down from the ceiling, its end lying coiled on the floor. With a feeling of something like horror. Malcolmson recognized the scene of the room as it stood, and gazed around him in an awestruck manner as though he expected to find some strange presence behind him. Then he looked over to the corner of the fireplace—and with a loud cry he let the lamp fall from his hands.

There, in the Judge's armchair, with the rope hanging behind, sat the rat with the Judge's baleful eyes, now intensified and with a fiendish leer. Save for the howling of the storm without there was silence.

The fallen lamp recalled Malcolmson to himself. Fortunately it was of metal, and so the oil was not spilt.

However, the practical need of attending to it settled at once his nervous apprehensions. When he had turned it out, he wiped his brow and thought for a moment.

"This will not do," he said to himself. "If I go on like this I shall become a crazy fool. This must stop! I promised the doctor I would not take tea. Faith, he was pretty right! My nerves must have been getting into a queer state. Funny I did not notice it. I never felt better in my life. However, it is all right now, and I shall not be such a fool again."

Then he mixed himself a good stiff glass of brandy and water and resolutely sat down to his work.

It was nearly an hour when he looked up from his book, disturbed by the sudden stillness. Without, the wind howled and roared louder than ever, and the rain drove in sheets against the windows, beating like hail on the glass; but within there was no sound whatever save the echo of the wind as it roared in the great chimney, and now and then a hiss as a few raindrops found their way down the chimney in a lull of the storm. The fire had fallen low and had ceased to flame, though it threw out a red glow. Malcolmson listened attentively, and presently heard a thin, squeaking noise, very faint. It came from the corner of the room where the rope hung down, and he thought it was the creaking of the rope on the floor as the swaying of the bell raised and lowered it. Looking up, however, he saw in the dim light the great rat clinging to the rope and gnawing it. The rope was already nearly gnawed through—he could see the lighter color where the strands were laid bare. As he looked the job was completed, and the severed end of the rope fell clattering on the oaken floor, whilst for an instant the great rat remained like a knob or tassel at the end of the rope, which now began to sway to and fro. Malcolmson felt for a moment another pang of terror as he thought that now the possibility of calling the outer world to his assistance was cut off, but an intense anger took its place, and seizing the book he was reading he hurled it at the rat. The blow was well aimed, but before the missile could reach him the rat dropped off and struck the floor with a soft thud. Malcolmson instantly rushed over toward him, but it darted away and disappeared in the darkness of the shadows of the room. Malcolmson felt that his work was over for the night, and determined then and there to vary the monotony of the proceedings by a hunt for the rat, and took off the green shade of the lamp so as to ensure a wider spreading light. As he did so the gloom of the upper part of the room was relieved, and in the new flood of light, great by comparison with the previous darkness, the pictures on the wall stood out boldly. From where he stood, Malcolmson saw right opposite to him the third picture on the wall from the right of the fireplace. He rubbed his eyes in surprise, and then a great fear began to come upon him.

In the center of the picture was a great irregular patch of brown canvas, as fresh as when it was stretched on the frame. The background was as before, with chair and chimney-corner and rope, but the figure of the Judge had disappeared.

Malcolmson, almost in a chill of horror, turned slowly round, and then he began to shake and tremble like a man in a palsy. His strength seemed to have left him, and he was incapable of action or movement, hardly even of thought. He could only see and hear.

There, on the great high-backed carved oak chair sat the Judge in his robes of scarlet and ermine, with his baleful eyes glaring vindictively, and a smile of triumph on the resolute, cruel mouth, as he lifted with his hands a *black cap*. Malcolmson felt as if the blood was running from his heart, as one does in moments of prolonged suspense. There was a singing in his ears. Without, he could hear the roar and howl of the tempest, and through it, swept on the storm came the striking of midnight by the great chimes in the market place. He stood for a space of time that seemed to him endless, still as a statue, and with wide-open horror-struck eyes, breathless. As the clock struck, so the smile of triumph on the Judge's face intensified, and at the last stroke of midnight he placed the black cap on his head.

Slowly and deliberately the Judge rose from his chair and picked up the piece of the rope of the alarm bell which lay on the floor, drew it through his hands as if he enjoyed its touch, and then deliberately began to knot one end of it, fashioning it into a noose. This he tightened and tested with his foot, pulling hard at it till he was satisfied and then making a running noose of it, which he held in his hand. Then he began to move along the table on the opposite side to Malcolmson, keeping his eyes on him until he had passed him, when with a quick movement he stood in front of the door. Malcolmson then began to feel that he was trapped, and tried to think of what he should do. There was some fascination in the Judge's eyes, which he never took off him, and he had perforce to look. He saw the Judge approach—still keeping between him and the door—and raise the noose and throw it toward him as if to entangle him. With a great effort he made a quick movement to one side, and saw the rope fall beside him, and heard it strike the oaken floor. After the Judge raised the noose and tried to ensnare him, ever keeping his baleful eyes fixed on him, and each time by a mighty effort the student just managed to evade it. So this went on for many times, the Judge seeming never discouraged nor discomposed at failure, but playing as a cat does with a mouse. At last in despair, which had reached its climax, Malcolmson cast a quick glance round him. The lamp seemed to have blazed up, and there was a fairly good light in the room. At the many rat-holes and the chinks and crannies of the wainscot he saw the rats' eyes; and this aspect, that was purely physical, gave him a gleam of comfort. He looked around and saw that the rope of the great alarm bell was laden with rats. Every inch of it was covered with them, and more and more were pouring through the small circular hole in the ceiling whence it emerged, so that with their weight the bell was beginning to sway.

Hark! it had swayed till the clapper had touched the bell. The sound was but a tiny one, but the bell was only beginning to sway, and it would increase.

At the sound the Judge, who had been keeping his eyes fixed on Malcolmson, looked up and a scowl of diabolical anger overspread his face. His eyes fairly glowed like hot coals, and he stamped his foot with a sound that seemed to make the house shake. A dreadful peal of thunder broke overhead as he raised the rope again, whilst the rats kept running up and down the rope as though working against time. This time, instead of throwing it, he drew close to his victim, and held open the noose as he approached. As he came closer there seemed something paralyzing in his very presence, and Malcolmson stood rigid as a corpse. He felt the Judge's icy fingers touch his throat as he adjusted the rope. The noose tightened—tightened. Then the Judge, taking the rigid form of the student in his arms, carried him over and placed him standing in the oak chair, and stepping up beside him, put is hand up and caught the end of the swaying rope of the alarm bell. As he raised his hand the rats fled squeaking and disappeared through the hole in the ceiling. Taking the end of the noose which was round Malcolmson's neck he tied it to the hanging-bell rope, and then descending pulled away from the chair.

When the alarm bell of the Judge's House began to sound a crowd soon assembled. Lights and torches of various kinds appeared, and soon a silent crowd was hurrying to the spot. They knocked loudly at the door, but there was no reply. Then they burst in the door, and poured into the great dining room, the doctor at the head.

There at the end of the rope of the great alarm bell hung the body of the student, and on the face of the Judge in the picture was a malignant smile.

H.P. LOVECRAFT

The Rats in the Walls

On July 16, 1923, I moved into Exham Priory after the last workman had finished his labors. The restoration had been a stupendous task, for little had remained of the deserted pile but a shell-like ruin; yet because it had been the seat of my ancestors, I let no expense deter me. The place had not been inhabited since the reign of James the First, when a tragedy of intensely hideous, though largely unexplained, nature had struck down the master, five of his children, and several servants; and driven forth under a cloud of suspicion and terror the third son, my lineal progenitor and the only survivor of the abhorred line.

With this sole heir denounced as a murderer, the estate had reverted to the crown, nor had the accused man made any attempt to exculpate himself or regain his property. Shaken by some horror greater than that of conscience or the law, and expressing only a frantic wish to exclude the ancient edifice from his sight and memory, Walter de la Poer, eleventh Baron Exham, fled to Virginia and there founded the family which by the next century had become known as Delapore.

Exham Priory had remained untenanted, though later allotted to the estates of the Norrys family and much studied because of its peculiarly composite architecture; an architecture involving Gothic towers resting on a Saxon or Romanesque substructure, whose foundation in turn was of a still earlier order or blend of orders—Roman, and even Druidic or native Cymric, if legends speak truly. This foundation was a very singular thing, being merged on one side with the solid limestone of the precipice from whose brink the priory overlooked a desolate valley three miles west of the village of Anchester.

Architects and antiquarians loved to examine this strange relic of forgotten centuries, but the country folk hated it. They had hated it hundreds of years before, when my ancestors lived there, and they hated it now, with the moss and mould of abandonment on it. I had not been a day in Anchester before I knew I came of an accursed house. And this week workmen have blown up Exham Priory, and are busy obliterating the traces of its foundations. The bare statistics of my ancestry I had always known, together with the fact that my first American forebear had come to the colonies under a strange cloud. Of details, however, I had been kept wholly ignorant through the policy of reticence always maintained by the Delapores. Unlike our planter neighbors, we seldom boasted of crusading ancestors or other mediaeval and Renaissance heroes; nor was any kind of tradition handed down except what may have been recorded in the sealed envelope left before the Civil War by every squire to his eldest son for posthumous opening. The glories we cherished were those achieved since the migration; the glories of a proud and honorable, if somewhat reserved and unsocial Virginia line.

During the war our fortunes were extinguished and our whole existence changed by the burning of Carfax, our home on the banks of the James. My grandfather, advanced in years, had perished in that incendiary outrage, and with him the envelope that had bound us all to the past. I can recall the fire today as I saw it then at the age of seven, with the Federal soldiers shouting, the women screaming, and the negroes howling and praying. My father was in the army, defending Richmond, and after many formalities my mother and I were passed through the lines to join him.

When the war ended we all moved north, whence my mother had come; and I grew to manhood, middle age, and ultimate wealth as a stolid Yankee. Neither my father nor I ever knew what our hereditary envelope had contained, and as I merged into the grayness of Massachusetts business life I lost all interest in the mysteries which evidently lurked far back in my family tree. Had I suspected their nature, how gladly I would have left Exham Priory to its moss, bats, and cobwebs!

My father died in 1904, but without any message to leave to me, or to my only child, Alfred, a motherless boy of ten. It was this boy who reversed the order of family information, for although I could give him only jesting conjectures about the past, he wrote me of some very interesting ancestral legends when the late war took him to England in 1917 as an aviation officer. Apparently the Delapores had a colorful and perhaps sinister history, for a friend of my son's, Capt. Edward Norrys of the Royal Flying Corps, dwelt near the family seat at Anchester and related some peasant superstitions which few novelists could equal for wildness and incredibility. Norrys himself, of course, did not take them so seriously; but they amused my son and made good material for his letters to me. It was this legendry which definitely turned my attention to my transatlantic heritage, and made me resolve to purchase and restore the family seat which Norrys showed to Alfred in its picturesque desertion, and offered to get for him at a surprisingly reasonable figure, since his own uncle was the present owner.

I bought Exham Priory in 1918, but was almost immediately distracted from my plans of restoration by the return of my son as a maimed invalid. During the two years that he lived I thought of nothing but his care, having even placed my business under the direction of partners.

In 1921, as I found myself bereaved and aimless, a retired manufacturer no longer young, I resolved to divert my remaining years with my new possession. Visiting Anchester in December, I was entertained by Capt. Norrys, a plump, amiable young man who had thought much of my son, and secured his assistance in gathering plans and anecdotes to guide in the coming restoration. Exham Priory itself I saw without emotion, a jumble of tottering medieval ruins covered with lichens and honeycombed with rooks' nests, perched perilously upon a precipice, and denuded of floors or other interior features save the stone walls of the separate towers.

As I gradually recovered the image of the edifice as it had been when my ancestors left it over three centuries before, I began to hire workmen for the reconstruction.

In every case I was forced to go outside the immediate locality, for the Anchester villagers had an almost unbelievable fear and hatred of the place. This sentiment was so great that it was sometimes communicated to the outside laborers, causing numerous desertions; whilst its scope appeared to include both the priory and its ancient family.

My son had told me that he was somewhat avoided during his visits because he was a de la Poer, and I now found myself subtly ostracized for a like reason until I convinced the peasants how little I knew of my heritage. Even then they sullenly disliked me, so that I had to collect most of the village traditions through the mediation of Norrys. What the people could not forgive, perhaps, was that I had come to restore a symbol so abhorrent to them; for, rationally or not, they viewed Exham Priory as nothing less than a haunt of fiends and werewolves.

Piecing together the tales which Norrys collected for me, and supplementing them with the accounts of several savants who had studied the ruins, I decided that Exham Priory stood on the site of a prehistoric temple; a Druidical or ante-Druidical thing which must have been contemporary with Stonehenge. That indescribable rites had been celebrated there, few doubted, and there were unpleasant tales of the transference of these rites into the Cybele-worship which the Romans had introduced.

Inscriptions still visible in the subcellar bore such unmistakable letters as "DIV ... OPS ... MAGNA. MAT ..." sign of the Magna Mater whose dark worship was once vainly forbidden to Roman citizens. Anchester had been the camp of the third Augustan legion, as many remains attest, and it was said that the temple of Cybele was splendid and thronged with worshippers who performed nameless ceremonies at the bidding of a Phrygian priest. Tales added that the fall of the old religion did not end the orgies at the temple, but that the priests lived on in the new faith without real change. Likewise was it said that the rites did not vanish with the Roman power, and that certain among the Saxons added to what remained of the temple, and gave it the essential outline it subsequently preserved, making it the center of a cult feared through half the heptarchy. About 1000 A.D. the place is mentioned in a chronicle as being a substantial stone priory housing a strange and powerful monastic order and surrounded by extensive gardens which needed no walls to exclude a frightened populace. It was never destroyed by the Danes, though after the Norman Conquest it must have declined tremendously; since there was no impediment when Henry the Third granted the site to my ancestor, Gilbert de la Poer, First Baron Exham, in 1261.

Of my family before this date there is no evil report, but something strange must have happened then. In one chronicle there is a reference to a de la Poer as "cursed of God" in 1307, whilst village legendry had nothing but evil and frantic fear to tell of the castle that went up on the foundations of the old temple and priory. The fireside tales were of the most grisly description, all the ghastlier because of their frightened reticence and cloudy evasiveness. They represented my ancestors as a race of hereditary daemons beside whom Gilles de Retz and the Marquis de Sade would seem the veriest tyros, and hinted whisperingly at their responsibility for the occasional disappearances of villagers through several generations.

The worst characters, apparently, were the barons and their direct heirs; at least, most was whispered about these. If of healtheir inclinations, it was said, an heir would early and mysteriously die to make way for another more typical scion. There seemed to be an inner cult in the family, presided over by the head of the house, and sometimes closed except to a few members. Temperament rather than ancestry was evidently the basis of this cult, for it was entered by several who married into the family. Lady Margaret Trevor from Cornwall, wife of Godfrey, the second son of the fifth baron, became a favorite bane of children all over the countryside, and the daemon heroine of a particularly horrible old ballad not yet extinct near the Welsh border. Preserved in balladry, too, though not illustrating the same point, is the hideous tale of Lady Mary de la Poer, who shortly after her marriage to the Earl of Shrewsfield was killed by him and his mother, both of the slayers being absolved and blessed by the priest to whom they confessed what they dared not repeat to the world.

These myths and ballads, typical as they were of crude superstition, repelled me greatly. Their persistence, and their application to so long a line of my ancestors, were especially annoying; whilst the imputations of monstrous habits proved unpleasantly reminiscent of the one known scandal of my immediate forebears—the case of my cousin, young Randolph Delapore of Carfax, who went among the negroes and became a voodoo priest after he returned from the Mexican War.

I was much less disturbed by the vaguer tales of wails and howlings in the barren, windswept valley beneath the limestone cliff; of the graveyard stenches after the spring rains; of the floundering, squealing white thing on which Sir John Clave's horse had trod one night in a lonely field; and of the servant who had gone mad at what he saw in the priory in the full light of day. These things were hackneyed spectral lore, and I was at that time a pronounced skeptic. The accounts of vanished peasants were less to be dismissed, though not especially significant in view of medieval custom. Prying curiosity meant death, and more than one severed head had been publicly shown on the bastions—now effaced—around Exham Priory.

A few of the tales were exceedingly picturesque, and made me wish I had learnt more of the comparative mythology in my youth. There was, for instance, the belief that a legion of batwinged devils kept witches' sabbath each night at the priory—a legion whose sustenance might explain the disproportionate abundance of coarse vegetables harvested in the vast gardens. And, most vivid of all, there was the dramatic epic of the rats—the scampering army of obscene vermin which had burst forth from the castle three months after the tragedy that doomed it to desertion—the lean, filthy, ravenous army which had swept all before it and devoured fowl, cats, dogs, hogs, sheep, and even two hapless human beings before its fury was spent. Around that unforgettable rodent army a whole separate cycle of myths revolves, for it scattered among the village homes and brought curses and horrors in its train.

Such was the lore that assailed me as I pushed to completion, with an elderly obstinacy, the work of restoring my ancestral home. It must not be imagined for a moment that these tales formed my principal psychological environment. On the other hand, I was constantly praised and encouraged by Capt. Norrys and the anti-quarians who surrounded and aided me. When the task was done, over two years after its commencement, I viewed the great rooms, wainscotted walls, vaulted ceil-ings, mullioned windows, and broad staircases with a pride which fully compensated for the prodigious ex-pense of the restoration.

Every attribute of the Middle Ages was cunningly re-produced, and the new parts blended perfectly with the original walls and foundations. The seat of my fathers was complete, and I looked forward to redeeming at last the local fame of the line which ended in me. I would reside here permanently, and prove that a de la Poer (for I had adopted again the original spelling of the name) need not be a fiend. My comfort was perhaps augmented by the fact that, although Exham Priory was mediaevally fitted, its interior was in truth wholly new and free from old vermin and old ghosts alike.

As I have said, I moved in on July 16, 1923. My household consisted of seven servants and nine cats, of which latter species I am particularly fond. My eldest cat, "Nigger-Man," was seven years old and had come with me from my home in Bolton, Massachusetts; the others I had accumulated whilst living with Capt. Norrys' fam-ily during the restoration of the priory.

For five days our routine proceeded with the utmost placidity, my time being spent mostly in the codification of old family data. I had now obtained some very circum-stantial accounts of the final tragedy and flight of Walter de la Poer, which I conceived to be the probable contents of the hereditary paper lost in the fire at Carfax. It appeared that my ancestor was accused with much reason of having killed all the other members of his household, except four servant confederates, in their sleep, about two weeks after a shocking discovery which changed his whole demeanor, but which, except by implication, he disclosed to no one save perhaps the servants who assisted him and afterward fled beyond reach.

This deliberate slaughter, which included a father, three brothers, and two sisters, was largely condoned by the villagers, and so slackly treated by the law that its perpe-trator escaped honored, unharmed, and undisguised to Virginia; the general whispered sentiment being that he had purged the land of immemorial curse. What discovery had prompted an act so terrible, I could scarcely even conjecture. Walter de la Poer must have known for years the sinister tales about his family, so that this material could have given him no fresh impulse. Had he, then, witnessed some appalling ancient rite, or stumbled upon some frightful and revealing symbol in the priory or its vicinity? He was reputed to have been a shy, gentle youth in England. In Virginia he seemed not so much hard or bitter as harassed and apprehensive. He was spoken of in the diary of another gentleman adventurer, Francis Harley of Bellview, as a man of unexampled justice, honor, and delicacy.

On July 22 occurred the first incident which, though lightly dismissed at the time, takes on a preternatural significance in relation to later events. It was so simple as to be almost negligible, and could not possibly have been noticed under the circumstances; for it must be recalled that since I was in a building practically fresh and new except for the walls, and surrounded by a well-balanced staff of servitors, apprehension would have been absurd despite the locality.

What I afterward remembered is merely this—that my old black cat, whose moods I know so well, was undoubtedly alert and anxious to an extent wholly out of keeping with his natural character. He roved from room to room, restless and disturbed, and sniffed contantly about the walls which formed part of the Gothic structure. I realize how trite this sounds—like the inevitable dog in the ghost story, which always growls before his master sees the sheeted figure—yet I cannot consistently suppress it.

The following day a servant complained of restlessness among all the cats in the house. He came to me in my study, a lofty west room on the second story, with groined arches, black oak panelling, and a triple Gothic window overlooking the limestone cliff and desolate valley; and even as he spoke I saw the jetty form of Nigger-man creeping along the west wall and scratching at the new panels which overlaid the ancient stone.

I told the man that there must be some singular odor or emanation from the old stonework, imperceptible to human senses, but affecting the delicate organs of cats even through the woodwork. This I truly believed, and when the fellow suggested the presence of mice or rats, I mentioned that there had been no rats there for three hundred years, and that even the field mice of the surrounding country could hardly be found in these high walls, where they had never been known to stray. That afternoon I called on Capt. Norrys, and he assured me that it would be quite incredible for field mice to infest the priory in such a sudden and unprecedented fashion.

That night, dispensing as usual with a valet, I retired in the west tower chamber which I had chosen as my own, reached from the study by a stone staircase and short gallery—the former partly ancient, the latter entirely restored. This room was circular, very high, and without wainscotting, being hung with arras which I had myself chosen in London.

Seeing that Nigger-man was with me, I shut the heavy Gothic door and retired by the light of the electric bulbs which so cleverly counterfeited candles, finally switching off the light and sinking on the carved and canopied four-poster, with the venerable cat in his accustomed place across my feet. I did not draw the curtains, but gazed out at the narrow north window which I faced. There was a suspicion of aurora in the sky, and the delicate traceries of the window were pleasantly silhouetted.

At some time I must have fallen quietly asleep, for I recall a distinct sense of leaving strange dreams, when the cat started violently from his placid position. I saw him in the faint aurora glow, head strained forward, forefeet on my ankles, and hind feet stretched behind. He was looking intensely at a point on the wall somewhat west of the window, a point which to my eye had nothing to mark it, but toward which all my attention was now directed.

And as I watched, I knew that Nigger-Man was not vainly excited. Whether the arras actually moved I cannot say. I think it did, very slightly. But what I can swear to is that behind it I heard a low, distinct scurrying as of rats or mice. In a moment the cat had jumped bodily on the screening tapestry, bringing the affected section to the floor with his weight, and exposing a damp, ancient wall of stone; patched here and there by the restorers, and devoid of any trace of rodent prowlers.

Nigger-Man raced up and down the floor by this part of the wall, clawing the fallen arras and seemingly trying at times to insert a paw between the wall and the oaken floor. He found nothing, and after a time returned wearily to his place across my feet. I had not moved, but I did not sleep again that night.

In the morning I questioned all the servants, and found that none of them had noticed anything unusual, save that the cook remembered the actions of a cat which had rested on her windowsill. This cat had howled at some unknown hour of the night, awaking the cook in time for her to see him dart purposefully out of the open door down the stairs. I drowsed away the noontime, and in the afternoon called again on Capt. Norrys, who became exceedingly interested in what I told him. The odd incidents—so slight yet so curious—appealed to his sense of the picturesque, and elicited from him a number of reminiscences of local ghostly lore. We were genuinely perplexed at the presence of rats, and Norrys lent me some traps and Paris green, which I had the servants place in strategic localities when I returned.

I retired early, being very sleepy, but was harassed by dreams of the most horrible sort, I seemed to be looking down from an immense height upon a twilit grotto, knee-deep with filth, where a white-bearded daemon swineherd drove about with his staff a flock of fungous, flabby beasts whose appearance filled me with unutterable loathing. Then, as the swineherd paused and nodded over his task, a mighty swarm of rats rained down on the sinking abyss and fell to devouring beasts and man alike.

From this terrific vision I was abruptly awakened by the motion of Nigger-man, who had been sleeping as usual across my feet. This time I did not have to question the source of his snarls and hisses, and of the fear which made him sink his claws into my ankle, unconscious of their effect; for on every side of the chamber the walls were alive with nauseous sound—the verminous slithering of ravenous, gigantic rats. There was now no aurora to show the state of the arras—the fallen section of which had been replaced—but I was not too frightened to switch on the light.

As the bulbs leapt into radiance I saw a hideous shaking all over the tapestry, causing the somewhat peculiar designs to execute a singular dance of death. This motion disappeared almost at once, and the sound with it. Springing out of bed, I poked at the arras with the long handle of a warming-pan that rested near, and lifted one section to see what lay beneath. There was nothing but the patched stone wall, and even the cat had lost his tense realization of abnormal presences. When I examined the circular trap that had been placed in the room, I found all of the openings sprung, though no trace remained of what had been caught and had escaped.

Further sleep was out of the question, so, lighting a candle, I opened the door and went out in the gallery toward the stairs to my study, Nigger-Man following at my heels. Before we had reached the stone steps, however, the cat darted ahead of me and vanished down the ancient flight. As I descended the stairs myself, I became suddenly aware of sounds in the great room below; sounds of a nature which could not be mistaken.

The oak-panelled walls were alive with rats, scampering and milling, whilst Nigger-Man was racing about with the fury of a baffled hunter. Reaching the bottom, I switched on the light, which did not this time cause the noise to subside. The rats continued their riot, stampeding with such force and distinctness that I could finally assign to their motions a definite direction. These creatures, in numbers apparently inexhaustible, were engaged in one stupendous migration from inconceivable heights to some depth conceivably or inconceivably below.

I now heard steps in the corridor, and in another moment two servants pushed open the massive door. They were searching the house for some unknown source of disturbance which had thrown all the cats into a snarling panic and caused them to plunge precipitately down several flights of stairs and squat, yowling, before the closed door to the sub-cellar. I asked them if they had heard the rats, but they replied in the negative. And when I turned to call their attention to the sounds in the panels, I realized that the noise had ceased.

With the two men, I went down to the door of the sub-cellar, but found the cats already dispersed. Later I resolved to explore the crypt below, but for the present I merely made a round of the traps. All were sprung, yet all were tenantless. Satisfying myself that no one had heard the rats save the felines and me, I sat in my study till morning, thinking profoundly and recalling every scrap of legend I had unearthed concerning the building I inhabited.

I slept some in the forenoon, leaning back in the one comfortable library chair which my mediaeval plan of furnishing could not banish. Later I telephoned to Capt. Norrys, who came over and helped me explore the sub-cellar.

Absolutely nothing untoward was found, although we could not repress a thrill at the knowledge that this vault was built by Roman hands. Every low arch and massive pillar was Roman—not the debased Romanesque of the bungling Saxons, but the severe and harmonious classicism of the age of the Caesars; indeed, the walls abounded with inscriptions familiar to the antiquarians who had repeatedly explored the place—things like "P.GETAE. PROP . . . TEMP . . . DONA . . ." and "L.PRAEC . . . VS . . . PONTIFI . . . ATYS. . . ."

The reference to Atys made me shiver, for I had read Catullus and knew something of the hideous rites of the Eastern god, whose worship was so mixed with that of Cybele. Norrys and I, by the light of lanterns, tried to interpret the odd and nearly effaced designs on certain irregularly rectangular blocks of stone generally held to be altars, but could make nothing of them. We remembered that one pattern, a sort of rayed sun, was held by students to imply a non-Roman origin, suggesting that these altars had merely been adopted by the Roman priests from some older and perhaps aboriginal temple on the same site. On one of these blocks were some brown stains which made me wonder. The largest, in the center of the room, had certain features on the upper surface which indicated its connection with fire—probably burnt offerings.

Such were the sights in that crypt before whose door the cats howled, and where Norrys and I now determined to pass the night. Couches were brought down by the servants, who were told not to mind any nocturnal actions of the cats, and Nigger-Man was admitted as much for help as for companionship. We decided to keep the great oak door—a modern replica with slits for ventilation—

tightly closed; and, with this attended to, we retired with lanterns still burning to await whatever might occur.

The vault was very deep in the foundations of the priory, and undoubtedly far down on the face of the beetling limestone cliff overlooking the waste valley. That it had been the goal of the scuffling and unexplainable rats I could not doubt, though why, I could not tell. As we lay there expectantly, I found my vigil occasionally mixed with half-formed dreams from which the uneasy motions of the cat across my feet would rouse me.

These dreams were not wholesome, but horribly like the one I had had the night before. I saw again the twilit grotto, and the swineherd with his unmentionable fungous beasts wallowing in filth, and as I looked at these things they seemed nearer and more distinct—so distinct that I could almost observe their features. Then I did observe the flabby features of one of them—and awakened with such a scream that Nigger-Man started up, whilst Capt. Norrys, who had not slept, laughed considerably. Norrys might have laughed more—or perhaps less—had he known what it was that made me scream. But I did not remember myself till later. Ultimate horror often paralyzes memory in a merciful way.

Norrys waked me when the phenomena began. Out of the same frightful dream I was called by his gentle shaking and his urging to listen to the cats. Indeed, there was much to listen to, for beyond the closed door at the head of the stone steps was a veritable nightmare of feline yelling and clawing, whilst Nigger-Man, unmindful of his kindred outside, was running excitedly around the bare stone walls, in which I heard the same babel of scurrying rats that had troubled me the night before.

An acute terror now rose within me, for here were anomalies which nothing normal could well explain. These rats, if not the creatures of a madness which I shared with the cats alone, must be burrowing and sliding in Roman walls I had thought to be of solid limestone blocks . . . unless perhaps the action of water through more than seventeen centuries had eaten winding tunnels which rodent bodies had worn clear and ample. . . . But even so, the spectral horror was no less; for if these were living vermin why did not Norrys hear their disgusting commotion? Why did he urge me to watch Nigger-Man and listen to the cats outside, and why did he guess wildly and vaguely at what could have aroused them?

By the time I had managed to tell him, as rationally as I could, what I thought I was hearing, my ears gave me the last fading impression of the scurrying; which had retreated *still downward*, far underneath this deepest of sub-cellars till it seemed as if the whole cliff below were riddled with questing rats. Norrys was not as skeptical as I had anticipated, but instead seemed profoundly moved. He motioned to me to notice that the cats at the door had ceased their clamor, as if giving up the rats for lost; whilst Nigger-man had a burst of renewed restlessness, and was clawing frantically around the bottom of the large stone altar in the center of the room, which was nearer Norrys' couch than mine.

My fear of the unknown was at this point very great. Something astounding had occurred, and I saw that Capt. Norrys, a younger, stouter, and presumably more naturally materialistic man, was affected fully as much as myself—perhaps because of his lifelong and intimate familiarity with local legend. We could for the moment do nothing but watch the old black cat as he pawed with decreasing fervor at the base of the altar, occasionally looking up and mewing to me in that persuasive manner which he used when he wished me to perform some favor for him.

Norrys now took a lantern close to the altar and examined the place where Nigger-Man was pawing; silently kneeling and scraping away the lichens of the centuries which joined the massive pre-Roman block to the tesselated floor. He did not find anything, and was about to abandon his efforts when I noticed a trivial circumstance which made me shudder, even though it implied nothing more than I had already imagined.

I told him of it, and we both looked at its almost imperceptible manifestation with the fixedness of fascinated discovery and acknowledgment. It was only this—that the flame of the lantern set down near the altar was slightly but certainly flickering from a draught of air which it had not before received, and which came indubitably form the crevice between floor and altar where Norrys was scraping away the lichens.

We spent the rest of the night in the brilliantly lighted

study, nervously discussing what we should do next. The discovery that some vault deeper than the deepest known masonry of the Romans underlay this accursed pile; some vault unsuspected by the curious antiquarians of three centuries; would have been sufficient to excite us without any background of the sinister. As it was, the fascination became two-fold; and we paused in doubt whether to abandon our search and quit the priory forever in superstitious caution, or to gratify our sense of adventure and brave whatever horrors might await us in the unknown depths.

By morning we had compromised, and decided to go to London to gather a group of archaeologists and scientific men fit to cope with the mystery. It should be mentioned that before leaving the sub-cellar we had vainly tried to move the central altar which we now recognized as the gate to a new pit of nameless fear. What secret would open the gate, wiser men than we would have to find.

During many days in London Capt. Norrys and I presented our facts, conjectures, and legendary anecdotes to five eminent authorities, all men who could be trusted to respect any familiar disclosures which future explorations might develop. We found most of them little disposed to scoff, but, instead, intensely interested and sincerely sympathetic. It is hardly necessary to name them all, but I may say that they included Sir William Brinton, whose excavations in the Troad excited most of the world in their day. As we all took the train for Anchester I felt myself poised on the brink of frightful revelations, a sensation symbolized by the air of mourning among the many Americans at the unexpected death of the President on the other side of the world.

On the evening of August 7 we reached Exham Priory, where the servants assured me that nothing unusual had occurred. The cats, even old Nigger-Man, had been perfectly placid; and not a trap in the house had been sprung. We were to begin exploring on the following day, awaiting which I assigned well-appointed rooms to all my guests.

I myself retired in my own tower chamber, with Nigger-Man across my feet. Sleep came quickly, but hideous dreams assailed me. There was a vision of a Roman feast like that of Trimalchio, with a horror in a covered platter. Then came that damnable, recurrent thing about the swineherd and his filthy drove in the twilit grotto. Yet when I awoke it was full daylight, with normal sounds in the house below. The rats, living or spectral, had not troubled me; and Nigger-Man was still quietly asleep. On going down, I found that the same tranquillity had prevailed elsewhere; a condition which one of the assembled savants—a fellow named Thornton, devoted to the psychic—rather absurdly laid to the fact that I had now been shown the thing which certain forces had wished to show me.

All was now ready, and at 11 A.M. our entire group of seven men, bearing powerful electric searchlights and implements of excavation, went down to the sub-cellar and bolted the door behind us. Nigger-Man was with us, for the investigators found no occasion to despise his excitability, and were indeed anxious that he be present in case of obscure rodent manifestations. We noted the Roman inscriptions and unknown altar designs only briefly, for three of the savants had already seen them, and all knew their characteristics. Prime attention was paid to the momentous central altar, and within an hour Sir William Brinton had caused it to tilt backward, balanced by some unknown species of counterweight.

There now lay revealed such a horror as would have overwhelmed us had we not been prepared. Through a nearly square opening in the tiled floor, sprawling on a flight of stone steps so prodigiously worn that it was little more than an inclined plane at the center, was a ghastly array of human or semi-human bones. Those which retained their collocation as skeletons showed attitudes of panic, fear, and over all were the marks of rodent gnawing. The skulls denoted nothing short of utter idiocy, cretinism, or primitive semiapedom.

Above the hellishly littered steps arched a descending passage seemingly chiseled from the solid rock, and conducting a current of air. This current was not a sudden and noxious rush as from a closed vault, but a cool breeze with something of freshness in it. We did not pause long, but shiveringly began to clear a passage down the steps. It was then that Sir William, examining the hewn walls, made the odd observation that the passage, according to the direction of the strokes, must have been chiseled *from beneath.*

I must be very deliberate now, and choose my words.

After ploughing down a few steps amidst the gnawed bones we saw that there was light ahead; not any mystic phosphorescence, but a filtered daylight which could not come except from unknown fissures in the cliff that overlooked the waste valley. That such fissures had escaped notice from outside was hardly remarkable, for not only is the valley wholly uninhabited, but the cliff is so high and beetling that only an aeronaut could study its face in detail. A few steps more, and our breaths were literally snatched from us by what we saw; so literally that Thornton, the psychic investigator, actually fainted in the arms of the dazed man who stood behind him. Norrys, his plump face utterly white and flabby, simply cried out inarticulately; whilst I think that what I did was to gasp or hiss, and cover my eyes.

The man behind me—the only one of the party older than I—croaked the hackneyed "My God!" in the most cracked voice I ever heard. Of seven cultivated men, only Sir William Brinton retained his composure, a thing the more to his credit because he led the party and must have seen the sight first.

It was a twilit grotto of enormous height, stretching away farther than any eye could see; a subterraneous world of limitless mystery and horrible suggestion. There were buildings and other architectural remains—in one terrified glance I saw a weird pattern of tumuli, a savage circle of monoliths, a low-domed Roman ruin, a sprawling Saxon pile, and an early English edifice of wood—but all these were dwarfed by the ghoulish spectacle presented by the general surface of the ground. For yards about the steps extended an insane tangle of human bones, or bones at least as human as those on the steps. Like a foamy sea they stretched, some fallen apart, but others wholly or partly articulated as skeletons; these latter invariably in postures of daemoniac frenzy, either fighting off some menace or clutching other forms with cannibal intent.

When Dr. Trask, the anthropologist, stopped to classify the skulls, he found a degraded mixture which utterly baffled him. They were mostly lower than the Piltdown man in the scale of evolution, but in every case definitely human. Many were of higher grade, and a very few were the skulls of supremely and sensitively developed types. All the bones were gnawed, mostly by rats, but somewhat by others of the half-human drove. Mixed with them were many tiny bones of rats—fallen members of the lethal army which closed the ancient epic.

I wonder that any man among us lived and kept his sanity through that hideous day of discovery. Not Hoffman or Huysmans could conceive a scene more wildly incredible, more frenetically repellent, or more Gothically grotesque than the twilit grotto through which we seven staggered; each stumbling on revelation after revelation, and trying to keep for the nonce from thinking of the events which must have taken place there three hundred, or a thousand, or two thousand, or ten thousand years ago. It was the antechamber of hell, and poor Thornton fainted again when Trask told him that some of the skeleton things must have descended as quadrupeds through the last twenty or more generations.

Horror piled on horror as we began to interpret the architectural remains. The quadruped things—with their occasional recruits from the biped class—had been kept in stone pens, out of which they must have broken in their last delirium of hunger or rat-fear. There had been great herds of them, evidently fattened on the coarse vegetables whose remains could be found as a sort of poisonous ensilage at the bottom of huge stone bins older than Rome. I knew now why my ancestors had had such excessive gardens—would to heaven I could forget! The purpose of the herds I did not have to ask.

Sir William, standing with his searchlight in the Roman ruin, translated aloud the most shocking ritual I have ever known; and told of the diet of the antediluvian cult which the priests of Cybele found and mingled with their own. Norrys, used as he was to the trenches, could not walk straight when he came out of the English building. It was a butcher shop and kitchen—he had expected that—but it was too much to see familiar English implements in such a place, and to read familiar English *graffiti* there, some as recent as 1610. I could not go in that building—that building whose demon activities were stopped only by the dagger of my ancestor Walter de la Poer.

What I did venture to enter was the low Saxon building whose oaken door had fallen, and there I found a terrible row of ten stone cells with rusty bars. Three had tenants, all skeletons of high grade, and on the bony forefinger of one I found a seal ring with my own coat-of-arms. Sir William found a vault with far older cells below the Roman chapel, but three cells were empty. Below them was a low crypt with cases of formally arranged bones, some of them bearing terrible parallel inscriptions carved in Latin, Greek, and the tongue of Phrygia.

Meanwhile, Dr. Trask had opened one of the prehistoric tumuli, and brought to light skulls which were slightly more human than a gorilla's, and which bore indescribably ideographic carvings. Through all this horror my cat stalked unperturbed. Once I saw him monstrously perched atop a mountain of bones, and wondered at the secrets that might lie behind his yellow eyes.

Having grasped to some slight degree the frightful revelations of this twilit area—an area so hideously foreshadowed by my recurrent dream—we turned to that apparently boundless depth of midnight cavern where no ray of light from the cliff could penetrate. We shall never know what sightless Stygian worlds yawn beyond the little distance we went, for it was decided that such secrets are not good for mankind. But there was plenty to engross us close at hand, for we had not gone far before the searchlights showed that accursed infinity of pits in which the rats had feasted, and whose sudden lack of replenishment had driven the ravenous rodent army first to turn on the living herds of starving things, and then to burst forth from the priority in that historic orgy of devastation which the peasants will never forget.

God! those carrion black pits of sawed, picked bones and opened skulls! Those nightmare chasms choked with the pithecanthropoid, Celtic, Roman, and English bones of countless unhallowed centuries! Some of them were full, and none can say how deep they had once been. Others were still bottomless to our searchlights, and peopled by unnameable fancies. What, I thought, of the hapless rats that stumbled into such traps amidst the blackness of their quests in this grisly Tartarus?

Once my foot slipped near a horribly yawning brink, and I had a moment of ecstatic fear. I must have been musing a long time, for I could not see any of the party but the plump Capt. Norrys. Then there came a sound from that inky, boundless, farther distance that I thought I knew; and I saw my old black cat dart past me like a winged Egyptian god, straight into the illimitable gulf of the unknown. But I was not far behind, for there was no doubt after another second. It was the eldritch scurrying of those fiend-born rats, always questing for new horrors, and determined to lead me on even into those grinning caverns of earth's center where Nyarlathotep, the mad faceless god, howls blindly in the darkness to the piping of two amorphous idiot flute-players.

My searchlight expired, but still I ran. I heard voices, and yowls, and echoes, but above all there gently rose that impious, insidious scurrying; gently rising, rising, as a stiff bloated corpse gently rises above an oily river that flows under endless onyx bridges to a black, putrid sea.

Something bumped into me—something soft and plump. It must have been the rats; the viscous, gelatinous, ravenous army that feast on the dead and the living. . . . Why shouldn't rats eat de la Poer as a de la Poer eats forbidden things? . . . The war ate my boy, damn them all . . . and the Yanks ate Carfax with flames and burned the Grandsire Delapore and the secret. . . . No, no, I tell you, I am *not* that demon swineherd in the twilit grotto! It was *not* Edward Norrys' fat face on that flabby fungous thing! Who says I am a de la Poer? He lived, but my boy died! . . . Shall a Norrys hold the lands of a de la Poer?. . . . It's voodoo, I tell you . . . that spotted snake. . . . Curse you, Thornton, I'll teach you to faint at what my family do! . . . 'Sblood, thou stinkard, I'll learn ye how to gust . . . wolde ye swynke me thilke wys? . . . *Magna Mater! Magna Mater! . . . Atys . . . Dia ad aghaidh's ad aodaun . . . agus bas dunach ort! Dhonas's dholas ort, agus leatsa! . . . Ungl . . . ungl . . . rrlh . . . chchch. . . .*

That is what they say I said when they found me in the blackness after three hours; found me crouching in the blackness over the plump, half-eaten body of Capt. Norrys, with my own cat leaping and tearing at my throat. Now they have blown up Exham Priory, taken my Nigger-Man away from me, and shut me into this barred room at Hanwell with fearful whispers about my heredity and experience. Thornton is in the next room, but they prevent me from talking to him. They are trying, too, to suppress most of the facts concerning the priory. When I speak of poor Norrys they accuse me of a hideous thing, but they must know that I did not do it. They must know it was the rats; the demon rats that race behind the padding in this room and beckon me down to greater horrors than I have ever known; the rats they can never hear; the rats, the rats in the walls.

ELIZABETH BOWEN

The Cat Jumps

After the Bentley murder, Rose Hill stood empty two years. Lawns mounted to meadows, white paint peeled from the balconies; the sun, looking more constantly, less fearfully, in than sightseers' eyes through the naked windows, bleached the floral wallpapers. The week after the execution Harold Bentley's legatees had placed the house on the books of the principal agents, London and local. But though sunny, modern and convenient, though so delightfully situate over the Thames valley (above flood level), within easy reach of a gold course, Rose Hill, while frequently viewed, remained unpurchased. Dreadful associations apart, the privacy of the place had been violated; with its terrace garden, lily-pond, and pergola cheerfully rose-encrusted, the public had been made too familiar. On the domestic scene, too many eyes had burnt the impression of their horror. Moreover, that pearly bathroom, bedroom with wide outlook over a loop of the Thames . . . "The Rose Hill Horror": headlines flashed up at the very sound of the name. "Oh *no*, dear!" many wives had exclaimed, drawing their husbands from the gate. "Come away!" they urged, crumpling the agent's order to view as though the house were advancing on them. And husbands came away—with a backward glance at the garage. Funny to think: a chap who was hanged had kept his car there.

The Harold Wrights, however, were not deterred. They had light, bright, shadowless, thoroughly disinfected minds. They believed that they disbelieved in most things but were unprejudiced; they enjoyed frank discussions. They dreaded nothing but inhibitions: they had no inhibitions. They were pious agnostics, earnest for social reform; they explained everything to their children and were annoyed to find their children could not sleep at nights because they thought there was a complex under the bed. They knew all crime to be pathological, and read their murders only in scientific books. They had Vita Glass put into all their windows. No family, in fact, could have been more unlike the mistaken Harold Bentleys.

Rose Hill, from the first glance, suited the Wrights admirably. They were in search of a cheerful weekend house with a nice atmosphere where their friends could join them for frank discussions, and their own and their friends' children "run wild" during the summer months. Harold Wright, who had a good head, got the agent to knock six hundred off the quoted price of the house. "The unfortunate affair," he murmured. Jocelyn commended his inspiration. Otherwise, they did not give the Bentleys another thought.

The Wrights had the floral wallpapers all stripped off and the walls cream-washed; they removed some disagreeably thick pink shades from the electricity, and had the paint renewed inside and out. (The front of the house was bracketed over with balconies, like an overmantel.) Their bedroom mantelpiece, stained by the late Mrs. Bentley's cosmetics, had to be scrubbed with chemicals. Also, they had removed from the rock-garden Mrs. Bentley's little dog's memorial tablet, with a quotation on it from "Indian Love Lyrics." Jocelyn Wright, looking into the unfortunate bath, *the* bath, so square and opulent with its surround of nacreous titles, said, laughing lightly, she supposed anyone *else* would have had that bath changed. "Not that that would be possible," she added; "the bath's built in. . . . I've always wanted a built-in bath."

Harold and Jocelyn turned from the bath to look down at the cheerful river shimmering under a spring haze. All the way down the slope cherry trees were in blossom. Life should be simplified for the Wrights—they were fortunate in their mentality.

After an experimental week-end, without guests or children, only one thing troubled them: a resolute stuffiness, upstairs and down—due, presumably, to the house's

having been so long shut up—a smell of unsavory habitation, of rich cigarette smoke stale in the folds of unaired
curtains, of scent spilled on unbrushed carpets; an alco-
holic smell—persistent in their perhaps too sensitive nos-
trils after days of airing, doors and windows open, in
rooms drenched thoroughly with sun and wind. They told
each other it came from the parquet—they didn't like it,
somehow. They had the parquet taken up—at great
expense—and put down plain oak floors.

In their practical way the Wrights now set out to expel,
live out, live down, almost (had the word had place in
their vocabulary) to "lay" the Bentleys. Deferred by
trouble over the parquet, their occupation of Rose Hill
(which should have dated from mid-April) did not begin
till the end of May. Throughout a week Jocelyn had
motored from town daily, so that the final installation of
themselves and the children was able to coincide with
their first week-end party—they asked down five of their
friends to warm the house.

That first Friday, everything was auspicious; afternoon
sky blue as the garden irises; later, a full moon pendant
over the river; a night so warm that, after midnight, their
enlightened friends, in pyjamas, could run on the blanched
lawns in a state of high though rational excitement.
Jane, John and Janet, their admirably spaced-out children, kept awake by the moonlight, hailed their elders
out of the nursery skylight. Jocelyn waved to them: they
never had been repressed.

The girl Muriel Barker was found looking up the ter-
races at the house a shade doubtfully. "You know," she
said, "I do rather wonder they don't feel . . . *sometimes*
. . . You know what I mean?"

"No," replied her companion, a young scientist.

Muriel sighed. "No one would mind if it had been just
a short, sharp shooting. But it was so . . . prolonged. It
went on all over the house. Do you remember?" she said
timidly.

"No," replied Mr. Cartaret; "it didn't interest me."

"Oh, nor me either!" agreed Muriel quickly, but added:
"How he must have hated her! . . ."

The scientist, sleepy, yawned frankly and referred her
to Krafft Ebing. But Muriel went to bed with *Alice in*

Wonderland; she went to sleep with the lights on. She was not, as Jocelyn realized later, the sort of girl to have asked at all.

Next morning was overcast; in the afternoon it rained, suddenly and heavily, interrupting, for some, tennis, for others a pleasant discussion, in a punt, on marriage under the Soviet. Defeated, they all rushed in. Jocelyn went round from room to room, shutting tightly the rain-lashed casements along the front of the house: these continued to rattle; the balconies creaked. An early dusk set in; an oppressive, almost visible moisture, up from the darkening river, pressed on the panes like a presence and slid through the house. The party gathered in the library, round an expansive but thinly burning fire. Harold circulated photographs of modern architecture; they discussed these tendencies. Then Mrs. Monkhouse, sniffing, exclaimed: "Who uses 'Trèfle Incarnat'?"

"Now *who*ever would——" her hostess began scornfully. Then from the hall came a howl, a scuffle, a thin shriek. They too sat still in the dusky library Mr. Cartaret laughed out loud. Harold Wright, indignantly throwing open the door, revealed Jane and John rolling at the foot of the stairs biting each other, their faces dark with uninhibited passion. Bumping alternate heads against the foot of the banisters, they shrieked in concord.

"Extraordinary," said Harold; "they've never done that before. They have always understood each other so well."

"I wouldn't do that," advised Jocelyn, raising her voice slightly; "you'll hurt your teeth. Other teeth won't grow at once, you know."

"You should let them find that out for themselves," disapproved Edward Cartaret, taking up the *New Statesman.* Harold, in perplexity, shut the door on his children, who soon stunned each other to silence.

Meanwhile, Sara and Talbot Monkhouse, Muriel Barker and Theodora Smith had drawn together over the fire in a tight little knot. Their voices twanged with excitement. By that shock just now, something seemed to have been released. Even Cartaret gave them half his attention. They were discussing *crime passionel.*

"Of course, if that's what they really *want* to discuss . . ." thought Jocelyn. But it did seem unfortunate. Partly from an innocent desire to annoy her visitors, partly because the room felt awful—you would have thought fifty people had been there for a week—she went across and opened one of the windows, admitting a pounce of damp wind. They all turned, started, to hear rain crash on the lead of an upstairs balcony. Muriel's voice was left in forlorn solo: "Dragged herself . . . whining 'Harold' . . ."

Harold Wright looked remarkably conscious. Jocelyn said brightly, "Whatever *are* you talking about?" But unfortunately Harold, on almost the same breath, suggested: "Let's leave that family alone, shall we?" Their friends all felt they might not be asked again. Though they did feel, plaintively, that they had been being natural. However, they disowned Muriel, who, getting up abruptly, said she thought she'd like to go for a walk in the rain before dinner. Nobody accompanied her.

Later, overtaking Mrs. Monkhouse on the stairs, Muriel confided: absolutely, she could not stand Edward Cartaret. She could hardly bear to be in the room with him. He seemed so . . . cruel. Cold-blooded? No, she meant cruel. Sara Monkhouse, going into Jocelyn's room for a chat (at her entrance Jocelyn started violently), told Jocelyn that Muriel could not stand Edward, could hardly bear to be in a room with him. "Pity," said Jocelyn; "I had thought they might do for each other." Jocelyn and Sara agreed that Muriel was unrealized: what she ought to have was a baby. But when Sara, dressing, told Talbot Monkhouse that Muriel could not stand Edward, and Talbot said Muriel was unrealized, Sara was furious. The Monkhouses, who never did quarrel, quarreled bitterly and were late for dinner. They would have been later if the meal itself had not been delayed by an outburst of sex-antagonism between the nice Jacksons, a couple imported from London to run the house. Mrs. Jackson, putting everything in the oven, had locked herself into her room.

"Curious," said Harold, "the Jacksons' relations to each other always seemed so modern. They have the most intelligent discussions."

Theodora said she had been re-reading Shakespeare— this brought them point-blank up against Othello. Harold, with titanic force, wrenched round the conversation to Relativity; about this no one seemed to have anything to say but Edward Cartaret. And Muriel, who by some mischance had again been placed beside him, sat deathly, turning down her dark-rimmed eyes. In fact, on the intelligent, sharp-featured faces all round the table, something, perhaps simply a clearness, seemed to be lacking, as though these were wax faces for one fatal instant exposed to a furnace. Voices came out from some dark interiority; in each conversational interchange a mutual vote of no confidence was implicit. You would have said that each personality had been attacked by some kind of decomposition.

"No moon tonight," complained Sara Monkhouse. Never mind, they would have a cozy evening, they would play paper games, Jocelyn promised.

"If you can see," said Harold. "Something seems to be going wrong with the light."

Did Harold think so? They had all noticed the light seemed to be losing quality, as though a film, smoke-like, were creeping over the bulbs. The light, thinning, darkening, seemed to contract round each lamp into a blurred aura. They had noticed, but, each with a proper dread of his own subjectivity, had not spoken.

"Funny stuff," Harold said, "electricity."

Mr. Cartaret could not agree with him.

Though it was late, though they yawned and would not play paper games, they were reluctant to go to bed. You would have supposed a delightful evening. Jocelyn was not gratified.

The library stools, rugs and divans were strewn with Krafft Ebing, Freud, Forel, Weiniger and the heterosexual volume of Havelock Ellis. (Harold had thought it right to install his reference library; his friends hated to discuss without basis.) The volumes were pressed open with paper-knives and small pieces of modern statuary; stooping from one to another, purposeful as a bee, Edward Cartaret read extracts aloud to Harold, to Talbot Monkhouse and to Theodora Smith, who stitched *gros point* with resolution. At the far end of the library, under a sallow drip from a group of electric candles, Mrs. Monkhouse and Miss Barker shared an ottoman, spines pressed rigid against the wall. Tensely, one spoke, one listened.

"And these," thought Jocelyn, leaning back with her

eyes shut between the two groups, "are friends I liked to have in my life. Pellucid, sane . . ."

It was remarkable how much Muriel knew. Sara, very much shocked, edged up till their thighs touched. You would have thought the Harold Bentleys had been Muriel's relatives. Surely, Sara attempted, in one's large, bright world one did not think of these things? Practically, they did not exist! Surely Muriel should not. . . . But Muriel looked at her strangely.

"Did you know," she said, "that one of Mrs. Bentley's hands was found in the library?"

Sara, smiling a little awkwardly, licked her lips. "Oh," she said.

"But the fingers were in the dining-room. He began there."

"Why isn't he in Broadmoor?"

"That defence failed. He didn't really subscribe to it. He said having done what he wanted was worth anything."

"Oh!"

"Yes, he was nearly lynched. . . . She dragged herself upstairs. She couldn't lock any doors—naturally. One maid, her maid, got shut into the house with them; he'd sent all the others away. For a long time everything seemed to quiet: the maid crept out and saw Harold Bentley sitting half-way upstairs, finishing a cigarette. All the lights were full on. He nodded to her and dropped the cigarette through the banisters. Then she saw the . . . state of the hall. He went upstairs after Mrs. Bentley, saying: 'Lucinda!' He looked into room after room, whistling, then he said, 'Here we are,' and shut a door after him.

"The maid fainted. When she came to it was still going on, upstairs. . . . Harold Bentley had locked all the garden doors, there were locks even on the french windows. The maid couldn't get out. Everything she touched was . . . sticky. At last she broke a pane and got through. As she ran down the garden—the lights were on all over the house—she saw Harold Bentley moving about in the bathroom. She fell right over the edge of a terrace and one of the tradesmen picked her up next day.

"Doesn't it seem odd, Sara, to think of Jocelyn in that bath?"

Finishing her recital, Muriel turned on Sara an ecstatic

and brooding look that made her almost beautiful. Sara fumbled with a cigarette; match after match failed her. "Muriel, you should see a specialist."

Muriel held out her hand for a cigarette. "He put her heart in her hat-box. He said it belonged there."

"You had no right to come here. It was most unfair to Jocelyn. Most . . . indelicate."

Muriel, to whom the word was, properly, unfamiliar, eyed incredulously Sara's lips.

"How dared you come?"

"I thought I might like it. I thought I ought to fulfill myself. I'd never had any experience of these things."

"Muriel! . . ."

"Besides, I wanted to meet Edward Cartaret. Several people said we were made for each other. Now, of course, I shall never marry. Look what comes of it. . . . I must say, Sara, I wouldn't be you or Jocelyn. Shut up all night with a man all alone—I don't know how you dare sleep. I've arranged to sleep with Theodora, and we shall barricade the door. I noticed something about Edward Cartaret the moment I arrived; a kind of insane glitter. He is utterly pathological. He's got instruments in his room, in that black bag. Yes, I looked. Did you notice the way he went on and on about cutting up that cat, and the way Talbot and Harold listened?"

Sara, looking furtively round the room, saw Mr. Cartaret making passes over the head of Theodora Smith with a paper-knife. Both appeared to laugh heartily, but in silence.

"Here we are," said Harold, showing his teeth, smiling.

He stood over Muriel with a siphon in one hand, glass in the other.

At this point Jocelyn, rising, said she, for one, intended to go to bed.

Jocelyn's bedroom curtains swelled a little over the noisy window. The room was stuffy and—insupportable, so that she did not know where to turn. The house, fingered outwardly by the wind that dragged unceasingly past the walls, was, within, a solid silence: silence heavy as flesh. Jocelyn dropped her wrap to the floor, then watched how its feathered edges crept a little—a draught came in under her bathroom door.

Jocelyn turned in despair and hostility from the strained, pale woman looking at her room from her oblong glass. She said aloud: "There *is* no fear," then within herself heard this taken up: "But the death fear, that one is not there to relate! If the spirit, dismembered in agony, dies before the body! If the spirit, in the whole knowledge of its dissolution, drags from chamber to chamber, drops from plane to plane of awareness (as from knife to knife down an oubliette) shedding, receiving agony! Till, long afterward, death with its little pain is established in the indifferent body." There was no comfort: death (now at every turn and instant claiming her) was in its every possible manifestation violent death: ultimately she was to be given up to terror.

Undressing, shocked by the iteration of her reflected movements, she flung a towel over the glass. With what desperate eyes of appeal, at Sara's door, she and Sara had looked at each other, clung with their looks—and parted. She could have sworn she heard Sara's bolt slide softly to. But what then, subsequently, of Talbot? And what—she eyed her own bolt, so bright (and for the late Mrs. Bentley so ineffective)—what of Harold?

"It's atavistic!" she said aloud, in the dark-lit room, and, kicking away her slippers, got into bed. She took *Erewhon* from the rack, but lay rigid, listening. As though snatched by a movement, the towel slipped from the mirror beyond her bed-end. She faced the two eyes of an animal in extremity, eyes black, mindless. The clock struck two: she had been waiting an hour.

On the floor her feathered wrap shivered again all over. She heard the other door of the bathroom very stealthily open, then shut. Harold moved in softly, heavily, knocked against the side of the bath and stood still. He was quietly whistling.

"Why didn't I understand? He must always have hated me. It's tonight he's been waiting for. . . . *He wanted this house*. His look, as we went upstairs . . ."

She shrieked: "Harold!"

Harold, so softly whistling, remained behind the imperturbable door, remained quite still. . . . "He's *listening* for me. . . ." One pin-point of hope at the tunnel end: to get to Sara, to Theodora, to Muriel. Unmasked, incautious, with a long tearing sound of displaced air, Jocelyn leapt from bed to the door.

But her door had been locked from the outside.

With a strange, rueful smile, like an actress, Jocelyn, skirting the foot of the two beds, approached the door of the bathroom. "At least I have still . . . my feet." For, for some time, the heavy body of Mrs. Bentley, tenacious of life, had been dragging itself from room to room. *"Harold!"* she said to the silence, face close to the door.

The door opened on Harold, looking more dreadfully at her than she had imagined. With a quick, vague movement he roused himself from his meditation. Therein he had assumed the entire burden of Harold Bentley. Forces he did not know of assembling darkly, he had faced for untold ages the imperturbable door to his wife's room. She would be there, densely, smotheringly there. She lay like a great cat, always, over the mouth of his life.

The Harolds, superimposed on each other, stood searching the bedroom strangely. Taking a step forward, shutting the door behind him:

"Here we are," said Harold.

Jocelyn went down heavily. Harold watched.

Harold Wright was appalled. Jocelyn had fainted: Jocelyn never have fainted before. He shook, he fanned, he applied restoratives. His perplexed thoughts fled to Sara—oh, Sara, certainly. "Hi!" he cried. "Sara!" and successively fled from each to each of the locked passage doors. There was no way out.

Across the passage a door throbbed to the maniac drumming of Sara Monkhouse. She had been locked in. For Talbot, agonized with solicitude, it was equally impossible to emerge from his dressing-room. Farther down the passage Edward Cartaret, interested by this nocturnal manifestation, wrenched and rattled his door-handle in vain.

Muriel, on her way through the house to Theodora's bedroom, had turned all the keys on the outside, impartially. She did not know which door was Edward Cartaret's. Muriel was a woman who took no chances.

DAVID H. KELLER

The Thing in the Cellar

It was a large cellar, entirely out of proportion to the house above it. The owner admitted that it was probably built for a distinctly different kind of structure from the one which rose above it. Probably the first house had been burned, and poverty had caused a diminution of the dwelling erected to take its place.

A winding stone stairway connected the cellar with the kitchen. Around the base of this series of steps, successive owners of the house had placed their firewood, winter vegetables, and junk. The junk had been pushed back till it rose, head high, in a barricade of uselessness. What was back of that barricade no one knew and no one cared. For some hundreds of years, no one had crossed it to penetrate to the black reaches of the cellar behind it.

At the top of the steps, separating the kitchen from the cellar, was a stout oaken door. This door was, in a way, as peculiar and out of relation to the rest of the house as the cellar. It was a strange kind of door to find in a modern house, and certainly a most unusual door to find in the inside of the house—thick, stoutly built, dexterously rabbeted together, with huge wrought-iron hinges, and a lock that looked as though it came from Castle Despair. Separating a house from the outside world, such a door would be excusable; swinging between kitchen and cellar, it seemed peculiarly inappropriate.

From the earliest months of his life, Tommy Tucker seemed unhappy in the kitchen. In the front parlor, in the formal dining-room, and especially on the second floor of the house, he acted like a normal, healthy child; but carry him to the kitchen, he at once began to cry. His parents, being plain people, ate in the kitchen, save when they had company. Being poor, Mrs. Tucker did most of her work, though occasionally she had a char-woman in to do the extra Saturday cleaning, and thus much of her time was spent in the kitchen. And Tommy stayed with her, at least as long as he was able to walk. Much of the time he was decidedly unhappy.

When Tommy learned to creep, he lost no time in leaving the kitchen. No sooner was his mother's back turned, than the little fellow crawled as fast as he could for the doorway opening into the front of the house—the dining-room, and the front parlor. Once away from the kitchen, he seemed happy; at least, he ceased to cry. On being returned to the kitchen, his howls so thoroughly convinced the neighbors that he had colic, that more than one bowl of catnip and sage tea were brought to his assistance.

It was not until the boy learned to talk, that the Tuck-ers had any idea as to what made the boy cry so hard when he was in the kitchen. In other words, the baby had to suffer for many months till he obtained at least a little relief, and even when he told his parents what was the matter, they were absolutely unable to comprehend. This is not to be wondered at, because they were both hard-working, rather simple-minded persons.

What they finally learned from their little son was this: That if the cellar door was shut and securely fastened with the heavy iron lock, Tommy could, at least, eat a meal in peace; if the door was simply closed and not locked, he shivered with fear, but kept quiet; but if the door was open, if even the slightest streak of black showed that it was not tightly shut, then the little three-year-old would scream himself to the point of exhaustion, espe-cially if his tired father would refuse him permission to leave the kitchen.

Playing in the kitchen, the child developed two inter-esting habits. Rags, scraps of paper, and splinters of wood were continually being shoved under the thick oak door to fill the space between the door and the sill. Whenever Mrs. Tucker opened the door, there was al-

ways some trash there, placed by her son. It annoyed
her, and more than once the little fellow was thrashed for
his conduct; but punishment acted in no way as a deter-
rent. The other habit was as singular. Once the door was
closed and locked, he would rather boldly walk over to it
and caress the old lock. Even when he was so small that
he had to stand on tiptoe to touch it with the tips of his
fingers, he could touch it with slow caressing strokes;
later on, as he grew older, he used to kiss it.

His father, who only saw the boy at the end of the day,
decided that there was no sense in such conduct, and, in
his masculine way, tried to break the lad of his foolishness. There was, of necessity, no effort on the part of the
hard-working man to understand the psychology back of
his son's conduct. All that the man knew was that his
little son was acting in a way that was decidedly queer.

Tommy loved his mother, and was willing to do anything he could to help her in the household chores; but
one thing he would not do, and never did do, and that
was to fetch and carry between the house and the cellar.
If his mother opened the door, he would run, screaming,
from the room, and he never returned voluntarily till he
was assured that the door was closed.

He never explained just why he acted as he did. In
fact, he refused to talk about it, at least to his parents,
and that was just as well, because had he done so, they
would simply have been more positive that there was
something wrong with their only child. They tried, in
their own ways, to break the child of his unusual habits;
failing to change him at all, they decided to ignore his
peculiarities.

That is, they ignored them till he became six years old
and the time came for him to go to school. He was a
sturdy little chap by that time, and more intelligent than
the usual boys beginning in the primer class. Mr. Tucker
was, at times, proud of him. The child's attitude toward
the cellar door was the one thing most disturbing to the
father's pride. Finally, nothing would do but that the
Tucker family call on the neighborhood physician. It was
an important event in the life of the Tuckers, so important that it demanded the wearing of Sunday clothes, and
all that sort of thing.

"The matter is just this, Doctor Hawthorn," said Mr. Tucker, in a somewhat embarrassed manner. "Our little Tommy is old enough to start to school, but he behaves childishly in regard to our cellar; and the Missus and I thought you could tell us how to do about it. It must be his nerves."

"Ever since he was a baby," continued Mrs. Tucker, taking up the thread of conversation where her husband had paused, "Tommy has had a great fear of the cellar. Even now, big boy that he is, he does not love me enough to fetch and carry for me through that door and down those steps. It is not natural for a child to act like he does, and what with chinking the cracks with rags and kissing the lock, he drives me to the point where I fear he may become daft-like as he grows older."

The doctor, eager to satisfy new customers, and dimly remembering some lectures on the nervous system received when he was a medical student, asked some general questions, listened to the boy's heart, examined his lungs, and looked at his eyes and fingernails. At last he commented:

"Looks like a fine, healthy boy to me."

"Yes, all except the cellar door," replied the father.

"Has he ever been sick?"

"Naught but fits once or twice, when he cried himself blue in the face," answered the mother.

"Frightened?"

"Perhaps. It was always in the kitchen."

"Suppose you go out, and let me talk to Tommy by myself?"

And there sat the doctor, very much at his ease, and the little six-year-old boy, very uneasy.

"Tommy, what is there in the cellar you are afraid of?"

"I don't know."

"Have you ever seen it?"

"No, sir."

"Then how do you know there is something there?"

"Because."

"Because what?"

"Because there is."

That was as far as Tommy would go, and, at last, his

seeming obstinacy annoyed the physician, even as it had for several years annoyed Mr. Tucker. He went to the door, and called the parents into the office.

"He thinks there is something down in the cellar," he stated.

The Tuckers simply looked at each other.

"That's foolish," commented Mr. Tucker.

" 'Tis just a plain cellar with junk, and firewood, and cider barrels in it," added Mrs. Tucker. "Since we moved into that house, I have not missed a day without going down those steps; and I know there is nothing there. But the lad has always screamed when the door was open. I recall now that since he was a child in arms, he has always screamed when the door was open."

"He thinks there is something there," said the doctor.

"That is why we brought him to you," replied the father. "It's the child's nerves. Perhaps 'as'f'tidy,' or something, will calm him."

"I'll tell you what to do," advised the doctor. "He thinks there is something there. Just as soon as he finds that he is wrong and that there is nothing there, he will forget about it. He has been humored too much. What you want to do is to open that cellar door, and make him stay by himself in the kitchen. Nail the door open so he cannot close it. Leave him alone there for an hour, and then go and laugh at him and show him how silly it was for him to be afraid of an empty cellar. I will give you some nerve and blood tonic and that will help, but the big thing is to show him that there is nothing to be afraid of."

On the way back to the Tucker home, Tommy broke away from his parents. They caught him after an exciting chase, and kept him between them the rest of the way home. Once in the house, he disappeared, and was found in the guest room under the bed. The afternoon being already spoiled for Mr. Tucker, he determined to keep the child under observation for the rest of the day. Tommy ate no supper, in spite of the urgings of the unhappy mother. The dishes were washed, the evening paper read, the evening pipe smoked; and then, and only then, did Mr. Tucker take down his tool box and get out a hammer and some long nails.

"And I am going to nail the door open, Tommy, so you cannot close it, as that was what the doctor said, Tommy; and you are to be a man and stay here in the kitchen alone for an hour, and we will leave the lamp a-burning, and then when you find there is naught to be afraid of, you will be well and a real man and not something for a man to be ashamed of being the father of."

But at the last, Mrs. Tucker kissed Tommy, and cried, and whispered to her husband not to do it, and to wait till the boy was larger; but nothing availed except to nail the thick door open so it could not be shut, and leave the boy there alone with the lamp burning and the dark open space of the doorway to look at with eyes that grew as hot and burning as the flame of the lamp.

That same day, Doctor Hawthorn took supper with a classmate of his, a man who specialized in psychiatry and who was particularly interested in children. Hawthorn told Johnson about his newest case, the little Tucker boy, and asked him for his opinion. Johnson frowned:

"Children are odd, Hawthorn. Perhaps they are like dogs. It may be their nervous system is more acute than in the adult. We know that our eyesight is limited, also our hearing and smell. I firmly believe that there are forms of life which exist in such a shape that we can neither see, hear, nor smell them. Fondly we delude ourselves into the fallacy of believing that they do not exist because we cannot prove their existence. This Tucker lad may have a nervous system that is peculiarly acute. He may dimly appreciate the existence of something in the cellar which is unappreciable to his parents. Evidently there is some basis to this fear of his. Now, I am not saying that there is anything in the cellar; but this boy, since he was a baby, has thought that something was there, and that is just as bad as though there actually were. What I would like to know is what makes him think so. Give me the address, and I will call tomorrow and have a talk with the little fellow."

"What do you think of my advice?"

"Sorry, old man, but I think it was perfectly rotten. If I were you, I would stop around there on my way home and prevent them from following it. The little fellow may be badly frightened. You see, he evidently thinks there is something there."

"But there isn't."

"Perhaps not. No doubt, he is wrong; but he thinks so."

It all worried Doctor Hawthorn so much that he decided to take his friend's advice. It was a chilly night, a foggy night, and the physician felt cold as he tramped along the London streets. At last, he came to the Tucker house. He remembered now that he had been there once before, long ago, when little Tommy Tucker came into the world. There was a light in the front window, and in no time at all Mr. Tucker came to the door.

"I have come to see Tommy," said the doctor.

"He is back in the kitchen," replied the father.

"He gave one cry, but since then he has been quiet," sobbed the wife.

"If I had let her have her way, she would have opened the door, but I said to her, 'Mother, now is the time to make a man out of our Tommy.' and I guess he knows by now that there was naught to be afraid of. Well, the hour is up. Suppose we go and get him, and put him to bed?"

"It has been a hard time for the little child," whispered the wife.

Carrying the candle, the man walked ahead of the woman and the doctor, and at last opened the kitchen door. The room was dark.

"Lamp has gone out," said the man. "Wait till I light it."

"Tommy! Tommy!" called Mrs. Tucker.

But the doctor ran to where a white form was stretched on the floor. Sharply, he called for more light. Trembling, he examined all that was left of little Tommy. Twitching, he looked into the open space down into the cellar. At last, he looked at Tucker and at Tucker's wife.

"Tommy—Tommy has been hurt—I guess he is dead!" he stammered.

The mother threw herself on the floor and picked up the torn, mutilated thing that had been, only a short while ago, her little Tommy.

The man took his hammer and drew the nails and closed the door and locked it, and then drove in a long spike to reinforce the lock. Then he took hold of the doctor's shoulders and shook him.

"What killed him, Doctor? What killed him?" he shouted into Hawthorn's ear.

The doctor looked at him bravely in spite of the fear in his throat.

"How do I know, Tucker?" he replied. "How do I know? Didn't you tell me that there was nothing there? Nothing down there? In the cellar?"

ROBERT BLOCH

Lizzie Borden Took An Axe . . .

"Lizzie Borden took an axe
And gave her mother forty whacks.
When she saw what she had done
She gave her father forty-one."

Men say that horror comes at midnight, born of whispers out of dreams. But horror came to me at high noon, heralded only by the prosaic jangling of a telephone.

I had been sitting in the office all morning, staring down the dusty road that led to the hills. It coiled and twisted before my aching eyes as a shimmering sun played tricks upon my vision. Nor were my eyes the only organs that betrayed me; something about the heat and the stillness seemed to invade my brain. I was restless, irritable, disturbed by a vague presentiment.

The sharp clangor of the phone bell crystallized my apprehension in a single, strident note.

My palms dripped perspiration-patterns across the receiver. The phone was warm, leaden weight against my ear. But the voice I heard was cold; icy cold, frozen with fear. The words congealed.

"Jim—come and help me!"

That was all. The receiver clicked before I could reply. The phone slid to the desk as I rose and ran to the door.

It was Anita's voice, of course.

It was Anita's voice that sent me speeding toward my car; sent me racing down the desolate, heat-riddled road toward the old house deep in the hills.

Something had happened out there. Something was

bound to happen, sooner or later. I'd known it, and now I cursed myself for not insisting on the sensible thing. Anita and I should have eloped weeks ago.

I should have had the courage to snatch her bodily away from this atmosphere of Faulkneresque melodrama, and I might have, if only I had been able to *believe* in it.

At the time it all seemed so improbable. Worse than that, it seemed *unreal*.

There are no legend-haunted houses looming on lonely hillsides. Yet Anita lived in one.

There are no gaunt, fanatical old men who brood over black books; no "hex doctors" whose neighbors shun them in superstitious dread. Yet Anita's uncle, Gideon Godfrey, was such a man.

Young girls cannot be kept virtual prisoners in this day and age; they cannot be forbidden to leave the house, to love, and marry the man of their choice. Yet Anita's uncle had her under lock and key, and our wedding was prohibited.

Yes, it was all sheer melodrama. The whole affair struck me as ridiculous when I thought about it; but when I was with Anita, I did not laugh.

When I heard Anita talk about her uncle, I almost believed; not that he had supernatural powers, but that he was cunningly, persistently attempting to drive her mad.

That's something you can understand, something evil, yet tangible.

There was a trust fund, and Gideon Godfrey was Anita's legal guardian. He had her out there in his rotting hulk of a house—completely at his mercy. It might easily occur to him to work on her imagination with wild stories and subtle confirmations.

Anita told me. Told me of the locked rooms upstairs where the old man sat mumbling over the moldering books he'd hidden away there. She told me of his feuds with farmers, his open boastings of the "hex" he put on cattle, the blights he claimed to visit upon crops.

Anita told me of her dreams. Something black came into her room at night. Something black and inchoate—a trailing mist that was nevertheless a definite and tangible presence. It had features, if not a face; a voice, if not a throat. It whispered.

And as it whispered, it caressed her. She would fight off the inky strands brushing her face and body; she would struggle to summon the scream which dispelled spectre and sleep simultaneously.

Anita had a name for the black thing, too.

She called it an *incubus*.

In ancient tracts on witchcraft, the incubus is mentioned—the dark demon that comes to women in the night. The black emissary of Satan the Tempter; the lustful shadow that rides the nightmare.

I knew of the incubus as a legend. Anita knew of it as a reality.

Anita grew thin and pale. I knew there was no magic concerned in her metamorphosis—confinement in that bleak old house was alchemy enough to work the change. That, plus the sadistically inspired hintings of Gideon Godfrey, and the carefully calculated atmosphere of dread which resulted in the dreams.

But I had been weak, I didn't insist. After all, there was no real proof of Godfrey's machinations, and any attempt to bring issues to a head might easily result in a sanity hearing for Anita, rather than the old man.

I felt that, given time, I would be able to make Anita come away with me voluntarily.

And now, there was no time.

Something had happened.

The car churned dust from the road as I turned in toward the tottering gambrels of the house on the hillside. Through the flickering heat of a midsummer afternoon, I peered at the ruined gables above the long porch.

I swung up the drive, shot the car past the barn and side-buildings, and parked hastily.

No figure appeared at the open windows, and no voice called a greeting as I ran up the porch steps and paused before the open door. The hall within was dark. I entered heedless of knocking, and turned towards the parlor.

Anita was standing there, waiting, on the far side of the room. Her red hair was disheveled about her shoulders; her face was pale—but she was obviously unharmed. Her eyes brightened when she saw me.

"Jim—you're here!"

She held out her arms to me, and I moved across the room to embrace her.

As I moved, I stumbled over something.

I looked down.

Lying at my feet was the body of Gideon Godfrey—the head split open and crushed to a bloody pulp.

2.

Then Anita was sobbing in my arms, and I was patting her shoulders and trying not to stare at the red horror on the floor.

"Help me," she whispered, over and over again. "Help me!"

"Of course I'll help you," I murmured. "But—what happened?"

"I don't—know."

"You don't *know?*"

Something in my intonation sobered her. She straightened up, pulled away, and began dabbing at her eyes. Meanwhile she whispered on, hastily:

"It was hot this morning. I was out in the barn. I felt tired and dozed off in the hayloft. Then, all at once, I woke and came back into the house. I found—him—lying here."

"There was no noise? Nobody around?"

"Not a soul."

"You can see how he was killed," I said. "Only an axe could do such a job. But—where is it?"

She averted her gaze. "The axe? I don't know. It should be beside the body, if someone killed him."

I turned and started out of the room.

"Jim—where are you going?"

"To call the police, naturally," I told her.

"No, you can't. Don't you see? If you call them now, they'll think *I* did it."

I could only nod. "That's right. It's a pretty flimsy story, isn't it Anita? If we only had a weapon; fingerprints, or footsteps, some kind of clue—"

Anita sighed. I took her hand. "Try to remember," I said, softly. "You're sure you were out in the barn when this happened? Can't you remember more than that?"

"No, darling. It's all so confused, somehow. I was sleeping—I had one of my dreams—the black thing came—"

I shuddered. I knew how *that* statement affected me,
and I could imagine the reaction of the police. She was
quite mad, I was sure of it; and yet another thought
struggled for realization. Somehow I had the feeling that
I had lived through this moment before. Pseudo-memory.
Or had I heard of it, read of it?

Read of it? Yes, that was it!

"Try hard, now," I muttered. "Can't you recall how it
all began? Don't you know why you went out to the barn
in the first place?"

"Yes. I think I can remember. I went out there for
some fishing sinkers."

"Fishing sinkers? In the barn?"

Something clicked, after all. I stared at her with eyes
as glassy as those of the corpse on the floor.

"Listen to me," I said. "You're not Anita Loomis.
You're—Lizzie Borden!"

She didn't say a word. Obviously the name had no
meaning for her. But it was all coming back to me now;
the old, old story, the unsolved mystery.

I guided her to the sofa, sat beside her. She didn't look
at me. I didn't look at her. Neither of us looked at the
thing on the floor. The heat shimmered all around us in
the house of death as I whispered the story to her—the
story of Lizzie Borden—

3.

It was early August of the year 1892. Fall River, Massachusetts lay gasping in the surge of a heat-wave.

The sun beat down upon the home of Fall River's
leading citizen, the venerable Andrew Jackson Borden.
Here the old man dwelt with his second wife, Mrs. Abby
Borden, stepmother of the two girls, Emma and Lizzie
Borden. The maid, Bridget "Maggie" Sullivan, completed
the small household. A house guest, John V. Morse, was
away at this time, visiting. Emma, the older Borden girl,
was also absent.

Only the maid and Lizzie Borden were present on
August 2nd, when Mr. and Mrs. Borden became ill. It
was Lizzie who spread the news—she told her friend,
Marion Russell, that she believed their milk had been
poisoned.

But it was too hot to bother, too hot to think. Besides, Lizzie's ideas weren't taken very seriously. At 32, the angular, unprepossessing younger daughter was looked upon with mixed opinion by the members of the community. It was known that she was "cultured" and "refined" —she had traveled in Europe; she was a churchgoer, taught a class in a church mission, and enjoyed a reputation for "good work" as a member of the WCTU and similar organizations. Yet some folks thought her temperamental, even eccentric. She had "notions."

So the illness of the elder Bordens was duly noted and ascribed to natural causes; it was impossible to think about anything more important than the omnipresent heat, and the forthcoming Annual Picnic of the Fall River Police Department, scheduled for August 4th.

On the 4th the heat was unabated, but the picnic was in full swing by 11 o'clock—the time at which Andrew Jackson Borden left his downtown office and came home to relax on the parlor sofa. He slept fitfully in the noonday swelter.

Lizzie Borden came in from the barn a short while later and found her father asleep no longer.

Mr. Borden lay on the sofa, his head bashed in so that his features were unrecognizable.

Lizzie Borden called the maid, "Maggie" Sullivan, who was resting in her room. She told her to run and fetch Dr. Bowen, a near neighbor. He was not at home.

Another neighbor, a Mrs. Churchill, happened by. Lizzie Borden greeted her at the door.

"Someone has killed father," were Lizzie's words.

"And where is your mother?" Mrs. Churchill asked.

Lizzie Borden hesitated. It was hard to think in all this heat. "Why—she's out. She received a note to go and help someone who is sick."

Mrs. Churchill didn't hesitate. She marched to a public livery stable and summoned help. Soon a crowd of neighbors and friends gathered; police and doctors were in attendance. And in the midst of growing confusion, it was Mrs. Churchill who went directly upstairs to the spare room.

Mrs. Borden rested there, her head smashed in.

By the time Dr. Dolan, the coroner, arrived, questioning was already proceeding. The Chief of Police and

several of his men were on hand, establishing the fact
that there had been no attempt at robbery. They began
to interrogate Lizzie.

Lizzie Borden said she was in the barn, eating pears
and looking for fishing sinkers—hot as it was. She dozed
off, was awakened by a muffled groan, and came into the
house to investigate. There she found her father's hacked
body. And that was all—

Now her story of a suspected poisoning was recalled,
with fresh significance. A druggist said that a woman had
indeed come into his shop several days before and attempted to procure some prussic acid—saying she needed
it to kill the moths in her fur coat. She had been refused,
and informed by the proprietor that she needed a doctor's prescription.

The woman was identified, too—as Lizzie Borden.

Lizzie's story of the note summoning her mother away
from the house now came in for scrutiny. No such note
was ever discovered.

Meanwhile, the investigators were busy. In the cellar,
they discovered a hatchet with a broken handle. It appeared to have been recently washed, then covered with
ashes. Water and ashes conceal stains. . . .

Shock, heat, embarrassment all played subtle parts in
succeeding events. The police presently withdrew without taking formal action, and the whole matter was held
over, pending an inquest. After all, Andrew Jackson
Borden was a wealthy citizen, his daughter was a promi-
nent and respectable woman, and no one wished to act
hastily.

Days passed in a pall of heat and gossip behind sweaty
palms. Lizzie's friend, Marion Russell, dropped in at the
house three days after the crime and discovered Lizzie
burning a dress.

"It was all covered with paint," Lizzie Borden explained.

Marion Russell remembered that dress—it was the one
Lizzie Borden had worn on the day of the murders.

The inevitable inquest was held, with the inevitable
verdict. Lizzie Borden was arrested and formally charged
with the slayings.

The press took over. The church members defended
Lizzie Borden. The sobsisters made much of her. During

the six months preceding the actual trial, the crime became internationally famous.

But nothing new was discovered.

During the thirteen days of the trial, the bewildering story was recounted without any sensational development.

Why should a refined New England spinster suddenly kill her father and stepmother with a hatchet, then boldly "discover" the bodies and summon the police?

The prosecution was unable to give a satisfactory answer. On June 20th, 1893, Lizzie Borden was acquitted by a jury of her peers, after one hour of deliberation.

She retired to her home and lived a life of seclusion for many, many years. The stigma had been erased, but the mystery remained unsolved with her passing.

Only the grave little girls remained, skipping their ropes and solemnly chanting:

> *"Lizzie Borden took an axe*
> *And gave her mother forty whacks.*
> *When she saw what she had done*
> *She gave her father forty-one."*

4.

That's the story I told Anita—the story you can read wherever famous crimes are chronicled.

She listened without comment, but I could hear the sharp intake of breath as I recounted some singularly significant parallel. *The hot day . . . the barn . . . the fishing sinkers . . . a sudden sleep, a sudden awakening . . . the return to the house . . . discovery of a body . . . took an axe. . . .*

She waited until I had finished before speaking.

"Jim, why do you tell me this? Is it your way of hinting that I—took an axe to my uncle?"

"I'm not hinting anything," I answered. "I was just struck by the amazing similarity of this case and the Lizzie Borden affair."

"What do you think happened, Jim? In the Lizzie Borden case, I mean."

"I don't know," I said slowly. "I was wondering if you had a theory."

Her opal eyes glinted in the shadowed room. "Couldn't it have been the same thing?" she whispered. "You know what I've told you about my dreams. About the incubus."

"Suppose Lizzie Borden had those dreams, too. Suppose an entity emerged from her sleeping brain; an entity that would take up an axe and kill—"

She sensed my protest and ignored it. "Uncle Gideon knew of such things. How the spirit descends upon you in sleep. Couldn't such a presence emerge into the world while she slept and kill her parents? Couldn't such a being creep into the house here while I slept and kill Uncle Gideon?"

I shook my head. "You know the answer I must give you," I said. "And you can guess what the police would say to that. Our only chance now, before calling them, is to find the murder weapon."

We went out into the hall together, and hand in hand we walked through the silent ovens that were the rooms of this old house. Everywhere was dust and desolation. The kitchen alone bore signs of recent occupancy—they had breakfasted there early in the day, Anita said.

There was no axe or hatchet to be found anywhere.

It took courage to tackle the cellar. I was almost certain of what we must find. But Anita did not recoil, and we descended the dark stairwell.

The cellar did not yield up a single sharp instrument.

Then we were walking up the stairs to the second floor. The front bedroom was ransacked, then Anita's little room, and at last we stood before the door of Gideon Godfrey's chamber.

"It's locked," I said. "That's funny."

"No," Anita demurred. "He always kept it locked. The key must be downstairs with—him."

"I'll get it," I said. And I did so. When I returned with the rusty key, Anita stood quaking in the hallway.

"I won't go inside with you," she breathed. "I've never been inside his room. I'm afraid. He used to lock himself in and I'd hear sounds late at night—he was praying, but not to God—"

"Wait here, then," I said.

I unlocked the door, opened it, stepped across the threshold.

*   *   *

Gideon Godfrey may have been a madman himself. He may have been a cunning schemer, bent on deluding his niece. But in either case, he did believe in sorcery.

That much was evident from the contents of his room. I saw the books, saw the crudely drawn chalk circles on the floor; literally dozens of them, hastily obliterated and repeated endlessly. There were queer geometric configurations traced in blue chalk upon one of the walls, and candle-drippings covered walls and floors alike.

The heavy, fetid air held a faint, acrid reek of incense. I noted one sharp instrument in the room—a long silver knife lying on a side-table next to a pewter bowl. The knife seemed rusty, and the rust was red. . . .

But it was not the murder weapon, that was certain. I was looking for an axe, and it wasn't here.

I joined Anita in the hall.

"Isn't there anywhere else?" I asked, Another room?"

"Perhaps the barn," she suggested.

"And we didn't really search in the parlor," I added.

"Don't make me go in there again," Anita begged. "Not in the same room where he is. You look there and I'll go through the barn."

We parted at the foot of the stairs. She went out the side entrance and I walked back into the parlor.

I looked behind the chairs, under the sofa. I found nothing. It was hot in there; hot and quiet. My head began to swim.

Heat—silence—and that grinning thing on the floor. I turned away, leaned against the mantel, and stared at my bloodshot eyes in the mirror.

All at once I saw it, standing behind me. It was like a cloud—a black cloud. But it wasn't a cloud. It was a *face*. A face, covered by a black mask of wavering smoke; a mask that leered and pressed closer.

Through heat and silence it came, and I couldn't move. I stared at the swirling, cloudy smoke that shrouded a face.

Then I heard something swish, and I turned.

Anita was standing behind me.

As I grasped her wrists she screamed and fell. I could only stare down at her, stare down as the black cloud over her face disappeared, oozed into air.

The search was over. I'd found the murder weapon, all right; it rested rigidly in her hands—the bloodstained axe!

5.

I carried Anita over to the sofa. She didn't move, and I made no attempt to revive her.

Then I went out into the hall, carrying the axe with me. No sense in taking any chances. I trusted Anita still, but not that thing—not that black mist, swirling up like smoke to take possession of a living brain and make it lust to kill.

Demoniac possession it was; the legend spoken of in ancient books like those in the room of the dead wizard.

I crossed the hall to the little study opposite the parlor. The wall telephone was here; I picked it up and rang the operator.

She got me the Highway Police headquarters. I don't know why I called them, rather than the sheriff. I was in a daze throughout the entire call. I stood there holding the axe in one hand, reporting the murder in a few words.

Questions rose from the other end of the wire; I did not answer them.

"Come on out to the Godfrey place," I said. "There's been a killing."

What else *could* I say?

What would we be telling the police, half an hour from now, when they arrived on the scene?

They wouldn't believe the truth—wouldn't believe that a demon could enter a human body and activate it as an instrument for murder.

But I believed it now. I had seen the fiend peering out of Anita's face when she tried to sneak up behind me with the axe. I had seen the black smoke, the conjuration of a demon lusting for bloody death.

Now I knew that it must have entered her as she slept; made her kill Gideon Godfrey.

Perhaps such a thing had happened to Lizzie Borden. Yes. The eccentric spinster with the overactive imagination, so carefully repressed; the eccentric spinster, sleeping in the barn on that hot summer day—

*"Lizzie Borden took an axe
And gave her mother forty whacks."*

I leaned back, the verse running through my head.

It was hotter than I had believed possible, and the stillness hinted of approaching storm.

I groped for coolness, felt the cold axeblade in my hand as I leaned the weapon across my lap. As long as I held onto this, we were safe. The fiend was foiled, now. Wherever that presence lurked, it must be raging, for it could not take possession.

Oh, that was madness! The heat was responsible, surely. Sunstroke caused Anita to kill her uncle. Sunstroke brought on her babblings about an incubus and dreams. Sunstroke impelled that sudden, murderous attack upon me before the mirror.

Sympathetic hallucination accounted for my image of a face veiled by a black mist. It had to be that way. The police would say so, doctors would say so.

*"When she saw what she had done
She gave her father forty-one."*

Police. Doctors. Lizzie Borden. The heat. The cool axe. Forty whacks. . . .

6.

The first crash of thunder awakened me. For a moment I thought the police had arrived, then realized that the heat-storm was breaking. I blinked and rose from the armchair. Then I realized that something was *missing*.

The axe no longer rested across my lap.

It wasn't on the floor. It wasn't visible anywhere. The axe had disappeared again!

"Anita," I gasped. I knew without conscious formulation of thought how it must have happened. She had awakened while I slept—come in here and stolen the axe from me.

What a fool I had been to sleep!

I might have guessed it . . . while she was unconscious, the lurking demon had another chance to gain possession. That was it; the demon had entered into Anita again.

I faced the door, stared at the floor, and saw my confirmation scrawled in a trail of red wetness dotting the carpet and outer hall.

It was blood. Fresh blood.

I rushed across the hall, re-entered the parlor.

Then I gasped, but with relief. For Anita was still lying on the couch, just as I had left her. I wiped the sudden perspiration from my eyes and forehead, then stared again at the red pattern on the floor.

The trail of blood ended beside the couch, all right. But did it lead *to* the couch—or *away* from it?

Thunder roared through the heat. A flicker of lightning seared the shadows of the room as I tried to puzzle it out.

What did it mean? It meant that perhaps Anita was not possessed of a demon now while she slept.

But I had slept, too.

Maybe—maybe the demon had come to *me* when *I* dozed off!

All at once, everything blurred. I was trying to remember. Where was the axe? Where could it possibly be, *now?*

Then the lightning came again and with it the final confirmation—the revelation.

I saw the axe now, crystal-clear—the axe—buried to the hilt in the top of Anita's head!

CORNELL WOOLRICH

The Moon of Montezuma

The hired car was very old. The girl in it was very
young. They were both American. Which was strange
here in this far-off place, this other world, as remote
from things American as anywhere could be.

The car was a vintage model, made by some concern
whose very name has been forgotten by now; a relic of
the Teens or early Twenties, built high and squared-off
at the top, like a box on wheels.

It crawled precariously to the top of the long, winding,
sharply ascending rutted road—wheezing, gasping, threat-
ening to slip backward at any moment, but never doing
so; miraculously managing even to inch on up.

It stopped at last, opposite what seemed to be a blank,
biscuit-colored wall. This had a thick door set into it, but
no other openings. A skimpy tendril or two of bougainvillaea, burningly mauve, crept downward over its top
here and there. There were cracks in the wall, and an
occasional place where the plaster facing had fallen off to
reveal the adobe underpart.

The girl peered out from the car. Her hair was blonde,
her skin fair. She looked unreal in these surroundings of
violent color; somehow completely out of key with them.
She was extremely tired-looking; there were shadows
under her blue eyes. She was holding a very young baby
wrapped into a little cone-shaped bundle in a blanket. A
baby not more than a few weeks old. And beside the
collar of her coat a rosebud was pinned. Scarcely opened,
yet dying already. Red as a glowing coal. Or a drop of

blood. She looked at the driver, then back to the blank wall again. "Is this where it is?"

He shrugged. He didn't understand her language. He said something to her. A great deal of something.

She shook her head bewilderedly. His language was as mysterious to her. She consulted the piece of paper she was holding in her hand, then looked again at the place where they'd stopped. "But there's no house here. There's just a wall."

He flicked the little pennant on his meter so that it sprang upright. Underneath it said "7.50". She could read that, at least. He opened the creaking door, to show her what he meant. "Pay me, Señorita. I have to go all the way back to the town."

She got out reluctantly, a forlorn, lost figure. "Wait here," she said. "Wait for me until I find out."

He understood the sense of her faltering gesture. He shook his head firmly. He became very voluble. He had to go back to where he belonged, he had no business being all the way out here. It would be dark soon. His was the only auto in the whole town.

She paid him, guessing at the unfamiliar money she still didn't understand. When he stopped nodding, she stopped giving it to him. There was very little left—a paper bill or two, a handful of coins. She reached in and dragged out a bulky bag and stood that on the ground beside her. Then she turned around and looked at the inscrutable wall.

The car turned creakily and went down the long, rutted road, back into the little town below.

She was left there, with child, with baggage, with a scrap of paper in her hand. She went over to the door in the wall, looked about for something to ring. There was a short length of rope hanging there against the side of the door. She tugged at it and a bell, the kind with hanging clapper, jangled loosely.

The child opened its eyes momentarily, then closed them again. Blue eyes, like hers.

The door opened, narrowly but with surprising quickness. An old woman stood looking at her. Glittering black eyes, gnarled face the color of tobacco, blue rebozo coifed about her head to hid every vestige of hair, one end of the scarf looped rearward over her throat. There was something malignant in the idol-like face, something almost Aztec.

"Señorita wishes?" she breathed suspiciously.

"Can you read?" The girl showed her the scrap of paper. That talisman that had brought her so far.

The old woman touched her eyes, shook her head. She couldn't read.

"But isn't this—isn't this—" Her tired tongue stumbled over the unfamiliar words. "Caminode . . ."

The old woman pointed vaguely in dismissal. "Go, ask them in the town, they can answer your questions there." She tried to close the heavy door again.

The girl planted her foot against it, held it open. "Let me in. I was told to come here. This is the place I was told to come. I'm tired, and I have no place to go." For a moment her face was wreathed in lines of weeping, then she curbed them. "Let me come in and rest a minute until I can find out. I've come such a long way. All night long, that terrible train from Mexico City, and before that the long trip down from the border. . . ." She pushed the door now with her free hand as well as her foot.

"I beg you, Señorita," the old woman said with sullen gravity, "do not enter here now. Do not force your way in here. There has been a death in this house."

"¿Qué pasa?" a younger, higher voice suddenly said, somewhere unseen behind her.

The crone stopped her clawing, turned her head. Suddenly she had whisked from sight as though jerked on a wire, and a young girl had taken her place in the door opening.

The same age as the intruder, perhaps even a trifle younger. Jet-black hair parted arrow-straight along the center of her head. Her skin the color of old ivory. The same glittering black eyes as the old one, but larger, younger. Even more liquid, as though they had recently been shedding tears. There was the same cruelty implicit in them too, but not yet as apparent. There was about her whole beauty, and she was beautiful, a tinge of cruelty, of barbarism, that same mask-like Aztec cast of expression, of age-old racial inheritance.

"¿Si?"

"Can you understand me?" the girl pleaded, hoping against hope for a moment.

There was a flash of perfect white teeth, but the black hair moved negatively. "The señorita is lost, perhaps?"

Somehow, the American sensed the meaning of the words. "This is where they told me to come. I inquired in Mexico City. The American consul. They even told me how to get here, what trains. I wrote him, and I never heard. I've been writing him and writing him, and I never heard. But this must be the place. This is where I've been writing, Camino de las Rosas. . . ." A dry sob escaped with the last.

The liquid black eyes had narrowed momentarily. "The señorita looks for who?"

"Bill. Bill Taylor." She tried to turn it into Spanish, with the pitiful resources at her command. "Señor Taylor. Señor Bill Taylor. Look, I'll show you his picture." She fumbled in her handbag, drew out a small snapshot, handed it to the waiting girl. It was a picture of herself and a young man. "Him. I'm looking for him. Now do you understand?"

For a moment there seemed to have been a sharp intake of breath, but it might have been an illusion. The dark-haired girl smiled ruefully. Then she shook her head.

"Don't you know him? Isn't he here? Isn't this his house?" She pointed to the wall alongside. "But it must be. Then whose house is it?"

The dark-haired girl pointed to herself, then to the old woman hovering and hissing surreptitiously in the background. "Casa de nosotros. The house of Chata and her mother. Nobody else."

"Then he isn't here?" The American leaned her back for a moment hopelessly against the wall, turning the other way, to face out from it. She let her head roll a little to one side. "What am I going to do? Where is he, what became of him? I haven't even enough money to go back. I have nowhere to go. They warned me back home not to come down here alone like this, looking for him—oh, I should have listened!"

The black eyes were speculatively narrow again, had been for some time. She pointed to the snapshot. "Hermano? He is the brother of the señorita, or—?"

The blonde stranger touched her own ring finger. This time the sob came first. "He's my husband! I had to pawn my wedding ring, to help pay my way here. I've got

to find him! He was going to send for me later—and then
he never did."

The black eyes had flicked downward to the child,
almost unnoticeably, then up again. Once more she pointed
to the snapshot.

The blonde nodded. "It's his. Ours. I don't think he
even knows about it. I wrote him, and I never heard
back. . . ."

The other's head turned sharply aside for a moment,
conferring with the old woman. In profile, her cameo-
like beauty was even more expressive. So was the razor-
sharpness of its latent cruelty.

Abruptly she had reached out with both hands. "Entra.
Entra. Come in. Rest. Refresh yourself." The door was
suddenly open at full width, revealing a patio in the
center of which was a profusion of white roses. The
bushes were not many, perhaps six all told, but they were
all in full bloom, weighted down with their masses of
flowers. They were arranged in a hollow square. Around
the outside ran a border of red-tiled flooring. In the
center there was a deep gaping hole—a well, either being
dug or being repaired. It was lined with a casing of
shoring planks that protruded above its lip. A litter of
construction tools lay around, lending a transient ugliness
to the otherwise beautiful little enclosure: a wheelbar-
row, several buckets, a mixing trough, a sack of cement,
shovels and picks, and an undulating mound of misplaced
earth brought up out of the cavity.

There was no one working at it now, it was too late in
the day. Silence hung heavily. In the background was the
house proper, its rooms ranged single file about three
sides of the enclosure, each one characteristically opening into it with its own individual doorway. The old
houses of Moorish Africa, of which this was a lineal
descendant, had been like that: blind to the street,
windowless, cloistered, each living its life about its own
inner, secretive courtyard. Twice transplanted—first to
Spain, then to the newer Spain across the waters.

Now that entry had at last been granted, the blonde
girl was momentarily hesitant about entering. "But if—
but if this isn't his house, what good is it to come in?"

The insistent hands of the other reached her, drew her,
gently but firmly, across the threshold. In the background

the old woman still looked on with a secretive malignancy that might have been due solely to the wizened lines in her face.

"Pase, pase," the dark-haired girl was coaxing her. Step in. "Descansa." Rest. She snapped her fingers with sudden, concealed authority behind her own back, and the old woman, seeming to understand the esoteric signal, sidled around to the side of them and out to the road for a moment, looked quickly up the road, then quickly down, picked up the bag standing there and drew it inside with her, leaning totteringly against its weight.

Suddenly the thick wall-door had closed behind her and the blonde wayfarer was in, whether she wanted to be or not.

The silence, the remoteness, was as if a thick, smothering velvet curtain had fallen all at once. Although the road had been empty, the diffuse, imponderable noises of the world had been out there somehow. Although this patio courtyard was unroofed and open to the same evening sky, and only a thick wall separated it from the outside, there was a stillness, a hush, as though it were a thousand miles away, or deep down within the earth.

They led her, one on each side of her—the girl with the slightest of forward-guiding hands just above her waist, the old woman still struggling with the bag—along the red-tiled walk skirting the roses, in under the overhanging portico of the house proper, and in through one of the doorways. It had no door as such; only a curtain of wooden-beaded strings was its sole provision for privacy and isolation. These clicked and hissed when they were stirred. Within were cool plaster walls painted a pastel color halfway up, allowed to remain undyed the rest of the way; an equally cool tiled flooring; an iron bedstead; an ebony chair or two, stiff, tortuously hand-carved, with rush-bottomed seats and backs. A serape of burning emerald and orange stripes, placed on the floor alongside the bed, served as a rug. A smaller one, of sapphire and cerise bands, affixed to the wall, served as the only decoration there was.

They sat her down in one of the chairs, the baby still in her arms. Chata, after a moment's hesitancy, summoned up a sort of defiant boldness, reached out and deliberately removed the small traveling-hat from her head without asking permission. Her expressive eyes widened for a moment, then narrowed again, as they took in the exotic blonde hair in all its unhampered abundance.

Her eyes now went to the child, but more as an afterthought than as if that were her primary interest, and she leaned forward and admired and played with him a little, as women do with a child, any women, of any race. Dabbing her finger at his chin, at his button of a nose, taking one of his little hands momentarily in hers, then relinquishing it again. There was something a trifle mechanical about her playing; there was no real feeling for the child at all.

She said something to the old woman, and the latter came back after a short interval with milk in an earthenware bowl.

"He'll have to drink it with a nipple," the young mother said. "He's too tiny." She handed him for a moment to Chata to hold for her, fumbled with her bag, opened it and got out his feeding-bottle. She poured some of the milk into that, then recapped it and took him up to feed him.

She had caught a curious look on Chata's face in the moment or two she was holding him. As though she were studying the child closely; but not with melting fondness, with a completely detached, almost cold, curiosity.

They remained looking on for a few moments; then they slipped out and left her, the old woman first, Chata a moment later, with a few murmured words and a half-gesture toward the mouth, that she sensed as meaning she was to come and have something to eat with them when she was ready.

She fed him first, and then she turned back the covers and laid him down on the bed. She found two large-size safety-pins in her bag and pinned the covers down tight on either side of him, so that he could not roll off and fall down. His eyes were already closed again, one tiny fist bent backward toward his head. She kissed him softly, with a smothered sob—that was for the failure of the long pilgrimage that had brought her all this way—then tiptoed out.

There was an aromatic odor of spicy cooking hovering disembodiedly about the patio, but just where it was originating from she couldn't determine. Of the surrounding six doorways, three were pitch-black. From one there was a dim, smoldering red glow peering. From another a paler, yellow light was cast subduedly. She mistakenly went toward this.

It was two doors down from the one from which she had just emerged. If they were together in there, they must be talking in whispers. She couldn't hear a sound, not even the faintest murmur.

It had grown darker now; it was full night already, with the swiftness of the mountainous latitudes. The square of sky over the patio was soft and dark as indigo velour, with magnificent stars like many-legged silver spiders festooned on its underside. Below them the white roses gleamed phosphorescently in the starlight, with a magnesium-like glow. There was a tiny splash from the depths of the well as a pebble or grain of dislodged earth fell in.

She made her way toward the yellow-ombre doorway. Her attention had been on other things: the starlight, the sheen of the roses; and she turned the doorway and entered the room too quickly, without stopping outside to look in first.

She was already well over the threshold and in before she stopped short, frozen there, with a stifled intake of fright and an instinctive clutching of both hands toward her throat.

The light came from two pairs of tapers. Between them rested a small bier that was perhaps only a trestled plank shrouded with a cloth. One pair stood at the head of it, one pair at the foot.

On the bier lay a dead child. An infant, perhaps days younger than her own. In fine white robes. Gardenias and white rosebuds disposed about it in impromptu arrangement, to form a little nest or bower. On the wall was a religious image; under it in a red glass cup burned a holy light.

The child lay there so still, as if waiting to be picked up and taken into its mother's arms. Its tiny hands were folded on its breast.

She drew a step closer, staring. A step closer, a step closer. Its hair was blond; fair, golden blond.

There was horror lurking in this somewhere. She was suddenly terribly frightened. She took another step, and then another. She wasn't moving her feet, something was drawing them.

She was beside it now. The sickening, cloying odor of the gardenias was swirling about her head like a tide. The infant's little eyes had been closed. She reached down gently, lifted an eyelid, then snatched her hand away. The baby's eyes had been blue.

Horror might have found her then, but it was given no time. She whirled suddenly, not in fright so much as mechanistic nervousness, and Chata was standing motionless in full-center of the doorway, looking in at her.

The black head gave a toss of arrogance. "My child, yes. My little son." And in the flowery language that can express itself as English never can, without the risk of being ridiculous: "The son of my heart." For a moment her face crumbled and a gust of violent emotion swept across it, instantly was gone again.

But it hadn't been grief, it had been almost maniacal rage. The rage of the savage who resents a loss, does not know how to accept it.

'I'm sorry, I didn't know—I didn't mean to come in here—'

"Come, there is some food for you," Chata cut her short curtly. She turned on her heel and went down the shadowy arcade toward the other lighted doorway, the more distant one her self-invited guest should have sought out in the first place.

The American went more slowly, turning in the murky afterglow beyond the threshold to look lingeringly back inside again: I will not think of this for a while. Later, I know, I must, but not now. That in this house where he said he lived there is a child lying dead whose hair is golden, whose eyes were blue.

Chata had reappeared in the designated doorway through which she wanted her to follow, to make it out for her, to hasten her coming. The American advanced toward it, and went in in turn.

They squatted on the floor to eat, as the Japanese do. The old woman palmed it, and Chata palmed it in turn, to have her do likewise, and to show her where.

She sank awkwardly down as they were, feeling her legs to be too long, but managing somehow to dispose of them with a fanned-out effect to the side. An earthenware bowl of rice and red beans was set down before her.

She felt a little faint for a moment, for the need of food, as the aroma reached her, heavy and succulent. She wanted to crouch down over it, and up-end the entire bowl against her face, to get its entire contents in all at one time.

The old woman handed her a tortilla, a round flat cake, paper-thin, of pestled maize, limp as a wet rag. She held it in her own hand helplessly, did not know what to do with it. They had no eating utensils.

The old woman took it back from her, deftly rolled it into a hollowed tube, returned it. She did with it as she saw them doing with theirs; held the bowl up closer to her mouth and scooped up the food in it by means of the tortilla.

The food was unaccustomedly piquant; it prickled, baffled the taste-buds of her tongue. A freakish thought from nowhere suddenly flitted through her mind: I should be careful. If they wanted to poison me. . . . And then: But why should they want to harm me? I've done them no harm; my being here certainly does them no harm.

And because it held no solid substance, the thought misted away again.

She was so exhausted, her eyes were already drooping closed before the meal was finished. She recovered with a start, and they had both been watching her fixedly. She could tell that by the way fluidity of motion set in again, as happens when people try to cover up the rigid intentness that has just preceded it. Each motion only started as she resumed her observation of it.

"Tienes sueño," Chata murmured. "¿Quieres acostarte?" And she motioned toward the doorway, without looking at it herself.

Somehow the American understood the intention of the words by the fact of the gesture, and the fact that Chata had not risen from the floor herself, but remained squatting. She was not being told to leave the house, she was being told that she might remain within the house and go and lie down with her child if she needed to.

She stumbled to her feet awkwardly, almost threatened to topple for a moment with fatigue. Then steadied herself.

"Gracia," she faltered. "Gracia, mucho." Two pitiful words.

They did not look at her. They were looking down at the emptied food bowls before them. They did not turn their eyes toward her as when somebody is departing from your presence. They kept them on the ground before them as if holding them leashed, waiting for the departure to have been completed.

She draggingly made the turn of the doorway and left them behind her.

The patio seemed to have brightened while she'd been away. It was bleached an almost dazzling white now, with the shadows of the roses and their leaves an equally intense black. Like splotches and drippings of ink beneath each separate component one. Or like a lace mantilla flung open upon a snowdrift.

A raging, glowering full moon had come up, was peering down over the side of the sky-well above the patio.

That was the last thing she saw as she leaned for a moment, inert with fatigue, against the doorway of the room in which her child lay. Then she dragged herself in to topple headlong upon the bed and, already fast asleep, to circle her child with one protective arm, moving as if of its own instinct.

Not the meek, the pallid, gentle moon of home. This was the savage moon that had shone down on Montezuma and Cuauhtemoc, and came back looking for them now. The primitive moon that had once looked down on terraced heathen cities and human sacrifices. The moon of Anahuac.

Now the moon of the Aztecs is at the zenith, and all the world lies still. Full and white, the white of bones, the white of a skull; blistering the center of the sky-well with its throbbing, not touching it on any side. Now the patio is a piebald place of black and white, burning in the downward-teeming light. Not a leaf moves, not a petal falls, in this fierce amalgam.

Now the lurid glow from within the brazero has dimmed, and is just a threaded crimson outline against contrasting surfaces, skipping the space in between. It traces, like a

fine wire, two figures coifed with rebozos. One against
the wall, inanimate, like one of the mummies of her race
that used to be sat upright in the rock catacombs. Eyes
alone move quick above the mouth-shrouded rebozo.

The other teetering slightly to and fro. Ever so slightly,
in time to a whispering. A whispering that is like a steady
sighing in the night; a whispering that does not come
through the muffling rebozos.

The whispering stops. She raises something. A small
stone. A whetstone. She spits. She returns it to the floor
again. The whispering begins once more. The whispering
that is not of the voice, but of a hungry panting in the
night. A hissing thirst.

The roses sleep pale upon the blackness of a dream.
The haunted moon looks down, lonely for Montezuma
and his nation, seeking across the land.

The whispering stops now. The shrouded figure in the
center of the room holds out something toward the one
propped passive against the wall. Something slim, sharp,
grip foremost. The wire-outline from the brazero-mouth
finds it for a moment, runs around it like a current,
flashes into a momentary highlight, a burnished blur,
then runs off it again and leaves it to the darkness.

The other takes it. Her hands go up briefly. The rebozo
falls away from her head, her shoulders. Two long plaits
of dark glossy hair hang down revealed against the cop-
per satin that is now her upper body. Her mouth opens
slightly. She places the sharp thing crosswise to it. Her
teeth fasten on it. Her hand leaves it there, rigid,
immovable.

Her hands execute a swift circling about her head. The
two long plaits whip from sight, like snakes scampering
to safety amidst rocks. She twines them, tucks them up.

She rises slowly with the grace of unhurried flexibility,
back continuing to the wall. She girds her skirt up high
about her thighs and interlaces it between, so that it
holds itself there. Unclothed now, save for a broad swath-
ing about the waist and hips, knife in mouth, she begins
to move. Sideward toward the entrance, like a ruddy
flame coursing along the wall, with no trace behind it.

Nothing is said. There is nothing to be said.

*   *   *

Nothing was said before. Nothing needed to be said. Dark eyes understood dark eyes. Dark thoughts met dark thoughts and understood, without the need of a word.

Nothing will be said after it is over. Never, not in a thousand days from now, not in a thousand months. Never again.

The old gods never had a commandment not to kill. That was another God in another land. The gods of Anahuac demanded the taking of human life, that was their nature. And who should know better than the gods what its real value is, for it is they who give it in the first place.

The flame is at the doorway now, first erect, then writhing, the way a flame does. Then the figure goes down on hands and knees, low, crouching, for craft, for stealth, for the approach to kill. The big cats in the mountains do it this way, belly-flat, and the tribe of Montezuma did it this way too, half a thousand years ago. And the blood remembers what the heart has never learned. The approach to kill.

On hands and knees the figure comes pacing along beside the wall that flanks the patio, lithe, sinuous, knife in mouth perpendicular to its course. In moonlight and out of it, as each successive archway of the portico circles high above it, comes down to join its support, and is gone again to the rear.

The moon is a caress on supple skin. The moon of Anahuac understands, the moon is in league, the moon will not betray.

Slowly along the portico creeps the death-approach, now borax-white in archway-hemisphere, now clay-blue in slanted support-ephemera. The knife-blade winks, like a little haze-puff of white dust, then the shadow hides it again.

The roses dream, the well lies hushed, not a straggling grain topples into it to mar it. No sound, no sound at all. Along the wall crawls life, bringing an end to life.

Past the opening where the death-tapers burn all night. She doesn't even turn her head as she passes. What is dead is gone. What is dead does not matter any more. There were no souls in Anahuac, just bodies that come to stir, then stop and stir no longer.

What is dead does not matter any more. The love of a
man, that is what matters to a woman. If she has not his
child, she cannot hold his love. If she loses his child, then
she must get another.

And now the other entrance is coming nearer as the
wraith-like figure creeps on, Like smoke, like mist, flickering along at the base of a wall. It seems to move of its
own accord, sidling along the wall as if it were a black
slab or panel traveling on hidden wheels or pulleys at the
end of a drawcord. Coming nearer all the time, black,
coffin-shaped, against the bluish-pale wall. Growing taller,
growing wider, growing greater.

And then a sound, a small night sound, a futile, helpless
sound—a child whimpers slightly in its sleep.

But instantly the figure stops, crouched. Is as still as if
it had never moved a moment ago, would never move
again. Not a further ripple, not a fluctuation, not a
belated muscular contraction, not even the pulsing of
breath. As the mountain lioness would stop as it stalked
an alerted kill.

The child whimpers troubledly again. It is having a
dream perhaps. Something, someone, stirs. Not the child.
A heavier, a larger body than the child. There is a faint
rustling, as when someone turns against overlying covers.

Then the sibilance of a soothing, bated voice, making a
hushing sound. "Sh-h-h. Sh-h-h." Vibrant with a light
motion. The motion of rocking interfolded arms.

A drowsy murmur of words, almost inchoate. "Sleep,
darling. We'll find your daddy soon."

The moon glares down patiently, remorselessly, waiting. The moon will wait. The night will wait.

Seconds of time pass. Breathing sounds from within
the doorway on the stillness now, in soft, slow, rhythmic
waves. With little ripples in the space between each
wave. Breathing of a mother, and elfin echo of her
arm-cradled child. The shadow moves along the wall.

The open doorway, from within, would be a sheet of
silver or of mercury, thin but glowing, if any eye were
open there upon it. Then suddenly, down low at its base,
comes motion, comes intrusion. A creeping, curved thing
circles the stone wall-breadth, loses itself again in the

darkness on the near side. Now once again the opening is an unmarred sheet of silver, fuming, sheeny.

Not even a shadow glides along the floor now, for there is no longer light to shape one. Nothing. Only death moving in invisibility.

The unseen current of the breathing still rides upon the darkness, to and fro, to and fro; lightly upon the surface of the darkness, like an evanescent pool of water stirring this way and that way.

Then suddenly it plunges deep, as if an unexpected vent, an outlet, had been driven through for it, gurgling, swirling, hollowing and sinking in timbre. A deep, spiraling breath that is the end of all breaths. No more than that. Then evaporation, the silence of death, in an arid, a denuded place.

The breathing of the child peers through again in a moment, now that its overshadowing counterpoint has been erased. It is taken up by other arms. Held pressed to another breast.

In the room of the smoldering brazero the other figure waits; patient, head inclined, rebozo-coifed. The soft pad of bare feet comes along the patio-tiles outside, exultant-quick. No need to crawl now. There are no longer other ears to overhear. Bare feet, proud and graceful; coolly firm, like bare feet wading through the moon-milk.

She comes in triumphant, erect and willowy, holding something in her arms, close to her breast. What a woman is supposed to hold. What a woman is born to hold.

She sinks down there on her knees before the other, the other who once held her thus in turn. She turns her head slightly in indication, holds it bent awkwardly askance, for her hands are not free. The old woman's hands go to her coil-wound hair, trace to the back of her head, draw out the knife for her.

Before her on the floor stands an earthenware bowl holding water. The knife splashes into it. The old woman begins to scrub and knead its blade dexterously between her fingers.

The younger one, sitting at ease now upon the backs of her heels, frees one hand, takes up the palmleaf, fans the brazero to a renewed glow. Scarlet comes back into the

room, then vermillion. Even light orange, in splashes
here and there, upon their bodies and their faces.

She speaks, staring with copper-plated mask into the
orange maw of the brazero. "My man has a son again. I
have his son again. I will not lose my man now."

"You have done well, my daughter. You have done as
a woman should." Thus a mother's approbation to her
daughter, in olden Anahuac.

She places the baby's head to her breast, the new-
made mother, and begins to suckle him.

The moon of Montezuma, well-content, is on the wane
now, slanting downward on the opposite side of the
patio. Such sights as these it once knew well in Anahuac;
now its hungering loneliness has been in a measure as-
suaged, for it has glimpsed them once again.

The moon has gone now; it is the darkness before
dawn. Soon the sun will come, the cosmic male-force.
The time of women is rapidly ending, the time of men
will be at hand.

They are both in the room with the trestle bier and the
flowers and the gold-tongued papers. The little wax doll
is a naked wax doll now, its wrappings taken from it, cast
aside. Lumpy, foreshortened, like a squat clay image
fashioned by the soft-slapping hands of some awkward,
unpractised potter.

The old woman is holding a charcoal sack, black-
smudged, tautly wide at its mouth. She brings it up just
under the bier, holds it steady, in the way of a catch-all.

Chata's hands reach out, scoop, roll something toward
her.

The bier is empty and the charcoal sack has swelled
full at the bottom.

The old woman quickly folds it over and winds it about
itself. She passes it to Chata. Deft swirling and tightening
of Chata's rebozo about her own figure, and it has gone,
and Chata's arms with it, hidden within.

The old woman takes apart the bier. Takes down the
two pitiful planks from the trestles that supported them.
A gardenia-petal or two slides down them to the floor.

"Go far," she counsels knowingly.

"I will go far up the mountain, where it is bare. Where
the buzzards can see it easily from overhead. By the time

the sun goes down it will be gone. Small bones like this they will even carry up with them and scatter."

The old woman pinches one taper-wick and it goes out.

She moves on toward another and pinches that.

Darkness blots the room. In the air a faint trace of gardenias remains. How long does the scent of gardenias last? How long does life last? And when each has gone, where is it each has gone?

They move across the moonless patio now, one back of the other. The wooden door in the street wall jars and creaks back aslant. The old woman sidles forth. Chata waits. The old woman reinserts herself. Her finger flicks permissive safety toward the aperture.

The girl slips out, just an Indian girl enswathed, a lump under her rebozo, the margin of it drawn up over her mouth against the unhealthful night air.

It is daybreak now. Clay-blue and dove-gray, rapidly paling with white. The old woman is sitting crouched upon her haunches, in patient immobility, just within the door.

She must have heard an almost wraith-like footfall that no other ears could have caught. She rose suddenly. She waited a bated moment, inclined toward the door, then she unfastened and swung open the door.

Chata slipped in on the instant, rebozo flat against her now. No more lump saddling her hip.

The old woman closed the door, went after her to deeper recesses of the patio. "You went far?"

Chata unhooded her rebozo from head and shoulders with that negligent racial grace she was never without. "I went far. I went up where it is bare rock. Where no weed grows that will hide it from the sailing wings in the sky. They will see it. Already they were coming from afar as I looked back from below. By sundown it will be gone."

The old woman nodded. "You have done well, my daughter," she praised her dignifiedly.

Beside the well in the patio there was something lying now. Another mound beside the mound of disinterred earth. And alongside it, parallel to one side of the well, a deep narrow trough lay dug, almost looking like a grave.

The rose bushes had all been pulled out and lay there

expiring on their sides now, roots striking skyward like frozen snakes.

"They were in the way," the old woman grunted. "I had to. I deepened it below where they left it when they were here last. The new earth I took out is apart, over there, in that smaller pile by itself. So we will know it from the earth they took out when they were last here. See, it is darker and fresher."

"He liked them," Chata said. "He will ask why it is, when he comes back."

"Tell him the men did it, Fulgencio and his helper."

"But if he asks them, when he goes to pay them for the work, they will say they did not, they left them in."

"Then we will plant them in again, lightly at the top, before they come back to resume their work. I will cut off their roots short, so that it can be done."

"They will die that way."

The old woman nodded craftily. "But only after a while. He will see them still in place, though dead. Then we will say it was the work of the men did it. Then Fulgencio and his helper will not be able to say they did not do it. For they were alive when the work began, and they will be dead when it was done."

Chata did not have to ask her to help. With one accord, with no further words between them, they went to the mound beside the mound of earth. The mound that was not earth. The mound that was concealing rags and bundled charcoal sacking. One went to one end, one to the other. Chata pried into the rags for a moment, made an opening, peered into it. It centered on a red rosebud, withered and falling apart, but still affixed by a pin to the dark-blue cloth of a coat.

"She wore a rose upon her coat," she hissed vengefully. "I saw it when she came in last night. She must have brought it with her from Tapatzingo, for there are none of that color growing here. He must have liked to see them on her." She swerved her head and spat into the trough alongside. "It is dead now," she said exultingly.

"As she is," glowered the old woman, tight-lipped.

"Let it go with her, for the worms to see."

They both scissored their arms, and the one mound overturned and dropped, was engulfed by the other.

Then Chata took up the shovel the workmen had left, and began lessening the second mound, the mound that was of earth. She knew just what they did and how they went about it, she had watched them for so many days now. The old woman, spreading her rebozo flat upon the ground nearby, busied herself palming and urging the newer fill over onto it, the fill that she herself had taken out to make more depth.

When it was filled, she tied the corners into a bundle and carried it from sight. She came back with the rebozo empty and began over again. After the second time, the pile of new fill was gone.

Chata had disappeared from the thighs down, was moving about as in a grave, trampling, flattening, with downbeating on her feet.

In midmorning, when Fulgencio and his nephew came, languid, to their slow-moving work, the white roses were all luxuriating around the well again, with a slender stick lurking here and there to prop them. Everything was as it had been. If the pile of disinterred earth they had left was a little lower, or if the depression waiting to take it back was a little shallower, who could tell? Who measured such things?

The old woman brought out a jug of pulque to them, so that they might refresh themselves. Their eyes were red when they left at sundown, and their breaths and their sweat were sour. But it had made their work go quicker, with snatches of song, and with laughter, and with stumblings of foot. And it had made the earth they shoveled back, the hollow they filled, the tiles they cemented back atop, the roses they brushed against and bent, all dance and blur in fumes of maguey.

But the task was completed, and when the door was closed upon their swaying, drooping-lidded forms, they needed to come back no more.

Seven times the sun rises, seven times it falls. Then fourteen. Then, perhaps, twenty-one. Who knows, who counts it? Hasn't it risen a thousand years in Anahuac, to fall again, to rise again?

Then one day, in its declining hours, there is a heavy knocking of men's hands on the outside of the wooden door in the street wall. The hands of men who have a right to enter, who may not be refused; their knocking tells that.

They know it for what it is at first sound, Chata and the old woman. They have known it was coming. There is another law in Anahuac now than the old one.

Eyes meet eyes. The trace of a nod is exchanged. A nod that confirms. That is all. No fear, no sudden startlement. No fear, because no sense of guilt. The old law did not depend on signs of fear, proofs and evidences, witnesses. The old law was wise, the new law is a fool.

The old woman struggles to her feet, pads forth across the patio toward the street-door, resounding now like a drum. Chata remains as she was, dexterously plaiting withes into a basket, golden-haired child on its back on the sun-cozened ground beside her, little legs fumbling in air.

The old woman comes back with two of mixed blood. Anahuac is in their faces, but so is the other race, with its quick mobility of feature that tells every thought. One in uniform of those who enforce the law, one in attire such as Chata's own man wears when he has returned from his prospecting trips in the distant mountains and walks the streets of the town with her on Sunday, or takes his ease without her in the cantina with the men of the other women.

They come and stand over her, where she squats at her work, look down on her. Their shadows shade her, blot out the sun in the corner of the patio in which she is. Are like thick blue stripes blanketing her and the child from some intangible serape.

Slowly her eyes go upward to them, liquid, dark, grave, respectful but not afraid, as a woman's do to strange men who come where she has a right to be.

"Stand. We are of the police. From Tapatzingo, on the other side of the mountain. We are here to speak to you."

She puts her basket-weaving aside and rises, graceful, unfrightened.

"And you are?" the one who speaks for the two of them, the one without uniform, goes on.

"Chata."

"Any last name?"

"We use no second name among us." That is the other race, two names for every one person.

"And the old one?"

"Mother of Chata."

"And who is the man here?"

"In the mountains. That way, far that way. He goes to look for silver. He works it when he finds it. He has been long gone, but he will come soon now, the time is drawing near."

"Now listen. A woman entered here, some time three weeks ago. A woman with a child. A norteña, a gringa, understand? One of those from up there. She has not been seen again. She did not go back to where she came from. To the great City of Mexico. In the City of Mexico the consul of her country has asked the police to find out where she is. The police of the City of Mexico have asked us to learn what became of her."

Both heads shake. "No. No woman entered here."

He turns to the one in uniform. "Bring him in a minute."

The hired-car driver shuffles forward, escorted by the uniform.

Chata looks at him gravely, no more. Gravely but untroubledly.

"This man says he brought her here. She got out. He went back without her."

Both heads nod now. The young one that their eyes are on, the old one disregarded in the background.

"There was a knock upon our door, one such day, many days ago. A woman with a child stood there, from another place. She spoke, and we could not understand her speech. She showed us a paper, but we cannot read writing. We closed the door. She did not knock again."

He turns on the hired-car driver. "Did you see them admit her?"

"No, Señor," the latter falters, too frightened to tell anything but the truth. "I only let her out somewhere along here. I did not wait to see where she went. It was late, and I wanted to get back to my woman. I had driven her all the way from Tapatzingo, where the train stops."

"Then you did not see her come in here?"

"I did not see her go in anywhere. I turned around and went the other way, and it was getting dark."

"This child here, does it look like the one she had with her?"

"I could not see it, she held it to her."

"This is the child of my man," Chata says with sultry dignity. "He has yellow hair like this. Tell, then."

"Her man is gringo, everyone has seen him. She had a gringo child a while ago, everyone knows that," the man stammers unhappily.

"Then you, perhaps, know more about where she went, than these two do! You did bring her out this way! Take him outside and hold him. At least I'll have something to report on."

The policeman drags him out again, pleading and whining. "No, Señor, no! I do not know—I drove back without her! For the love of God, Señor, the love of God!"

He turns to Chata. "Show me this house. I want to see it."

She shows it to him, room by room. Rooms that know nothing, can tell nothing. Then back to the patio again. The other one is waiting for him there, alone now.

"And this pozo? It seems cleaner, newer, this tiling, than elsewhere around it." He taps his foot on it.

"It kept falling in, around the sides. Cement was put around them to hold the dirt back."

"Who had it done?"

"It was the order of my man, before he left. It made our water bad. He told two men to do it for him while he was away."

"And who carried it out?"

"Fulgencio and his nephew, in the town. They did not come right away, and they took long, but finally they finished."

He jotted the name. "We will ask."

She nodded acquiescently. "They will tell."

He takes his foot off it at last, moves away. He seems to be finished, he seems to be about to go. Then suddenly, curtly, "Come." And he flexes his finger for her benefit.

For the first time her face shows something. The skin draws back rearward of her eyes, pulling them oblique.

"Where?" she whispers.

"To the town. To Tapatzingo. To the headquarters."

She shakes her head repeatedly, mutely appalled. Creeps backward a step with each shake. Yet even now it is less than outright fear; it is more an unreasoning obstinacy. An awe in the face of something one is too simple to understand. The cringing of a wide-eyed child.

"Nothing will happen to you," he says impatiently. "You won't be held. Just to sign a paper. A statement for you to put your name to."

Her back has come to rest against one of the archway supports now. She can retreat no further. She cowers against it, then sinks down, then turns and clasps her arms about it, holding onto it in desperate appeal.

"I cannot write. I do not know how to make those marks."

He is standing over her now, trying to reason with her. "Valgame dios! What a criatura!"

She transfers her embrace suddenly from the inanimate pilaster to his legs, winding her arms about them in supplication.

"No, patrón, no! Don't take me to Tapatzingo! They'll keep me there. I know how they treat our kind. I'll never get back again."

Her eyes plead upward at him, dark pools of mournfulness.

He looks more closely at her, as if seeming to see her face for the first time. Or at least as if seeming to see it as a woman's face and not just that of a witness.

"And you like this gringo you house with?" he remarks at a tangent. "Why did you not go with one of your own?"

"One goes with the man who chooses one."

"Women are thus," he admits patronizingly. Asi son las mujeres.

She releases his pinioned legs, but still crouches at his feet, looking questioningly upward.

He is still studying her face. "He could have done worse." He reaches down and wags her chin a little with two pinched fingers.

She rises, slowly turns away from him. She does not smile. Her coquetry is more basic than the shallow superficiality of a smile. More gripping in its pull. It is in the slow, enfolding way she draws her rebozo tight about her and hugs it to her shoulders and her waist. It is the very way she walks. It is in the coalescing of the sunlight dust-motes all about her in the air as she passes, forming almost a haze, a passional halo.

In fact, she gives him not another look. Yet every step of the way she pulls his eyes with her. And as she passes where a flowering plant stands in a green glazed mold, she tears one of the flowers off. She doesn't drop it, just carries it along with her in her hand.

She approaches one of the room-openings, and still without turning, still without looking back, goes within.

He stands there staring at the empty doorway.

The old woman squats down by the child, takes it up, and lowers her head as if attentively waiting.

He looks at the policeman, and the policeman at him, and everything that was unspoken until now is spoken in that look between them.

"Wait for me outside the house. I'll be out later."

The policeman goes outside and closes the wall-door after him.

Later she comes out of the room by herself, ahead of the man. She rejoins the old woman and child, and squats down by them on her knees and heels. The old woman passes the child into her arms. She rocks it lullingly, looks down at it protectively, touches a speck from its brow with one finger. She is placid, self-assured.

Then the man comes out again. He is tracing one side of his mustache with the edge of one finger.

He comes and stops, standing over her, as he did when he and the other one first came in here.

He smiles a little, very sparingly, with only the corner of his mouth. Half-indulgently, half-contemptuously.

He speaks. But to whom? Scarcely to her, for his eyes go up over her, stare thoughtfully over her head; and the policeman isn't present to be addressed. To his own sense of duty, perhaps, reassuring it. "Well—you don't need to come in, then, most likely. You've told me all you can. No need to question you further. I can attend to the paper myself. And we always have the driver, anyway, if they want to go ahead with it."

He turns on his heel. His long shadow undulates off her.

"Adios, india," he flings carelessly at her over his shoulder, from the wall-door.

"Adios, patrón," she murmurs obsequiously.

The old woman goes over to the door in his wake, to make sure it is shut fast from the inside. Comes back, sinks down again.

Nothing is said.

In the purple bloodshed of a sunset afterglow, the tired horse brings its tired rider to a halt before the biscuit-colored wall with the bougainvillaea unravelling along it. Having ridden the day, having ridden the night, and many days and many nights, the ride is at last done.

For a moment they stand there, both motionless, horse with its neck slanted to ground, rider with his head dropped almost to saddle-grip. He has been riding asleep for the past hour or so. But riding true, for the horse knows the way.

Then the man stirs, raises his head, slings his leg off, comes to the ground. Face mahogany from the high sierra sun, golden glisten filming its lower part, like dust of that other metal, the one even more precious than that he seeks and lives by. Dust-paled shirt opened to the navel. Service automatic of another country, of another army, that both once were his, bedded at his flank. Bulging saddle-bags upon the burro tethered behind, of ore, of precious crushed rock, to be taken to the assay office down at Tapatzingo. Blue eyes that have forgotten all their ties, and thus will stay young as they are now forever. Bill Taylor's home. Bill Taylor, once of Iowa, once of Colorado.

Home? What is home? Home is where a house is that you come back to when the rainy season is about to begin, to wait until the next dry season comes around. Home is where your woman is, that you come back to in the intervals between a greater love—the only real love—the lust for riches buried in the earth, that are your own if you can find them.

Perhaps you do not call it home, even to yourself. Perhaps you call them "my house," "my woman." What if there was another "my house," "my woman," before this one? It makes no difference. This woman is enough for now.

Perhaps the guns sounded too loud at Anzio or at Omaha Beach, at Guadalcanal or at Okinawa. Perhaps when they stilled again some kind of strength had been blasted from you that other men still have. And then again perhaps it was some kind of weakness that other men still have. What is strength, what is weakness, what is loyalty, what is perfidy?

The guns taught only one thing, but they taught it well: of what consequence is life? Of what consequence is a man? And, therefore, of what consequence if he tramples love in one place and goes to find it in the next? The little moment that he has, let him be at peace, far from the guns and all that remind him of them.

So the man who once was Bill Taylor has come back to his house, in the dusk, in the mountains, in Anahuac.

He doesn't have to knock, the soft hoof-plod of his horse has long ago been heard, has sent its long-awaited message. Of what use is a house to a man if he must knock before he enters? The door swings wide, as it never does and never will to anyone but him. Flitting of a figure, firefly-quick, and Chata is entwined about him.

He goes in, faltering a little from long weariness, from long disuse of his legs, she welded to his side, half-supporting, already resting, restoring him, as is a woman's reason for being.

The door closes behind them. She palms him to wait, then whisks away.

He stands there, looking about.

She comes back, holding something bebundled in her arms.

"What happened to the roses?" he asks dimly.

She does not answer. She is holding something up toward him, white teeth proudly displayed in her face. The one moment in a woman's whole life. The moment of fulfilment. "Your son," she breathes dutifully.

Who can think of roses when he has a son?

Two of the tiles that Fulgencio had laid began to part. Slowly. So slowly who could say they had not always been that way? And yet they had not. Since they could not part horizontally because of the other tiles all around them, their parting was vertical, they began to slant upward out of true. At last the strain became too great.

They had no resiliency by which to slant along the one side, remain flat along the other. They cracked along the line of greatest strain, and then they crumbled there, disintegrated into a mosaic. And then the smaller, lighter pieces were disturbed still more, and finally lay about like scattered pebbles, out of their original bed.

And then it began to grow. The new rosebush.

There had been rosebushes there before. Why should there not be one there now again?

It was full-grown now, the new rosebush. And he had gone and come again, Bill Taylor; and gone, and come again. Then suddenly, in the time for roses to bloom, it burst into flower. Like a splattering of blood, drenching that one particular part of the patio. Every rose as red as the heart.

He smiled with pleasant surprise when he first saw it, and he said how beautiful it was. He called to her and made her come out there where he was and stand beside him and take the sight in.

"Look. Look what we have now. I always liked them better than the white ones."

"I already saw them," she said sullenly. "You are only seeing them now for the first time, but I saw them many days ago, coming through little by little."

And she tried to move away, but he held her there by the shoulder, in command. "Take good care of it now. Water it. Treat it well."

In a few days he noticed that the sun was scorching it, that the leaves were burning here and there.

He called her out there, and his face was dark. His voice was harsh and curt, as when you speak to a disobedient dog. "Didn't I tell you to look after this rosebush? Why haven't you? Water it now! Water it well!"

She obeyed him. She had to. But as she moved about it, tending to it, on her face, turned from him, there was the ancient hatred of woman for woman, when there is but one man between the two of them.

She watered it the next day, and the next. It throve, it flourished, jeering at her with liquid diamonds dangling from each leaf, and pearls of moisture rolling lazily about the crevices of its tight-packed satin petals. And when his eyes were not upon her, and she struck at it viciously with her hand, it bit back at her, and tore a drop of blood from her palm.

Of what use to move around the ground on two firm feet, to be warm, to be flesh, if his eyes scarce rested on you any more? Or if they did, no longer saw you as they once had, but went right through you as if you were not there?

Of what use to have buried her in the ground if he stayed now always closer to her than to you, moving his chair now by her out there in the sun? If he put his face down close to her and inhaled the memory of her and the essence of her soul?

She filled the patio with her sad perfume, and even in the very act of breathing in itself, he drew something of her into himself, and they became one.

She held sibilant conference with the old woman beside the brazero in the evening as they prepared his meal. "It is she. She has come back again. He puts his face down close, down close to her many red mouths, and she whispers to him. She tries to tell him that she lies there, she tries to tell him that his son was given him by her and not by me."

The old woman nodded sagely. These things are so. "Then you must do again as you did once before. There is no other way."

"He will be angered as the thunder rolling in a mountain gorge."

"Better a blow from a man's hand than to lose him to another woman."

Again the night of a full moon, again she crept forth, hands to ground, as she had once before. This time from his very side, from his very bed. Again a knife between her teeth blazed intermittently in the moonlight. But this time she didn't creep sideward along the portico, from room-entry to room-entry; this time she paced her way straight outward into mid-patio. And this time her rebozo was twined tight about her, not cast off; for the victim had no ears with which to hear her should the garment impede or betray; and the victim had no feet on which to start up and run away.

Slowly she toiled and undulated under the enormous

spot-light of the moon. Nearer, nearer. Until the shadows of the little leaves made black freckles on her back.

Nearer, nearer. To kill a second time the same rival.

Nearer, nearer. To where the rosebush lay floating on layers of moon-smoke.

They found her the next morning, he and the old woman. They found the mute evidence of the struggle there had been; like a contest between two active agencies, between two opposing wills. A struggle in the silent moonlight.

There was a place where the tiled surfacing, the cement shoring, faultily applied by the pulque-drugged Fulgencio and his nephew, had given way and dislodged itself over the lip of the well and down into it, as had been its wont before the repairs were applied. Too much weight incautiously brought too near the edge, in some terrible, oblivious throe of fury or of self-preservation.

Over this ravage the rosebush, stricken, gashed along its stem, stretched taut, bent like a bow; at one end its manifold roots still clinging tenaciously to the soil, like countless crooked grasping fingers; at the other its flowered head, captive but unsubdued, dipping downward into the mouth of the well.

And from its thorns, caught fast in a confusion hopeless of extrication, it supported two opposite ends of the rebozo, whipped and wound and spiraled together into one, from some aimless swaying and counter-swaying weight at the other end.

A weight that had stopped swaying long before the moon waned; that hung straight and limp now, hugging the wall of the well. Head sharply askew, as if listening to the mocking voice whispering through from the soil alongside, where the roots of the rosebush found their source.

No water had touched her. She had not died the death of water. She had died the death that comes without a sound, the death that is like the snapping of a twig, of a broken neck.

They lifted her up. They laid her tenderly there upon the ground.

She did not move. The rosebush did; it slowly righted

to upward. Leaving upon the ground a profusion of petals, like drops of blood shed in combat.

The rosebush lived, but she was dead.

Now he sits there in the sun, by the rosebush; the world forgotten, other places that once were home, other times, other loves, forgotten. It is good to sit there in the sun, your son playing at your feet. This is a better love, this is the only lasting love. For a woman dies when you do, but a son lives on. He is you and you are he, and thus you do not die at all.

And when his eyes close in the sun and he dozes, as a man does when his youth is running out, perhaps now and then a petal will fall upon his head or upon his shoulder from some near-curving branch, and lie there still. Light as a caress. Light as a kiss unseen from someone who loves you and watches over you.

The old woman squats at hand, watchful over the child. The old woman has remained, ignored. Like a dog, like a stone. Unspeaking and unspoken to.

Her eyes reveal nothing. Her lips say nothing. They will never say anything, for thus it is in Anahuac.

But the heart knows. The skies that look forever down on Anahuac know. The moon that shone on Montezuma once; it knows.

MARGARET ST. CLAIR

The House In Bel Aire

A solid gold toilet seat is unsettling to the mind. Alfred Gluckshoffer, proprietor of the Round the Clock Plumbing Company, raised and lowered the lid several times experimentally and decided that it, too, was gold. It looked like gold, it felt like gold: Gluckshoffer, whose brother-in-law Milt was a salesman for a firm of manufacturing jewelers, and who had heard Milt talking about carats and alloys as long as he had known him, was sure it *was* gold. About fourteen carat.

From the doorway the elderly party in the dusty dress suit cleared his throat. It was not a menacing sound, but Alfred jumped. Hastily he picked up his screwdriver and began prying at the valve in the float again.

"Oh, it's a genuine stone," Milt said later that day. "They cut the synthetics out of a boule, see, and they always show the curved lines. Yours has a good color, too. The deeper the color in sapphire, the more valuable, and this one is nearly true cornflower blue. A beauty. Worth maybe four or five hundred. Where'd you get it, Al?"

Gluckshoffer decided to be frank. "Out of that house I was telling you about. The one where they called me to fix the can in the middle of the night. I dropped my pliers under the washbasin, and when I got down to pick them up, I found it. There was a sort of patch of inlaid work over the tub, wire and stone and tile and stuff, and I guess it must have fallen out of that."

Milt stuck his hands in his pockets and began to walk up and down the shop. Cupidity was coating his features

159

with a dreamy, romantic glaze. "Think you could find the house again, Al?" he asked.

"I don't know. Like I told you, they called for me in a car with all the blinds down, and before I got out they tied a cloth over my eyes. I couldn't see a thing. There was a swimming pool on the left as we went in—I could tell by the way it echoed—and when I was getting out of the car I brushed up against a big tall hedge. Oh, yes, and from the way the streets felt, I think it was out in Bel Aire."

Milt sagged. "A house with a hedge and a swimming pool in Bel Aire. That's about like looking for a girl with brown eyes."

"Oh, I don't know," Gluckshoffer said perversely. "I might be able to tell it if I ran across it again. There was a kind of funny feel to the place, Milt. Sleepy. Dead. Why? Why're you so keen on locating it?"

"Don't be a dope," Milt said. "You want to be a plumber all your life?"

They located the house on the fifth night. It stood by itself on what must have been nearly two acres of ground, a whitely glimmering bulk, lightless and somnolent.

"Looks like there's nobody home," Milt said as he brought the car to a noiseless halt. "You oughtn't to have any trouble, Al."

Gluckshoffer snorted softly. "There's at least two people on the place," he whispered, "the chauffeur and the old geezer in the dress suit that called for me that night. Remember what you promised, Milt, about coming in for me if I'm not back in forty-five minutes. After all, this was your idea. And don't forget about honking twice if a patrol car comes by, either." His tone, though subdued, was fierce.

"Oh, sure," Milt said easily. "Don't worry about it. I won't forget."

Al Gluckshoffer got out of the car and began to worm his way through the pale green leaves of a tall pittosporum hedge. As he padded past the swimming pool (on the left, as he had remembered it) in his tennis shoes, he found himself swallowing a yawn.

This was the darnedest place. As he'd told Milt, there were two people at home—probably more, since you wouldn't keep a chauffeur unless there was somebody for him to drive—and the old party in the dress suit must sleep in the house because he'd said something to Al about the noise of the can having awakened him. But the feel in the air was so sleepy and dead that you'd think everybody on the place had been asleep for the last hundred years.

At the back of the house a window looked promising. Al tried it and found it unlocked. Stifling a yawn, and then another one, he raised the window and slipped inside.

He went into a lavatory on the ground floor first. He had unscrewed the gold faucets on the washbasin and pried eight or ten stones out of the mosaic on the wall before it occurred to him that he was wasting his time. Would people in a house like this put their best stuff in the cans. Obviously not. The place to look for the hot stuff—the really *hot* hot stuff—would be in the bedrooms upstairs. Palladium-backed clothes brushes. Mirrors set with big diamonds all around the edges. He was a dope not to have thought of it before.

Al wrapped the faucets carefully in the old rags he had brought to muffle their chinking and put them in his little satchel. Noiselessly as a shadow, he stole up the stair.

In the upper hall he hesitated. His idea about the bedrooms was all very well, but it wouldn't do to pick one where the old geezer in the dress suit, say, was asleep.

The moonlight slanting through the big windows in the hall and falling on the door to his right put an end to Al's difficulties. There were cobwebs thick between the door itself and the jamb, cobwebs all over the frame. A room like that must be perfectly safe. There couldn't be anybody in a room like that. Softly he turned the knob.

The bed, swathed in shimmering gauze, was at one end of the room. Al paid no attention to it. His eyes were fixed on the dressing table where, even in the subdued light, he could make out jewelry—earrings, rings, tiara, bracelets—lying in a corruscating heap. The pendants at the corners of the tiara were teardrop-shaped things, big as bantam's eggs, and the earrings and bracelets were set all over with flashing gems.

Al licked his lips. He put out a skeptical hand toward
the tiara and touched the pendants very cautiously. They
were cold, and from the motion his hand imparted to
them, they started to swing back and forth and give out
rays of colored light.

From sheer nervous excitement he was on the edge of
bursting into tears or something. The stones in the bracelets seemed to be square-cut diamonds, and the pendants
on the tiara surpassed anything he had ever imagined.
They made him feel like getting down and kowtowing in
a paroxysm of unworthiness. He controlled himself and
began to put the jewels away in his bag.

The earrings were following the bracelets into custody
when there was a slight creak from the bed. Al turned to
stone. In very much less than a second (nervous im-
pulses, being electrical in origin, move at the speed of
light, which is 186,000 m.p.s.), he had decided that the
jewelry was a trap, that the trap was being sprung, and
that he was hauling tail out. He began backing toward
the door. There was another creak from the bed. This
time it was accompanied by a wonderful, a glorious, flash
of prismatic light.

Al Gluckshoffer faltered, torn cruelly between cupidity
and fear. It if *wasn't* a trap, the biggest diamond in the
whole world must be hanging around the throat, or otherwise depending from the person, or whoever was sleeping in the bed. Indecision almost made him groan. Then
he made up his mind and, the sweat starting out on his
forehead, tiptoed in the direction of the flash of light.

The beauty of the girl lying on the bed in the moonlight was so extreme that he forgot all about the necklace
which clasped her throat. He stared down at her for an
instant. Then he put his bag on the floor, knelt beside
the bed and drew the curtains back. He leaned forward
and kissed her on the lips.

His heart was beating like a hammer. Slowly her shadowy lids opened and she looked into his eyes. A faint,
joyous smile began to curve her lips.

The expression was succeeded almost instantly by a
look of regal rage. "By the scepter of Mab," the girl
said, sitting up in bed and glaring at him, "you are not
His Highness at all! In fact, I perceive clearly from your

attitude and bearing that you are not *any* Highness. You are some low creature who has no proper business of any sort in the palace. You are Another One."

With the words, she pressed a button beside her bed. While Al cowered back, there was a clamor as strident as that of a burglar alarm, and then the elderly party in the dress suit came in, yawning and rubbing his eyes.

"He awakened me in the proper way," the girl said, gesturing in Al's direction, "but he is by no means the proper person."

"So I see, Your Highness," the old gent said with a bow. "I believe—" He peered closely at Gluckshoffer, who pushed himself hard against the wall and tried to pretend that he wasn't there. "I believe he is the plumber whom I called in last week to repair the lavatory. I am sorry. What disposition does Your Highness wish me to make of him?"

"Use the transformation machine to make him into something," the princess said, turning around and punching at the pillows on her bed. They were embroidered with a little crown.

"What would Your Highness suggest?"

"Anything you like," the princess replied. The pillows arranged to her satisfaction, she lay back on them once more. "Something appropriate, of course. Frankly, Norfreet, I'm getting tired of being waked once or twice a year by some incompetent idiot who has no legitimate business in the palace in the first place. The next bungler who wakes me up, I want you to turn into a mouse and give to the cat next door to play with. Good night." Delicately she closed her eyes.

"Good night, Your Highness," the chamberlain replied with another low bow. He turned to Al, who had been listening to this talk of transformations with a comforting sense of its impossibility, and fixed him with a hypnotic gaze. "Come with me," he said sternly. "Before I transform you, you must repair the damage you have done."

Some twenty minutes later, the chamberlain gave the solid brass cuspidor which had been Al Gluckshoffer a contemptuous shove with his foot. He ought to take the thing up to the attic and leave it, but he was getting dreadfully sleepy. He needed his rest at his age. Some other time.

He got into bed, his joints creaking. Her Highness was right; there were altogether too many intruders in the palace these days. They needed to be shown their place, made an example of. The next person who woke him up was going to be the object of something special in the way of transformations. Norfreet began to snore.

And on the other side of the pittosporum hedge, Milt looked at his watch and decided that it was time to go in and see what had happened to Al. He started to worm his way through the hedge.

ROBERT AICKMAN

The School Friend

To be taken advantage of is every woman's secret wish.
—PRINCESS ELIZABETH BIBESCO

It would be false modesty to deny that Sally Tessler and I were the bright girls of the school. Later it was understood that I went more and more swiftly to the bad; but Sally continued being bright for some considerable time. Like many males, but few females, even among those inclined to scholarship, Sally combined a true love for the Classics, the ancient ones, with an insight into mathematics which, to the small degree that I was interested, seemed to me almost magical. She won three scholarships, two gold medals, and a sojourn among the Hellenes with all expenses paid. Before she had graduated, she had published a little book of popular mathematics which, I understood, made her a surprising sum of money. Later she edited several lesser Latin authors, published in editions so small that they can have brought her nothing but inner satisfaction.

The foundations of all this erudition had almost certainly been laid in Sally's earliest childhood. The tale went that Dr. Tessler had once been the victim of some serious injustice, or considered that he had: certainly it seemed to be true that, as his neighbors put it, he "never went out." Sally herself once told me that she not only could remember nothing of her mother but had never come across any trace or record of her. From the very beginning Sally had been brought up, it was said, by her father alone. Rumor suggested that Dr. Tessler's regi-

men was threefold: reading, domestic drudgery, and obe-
dience. I deduced that he used the last to enforce the two
first: when Sally was not scrubbing the floor or washing
up, she was studying Vergil and Euclid. Even then I
suspected that the doctor's ways of making his will felt
would not have borne examination by the other parents.
Certainly, however, when Sally first appeared at school,
she had much more than a grounding in almost every
subject taught, and in several which were not taught.
Sally, therefore, was from the first a considerable irritant
to the mistresses. She was always two years or more
below the average age of her form. She had a real tech-
nique of acquiring knowledge. She respected learning in
her preceptors, and detected its absence. . . . I once
tried to find out in what subject Dr. Tessler had obtained
his doctorate. I failed; but, of course, one then expected
a German to be a doctor.

It was the first school Sally had attended. I was a
member of the form to which she was originally assigned
but in which she remained for less than a week, so
eclipsing to the rest of us was her mass of information.
She was thirteen years and five months old at the time,
nearly a year younger than I. (I owe it to myself to say
that I was promoted at the end of the term and thereafter
more or less kept pace with the prodigy, although this,
perhaps, was for special reasons.) Her hair was remarkably beautiful; a perfect light blonde and lustrous with
brushing, although cut short and done in no particular
way, indeed usually very untidy. She had dark eyes, a
pale skin, a large distinguished nose, and a larger mouth.
She had also a slim but precocious figure, which later put
me in mind of Tessa in "The Constant Nymph." For
better or for worse, there was no school uniform, and
Sally invariably appeared in a dark-blue dress of foreign
aspect and extreme simplicity, which nonetheless distinctly became her looks. As she grew, she seemed to
wear later editions of the same dress, new and enlarged,
like certain publications.

Sally, in fact, was beautiful; but one would be unlikely
ever to meet another so lovely who was so entirely and
genuinely unaware of the fact and of its implications.
And, of course, her casualness about her appearance,

and her simple clothes, added to her charm. Her disposition seemed kindly and easy-going in the extreme, and her voice was lazy to drawling. But Sally nonetheless seemed to live only in order to work, and although I was, I think, her closest friend (it was the urge to keep up with her which explained much of my own progress in the school), I learnt very little about her. She seemed to have no pocket money at all: as this amounted to a social deficiency of the vastest magnitude, and as my parents could afford to be and were generous, I regularly shared with her. She accepted the arrangement simply and warmly. In return she gave me frequent little presents of books: a copy of Goethe's *Faust* in the original language and bound in somewhat discouraging brown leather, and an edition of Petronius, with some remarkable drawings. . . . Much later, when in need of money for a friend, I took the *Faust,* in no hopeful spirit, to Sotheby's. It proved to be a rebound first edition . . .

But it was a conversation about the illustrations in the Petronius (I was able to construe Latin fairly well for a girl, but the italics and long *s*'s daunted me) which led me to the discovery that Sally knew more than any of us about the subject illustrated. Despite her startling range of information she seemed then, and certainly for long after, completely disinterested in any personal way. It was as if she discoursed, in the gentlest, sweetest manner, about some distant far off thing, or, to use a comparison absurdly hackneyed but here appropriate, about botany. It was an ordinary enough school, and sex was a preoccupation among us. Sally's attitude was surprisingly new and unusual. In the end she did ask me not to tell the others what she had just told me.

"As if I would," I replied challengingly, but still musingly.

And in fact I didn't tell anyone until considerably later, when I found that I had learned from Sally things which no one lse at all seemed to know, things which I sometimes think have in themselves influenced my life, so to say, not a little. Once I tried to work out how old Sally was at the time of this conversation. I think she could hardly have been more than fifteen.

In the end Sally won her university scholarship, and I just failed, but won the school's English Essay Prize and also the Good Conduct Medal, which I deemed (and still deem) in the nature of a stigma, but believed, consolingly, to be awarded more to my prosperous father than to me. Sally's conduct was in any case much better than mine, being indeed irreproachable. I had entered for the scholarship with the intention of forcing the examiners, in the unlikely event of my winning it, to bestow it upon Sally, who really needed it. When this doubtless impracticable scheme proved unnecessary, Sally and I parted company, she to her triumphs of the intellect, I to my lesser achievements. We corresponded intermittently, but decreasingly as our areas of common interest diminished. Ultimately, for a very considerable time, I lost sight of her altogether, although occasionally over the years I used to see reviews of her learned books and encounter references to her in leading articles about the Classical Association and similar indispensable bodies. I took it for granted that by now we should have difficulty in communicating at all. I observed that Sally did not marry. One couldn't wonder, I foolishly and unkindly drifted into supposing . . .

When I was forty-one, two things happened which have a bearing on this narrative. The first was that a catastrophe befell me which led to my again taking up residence with my parents. Details are superfluous. The second thing was the death of Dr. Tessler.

I should probably have heard of Dr. Tessler's death in any case, for my parents, who, like me and the rest of the neighbors, had never set eyes upon him, had always regarded him with mild curiosity. As it was, the first I knew of it was when I saw the funeral. I was shopping on behalf of my mother and reflecting upon the vileness of things when I observed old Mr. Orbit remove his hat, in which he always served, and briefly sink his head in prayer. Between the aggregations of "Shredded Wheat" in the window, I saw the passing shape of a very old-fashioned and therefore very ornate horse-drawn hearse. It bore a coffin covered in a pall of worn purple velvet, but there seemed to be no mourners at all.

"Didn't think never to see a 'orse 'earse again, Mr. Orbit," remarked old Mrs. Rind, who was ahead of me in the queue.

"Pauper funeral, I expect," said her friend old Mrs. Edge.

"No such thing no more," said Mr. Orbit quite sharply, and replacing his hat. "That's Dr. Tessler's funeral. Don't suppose 'e 'ad no family come to look after things."

I believe the three white heads then got together and began to whisper; but, on hearing the name, I had made toward the door. I looked out. The huge ancient hearse, complete with the vast black plumes, looked much too big for the narrow autumnal street. It put me in mind of how toys are often so grossly out of scale with one another. I could now see that instead of mourners, a group of urchins, shadowy in the fading light, ran behind the bier, shrieking and jeering: a most regrettable scene in a well-conducted township.

For the first time in months, if not years, I wondered about Sally.

Three days later she appeared without warning at my parents' front door. It was I who opened it.

"Hallo, Mel."

One hears of people who after many years take up a conversation as if the same number of hours had passed. This was a case in point. Sally, moreover, looked almost wholly unchanged. Possibly her lustrous hair was one half-shade darker, but it was still short and wild. Her lovely white skin was unwrinkled. Her large mouth smiled sweetly but, as always, somewhat absently. She was dressed in the most ordinary clothes but still managed to look like anything but a don or a dominie: although neither did she look like a woman of the world. It was, I reflected, hard to decide what she did look like.

"Hallo, Sally."

I kissed her and began to condole.

"Father really died before I was born. You know that."

"I have heard something." I should not have been sorry to hear more; but Sally threw off her coat, sank down before the fire, and said:

"I've read all your books. I loved them. I should have written."

"Thank you," I said. "I wish there were more who felt like you."

"You're an artist, Mel. You can't expect to be a suc-

cess at the same time." She was warming her white hands.
I was not sure that I was an artist, but it was nice to be
told.

There was a circle of leather-covered armchairs round
the fire. I sat down beside her. "I've read about you
often in the *Times Lit*," I said, "but that's all. For years.
Much too long."

"I'm glad you're still living here," she replied.

"Not *still*. Again."

"Oh?" She smiled in her gentle, absent way.

"Following a session in the frying pan, and another
one in the fire . . . I'm sure you've been conducting
yourself more sensibly." I was still fishing.

But all she said was, "Anyway I'm still glad you're
living here."

"Can't say *I* am. But why in particular?"

"Silly Mel! Because I'm going to live here too."

I had never even thought of it.

I could not resist a direct question.

"Who told you your father was ill?"

"A friend. I've come all the way from Asia Minor. I've
been looking at potsherds." She was remarkably un-
tanned for one who had been living under the sun; but
her skin was of the kind which does not tan readily.

"It will be lovely to have you about again. Lovely,
Sally. But what will you do here?"

"What do *you* do?"

"I write . . . In other ways my life is rather over, I
feel."

"*I* write too. Sometimes. At least I edit . . . And I
don't think my life, properly speaking, has ever begun."

I had spoken in self-pity, although I had not wholly
meant to do so. The tone of her reply I found it impossible to define. Certainly, I thought with slight malice,
certainly she does look absurdly virginal.

A week later a van arrived at Dr. Tessler's house, containing a great number of books, a few packed trunks,
and little else; and Sally moved in. She offered no further
explanation for this gesture of semiretirement from the
gay world (for we lived about forty miles from London,
too many for urban participation, too few for rural self-

sufficiency); but it occurred to me that Sally's resources were doubtless not so large that she could disregard an opportunity to live rent free, although I had no idea whether the house was freehold, and there was no mention even of a will. Sally was and always had been so vague about practicalities that I was a little worried about these matters; but she declined ideas of help. There was no doubt that if she were to offer the house for sale, she could not expect from the proceeds an income big enough to enable her to live elsewhere; and I could imagine that she shrank from the bother and uncertainty of letting.

I heard about the contents of the van from Mr. Ditch, the remover; and it was, in fact, not until she had been in residence for about ten days that Sally sent me an invitation. During this time, and after she had refused my help with her affairs, I had thought it best to leave her alone. Now, although the house which I must thenceforth think of as hers, stood only about a quarter of a mile from the house of my parents, she sent me a postcard. It was a picture postcard of Mitylene. She asked me to tea.

The way was through the avenues and round the corners of a mid-nineteenth-century housing estate for merchants and professional men. My parents' house was intended for the former; Sally's for the latter. It stood, in fact, at the very end of a cul-de-sac; even now the house opposite bore the plate of a dentist.

I had often stared at the house during Dr. Tessler's occupancy and before I knew Sally; but not until that day did I enter it. The outside looked much as it had ever done. The house was built in a gray brick so depressing that one speculated how anyone could ever come to choose it (as many once did, however, throughout the Home Counties). To the right of the front door (approached by twelve steps, with blue and white tessellated risers) protruded a greatly disproportionate obtuse-angled bay window: it resembled the thrusting nose on a gray and wrinkled face. This bay window served the basement, the ground floor, and the first floor: between the two latter ran a dull red string course "in an acanthus pattern," like a chaplet round the temples of a dowager. From the second floor window it might have been possible to step onto the top of the projecting bay, the better to view the surgery opposite, had not the second floor window been barred, doubtless as protection for a nursery. The wooden gate had fallen from its hinges and had to be lifted open and shut. It was startlingly heavy.

The bell was in order.

Sally was, of course, alone in the house.

Immediately she opened the door (which included two large tracts of colored glass), I apprehended a change in her, essentially the first change in all the time I had known her, for the woman who had come to my parents' house a fortnight or three weeks before had seemed to me very much the girl who had joined my class when we were both children. But now there was a difference . . .

In the first place she looked different. Previously there had always been a distinction about her appearance, however inexpensive her clothes. Now she wore a fawn jumper which needed washing and stained, creaseless gray slacks. When a woman wears trousers, they need to be smart. These were slacks indeed. Sally's hair was not so much picturesquely untidy as in the past, but, more truly, in bad need of trimming. She wore distasteful sandals. And her expression had altered.

"Hallo, Mel. Do you mind sitting down and waiting for the kettle to boil?" She showed me into the ground floor room (although to make possible the basement, it was cocked high in the air) with the bay window. "Just throw your coat on a chair." She bustled precipitately away. It occurred to me that Sally's culinary aplomb had diminished since her busy childhood of legend.

The room was horrible. I had expected eccentricity, discomfort, bookworminess, even perhaps the slightly macabre. But the room was entirely commonplace and in the most unpleasing fashion. The furniture had probably been mass-produced in the early twenties. It was of the kind which it is impossible, by any expenditure of time and polish, to keep in good order. The carpet was dingy jazz. There were soulless little pictures in gilt frames. There were dreadful modern knickknacks. There was a wireless set, obviously long broken . . . For the time of year, the rickety smoky fire offered none too much heat. Rejecting Sally's invitation, I drew my coat about me.

There was nothing to read except a prewar copy of

"Tit-Bits" which I found on the floor under the lumpy settee. Like Sally's jumper, the dense lace curtains could have done with a wash. But before long Sally appeared with tea: six uniform pink cakes from the nearest shop and a flavorless liquid full of floating "strangers." The crockery accorded with the other appurtenances.

I asked Sally whether she had started work of any kind.

"Not yet," she replied, a little dourly. "I've got to get things going in the house first."

"I suppose your father left things in a mess?"

She looked at me sharply. "Father never went out of his library."

She seemed to suppose that I knew more than I did. Looking round me, I found it hard to visualize a "library." I changed the subject.

"Aren't you going to find it rather a big house for one?"

It seemed a harmless, though uninspired, question. But Sally, instead of answering, simply sat staring before her. Although it was more as if she stared within her at some unpleasant thought.

I believe in acting upon impulse. "Sally," I said, "I've got an idea. Why don't you sell this house, which *is* much too big for you and come and live with me? We've plenty of room, and my father is the soul of generosity."

She only shook her head. "Thank you, Mel. No." She still seemed absorbed by her own thoughts, disagreeable thoughts.

"You remember what you said the other day. About being glad I was living here. I'm likely to go on living here. I'd love to have you with me, Sally. Please think about it."

She put down her ugly little teaplate on the ugly little table. She had taken a single small bite out of her pink cake. She stretched out her hand toward me, very tentatively, not nearly touching me. She gulped slightly. "Mel—"

I moved to take her hand, but she drew it back. Suddenly she shook her head violently. Then she began to talk about her work.

She did not resume eating or drinking; and indeed

both the cakes and tea, which every now and then she pressed upon me in a casual way more like her former manner, were remarkably unappetizing. But she talked interestingly and familiarly for about half an hour—about indifferent matters. Then she said, "Forgive me, Mel. But I must be getting on."

She rose. Of course I rose too. Then I hesitated.

"Sally . . . Please think about it. I'd like it so much. Please."

"Thank you, Mel. I'll think about it."

"Promise?"

"Promise . . . Thank you for coming to see me."

"I want to see much more of you."

She stood in the open front door. In the dusk she looked inexplicably harassed and woebegone.

"Come and see me whenever you want. Come to tea tomorrow and stay to dinner." Anything to get her out of that horrible, horrible house.

But, as before, she only said, "I'll think about it."

Walking home it seemed to me that she could only have invited me out of obligation. I was much hurt and much frightened by the change in her. As I reached my own gate it struck me that the biggest change of all was that she had never once smiled.

When five or six days later I had neither seen nor heard from Sally, I wrote asking her to visit me. For several days she did not reply at all: then she sent me another picture postcard this time of some ancient bust in a museum, informing me that she would love to come when she had a little more time. I noticed that she had made a slight error in my address, which she had hastily and imperfectly corrected. The postman, of course, knew me. I could well imagine that there was much to do in Sally's house. Indeed, it was a house of the kind in which the work is never either satisfying or complete: an ever-open mouth of a house. But, despite the tales of her childhood, I could not imagine the Sally I knew doing it . . . I could not imagine what she was doing, and I admit that I did want to know.

Some time after that I came across Sally in the International Stores. It was not a shop I usually patronized, but

Mr. Orbit was out of my father's particular pickles. I could not help wondering whether Sally did not remember perfectly well that it was a shop in which I was seldom found.

She was there when I entered. She was wearing the same grimy slacks and this time a white blouse which was worse than her former jumper, being plainly filthy. Against the autumn she wore a blue raincoat which I believed to be the same she had worn to school. She looked positively unkempt and far from well. She was nervously shoving a little heap of dark blue bags and gaudy packets into a very ancient holdall. Although the shop was fairly full, no one else was waiting to be served at the part of the counter where Sally stood. I walked up to her.

"Good morning, Sally."

She clutched the ugly holdall to her, as if I were about to snatch it. Then at once she became ostentatiously relaxed.

"Don't look at me like that," she said. There was an upsetting little rasp in her voice. "After all, Mel, you're not my mother." Then she walked out of the shop.

"Your change, miss," cried the International Stores shopman after her.

But she was gone. The other women in the shop watched her go as if she were the town tart. Then they closed up along the section of the counter where she had been standing.

"Poor thing," said the shopman unexpectedly. He was young. The other women looked at him malevolently and gave their orders with conscious briskness.

Then came Sally's accident.

By this time there could be no doubt that something was much wrong with her; but I had always been very nearly her only friend in the town, and her behavior to me made it difficult for me to help. It was not that I lacked will or, I think, courage, but that I was unable to decide how to set about the task. I was still thinking about it when Sally was run over. I imagine that her trouble, whatever it was, had affected her ordinary judgment. Apparently she stepped right under a lorry in the High Street, having just visited the post office. I learned shortly afterward that she refused to have letters deliv-

ered at her house but insisted upon them being left *Poste
Restante*.

When she had been taken to the Cottage Hospital, the
matron, Miss Garvice, sent for me. Everyone knew that I
was Sally's friend.

"Do you know who is her next of kin?"

"I doubt whether she has such a thing in this country."

"Friends?"

"Only me that I know of." I had always wondered
about the mysterious informant of Dr. Tessler's passing.

Miss Garvice considered for a moment.

"I'm worried about her house. Strictly speaking, in all
the circumstances, I suppose I ought to tell the police
and ask them to keep an eye on it. But I am sure she
would prefer me to ask you."

From her tone I rather supposed that Miss Garvice
knew nothing of the recent changes in Sally. Or perhaps
she thought it best to ignore them.

"As you live so close, I wonder if it would be too much
to ask you just to look in every now and then? Perhaps
daily might be best?"

I think I accepted mainly because I suspected that
something in Sally's life might need, for Sally's sake, to
be kept from the wrong people.

"Here are her keys."

It was a numerous assembly for such a commonplace
establishment as Sally's.

"I'll do it as I say, Miss Garvice. But how long do you
think it will be?"

"Hard to say. But I don't think Sally's going to die."

One trouble was that I felt compelled to face the assign-
ment unaided because I knew no one in the town who
seemed likely to regard Sally's predicament with the sen-
sitiveness and delicacy—and indeed love—which I suspected were essential. There was also a dilemma about
whether or not I should explore the house. Doubtless I
had no right; but to do so might, on the other hand,
possibly be regarded as in Sally's "higher interests." I
must acknowledge, nonetheless, that my decision to pro-
ceed was considerably inspired by curiosity. This did not
mean that I should involve others in whatever might be

disclosed. Even that odious sitting room would do Sally's reputation no good . . .

Miss Garvice had concluded by suggesting that I perhaps ought to pay my first visit at once. I went home to lunch. Then I set out.

Among the first things I discovered were that Sally kept every single door in the house locked: and that the remains of the tea I had taken with her weeks before still lingered in the sitting room; not, mercifully, the food, but the plates, and cups, and genteel little knives, and the teapot with leaves and liquor at the bottom of it.

Giving on to the passage from the front door was a room adjoining the sitting room and corresponding to it at the back of the house. Presumably one of these rooms was intended by the builder (the house was not of a kind to have had an architect) for use as a dining room, the other as a drawing room. I went through the keys. They were big keys, the doors and locks being pretentiously oversized. In the end the door opened. I noticed a stale cold smell. The room appeared to be in complete darkness. Possibly Dr. Tessler's library?

I groped round the inside of the door frame for an electric light switch but could find nothing. I took another half step inside. The room seemed blacker than ever and the stale cold smell somewhat stronger. I decided to defer exploration until later.

I shut the door and went upstairs. The ground floor rooms were high, which made the stairs many and steep.

On the first floor were two rooms corresponding in plan to the two rooms below. It could be called neither an imaginative design, nor a convenient one. I tried the front room first, again going through the rigmarole with the keys. The room was in a dilapidated condition and contained nothing but a considerable mass of papers. They appeared once to have been stacked on the bare floor; but the stacks had long since fallen over, and their component elements accumulated a deep top-dressing of flaky black particles. The grime was of that ultimate kind which seems to have an actually greasy consistency: the idea of further investigating those neglected masses of scroll and manuscript made me shudder.

The back room was a bedroom, presumably Sally's. All

the curtains were drawn, and I had to turn on the light. It contained what must truly be termed, in the worn phrase, "a few sticks of furniture," all in the same period as the pieces in the sitting room, though more exiguous and spidery-looking. The inflated size and height of the room, the heavy plaster cornice and even heavier plaster rose in the center of the cracked ceiling emphasized the sparseness of the anachronistic furnishing. There was, however, a more modern double-divan bed, very low on the floor and looking as if it had been slept in but not remade for weeks. Someone seemed to have arisen rather suddenly, as at an alarm clock. I tried to pull open a drawer in the rickety dressing table. It squeaked and stuck and proved to contain some pathetic-looking underclothes of Sally's. The long curtains were very heavy and dark green.

It was a depressing investigation, but I persisted.

The second floor gave the appearance of having been originally one room, reached from a small landing. There was marked evidence of unskilled cuttings and bodgings; aimed, it was clear, at partitioning off this single vast room in order to form a bathroom and lavatory and a passage giving access thereto. Could the house have been originally built without these necessary amenities? Anything seemed possible. I remembered the chestnut about the architect who forgot the staircase.

But there was something here which I found not only squalid but vaguely frightening. The original door, giving from the small landing into the one room, showed every sign of having been forcibly burst open, and from the inside (characteristically, it had been hung to open outward). The damage was seemingly not recent (although it is not easy to date such a thing); but the shattered door still hung dejectedly outward from its weighty lower hinge only and, in fact, made it almost impossible to enter the room at all. Gingerly I forced it a little more forward. The ripped woodwork of the heavy door shrieked piercingly as I dragged at it. I looked in. The room, such as it had ever been, had been finally wrecked by the introduction of the batten partition which separated it from the bathroom and was covered with blistered dark brown varnish. The only contents were a few decaying toys. The nursery, as I remembered from the exterior prospect.

Through the gap between the sloping door and its frame I looked at the barred windows. Like everything else in the house, the bars seemed very heavy. I looked again at the toys. I observed that *all* of them seemed to be woolly animals. They were rotted with moth and mold, but not so much so as to conceal the fact that at least some of them appeared also to have been mutilated. There were the decomposing leg of a teddy bear, inches away from the main torso; the severed head of a fanciful stuffed bird. It was as unpleasant a scene as every other in the house.

What had Sally been doing all day? As I had suspected, clearly not cleaning the house. There remained the kitchen quarters; and, of course, the late doctor's library.

There were odd scraps of food about the basement and signs of recent though sketchy cooking. I was almost surprised to discover that Sally had not lived on air. In general, however, the basement suggested nothing more unusual than the familiar feeling of wonder at the combined magnitude and cumbrousness of cooking operations in the homes of our middle class great-grandfathers.

I looked round for a candle with which to illumine the library. I even opened various drawers, bins, and cupboards. It seemed that there were no candles. In any case, I thought, shivering slightly in the descending dusk, the library was probably a job for more than a single candle. Next time I would provide myself with my father's imposing flashlamp.

There seemed nothing more to be done. I had not even taken off my coat. I had discovered little which was calculated to solve the mystery. Could Sally be doping herself? It really seemed a theory. I turned off the kitchen light, ascended to the ground floor, and, shutting the front door, descended again to the garden. I eyed the collapsed front gate with new suspicion. Some time later I realized that I had relocked none of the inside doors.

Next morning I called at the Cottage Hospital.

"In a way," said Miss Garvice, "she's much better. Quite surprisingly so."

"Can I see her?"

"I am afraid not. She's unfortunately had a very restless night." Miss Garvice was sitting at her desk with a large yellow cat in her lap. As she spoke, the cat gazed up into her face with a look of complacent interrogation.

"Not pain?"

"Not exactly, I think." Miss Garvice turned the cat's head downward toward her knee. She paused before saying: "She's been weeping all night. And talking too. More hysterical than delirious. In the end we had to move her out of the big ward."

"What does she say?"

"It wouldn't be fair to our patients if we repeated what they say when they're not themselves."

"I suppose not. Still—"

"I admit that I cannot at all understand what's the matter with her. With her mind, I mean, of course."

"She's suffering from shock."

"Yes . . . But when I said 'mind,' I should perhaps have said 'emotions.' " The cat jumped from Miss Garvice's lap to the floor. It began to rub itself against my stockings. Miss Garvice followed it with her eyes. "Were you able to get to her house?"

"I looked in for a few minutes."

Miss Garvice wanted to question me; but she stopped herself and only asked, "Everything in order?"

"As far as I could see."

"I wonder if you would collect together a few things and bring them when you next come. I am sure I can leave it to you."

"I'll see what I can do." Remembering the house, I wondered what I *could* do. I rose. "I'll look in tomorrow, if I may." The cat followed me to the door purring. "Perhaps I shall be able to see Sally then."

Miss Garvice only nodded.

The truth was that I could not rest until I had investigated that back room. I was afraid, of course, but much more curious. Even my fear, I felt, perhaps wrongly, was more fear of the unknown than of anything I imagined myself likely in fact to find. Had there been a sympathetic friend available, I should have been glad of his company (it was a job for a man, or for no one). As it was, loyalty to Sally sent me, as before, alone.

During the morning it had become more and more overcast. In the middle of lunch it began to rain. Throughout the afternoon it rained more and more heavily. My mother said I was mad to go out, but I donned a pair of heavy walking shoes and my riding mackintosh. I had borrowed my father's flashlamp before he left that morning for his business.

I first entered the sitting room, where I took off my mackintosh and saturated beret. It would perhaps have been more sensible to hang the dripping object in the lower regions; but I think I felt it was wise not to leave them too far from the front door. I stood for a time in front of the mirror combing my matted hair. The light was fading fast, and it was difficult to see very much. The gusty wind hurled the rain against the big bay window, down which it descended like a rippling membrane of wax, distorting what little prospect remained outside. The window frame leaked copiously, making little pools on the floor.

I pulled up the collar of my sweater, took the flashlamp, and entered the back room. Almost at once in the beam of light, I found the switch. It was placed at the normal height, but about three feet from the doorway: as if the intention were precisely to make it impossible for the light to be switched on—or off—from the door. I turned it on.

I had speculated extensively, but the discovery still surprised me. Within the original walls had been laid three courses of stonework, which continued overhead to form an arched vault under the ceiling. The gray stones had been unskillfully laid, and the vault in particular looked likely to collapse. The inside of the door was reinforced with a single sheet of iron. There remained no window at all. A crude system of electric lighting had been installed, but there seemed provision for neither heating nor ventilation. Conceivably the room was intended for use in air raids; it had palpably been in existence for some time. But in that case it was hard to see why it should still be inhabited as it so plainly was . . .

For within the dismal place were many rough wooden shelves laden with crumbling brown books; several battered wooden armchairs; a large desk covered with pa-

pers; and a camp bed, showing, like the bed upstairs,
signs of recent occupancy. Most curious of all were a
small ashtray by the bedside choked with cigarette ends,
and an empty coffee cup. I lifted the pillow; underneath
it were Sally's pajamas, not folded, but stuffed away out
of sight. It was difficult to resist the unpleasant idea that
she had begun by sleeping in the room upstairs but for
some reason had moved down to this stagnant cavern;
which, moreover, she had stated that her father had
never left.

I like to think of myself as more imaginative than
sensible. I had, for example, conceived it as possible that
Dr. Tessler had been stark raving mad, and that the
room he never left would prove to be padded. But no
room could be less padded than this one. It was much
more like a prison. It seemed impossible that all through
her childhood Sally's father had been under some kind of
duress. The room also—and horribly—resembled a tomb.
Could the doctor have been one of those visionaries who
are given to brooding upon The End and to decking
themselves with the symbols of mortality, like Donne
with his shroud? It was difficult to believe in Sally emu-
lating her father in this . . . For some time, I think, I
fought off the most probable solution, carefully giving
weight to every other suggestion which my mind could
muster up. In the end I faced the fact that more than an
oubliette or a grave, the place resembled a fortress; and
the suggestion that there was something in the house
against which protection was necessary, was imperative.
The locked doors, the scene of ruin on the second floor,
Sally's behavior. I had known it all the time.

I turned off the bleak light, hanging by its kinked flex.
As I locked the library door, I wondered upon the unknown troubles which might have followed my failure of
yesterday to leave the house as I had found it. I walked
the few steps down the passage from the library to the
sitting room, at once preoccupied and alert. But, for my
peace of mind, neither preoccupied nor alert enough.
Because, although only for a moment, a second, a gleam,
when in that almost vanished light I reentered the sitting
room, I saw him.

As if, for my benefit, to make the most of the little

light, he stood right up in the big bay window. The view he presented to me was what I should call three-quarters back. But I could see a fraction of the outline of his face; entirely white (a thing which has to be seen to be believed) and with the skin drawn tight over the bones as by a tourniquet. There was a suggestion of wispy hair. I think he wore black; a garment, I thought, like a frock coat. He stood stooped and shadowy, except for the glimpse of white face. Of course I could not see his eyes. Needless to say, he was gone almost as soon as I beheld him; but it would be inexact to say that he went quite immediately. I had a scintilla of time in which to blink. I thought at first that dead or alive, it was Dr. Tessler; but immediately afterward I thought not.

That evening I tried to take my father into my confidence. I had always considered him the kindest of men, but one from whom I had been carried far out to sea. Now I was interested, as often with people, by the unexpectedness of his response. After I had finished my story (although I did not tell him everything), to which he listened carefully, sometimes putting an intelligent question about a point I had failed to illuminate, he said, "If you want my opinion, I'll give it to you."

"Please."

"It's simple enough. The whole affair is no business of yours." He smiled to take the sting out of the words, but underneath he seemed unusually serious.

"I'm fond of Sally. Besides, Miss Garvice asked me."

"Miss Garvice asked you to look in and see if there was any post; not to poke and pry about the house."

It was undoubtedly my weak point. But neither was it an altogether strong one for him. "Sally wouldn't let the postman deliver," I countered. "She was collecting her letters from the post office at the time she was run over. I can't imagine why."

"Don't try," said my father.

"But," I said, "what I saw? Even if I *had* no right to go all over the house."

"Mel," said my father, "you're supposed to write novels. Haven't you noticed by this time that everyone's lives are full of things you can't understand? The exceptional thing is the thing you *can* understand. I remember a man I knew when I was first in London . . ." He broke off. "But fortunately we don't *have* to understand. And for that reason we've no right to scrutinize other people's lives too closely."

Completely baffled, I said nothing.

My father patted me on the shoulder. "You can fancy you see things when the light's not very good, you know. Particularly an artistic girl like you, Mel."

Even by my parent I still liked occasionally to be called a girl.

When I went up to bed it struck me that again something had been forgotten. This time it was Sally's "few things."

Naturally it was the first matter Miss Garvice mentioned.

"I'm very sorry. I forgot. I think it must have been the rain," I continued, excusing myself like an adolescent to authority.

Miss Garvice very slightly clucked her tongue. But her mind was on something else. She went to the door of her room.

"Serena!"

"Yes, Miss Garvice?"

"See that I'm not disturbed for a few minutes, will you please? I'll call you again."

"Yes, Miss Garvice." Serena disappeared, mousily shutting the door.

"I want to tell you something in confidence."

I smiled. Confidences preannounced are seldom worthwhile.

"You know our routine here. We've been making various tests on Sally. One of them roused our suspicion." Miss Garvice scraped a Swan vesta on the composition striker which stood on her desk. For the moment she had forgotten the relative cigarette. "Did you know that Sally was pregnant?"

"No," I replied. But it might provide an explanation. Of a few things.

"Normally, of course, I shouldn't tell you. Or anyone else. But Sally is in such a hysterical state. And you say you know of no relatives?"

"None. What can I do?"

"I wonder if you would consider having her to stay with you? Not at once, of course. When we discharge her. Sally's going to need a friend."

"She won't come. Or she wouldn't. I've already pressed her."

Miss Garvice now was puffing away like a traction engine. "Why did you do that?"

"I'm afraid that's my business."

"You don't know who the father is?"

I said nothing.

"It's not as if Sally were a young girl. To be perfectly frank, there are things about her condition which I don't like."

It was my turn for a question.

"What about the accident? Hasn't that affected matters?"

"Strangely enough, no. Although it's nothing less than a miracle. Of one kind or the other," said Miss Garvice, trying to look broadminded.

I felt that we were unlikely to make further progress. Assuring Miss Garvice that in due course I should invite Sally once more, I asked again if I could see her.

"I am sorry. But it's out of the question for Sally to see anyone."

I was glad that Miss Garvice did not revert to the subject of Sally's few things, although, despite everything, I felt guilty for having forgotten them. Particularly because I had no wish to go back for them. It was out of the question even to think of explaining my real reasons to Miss Garvice, and loyalty to Sally continued to weigh heavily with me; but something must be devised. Moreover I must not take any step which might lead to someone else being sent to Sally's house. The best I could think of was to assemble some of my own "things" and say they were Sally's. It would be for Sally to accept the substitution.

But the question which struck me next morning was whether the contamination in Sally's house could be brought to an end by steps taken in the house itself; or whether it could have influence outside. Sally's mysterious restlessness, as reported by Miss Garvice, was far from reassuring; but on the whole I inclined to see it as an aftermath or revulsion. (Sally's pregnancy I refused at

this point to consider at all.) It was impossible to doubt
that immediate action of some kind was vital. Exorcism?
Or, conceivably, arson? I doubt whether I am one to
whom the former would ever strongly appeal: certainly
not as a means of routing something so apparently sensible to feeling as to sight. The latter, on the other hand,
might well be defeated (apart from other difficulties) by
that stone strongbox of a library. Flight? I considered it
long and seriously. But still it seemed that my strongest
motive in the whole affair was pity for Sally. So I stayed.

I did not visit the hospital that morning, from complete
perplexity as to what there to do or say; but instead,
during the afternoon, wandered back to the house. Despite my horror of the place, I thought that I might hit
upon something able to suggest a course of action. I
would look more closely at those grimy papers and even
at the books in the library. The idea of burning the place
down was still by no means out of my mind. I would
further ponder the inflammability of the house and the
degree of risk to the neighbors . . . All the time, of
course, I was completely miscalculating my own strength
and what was happening to me.

But as I hoisted the fallen gate, my nerve suddenly left
me; again, something which had never happened to me
before, either in the course of these events or at any
previous time. I felt very sick. I was much afraid lest I
faint. My body felt simultaneously tense and insubstantial.

Then I became aware that Mr. Orbit's delivery boy
was staring at me from the gate of the dentist's house
opposite. I must have presented a queer spectacle because the boy seemed to be standing petrified. His mouth,
I saw, was wide open. I knew the boy quite well. It was
essential for all kinds of reasons that I conduct myself
suitably. The boy stood, in fact, for public opinion. I
took a couple of deep breaths, produced the weighty
bunch of keys from my handbag and ascended the steps
as steadily as possible.

Inside the house, I made straight for the basement,
with a view to a glass of water. With Mr. Orbit's boy no
longer gaping at me, I felt worse than ever; so that,
even before I could look for a tumbler or reach the tap, I
had to sink upon one of the two battered kitchen chairs.

All my hair was damp, and my clothes felt unbearably heavy.

Then I became aware that steps were descending the basement staircase.

I completed my sequence of new experiences by fainting indeed.

I came round to the noise of an animal; a snuffling, grunting cry, which seemed to come, with much presistence, from the floor above. I seemed to listen to it for some time, even trying, though failing, to identify what animal it was; before recovering more fully and realizing that Sally was leaning back against the dresser and staring at me.

"Sally! It was you."

"Who did you think it was? It's my house."

She no longer wore the stained gray slacks but was dressed in a very curious way about which I do not think it fair to say more. In other ways also, the change in her had become complete: her eyes had a repulsive lifelessness; the bone structure of her face, previously so fine, had altered unbelievably. There was an unpleasant croak in her voice, precisely as if her larynx had lost flexibility.

"Will you please return my keys?"

I even had difficulty in understanding what she said, although doubtless my shaky condition did not help. Very foolishly, I rose to my feet while Sally glared at me with her changed eyes. I had been lying on the stone floor. There was a bad pain in the back of my head and neck.

"Glad to see you're better, Sally. I didn't expect you'd be about for some time yet." My words were incredibly foolish.

She said nothing but only stretched out her hand. It too was changed: it had become gray and bony, with protruding knotted veins.

I handed her the big bunch of keys. I wondered how she had entered the house without them. The animal wailing above continued without intermission. To it now seemed to be added a noise which struck me as resembling that of a pig scrabbling. Involuntarily I glanced upward to the ceiling.

Sally snatched the keys, snatched them gently and

softly, not violently, then cast her unblinking eyes upwards in parody of mine and emitted an almost deafening shriek of laughter.

"Do you love children, Mel? Would you like to see my baby?"

Truly it was the last straw; and I do not know quite how I behaved.

Now Sally seemed filled with terrible pride. "Let me tell you, Mel," she said, "that it's possible for a child to be born in a manner you'd never dream of."

I had begun to shudder again, but Sally clutched hold of me with her gray hand and began to drag me up the basement stairs.

"Will you be godmother? Come and see your godchild, Mel."

The noise was coming from the library. I clung to the top of the basement baluster. Distraught as I was, I now realized that the scrabbling sound was connected with the tearing to pieces of Dr. Tessler's books. But it was the wheezy, throaty cry of the creature which most turned my heart and sinews to water.

Or to steel. Because as Sally tugged at me, trying to pull me away from the baluster and into the library, I suddenly realized that she had no strength at all. Whatever else had happened to her, she was weak as a wraith.

I dragged myself free from her, let go of the baluster, and made toward the front door. Sally began to scratch my face and neck, but I made a quite capable job of defending myself. Sally then began to call out in her unnatural voice: she was trying to summon the creature into the passage. She scraped and tore at me, while panting out a stream of dreadful endearments to the thing in the library.

In the end, I found that my hands were about her throat, which was bare despite the cold weather. I could stand no more of that wrecked voice. Immediately she began to kick; and the shoes she was wearing seemed to have metal toes. I had the final awful fancy that she had acquired iron feet. Then I threw her from me on the floor of the passage and fled from the house.

It was now dark, somehow darker outside the house than inside it, and I found that I still had strength enough to run all the way home.

*   *   *

I went away for a fortnight, although on general grounds
it was the last thing I had wanted to do. At the end of
that time, and with Christmas drawing near, I returned
to my parents' house; I was not gong to permit Sally to
upset my plan for a present way of life.

At intervals through the winter I peered at Sally's
house from the corner of the cul-de-sac in which it stood,
but never saw a sign of occupancy or change.

I had learned from Miss Garvice that Sally had simply
"disappeared" from the Cottage Hospital.

"Disappeared?"

"Long before she was due for discharge, I need hardly
say."

"How did it happen?"

"The night nurse was going her rounds and noticed
that the bed was empty."

Miss Garvice was regarding me as if I were a material
witness. Had we been in Miss Garvice's room at the
hospital, Serena would have been asked to see that we
were not disturbed.

Sally had not been back long enough to be much noticed
in the town; and I observed that soon no one mentioned
her at all.

Then, one day between Easter and Whitsun, I found
she was at the front door.

"Hallo, Mel."

Again she was taking up the conversation. She was as
until last autumn she had always been; with that strange,
imperishable, untended prettiness of hers and her sweet
absent smile. She wore a white dress.

"Sally!" What could one say?

Our eyes met. She saw that she would have to come
straight to the point.

"I've sold my house."

I kept my head. "I said it was too big for you. Come
in."

She entered.

"I've bought a villa. In the Cyclades."

"For your work?"

She nodded. "The house fetched a price of course.
And my father left me more than I expected."

I said something banal.

Already she was lying on the big sofa and looking at me over the arm. "Mel, I should like you to come and stay with me. For a long time. As long as you can. You're a free agent, and you can't want to stay here."

Psychologists, I recollected, have ascertained that the comparative inferiority of women in contexts described as purely intellectual is attributable to the greater discouragement and repression of their curiosity when children.

"Thank you, Sally. But I'm quite happy here, you know."

"You're *not*. Are you, Mel?"

"No. I'm not."

"Well then?"

One day I shall probably go.

WILLIAM WOOD

One of the Dead

We couldn't have been more pleased. Deep in Clay Canyon we came upon the lot abruptly at a turn in the winding road. There was a crudely lettered board nailed to a dead tree which read, LOT FOR SALE—$1500 OR BEST OFFER, and a phone number.

"Fifteen hundred dollars—in Clay Canyon? I can't believe it," Ellen said.

"Or best offer," I corrected.

"I've heard you can't take a step without bumping into some movie person here."

"We've come three miles already without bumping into one. I haven't seen a soul."

"But there are the houses." Ellen looked about breathlessly.

There indeed were the houses—to our left and our right, to our front and our rear—low, ranch-style houses, unostentatious, prosaic, giving no hint of the gay and improbable lives we imagined went on inside them. But as the houses marched up the gradually climbing road there was not a single person to be seen. The cars—the Jaguars and Mercedeses and Cadillacs and Chryslers—were parked unattended in the driveways, their chrome gleaming in the sun; I caught a glimpse of one corner of a pool and a white diving board, but no one swam in the turquoise water. We climbed out of the car, Ellen with her rather large, short-haired head stooped forward as if under a weight. Except for the fiddling of a cicada somewhere on the hill, a profound hush lay over us in the

191

stifling air. Not even a bird moved in the motionless trees.

"There must be something wrong with it," Ellen said.

"It's probably already been sold, and they just didn't bother to take down the sign. . . . There was something here once, though." I had come across several ragged chunks of concrete that lay about randomly as if heaved out of the earth.

"A house, do you think?"

"It's hard to say. If it was a house it's been gone for years."

"Oh, Ted," Ellen cried. "It's perfect! Look at the view!" She pointed up the canyon toward the round, parched hills. Through the heat shimmering on the road they appeared to be melting down like wax.

"Another good thing," I said. "There won't be much to do to get the ground ready except for clearing the brush away. This place has been graded once. We save a thousand dollars right there."

Ellen took both my hands. Her eyes shone in her solemn face. "What do you think, Ted? What do you think?"

Ellen and I had been married four years, having both taken the step relatively late—in our early thirties—and in that time had lived in two different places, first an apartment in Santa Monica, then, when I was promoted to office manager, in a partly furnished house in the Hollywood Hills, always with the idea that when our first child came we would either buy or build a larger house of our own. But the child had not come. It was a source of anxiety and sadness to us both and lay between us like an old scandal for which each of us took on the blame.

Then I made an unexpected killing on the stock market and Ellen suddenly began agitating in her gentle way for the house. As we shopped around she dropped hints along the way—"This place is really too small for us, don't you think?" or "We'd have to fence off the yard, of course"—that let me know that the house had become a talisman for her; she had conceived the notion that perhaps, in some occult way, if we went ahead with our accommodations for a child the child might come. The notion gave her happiness. Her face filled out, the gray circles under her eyes disappeared, the quiet gaiety, which did not seem like gaiety at all but a form of peace, returned.

As Ellen held on to my hands, I hesitated. I am convinced now that there was something behind my hesitation—something I felt then only as a quality of silence, a fleeting twinge of utter desolation. "It's so safe," she said. "There's no traffic at all."

I explained that. "It's not a through street. It ends somewhere up in the hills."

She turned back to me again with her bright, questioning eyes. The happiness that had grown in her during our months of house-hunting seemed to have welled into near rapture.

"We'll call the number," I said, "but don't expect too much. It must have been sold long ago."

We walked slowly back to the car. The door handle burned to the touch. Down the canyon the rear end of a panel truck disappeared noiselessly around a bend.

"No," Ellen said, "I have a feeling about this place. I think it was meant to be ours."

And she was right, of course.

Mr. Carswell Deeves, who owned the land, was called upon to do very little except take my check for $1500 and hand over the deed to us, for by the time Ellen and I met him we had already sold ourselves. Mr. Deeves, as we had suspected from the unprofessional sign, was a private citizen. We found his house in a predominantly Mexican section of Santa Monica. He was a chubby, pink man of indeterminate age dressed in white ducks and soft white shoes, as if he had had a tennis court hidden away among the squalid, asphalt-shingled houses and dry kitchen gardens of his neighbors.

"Going to live in Clay Canyon, are you?" he said. "Ros Russell lives up there, or used to." So, we discovered, did Joel McCrea, Jimmy Stewart and Paula Raymond, as well as a cross-section of producers, directors and character actors. "Oh, yes," said Mr. Deeves, "it's an address that will look extremely good on your stationery."

Ellen beamed and squeezed my hand.

Mr. Deeves turned out to know very little about the land other than that a house had been destroyed by fire there years ago and that the land had changed hands

many times since. "I myself acquired it in what may
strike you as a novel way," he said as we sat in his
parlor—a dark, airless box which smelled faintly of cam-
phor and whose walls were obscured with yellowing
autographed photographs of movie stars. "I won it in a
game of hearts from a makeup man on the set of *Quo
Vadis.* Perhaps you remember me. I had a close-up in
one of the crowd scenes."

"That was a number of years ago, Mr. Deeves," I said.
"Have you been trying to sell it all this time?"

"I've nearly sold it dozens of times," he said, "but
something always went wrong somehow."

"What kind of things?"

"Naturally, the fire-insurance rates up there put off a
lot of people. I hope you're prepared to pay a high
premium——"

"I've already checked into that."

"Good. You'd be surprised how many people will let
details like that go till the last minute."

"What other things have gone wrong?"

Ellen touched my arm to discourage my wasting any
more time with foolish questions.

Mr. Deeves spread out the deed before me and
smoothed it with his forearm. "Silly things, some of
them. One couple found some dead doves. . . ."

"Dead doves?" I handed him the signed article. With
one pink hand Mr. Deeves waved it back and forth to
dry the ink. "Five of them, if I remember correctly. In
my opinion they'd sat on a wire and were electrocuted
somehow. The husband thought nothing of it, of course,
but his wife became so hysterical that we had to call off
the transaction."

I made a sign at Mr. Deeves to drop this line of
conversation. Ellen loves animals and birds of all kinds
with a devotion that turns the loss of a household pet
into a major tragedy, which is why, since the death of
our cocker spaniel, we have had no more pets. But Ellen
appeared not to have heard; she was watching the paper
in Mr. Deeve's hand fixedly, as if she were afraid it
might vanish.

Mr. Deeves sprang suddenly to his feet. "Well!" he
cried. "It's all yours now. I know you'll be happy there."

Ellen flushed with pleasure. "I'm sure we will," she said, and took his pudgy hand in both of hers.

"A prestige address," called Mr. Deeves from his porch as we drove away. "A real prestige address."

Ellen and I are modern people. Our talk in the evenings is generally on issues of the modern world. Ellen paints a little and I do some writing from time to time—mostly on technical subjects. The house that Ellen and I built mirrored our concern with present-day aesthetics. We worked closely with Jack Salmanson, the architect and a friend, who designed a steel module house, low and compact and private, which could be fitted into the irregularities of our patch of land for a maximum of space. The interior *décor* we left largely up to Ellen, who combed the home magazines and made sketches as if she were decorating a dozen homes.

I mention these things to show that there is nothing Gothic about my wife and me: We are as thankful for our common sense as for our sensibilities, and we flattered ourselves that the house we built achieved a balance between the aesthetic and the functional. Its lines were simple and clean; there were no dark corners, and it was surrounded on three sides by houses, none of which were more than eight years old.

There were, however, signs from the very beginning, ominous signs which can be read only in retrospect, though it seems to me now that there were others who suspected but said nothing. One was the Mexican who cut down the tree.

As a money-saving favor to us, Jack Salmanson agreed to supervise the building himself and hire small, independent contractors to do the labor, many of whom were Mexicans or Negroes with dilapidated equipment that appeared to run only by some mechanical miracle. The Mexican, a small, forlorn workman with a stringy moustache, had already burned out two chain-saw blades and still had not cut halfway through the tree. It was inexplicable. The tree, the same one on which Ellen and I had seen the original FOR SALE sign, had obviously been dead for years, and the branches that already lay scattered on the ground were rotted through.

"You must have run into a batch of knots," Jack said. "Try it again. If the saw gets too hot, quit and we'll pull it down with the bulldozer." As if answering to its name, the bulldozer turned at the back of the lot and lumbered toward us in a cloud of dust, the black shoulders of the Negro operator gleaming in the sun.

The Mexican need not have feared for his saw. He had scarcely touched it to the tree when it started to topple of its own accord. Startled, he backed away a few steps. The tree had begun to fall toward the back of the lot, in the direction of his cut, but now it appeared to arrest itself, its naked branches trembling as if in agitation; then with an awful rending sound it writhed upright and fell back on itself, gaining momentum and plunging directly at the bulldozer. My voice died in my throat, but Jack and the Mexican shouted, and the operator jumped and rolled on the ground just as the tree fell high on the hood, shattering the windshield to bits. The bulldozer, out of control and knocked off course, came directly at us, gears whining and gouging a deep trough in the earth. Jack and I jumped one way, the Mexican the other; the bulldozer lurched between us and ground on toward the street, the Negro sprinting after it.

"The car!" Jack shouted. "The car!"

Parked in front of the house across the street was a car, a car which was certainly brand-new. The bulldozer headed straight for it, its blade striking clusters of sparks from the pavement. The Mexican waved his chain saw over his head like a toy and shouted in Spanish. I covered my eyes with my hands and heard Jack grunt softly, as if he had been struck in the mid-section, just before the crash.

Two woman stood on the porch of the house across the street and gaped. The car had caved in at the center, its steel roof wrinkled like tissue paper; its front and rear ends were folded around the bulldozer as if embracing it. Then, with a low whoosh, both vehicles were enveloped in creeping blue flame.

"Rotten luck," Jack muttered under his breath as we ran into the street. From the corner of my eye I caught the curious sight of the Mexican on the ground, praying, his chain saw lying by his knees.

In the evening Ellen and I paid a visit to the Sheffits', Sondra and Jeff, our neighbors across the canyon road, where we met the owner of the ruined car, Joyce Castle, a striking blonde in lemon-colored pants. The shock of the accident itself wore off with the passing of time and cocktails, and the three of them treated it as a tremendous joke.

Mrs. Castle was particularly hilarious. "I'm doing better," she rejoiced. "The Alfa-Romeo only lasted two days, but I held on to this one a whole six weeks. I even had the permanent plates on."

"But you mustn't be without a car, Mrs. Castle," Ellen said in her serious way. "We'd be glad to loan you our Plymouth until you can—"

"I'm having a new car delivered tomorrow afternoon. Don't worry about me. A Daimler, Jeff, you'll be interested to know. I couldn't resist after riding in yours. What about the poor bulldozer man? Is he absolutely wiped out?"

"I think he'll survive," I said. "In any case he has two other 'dozers."

"Then you won't be held up," Jeff said.

"I wouldn't think so."

Sondra chuckled softly. "I just happened to look out the window," she said. "It was just like a Rube Goldberg cartoon. A chain reaction."

"And there was my poor old Cadillac at the end of it," Mrs. Castle sighed.

Suey, Mrs. Castle's dog, who had been lying on the floor beside his mistress glaring dourly at us between dozes, suddenly ran to the front door barking ferociously, his red mane standing straight up.

"Suey!" Mrs. Castle slapped her knee. "Suey! Come here!"

The dog merely flattened its ears and looked from his mistress toward the door again as if measuring a decision. He growled deep in his throat.

"It's the ghost," Sondra said lightly. "He's behind the whole thing." Sondra sat curled up in one corner of the sofa and tilted her head to one side as she spoke, like a very clever child.

Jeff laughed sharply. "Oh, they tell some very good stories."

With a sigh Mrs. Castle rose and dragged Suey back by his collar. "If I didn't feel so self-conscious about it I'd take him to an analyst," she said. "Sit, Suey! Here's a cashew nut for you."

"I'm very fond of ghost stories," I said, smiling.

"Oh, well," Jeff murmured, mildly disparaging.

"Go ahead, Jeff," Sondra urged him over the rim of her glass. "They'd like to hear it."

Jeff was a literary agent, a tall, sallow man with dark oily hair that he was continually pushing out of his eyes with his fingers. As he spoke he smiled lopsidedly as if defending against the probability of being taken seriously. "All I know is that back in the late seventeenth century the Spanish used to have hangings here. The victims are supposed to float around at night and make noises."

"Criminals?" I asked.

"Of the worst sort," said Sondra. "What was the story Guy Relling told you, Joyce?" She smiled with a curious inward relish that suggested she knew the story perfectly well herself.

"Is that Guy Relling, the director?" I asked.

"Yes," Jeff said. "He owns those stables down the canyon."

"I've seen them," Ellen said. "Such lovely horses."

Joyce Castle hoisted her empty glass into the air. "Jeff, love, will you find me another?"

"We keep straying from the subject," said Sondra gently. "Fetch me another too, darling"—she handed her glass to Jeff as he went by—"like a good boy. . . . I didn't mean to interrupt, Joyce. Go on." She gestured toward us as the intended audience. Ellen stiffened slightly in her chair.

"It seems that there was one *hombre* of outstanding depravity," Joyce Castle said languidly. "I forgot the name. He murdered, stole, raped . . . one of those endless Spanish names with a 'Luis' in it, a nobleman I think Guy said. A charming sort. Mad, of course, and completely unpredictable. They hanged him at last for some unsavory escapade in a nunnery. You two are moving into a neighborhood rich with tradition."

We all laughed.

"What about the noises?" Ellen asked Sondra. "Have you heard anything?"

"Of course," Sondra said, tipping her head prettily.

Every inch of her skin was tanned to the color of coffee from afternoons by the pool. It was a form of leisure that her husband, with his bilious coloring and lank hair, apparently did not enjoy.

"Everywhere I've ever lived," he said, his grin growing crookeder and more apologetic, "there were noises in the night that you couldn't explain. Here there are all kinds of wildlife— foxes, coons, possums—even coyotes up on the ridge. They're all active after sundown."

Ellen's smile of pleasure at this news turned to distress as Sondra remarked in her offhand way, "We found our poor kitty-cat positively torn to pieces one morning. He was all blood. We never did find his head."

"A fox," Jeff put in quickly. Everything he said seemed hollow. Something came from him like a vapor. I thought it was grief.

Sondra gazed smugly into her lap as if hugging a secret to herself. She seemed enormously pleased. It occurred to me that Sondra was trying to frighten us. In a way it relieved me. She was enjoying herself too much, I thought, looking at her spoiled, brown face, to be frightened herself.

After the incident of the tree everything went well for some weeks. The house went up rapidly. Ellen and I visited it as often as we could, walking over the raw ground and making our home in our mind's eye. The fireplace would go here, the refrigerator here, our Picasso print there. "Ted," Ellen said timidly, "I've been thinking. Why don't we fix up the extra bedroom as a children's room?"

I waited.

"Now that we'll be living out here our friends will have to stay overnight more often. Most of them have young children. It would be nice for them."

I slipped my arm around her shoulders. She knew I understood. It was a delicate matter. She raised her face and I kissed her between her brows. Signal and counter-signal, the keystones of our life together—a life of sensibility and tact.

"Hey, you two!" Sondra Sheffits called from across the street. She stood on her front porch in a pink bathing suit, her skin brown, her hair nearly white. "How about a swim?"

"No suits!"

"Come on, we've got plenty."

Ellen and I debated the question with a glance, settled it with a nod.

As I came out onto the patio in one of Jeff's suits, Sondra said, "Ted, you're pale as a ghost. Don't you get any sun where you are?" She lay in a chaise longue behind huge elliptical sunglasses encrusted with glass gems.

"I stay inside too much, writing articles," I said.

"You're welcome to come here any time you like" —she smiled suddenly, showing me a row of small, perfect teeth—"and swim."

Ellen appeared in her borrowed suit, a red one with a short, limp ruffle. She shaded her eyes as the sun, glittering metallically on the water, struck her full in the face.

Sondra ushered her forward as if to introduce my wife to me. "You look much better in that suit than I ever did." Her red nails flashed on Ellen's arm. Ellen smiled guardedly. The two women were about the same height, but Ellen was narrower in the shoulders, thicker through the waist and hips. As they came toward me it seemed to me that Ellen was the one I did not know. Her familiar body became strange. It looked out of proportion. Hairs that on Sondra were all but invisible except when the sun turned them to silver, lay flat and dark on Ellen's pallid arm.

As if sensing the sudden distance between us, Ellen took my hand. "Let's jump in together," she said gaily. "No hanging back."

Sondra retreated to the chaise longue to watch us, her eyes invisible behind her outrageous glasses, her head on one side.

Incidents began again and continued at intervals. Guy Relling, whom I never met but whose pronouncements on the supernatural reached me through others from time to time like messages from an oracle, claims that the existence of the living dead is a particularly excruciating one as they hover between two states of being. Their memories keep the passions of life forever fresh and sharp, but they are able to relieve them only at a monstrous expense of will and energy which leaves them literally helpless for months or sometimes even years afterward. This was why materializations and other forms of tangible action are relatively rare. There are of course exceptions, Sondra, our most frequent translator of Relling's theories, pointed out one evening with the odd joy that accompanied all of her remarks on the subject; some ghosts are terrifically active—particularly the insane ones who, ignorant of the limitations of death as they were of the impossibilities of life, transcend them with the dynamism that is exclusively the property of madness. Generally, however, it was Relling's opinion that a ghost was more to be pitied than feared. Sondra quoted him as having said, "The notion of a haunted house is a misconception semantically. It is not the house but the soul itself that is haunted."

On Saturday, August 6, a workman laying pipe was blinded in one eye by an acetylene torch.

On Thursday, September 1, a rockslide on the hill behind us dumped four tons of dirt and rock on the half-finished house and halted work for two weeks.

On Sunday, October 9—my birthday, oddly enough—while visiting the house alone, I slipped on a stray screw and struck my head on a can of latex paint which opened up a gash requiring ten stitches. I rushed across to the Sheffits'. Sondra answered the door in her bathing suit and a magazine in her hand. "Ted?" She peered at me. "I scarcely recognized you through the blood. Come in, I'll call the doctor. Try not to drip on the furniture, will you?"

I told the doctor of the screw on the floor, the big can of paint. I did not tell him that my foot had slipped because I had turned too quickly and that I had turned too quickly because the sensation had grown on me that there was someone behind me, close enough to touch me, perhaps, because something hovered there, fetid and damp and cold and almost palpable in its nearness; I remember shivering violently as I turned, as if the sun of this burning summer's day had been replaced by a mysterious star without warmth. I did not tell the doctor this nor anyone else.

In November Los Angeles burns. After the long drought of summer the sap goes underground and the baked hills seem to gasp in pain for the merciful release of either life or death—rain or fire. Invariably fire comes first, spreading through the outlying parts of the country like an epidemic, till the sky is livid and starless at night and overhung with dun-colored smoke during the day.

There was a huge fire in Tujunga, north of us, the day Ellen and I moved into our new house—handsome, severe, aggressively new on its dry hillside—under a choked sky the color of earth and a muffled, flyspeck sun. Sondra and Jeff came over to help, and in the evening Joyce Castle stopped by with Suey and a magnum of champagne.

Ellen clasped her hands under her chin. "What a lovely surprise!"

"I hope it's cold enough. I've had it in my refrigerator since four o'clock. Welcome to the canyon. You're nice people. You remind me of my parents. God, it's hot. I've been weeping all day on account of the smoke. You'll have air conditioning I suppose?"

Jeff was sprawled in a chair with his long legs straight in front of him in the way a cripple might put aside a pair of crutches. "Joyce, you're an angel. Excuse me if I don't get up. I'm recuperating."

"You're excused, doll, you're excused."

"Ted," Ellen said softly. "Why don't you get some glasses?"

Jeff hauled in his legs. "Can I give you a hand?"

"Sit still, Jeff."

He sighed. "I hadn't realized I was so out of shape." He looked more cadaverous than ever after our afternoon of lifting and shoving. Sweat had collected in the hollows under his eyes.

"Shall I show you the house, Joyce? While Ted is in the kitchen?"

"I love you, Ellen," Joyce said. "Take me on the whole tour."

Sondra followed me into the kitchen. She leaned against the wall and smoked, supporting her left elbow in the palm of her right hand. She didn't say a word. Through the open door I could see Jeff's outstretched legs from the calves down.

"Thanks for all the help today," I said to Sondra in a voice unaccountably close to a whisper. I could hear Joyce and Ellen as they moved from room to room, their voices swelling and dying: "It's all steel? You mean everything? Walls and all? Aren't you afraid of lightning?"

"Oh, we're all safely grounded, I think."

Jeff yawned noisily in the living room. Wordlessly Sondra put a tray on the kitchen table as I rummaged in an unpacked carton for the glasses. She watched me steadily and coolly, as if she expected me to entertain her. I wanted to say something further to break a silence which was becoming unnatural and oppressive. The sounds around us seemed only to isolate us in a ring of intimacy. With her head on one side Sondra smiled at me. I could hear her rapid breathing.

"What's this, a nursery? Ellen, love!"

"No, no! It's only for our friends' children."

Sondra's eyes were blue, the color of shallow water. She seemed faintly amused, as if we were sharing in a conspiracy—a conspiracy I was anxious to repudiate by making some prosaic remark in a loud voice for all to hear, but a kind of pain developed in my chest as the words seemed dammed there, and I only smiled at her foolishly. With every passing minute of silence, the more impossible it became to break through and the more I felt drawn into the intrigue of which, though I was ignorant, I was surely guilty. Without so much as a touch she had made us lovers.

Ellen stood in the doorway, half turned away as if her first impulse had been to run. She appeared to be deep in thought, her eyes fixed on the steel, cream-colored doorjamb.

Sondra began to talk to Ellen in her dry, satirical voice. It was chatter of the idlest sort, but she was destroying, as I had wished to destroy, the absurd notion that there was something between us. I could see Ellen's confusion. She hung on Sondra's words, watching her lips attentively, as if this elegant, tanned woman, calmly smoking and talking of trifles, were her savior.

As for myself, I felt as if I had lost the power of speech entirely. If I joined in with Sondra's carefully innocent chatter I would only be joining in the deception against my wife; if I proclaimed the truth and ended everything by bringing it into the open. . . . but what truth? What was there in fact to bring into the open? What was there to end? A feeling in the air? An intimation? The answer was nothing, of course. I did not even like Sondra very much. There was something cold and unpleasant about her. There was nothing to proclaim because nothing had happened. "Where's Joyce?" I asked finally, out of a dry mouth. "Doesn't she want to see the kitchen?"

Ellen turned slowly toward me, as if it cost her a great effort. "She'll be here in a minute," she said tonelessly, and I became aware of Joyce's and Jeff's voices from the living room. Ellen studied my face, her pupils oddly dilated under the pinkish fluorescent light, as if she were trying to penetrate to the bottom of a great darkness that lay beneath my chance remark. Was it a code of some kind, a new signal for her that I would shortly make clear? What did it mean? I smiled at her and she responded with a smile of her own, a tentative and formal upturning of her mouth, as if I were a familiar face whose name escaped her for the moment.

Joyce came in behind Ellen. "I hate kitchens. I never go into mine." She looked from one to the other of us. "Am I interrupting something?"

At two o'clock in the morning I sat up in bed, wide awake. The bedroom was bathed in the dark red glow of the fire which had come closer in the night. A thin, autumnal veil of smoke hung in the room. Ellen lay on her side, asleep, one hand cupped on the pillow next to her face as if waiting for something to be put in it. I had no idea why I was so fully awake, but I threw off the covers and went to the window to check on the fire. I could see no flame, but the hills stood out blackly against a turgid sky that belled and sagged as the wind blew and relented.

Then I heard the sound.

I am a person who sets store by precision in the use of words—in the field of technical writing this is a necessity. But I can think of no word to describe that sound. The closest I can come with a word of my own invention is "vlump." It came erratically, neither loud nor soft. It was, rather, pervasive and without location. It was not a *solid* sound. There was something vague and whispering about it, and from time to time it began with the suggestion of a sigh—a shuffling dissipation in the air that seemed to take form and die in the same instant. In a way I cannot define, it was mindless, without will or reason, yet implacable. Because I could not explain it immediately I went to seek an explanation.

I stepped into the hall and switched on the light, pressing the noiseless button. The light came down out of a fixture set flush into the ceilings and diffused through a milky plastic-like Japanese rice paper. The clean, indestructible walls rose perpendicularly around me. Through the slight haze of smoke came the smell of the newness, sweet and metallic—more like a car than a house. And still the sound went on. It seemed to be coming from the room at the end of the hall, the room we had designed for our friends' children. The door was open and I could see a gray patch that was a west window. Vlump . . . vlump . . . vlumpvlump. . . .

Fixing on the gray patch, I moved down the hall while my legs made themselves heavy as logs, and all the while I repeated to myself, "The house is settling. All new houses settle and make strange noises." And so lucid was I that I believed I was not afraid. I was walking down the bright new hall of my new steel house to investigate a noise, for the house might be settling unevenly, or an animal might be up to some mischief—raccoons regularly raided the garbage cans, I had been told. There might be something wrong with the plumbing or with the radiant-heating system that warmed our steel and vinyl floors. And now, like the responsible master of the house, I had located the apparent center of the sound and was going responsibly toward it. In a second or two, very likely, I would know. Vlump vlump. The gray of the window turned rosy as I came near enough to see the hillside beyond it. That black was underbrush and that pink the dusty swath cut by the bulldozer before it had run amok. I had watched the accident from just about the spot where I stood now, and the obliterated hole where the tree had been, laid firmly over with the prefabricated floor of the room whose darkness I would eradicate by touching with my right hand the light switch inside the door.

"Ted?"

Blood boomed in my ears. I had the impression that my heart had burst. I clutched at the wall for support. Yet of course I knew it was Ellen's voice, and I answered her calmly. "Yes, it's me."

"What's the matter?" I heard the bedclothes rustle.

"Don't get up, I'm coming right in." The noise had

stopped. There was nothing. Only the almost inaudible hum of the refrigerator, the stirring of the wind.

Ellen was sitting up in bed. "I was just checking on the fire," I said. She patted my side of the bed and in the instant before I turned out the hall light I saw her smile.

"I was just dreaming about you," she said softly, as I climbed under the sheets. She rolled against me. "Why, you're trembling."

"I should have worn my robe."

"You'll be warm in a minute." Her fragrant body lay against mine, but I remained rigid as stone and just as cold, staring at the ceiling, my mind a furious blank. After a moment she said, "Ted?" It was her signal, always hesitant, always tremulous, that meant I was to roll over and take her in my arms.

Instead I answered, "What?" just as if I had not understood.

For a few seconds I sensed her struggling against her reserve to give me a further sign that would pierce my peculiar distraction and tell me she wanted love. But it was too much for her—too alien. My coldness had created a vacuum she was too unpracticed to fill—a coldness sudden and inexplicable, unless . . .

She withdrew slowly and pulled the covers up under her chin. Finally she asked, "Ted, is there something happening that I should know about?" She had remembered Sondra and the curious scene in the kitchen. It took, I knew, great courage for Ellen to ask that question, though she must have known my answer.

"No, I'm just tired. We've had a busy day. Goodnight, dear." I kissed her on the cheek and sensed her eyes, in the shadow of the fire, searching mine, asking the question she could not give voice to. I turned away, somehow ashamed because I could not supply the answer that would fulfill her need. Because there was no answer at all.

The fire was brought under control after burning some eight hundred acres and several homes, and three weeks later the rains came. Jack Salmanson came out one Sunday to see how the house was holding up, checked the foundation, the roof and all the seams and pronounced it tight as a drum. We sat looking moodily out the glass doors onto the patio—a flatland of grayish mud which threatened to swamp with a thin ooze of silt and gravel the few flagstones I had set in the ground. Ellen was in the bedroom lying down; she had got into the habit of taking a nap after lunch, though it was I, not she, who lay stark awake night after night explaining away sounds that became more and more impossible to explain away. The gagging sound that sometimes accompanied the vlump and the strangled expulsion of air that followed it were surely the result of some disturbance in the water pipes; the footsteps that came slowly down the hall and stopped outside our closed door and then went away again with something like a low chuckle were merely the night contracting of our metal house after the heat of the day. Through all this Ellen slept as if in a stupor; she seemed to have become addicted to sleep. She went to bed at nine and got up at ten the next morning; she napped in the afternoon and moved about lethargically the rest of the time with a Mexican shawl around her shoulders, complaining of the cold. The doctor examined her for mononucleosis but found nothing. He said perhaps it was her sinuses and that she should rest as much as she wanted.

After a protracted silence Jack put aside his drink and stood up. "I guess I'll go along."

"I'll tell Ellen."

"What the hell for? Let her sleep. Tell her I hope she feels better." He turned to frown at the room of the house he had designed and built. "Are you happy here?" he asked suddenly.

"Happy?" I repeated the word awkwardly. "Of course we're happy. We love the house. It's . . . just a little noisy at night, that's all." I stammered it out, like the first word of a monstrous confession, but Jack seemed hardly to hear it. He waved a hand. "House settling." He squinted from one side of the room to the other. "I don't know. There's something about it. . . . It's not right. Maybe it's just the weather . . . the light. . . . It could be friendlier, you know what I mean? It seems cheerless."

I watched him with a kind of wild hope, as if he might magically fathom my terror—do for me what I could not do for myself, and permit it to be discussed calmly between two men of temperate mind. But Jack was not looking for the cause of the gloom but the cure for it.

"Why don't you try putting down a couple of orange rugs in this room?" he said.

I stared at the floor as if two orange rugs were an infallible charm. "Yes," I said, "I think we'll try that."

Ellen scuffed in, pushing back her hair, her face puffy with sleep. "Jack," she said, "when the weather clears and I'm feeling livelier, you and Anne and the children must come and spend the night."

"We'd like that. After the noises die down," he added satirically to me.

"Noises? What noises?" A certain blankness came over Ellen's face when she looked at me now. The expression was the same, but what had been open in it before was now merely empty. She had put up her guard against me; she suspected me of keeping things from her.

"At night," I said. "The house is settling. You don't hear them."

When Jack had gone, Ellen sat with a cup of tea in the chair where Jack had sat, looking out at the mud. Her long purple shawl hung all the way to her knees and made her look armless. There seemed no explanation for the two white hands that curled around the teacup in her lap. "It's a sad thing," she said tonelessly. "I can't help but feel sorry for Sondra."

"Why is that?" I asked guardedly.

"Joyce was here yesterday. She told me that she and Jeff have been having an affair off and on for six years." She turned to see how I would receive this news.

"Well, that explains the way Joyce and Sondra behave toward each other," I said, with a pleasant glance straight into Ellen's eyes; there I encountered only the reflection of the glass doors, even to the rain trickling down them, and I had the eerie sensation of having been shown a picture of the truth, as if she were weeping secretly in the depths of a soul I could no longer touch. For Ellen did not believe in my innocence; I'm not sure I still believed in it myself; very likely Jeff and Joyce didn't either. It is impossible to say what Sondra believed. She behaved as if our infidelity were an accomplished fact. In its way it was a performance of genius, for Sondra never touched me except in the most accidental or impersonal way; even her glances, the foundation on which she built the myth of our liaison, had nothing soft in them; they were

probing and sly and were always accompanied by a fur-
tive smile, as if we merely shared some private joke. Yet
there was something in the way she did it—in the tilt of
her head perhaps—that plainly implied that the joke was
at everyone else's expense. And she had taken to calling
me "darling."

"Sondra and Jeff have a feebleminded child off in an
institution somewhere," Ellen said. "That set them against
each other, apparently."

"Joyce told you all this?"

"She just mentioned it casually as if it were the most
natural thing in the world—she assumed we must have
known. . . . But I don't want to know things like that
about my friends."

"That's show biz, I guess. You and I are just provin-
cials at heart."

"Sondra must be a very unhappy girl."

"It's hard to tell with Sondra."

"I wonder what she tries to do with her life. . . . If she
looks for anything—outside."

I waited.

"Probably not," Ellen answered her own question.
"She seems very self-contained. Almost cold . . ."

I was treated to the spectacle of my wife fighting with
herself to delay a wound that she was convinced would
come home to her sooner or later. She did not want to
believe in my infidelity. I might have comforted her with
lies. I might have told her that Sondra and I rendezvoused
downtown in a cafeteria and made love in a second-rate
hotel on the evenings when I called to say that I was
working late. Then the wound would be open and could
be cleaned and cured. It would be painful of course, but
I would have confided in her again and our old system
would be restored. Watching Ellen torture herself with
doubt, I was tempted to tell her those lies. The truth
never tempted me: To have admitted that I knew what
she was thinking would have been tantamount to an
admission of guilt. How could I suspect such a thing
unless it were true? And was I to explain my coldness by
terrifying her with vague stories of indescribable sounds
which she never heard?

And so the two of us sat on, dumb and chilled, in our
watertight house as the daylight began to go. And then a

sort of exultation seized me. What if my terror were no more real than Ellen's? What if both our ghosts were only ghosts of the mind which needed only a little common sense to drive them away? And I saw that if I could drive away my ghost, Ellen's would soon follow, for the secret that shut me away from her would be gone. It was a revelation, a triumph of reason.

"What's that up there?" Ellen pointed to something that looked like a leaf blowing at the top of the glass doors. "It's a tail, Ted. There must be some animal on the roof."

Only the bushy tip was visible. As I drew close to it I could see raindrops clinging as if by a geometrical system to each black hair. "It looks like a raccoon tail. What would a coon be doing out so early?" I put on a coat and went outside. The tail hung limply over the edge, ringed with white and swaying phlegmatically in the breeze. The animal itself was hidden behind the low parapet. Using the ship's ladder at the back of the house I climbed up to look at it.

The human mind, just like other parts of the anatomy, is an organ of habit. Its capabilities are bounded by the limits of precedent; it thinks what it is used to thinking. Faced with a phenomenon beyond its range it rebels, it rejects, sometimes it collapses. My mind, which for weeks had steadfastly refused to honor the evidence of my senses that there was Something Else living in the house with Ellen and me, something unearthly and evil, largely on the basis of insufficient evidence, was now forced to the subsequent denial by saying, as Jeff had said, "fox." It was of course, ridiculous. The chances of a fox's winning a battle with a raccoon were very slight at best, let alone what had been done to this raccoon. The body lay on the far side of the roof. I didn't see the head at all until I had stumbled against it and it had rolled over and over to come to rest against the parapet where it pointed its masked, ferret face at me.

Only because my beleaguered mind kept repeating, like a voice, "Ellen mustn't know, Ellen mustn't know," was I able to take up the dismembered parts and hurl them with all my strength onto the hillside and answer when Ellen called out, "What is it, Ted?" "Must have been a coon. It's gone now," in a perfectly level voice before I went to the back of the roof and vomited.

I recalled Sondra's mention of their mutilated cat and phoned Jeff at his agency. "We will discuss it over lunch," I told myself. I had a great need to talk, an action impossible within my own home, where every day the silence became denser and more intractable. Once or twice Ellen ventured to ask, "What's the matter, Ted?" but I always answered, "Nothing." And there our talk ended. I could see it in her wary eyes; I was not the man she had married; I was cold, secretive. The children's room, furnished with double bunks and wallpaper figured with toys, stood like a rebuke. Ellen kept the door closed most of the time though once or twice, in the late afternoon, I had found her in there moving about aimlessly, touching objects as if half in wonder that they should still linger on after so many long, sterile months; a foolish hope had failed. Neither did our friends bring their children to stay. They did not because we did not ask them. The silence had brought with it a profound and debilitating inertia. Ellen's face seemed perpetually swollen, the features cloudy and amorphous, the eyes dull; her whole body had become bloated, as if an enormous cache of pain had backed up inside her. We moved through the house in our orbits like two sleepwalkers, going about our business out of habit. Our friends called at first, puzzled, a little hurt, but soon stopped and left us to ourselves. Occasionally we saw the Sheffitses. Jeff was looking seedier and seedier, told bad jokes, drank too much and seemed always ill at ease. Sondra did most of the talking, chattering blandly on indifferent subjects and always hinting by gesture, word or glance at our underground affair.

Jeff and I had lunch at the Brown Derby on Vine Street under charcoal caricatures of show folk. At a table next to ours an agent was eulogizing an actor in a voice hoarse with trumped-up enthusiasm to a large, purple-faced man who was devoting his entire attention to a bowl of vichyssoise.

"It's a crazy business," Jeff said to me. "Be glad you're not in it."

"I see what you mean," I replied. Jeff had not the

faintest idea of why I had brought him there, nor had I given him any clue. We were "breaking the ice." Jeff grinned at me with that crooked trick of his mouth, and I grinned back. "We are friends"—presumably that is the message we were grinning at each other. Was he my friend? Was I his friend? He lived across the street; our paths crossed perhaps once a week; we joked together; he sat always in the same chair in our living room twisting from one sprawl to another; there was a straight white chair in his living room that I preferred. Friendships have been founded on less, I suppose. Yet he had an idiot child locked off in an asylum somewhere and a wife who amused herself with infidelity by suggestion; I had a demon loose in my house and a wife gnawed with suspicion and growing remote and old because of it. And I had said, "I see what you mean." It seemed insufferable. I caught Jeff's eye. "You remember we talked once about a ghost?" My tone was bantering; perhaps I meant to make a joke.

"I remember."

"Sondra said something about a cat of yours that was killed."

"The one the fox got."

"That's what you said. That's not what Sondra said."

Jeff shrugged. "What about it?"

"I found a dead raccoon on our roof."

"Your roof!"

"Yes. It was pretty awful."

Jeff toyed with his fork. All pretense of levity was at an end. "No head?"

"Worse."

For a few moments he was silent. I felt him struggle with himself before he spoke. "Maybe you'd better move out, Ted," he said.

He was trying to help—I knew it. With a single swipe he had tried to push through the restraint that hung between us. He was my friend; he was putting out his hand to me. And I suppose I must have known what he'd suggest. But I could not accept it. It was not what I wanted to hear. "Jeff, I can't do that," I said tolerantly, as if he had missed my point. "We've only been living there five months. It cost me twenty-two thousand to build that place. We have to live in it at least a year under the GI loan.''

"Well, you know best, Ted." The smile dipped at me again.

"I just wanted to talk," I said, irritated at the ease with which he had given in. "I wanted to find out what you knew about this ghost business.''

"Not very much. Sondra knows more than I do.''

"I doubt that you would advise me to leave a house I had just built for no reason at all.''

"There seems to be some sort of jinx on the property, that's all. Whether there's a ghost or not I couldn't tell you," he replied, annoyed in his turn at the line the conversation was taking. "How does Ellen feel about this?''

"She doesn't know.''

"About the raccoon?''

"About anything.''

"You mean there's more?''

"There are noises—at night. . . .''

"I'd speak to Sondra if I were you. She's gone into this business much more deeply than I. When we first moved in, she used to hang around your land a good deal . . . just snooping . . . particularly after that cat was killed . . .'' He was having some difficulty with his words. It struck me that the conversation was causing him pain. He was showing his teeth now in a smiling grimace. Dangling an arm over the back of his chair he seemed loose to the point of collapse. We circled warily about his wife's name.

"Look, Jeff," I said, and took a breath, "about Sondra. . .''

Jeff cut me off with a wave of his hand. "Don't worry, I know Sondra.''

"Then you know there's nothing between us?''

"It's just her way of amusing herself. Sondra's a strange girl. She does the same thing with me. She flirts with me but we don't sleep together.'' He picked up his spoon and stared at it unseeingly. "It started when she became pregnant. After she had the boy, everything between us stopped. You knew we had a son? He's in a sanitarium in the Valley.''

"Can't you do anything?''

"Sure. Joyce Castle. I don't know what I'd have done without her."

"I mean divorce."

"Sondra won't divorce me. And I can't divorce her. No grounds." He shrugged as if the whole thing were of no concern at all to him. "What could I say? I want to divorce my wife because of the way she looks at other men? She's scrupulously faithful."

"To whom, Jeff? To you? To whom?"

"I don't know—to herself, maybe," he mumbled.

Whether with encouragement he might have gone on I don't know, for I cut him off. I sensed that with the enigmatic remark he was giving me my cue and that if I had chosen to respond to it he would have told me what I had asked him to lunch to find out—and all at once I was terrified; I did not want to hear it; I did not want to hear it at all. And so I laughed in a quiet way and said, "Undoubtedly, undoubtedly," and pushed it behind the closed door of my mind where I had stored all the impossibilities of the last months—the footsteps, the sounds in the night, the mutilated raccoon—or else, by recognizing them, go mad.

Jeff suddenly looked me full in the face; his cheeks were flushed, his teeth clamped together. "Look, Ted," he said, "can you take the afternoon off? I've got to go to the sanitarium and sign some papers. They're going to transfer the boy. He has fits of violence and does . . . awful things. He's finally gotten out of hand."

"What about Sondra?"

"Sondra's signed already. She likes to go alone to visit him. She seems to like to have him to herself. I'd appreciate it, Ted—the moral support. . . . You don't have to come in. You can wait in the car. It's only about thirty miles from here, you'd be back by dinnertime. . . ." His voice shook, tears clouded the yellow-stained whites of his eyes. He looked like a man with fever. I noticed how shrunken his neck had become as it revolved in his collar, how his head caved in sharply at the temples. He fastened one hand on my arm, like a claw. "Of course I'll go, Jeff," I said. "I'll call the office. They can get along without me for one afternoon."

He collected himself in an instant. "I'd appreciate it, Ted. I promise you it won't be so bad."

The sanitarium was in the San Fernando Valley, a complex of new stucco buildings on a newly seeded lawn. Everywhere there were signs that read, PLEASE KEEP OFF, FOLKS. Midget saplings stood in discs of powdery earth along the cement walks angling white and hot through the grass. On these walks, faithfully observing the signs, the inmates strolled. Their traffic, as it flowed somnolently from one avenue to another, was controlled by attendants stationed at intersections, conspicuous in white uniforms and pith helmets.

After a time it became unbearably hot in the car, and I climbed out. Unless I wished to pace in the parking lot among the cars, I had no choice but to join the inmates and their visitors on the walks. I chose a nearly deserted walk and went slowly toward a building that had a yard attached to it surrounded by a wire fence. From the slide and the junglegym in it I judged it to be for the children. Then I saw Jeff come into it. With him was a nurse pushing a kind of cart railed around like an oversized toddler. Strapped into it was "the boy."

He was human, I suppose, for he had all the equipment assigned to humans, yet I had the feeling that if it were not for the cart the creature would have crawled on his belly like an alligator. He had the eyes of an alligator too—sleepy, cold and soulless—set in a swarthy face and a head that seemed to run in a horizontal direction rather than the vertical, like an egg lying on its side. The features were devoid of any vestige of intelligence; the mouth hung open and the chin shone with saliva. While Jeff and the nurse talked, he sat under the sun, inert and repulsive.

I turned on my heel and bolted, feeling that I had intruded on a disgrace. I imagined that I had been given a glimpse of a diseased universe, the mere existence of which constituted a threat to my life; the sight of that monstrous boy with his cold, bestial eyes made me feel as if, by stumbling on this shame I somehow shared in it with Jeff. Yet I told myself that the greatest service I could do him was to pretend that I had seen nothing, knew nothing, and not place on him the hardship of talking about something which obviously caused him pain.

He returned to the car pale and shaky and wanting a drink. We stopped first at a place called Joey's on Hollywood Way. After that it was Cherry Lane on Vine Street, where a couple of girls propositioned us, and then a stop at the Brown Derby again, where I had left my car. Jeff downed the liquor in a joyless, businesslike way and talked to me in a rapid, confidential voice about a book he had just sold to Warner Brothers Studio for an exorbitant sum of money—trash in his opinion, but that was always the way—the parasites made it. Pretty soon there wouldn't be any good writers left: "There'll only be competent parasites and incompetent parasites." This was perhaps the third time we had had this conversation. Now Jeff repeated it mechanically, all the time looking down at the table where he was painstakingly breaking a red swizzle stick into ever tinier pieces.

When we left the restaurant, the sun had gone down, and the evening chill of the desert on which the city had been built had settled in. A faint pink glow from the vanished sun still lingered on the top of the Broadway Building. Jeff took a deep breath, then fell into a fit of coughing. "Goddamn smog," he said. "Goddamn city. I can't think of a single reason why I live here." He started toward his Daimler, tottering slightly.

"How about driving home with me?" I said. "You can pick your car up tomorrow."

He fumbled in the glove compartment and drew out a packet of small cigars. He stuck one between his teeth where it jutted unlit toward the end of his nose. "I'm not going home tonight, Ted friend," he said. "If you'll just drop me up the street at the Cherry Lane I'll remember you for life."

"Are you sure? I'll go with you if you want."

Jeff shook a forefinger at me archly. "Ted, you're a gentleman and a scholar. But my advice to you is to go home and take care of your wife. No, seriously. Take care of her, Ted. As for myself I shall go quietly to seed in the Cherry Lane Café." I had started toward my car when Jeff called out to me again. "I just want to tell you, Ted friend. . . . My wife was once just as nice as your wife. . . ."

I had gone no more than a mile when the last glimmer of light left the sky and night fell like a shutter. The sky above the neon of Sunset Boulevard turned jet black, and a sickly half-moon rose and was immediately obscured by thick fog that lowered itself steadily as I trav-

eled west, till at the foot of Clay Canyon it began to pat
my windshield with little smears of moisture.

The house was dark, and at first I thought Ellen must
have gone out, but then seeing her old Plymouth in the
driveway I felt the grip of a cold and unreasoning fear.
The events of the day seemed to crowd around and hover
at my head in the fog; and the commonplace sight of that
car, together with the blackness and silence of the house,
sent me into a panic as I ran for the door. I pushed at it
with my shoulder as if expecting it to be locked, but it
swung open easily and I found myself in the darkened
living room with no light anywhere and the only sound
the rhythm of my own short breathing. "Ellen!" I called
in a high, querulous voice I hardly recognized. "Ellen!" I
seemed to lose my balance; my head swam; it was as if
this darkness and silence were the one last iota that the
chamber of horrors in my mind could not hold, and the
door snapped open a crack, emitting a cloudy light that
stank of corruption, and I saw the landscape of my denial, like a tomb. It was the children's room. Rats nested
in the double bunks, mold caked the red wallpaper, and
in it an insane Spanish don hung by his neck from a dead
tree, his heels vlumping against the wall, his foppish
clothes rubbing as he revolved slowly in invisible currents
of bad air. And as he swung toward me, I saw his
familiar reptile eyes open and stare at me with loathing
and contempt.

I conceded: It is here and It is evil, and I have left my
wife alone in the house with It, and now she has been
sucked into that cold eternity where the dumb shades
store their plasms against an anguished centenary of
speech—a single word issuing from the petrified throat, a
scream or a sigh or a groan, syllables dredged up from a
lifetime of eloquence to slake the bottomless thirst of
living death.

And then a light went on over my head, and I found
myself in the hall outside the children's room. Ellen
was in her nightgown, smiling at me. "Ted? Why on
earth are you standing here in the dark? I was just taking
a nap. Do you want some dinner? Why don't you say
something? Are you all right?" She came toward me; she
seemed extraordinarily lovely; her eyes, a deeper blue
than Sondra's, looked almost purple; she seemed young

and slender again; her old serenity shone through like a restored beacon.

"I'm all right," I said hoarsely. "Are you sure you are?"

"Of course I am," she laughed. "Why shouldn't I be? I'm feeling much, much better." She took my hand and kissed it gaily. "I'll put on some clothes and then we'll have our dinner." She turned and went down the hall to our bedroom, leaving me with a clear view into the children's room. Though the room itself was dark, I could see by the hall light that the covers on the lower bunk had been turned back and that the bed had been slept in. "Ellen," I said. "Ellen, were you sleeping in the children's room?"

"Yes," she said, and I heard the rustle of a dress as she carried it from the closet. "I was in there mooning around, waiting for you to come home. I got sleepy and lay down on the bunk. What were *you* doing, by the way? Working late?"

"And nothing happened?"

"Why? What should have happened?"

I could not answer; my head throbbed with joy. It was over—whatever it was, it was over. All unknowing Ellen had faced the very heart of the evil and had slept through it like a child, and now she was herself again without having been tainted by the knowledge of what she had defeated; I had protected her by my silence, by my refusal to share my terror with this woman whom I loved. I reached inside and touched the light button; there was the brave red wallpaper scattered over with toys, the red-and-white curtains, the blue-and-red bedspreads. It was a fine room. A fine, gay room fit for children.

Ellen came down the hall in her slip. "Is anything wrong, Ted? You seem do distraught. Is everything all right at the office?"

"Yes, yes," I said. "I was with Jeff Sheffits. We went to see his boy in the asylum. Poor Jeff; he leads a rotten life." I told Ellen the whole story of our afternoon, speaking freely in my house for the first time since we had moved there. Ellen listened carefully as she always did, and wanted to know, when I had finished, what the boy was like.

"Like an alligator," I said with disgust. "Just like an alligator."

Ellen's face took on an unaccountable expression of private glee. She seemed to be looking past me into the children's room, as if the source of her amusement lay there. At the same moment I shivered in a breath of profound cold, the same clammy draft that might have warned me on my last birthday had I been other than what I am. I had a sense of sudden dehydration, as if all the blood had vanished from my veins. I felt as if I were shrinking. When I spoke, my voice seemed to come from a throat rusty and dry with disuse. "Is that funny?" I whispered.

And my wife replied, "Funny? Oh, no, it's just that I'm feeling so much better. I think I'm pregnant, Ted." She tipped her head to one side and smiled at me.

STEPHEN KING

The Boogeyman

"I came to you because I want to tell my story," the man on Dr. Harper's couch was saying. The man was Lester Billings from Waterbury, Connecticut. According to the history taken from Nurse Vickers, he was twenty-eight, employed by an industrial firm in New York, divorced, and the father of three children. All deceased.

"I can't go to a priest because I'm not Catholic. I can't go to a lawyer because I haven't done anything to consult a lawyer about. All I did was kill my kids. One at a time. Killed them all."

Dr. Harper turned on the tape recorder.

Billings lay straight as a yardstick on the couch, not giving it an inch of himself. His feet protruded stiffly over the end. Picture of a man enduring necessary humiliation. His hands were folded corpselike on his chest. His face was carefully set. He looked at the plain white composition ceiling as if seeing scenes and pictures played out there.

"Do you mean you actually killed them, or—"

"No." Impatient flick of the hand. "But I was responsible. Denny in 1967. Shirl in 1971. And Andy this year. I want to tell you about it."

Dr. Harper said nothing. He thought that Billings looked haggard and old. His hair was thinning, his complexion sallow. His eyes held all the miserable secrets of whiskey.

"They were murdered, see? Only no one believes that. If they would, things would be all right."

"Why is that?"

"Because . . ."

Billings broke off and darted up on his elbows, staring across the room. "What's that?" he barked. His eyes had narrowed to black slots.

"What's what?"

"That door."

"The closet," Dr. Harper said. "Where I hang my coat and leave my overshoes."

"Open it. I want to see."

Dr. Harper got up wordlessly, crossed the room, and opened the closet. Inside, a tan raincoat hung on one of four or five hangers. Beneath that was a pair of shiny galoshes. The New York *Times* had been carefully tucked into one of them. That was all.

"All right?" Dr. Harper said.

"All right." Billings removed the props of his elbows and returned to his previous position.

"You were saying," Dr. Harper said as he went back to his chair, "that if the murder of your three children could be proved, all your troubles would be over. Why is that?"

"I'd go to jail," Billings said immediately. "For life. And you can see into all the rooms in a jail. All the rooms." He smiled at nothing.

"How were your children murdered?"

"Don't try to jerk it out of me!"

Billings twitched around and stared balefully at Harper.

"I'll tell you, don't worry. I'm not one of your freaks strutting around and pretending to be Napoleon or explaining that I got hooked on heroin because my mother didn't love me. I know you won't believe me. I don't care. It doesn't matter. Just to tell will be enough."

"All right." Dr. Harper got out his pipe.

"I married Rita in 1965—I was twenty-one and she was eighteen. She was pregnant. That was Denny." His lips twisted in a rubbery, frightening grin that was gone in a wink. "I had to leave college and get a job, but I didn't mind. I loved both of them. We were very happy.

"Rita got pregnant just a little while after Denny was born, and Shirl came along in December of 1966. Andy came in the summer of 1969, and Denny was already dead by then. Andy was an accident. That's what Rita said. She said sometimes that birth-control stuff doesn't work. I think that it was more than an accident. Children tie a man down, you know. Women like that, especially when the man is brighter than they. Don't you find that's true?"

Harper grunted noncommittally.

"It doesn't matter, though. I loved him anyway." He said it almost vengefully, as it he had loved the child to spite his wife.

"Who killed the children?" Harper asked.

"The boogeyman," Lester Billings answered immediately. "The boogeyman killed them all. Just came out of the closet and killed them." He twisted around and grinned. "You think I'm crazy, all right. It's written all over you. But I don't care. All I want to do is tell you and then get lost."

"I'm listening," Harper said.

"It started when Denny was almost two and Shirl was just an infant. He started crying when Rita put him to bed. We had a two-bedroom place, see. Shirl slept in a crib in our room. At first I thought he was crying because he didn't have a bottle to take to bed anymore. Rita said don't make an issue of it, let it go, let him have it and he'll drop it on his own. But that's the way kids start off bad. You get permissive with them, spoil them. Then they break your heart. Get some girl knocked up, you know, or start shooting dope. Or they get to be sissies. Can you imagine waking up some morning and finding your kid—your *son*—is a sissy?

"After a while, though, when he didn't stop, I started putting him to bed myself. And if he didn't stop crying I'd give him a whack. Then Rita said he was saying 'light' over and over again. Well, I didn't know. Kids that little, how can you tell what they're saying. Only a mother can tell.

"Rita wanted to put in a nightlight. One of those wall-plug things with Mickey Mouse or Huckleberry Hound or something on it. I wouldn't let her. If a kid doesn't get over being afraid of the dark when he's little, he never gets over it.

"Anyway, he died the summer after Shirl was born. I put him to bed that night and he started to cry right off. I heard what he said that time. He pointed right at the closet when he said it. 'Boogeyman,' the kid says. 'Boogeyman, Daddy.'

"I turned off the light and went into our room and asked Rita why she wanted to teach the kid a word like that. I was tempted to slap her around a little, but I didn't. She said she never taught him to say that. I called her a goddamn liar.

"That was a bad summer for me, see. The only job I could get was loading Pepsi-Cola trucks in a warehouse, and I was tired all the time. Shirl would wake up and cry every night and Rita would pick her up and sniffle. I tell you, sometimes I felt like throwing them both out a window. Christ, kids drive you crazy sometimes. You could kill them.

"Well, the kid woke me at three in the morning, right on schedule. I went to the bathroom, only a quarter awake, you know, and Rita asked me if I'd check on Denny. I told her to do it herself and went back to bed. I was almost asleep when she started to scream.

"I got up and went in. The kid was dead on his back. Just as white as flour except for where the blood had . . . had sunk. Back of the legs, the head, the a—the buttocks. His eyes were open. That was the worst, you know. Wide open and glassy, like the eyes you see on a moosehead some guy put over his mantel. Like pictures you see of those gook kids over in Nam. But an American kid shouldn't look like that. Dead on his back. Wearing diapers and rubber pants because he'd been wetting himself again the last couple of weeks. Awful, I loved that kid."

Billings shook his head slowly, then offered the rubbery, frightening grin again. "Rita was screaming her head off. She tried to pick Denny up and rock him, but I wouldn't let her. The cops don't like you to touch any of the evidence. I know that—"

"Did you know it was the boogeyman then?" Harper asked quietly.

"Oh, no. Not then. But I did see one thing. It didn't mean anything to me then, but my mind stored it away."

"What was that?"

"The closet door was open. Not much. Just a crack. But I knew I left it shut, see. There's dry-cleaning bags in there. A kid messes around with one of those and bango. Asphyxiation. You know that?"

"Yes. What happened then?"

Billings shrugged. "We planted him." He looked morbidly at his hands, which had thrown dirt on three tiny coffins.

"Was there an inquest?"

"Sure." Billings eyes flashed with sardonic brilliance. "Some back-country fuckhead with a stethoscope and a black bag full of Junior Mints and a sheepskin from some cow college. Crib death, he called it! You ever hear such a pile of yellow manure? The kid was three years old!"

"Crib death is most common during the first year," Harper said carefully, "but that diagnosis has gone on death certificates for children up to age five for want of a better—"

"*Bullshit!*" Billings spat out violently.

Harper relit his pipe.

"We moved Shirl into Denny's old room a month after the funeral. Rita fought it tooth and nail, but I had the last word. It hurt me, of course it did. Jesus, I loved having the kid in with us. But you can't get overprotective. You make a kid a cripple that way. When I was a kid my mom used to take me to the beach and then scream herself hoarse. 'Don't go out so far! Don't go there! It's got an undertow! You only ate an hour ago! Don't go over your head!' Even to watch out for sharks, before God. So what happens? I can't even go near the water now. It's the truth. I get the cramps if I go near a beach. Rita got me to take her and the kids to Savin Rock once when Denny was alive. I got sick as a dog. I know, see? You can't overprotect kids. And you can't coddle yourself either. Life goes on. Shirl went right into Denny's crib. We sent the old mattress to the dump, though. I didn't want my girl to get any germs.

"So a year goes by. And one night when I'm putting Shirl into her crib she starts to yowl and scream and cry. 'Boogeyman, Daddy, boogeyman, boogeyman!'

"That threw a jump into me. It was just like Denny. And I started to remember about that closet door, open just a crack when we found him. I wanted to take her into our room for the night."

"Did you?"

"No." Billings regarded his hands and his face twitched. "How could I go to Rita and admit I was wrong? I *had* to be strong. She was always such a jellyfish . . . look how easy she went to bed with me when we weren't married."

Harper said, "On the other hand, look how easily *you* went to bed with *her*."

Billings froze in the act of rearranging his hands and slowly turned his head to look at Harper. "Are you trying to be a wise guy?"

"No, indeed," Harper said.

"Then let me tell it my way," Billings snapped. "I came here to get this off my chest. To tell my story. I'm not going to talk about my sex life, if that's what you expect. Rita and I had a very normal sex life, with none of that dirty stuff. I know it gives some people a charge to talk about that, but I'm not one of them."

"Okay," Harper said.

"Okay," Billings echoed with uneasy arrogance. He seemed to have lost the thread of his thought, and his eyes wandered uneasily to the closet door, which was firmly shut.

"Would you like that open?" Harper asked.

"No!" Billings said quickly. He gave a nervous little laugh. "What do I want to look at your overshoes for?

"The boogeyman got her, too," Billings said. He brushed at his forehead, as if sketching memories. "A month later. But something happened before that. I heard a noise in there one night. And then she screamed. I opened the door real quick—the hall light was on—and . . . she was sitting up in the crib crying and . . . something *moved*. Back in the shadows, by the closet. Something *slithered*."

"Was the closet door open?"

"A little. Just a crack." Billings licked his lips. "Shirl was screaming about the boogeyman. And something else that sounded like 'claws.' Only she said 'craws,' you know. Little kids have trouble with that 'l' sound. Rita ran upstairs and asked what the matter was. I said she got scared by the shadows of the branches moving on the ceiling."

"Crawset?" Harper said.

"Huh?"

"Crawset . . . closet. Maybe she was trying to say 'closet.' "

"Maybe," Billings said. "Maybe that was it. But I

don't think so. I think it was 'claws.' " His eyes began seeking the closet door again. "Claws, long claws." His voice had sunk to a whisper.

"Did you look in the closet?"

"Y-yes." Billings' hands were laced tightly across his chest, laced tightly enough to show a white moon at each knuckle.

"Was there anything in there? Did you see the—"

"*I didn't see anything!*" Billings screamed suddenly. And the words poured out, as if a black cork had been pulled from the bottom of his soul: "When she died I found her, see. And she was black. All black. She swallowed her own tongue and she was just as black as a nigger in a minstrel show and she was staring at me. Her eyes, they looked like those eyes you see on stuffed animals, all shiny and awful, like live marbles, and they were saying it got me, Daddy, you let it get me, you killed me, you helped it kill me . . ." His words trailed off. One single tear very large and silent, ran down the side of his cheek.

"It was a brain convulsion, see? Kids get those sometimes. A bad signal from the brain. They had an autopsy at Hartford Receiving and they told us she choked on her tongue from the convulsion. And I had to go home alone because they kept Rita under sedation. She was out of her mind. I had to go back to that house all alone, and I know a kid don't just get convulsions because their brain frigged up. You can scare a kid into convulsions. And I had to go back to the house where *it* was."

He whispered, "I slept on the couch. With the light on."

"Did anything happen?"

"I had a dream," Billings said. "I was in a dark room and there was something I couldn't . . . couldn't quite see, in the closet. It made a noise . . . a squishy noise. It reminded me of a comic book I read when I was a kid. *Tales from the Crypt,* you remember that? Christ! They had a guy named Graham Ingles; he could draw every god-awful thing in the world—and some out of it. Anyway, in this story this woman drowned her husband, see? Put cement blocks on his feet and dropped him into a quarry. Only he came back. He was all rotted and black-green and the fish had eaten away one of his eyes and there was seaweed in his hair. He came back and killed her. And when I woke up in the middle of the night, I thought that would be leaning over me. With claws . . . long claws . . ."

Dr. Harper looked at the digital clock inset into his desk. Lester Billings had been speaking for nearly half an hour. He said, "When your wife came back home, what was her attitude toward you?"

"She still loved me," Billings said with pride. "She still wanted to do what I told her. That's the wife's place, right? This women's lib only makes sick people. The most important thing in life is for a person to know his place. His . . . his . . . uh . . ."

"Station in life?"

"That's it!" Billings snapped his fingers. "That's it exactly. And a wife should follow her husband. Oh, she was sort of colorless the first four or five months after— dragged around the house, didn't sing, didn't watch the TV, didn't laugh. I knew she'd get over it. When they're that little, you don't get so attached to them. After a while you have to go to the bureau drawer and look at a picture to even remember exactly what they looked like.

"She wanted another baby," he added darkly. "I told her it was a bad idea. Oh, not forever, but for a while. I told her it was a time for us to get over things and begin to enjoy each other. We never had a chance do that before. If you wanted to go to a movie, you had to hassle around for a baby-sitter. You couldn't go into town to see the Mets unless her folks would take the kids, because my mom wouldn't have anything to do with us. Denny was born too soon after we were married, see? She said Rita was just a tramp, a common little corner-walker. Corner-walker is what my mom always called them. Isn't that a sketch? She sat me down once and told me diseases you can get if you went to a cor . . . to a prostitute. How your pri . . . your penis has just a little tiny sore on it one day and the next day it's rotting right off. She wouldn't even come to the wedding."

Billings drummed his chest with his fingers.

"Rita's gynecologist sold her on this thing called an IUD—interuterine device. Foolproof, the doctor said. He just stick it up the woman's . . . her place, and that's it. If there's anything in there, the egg can't fertilize. You don't even know it's there." He smiled at the ceiling with dark sweetness. "No one knows if it's there or not. And next year she's pregnant again. Some foolproof.

"No birth-control method is perfect," Harper said. "The pill is only ninety-eight percent. The IUD may be ejected by cramps, strong menstrual flow, and, in exceptional cases, by evacuation."

"Yeah. Or you can take it out."

"That's possible."

"So what's next? She's knitting little things, singing in the shower, and eating pickles like crazy. Sitting on my lap and saying things about how it must have been God's will. *Piss.*"

"The baby came at the end of the year after Shirl's death?"

"That's right. A boy. She named it Andrew Lester Billings. I didn't want anything to do with it, at least at first. My motto was she screwed up, so let her take care of it. I know how that sounds but you have to remember that I'd been through a lot.

"But I warmed up to him, you know it? He was the only one of the litter that looked like me, for one thing. Denny looked like his mother, and Shirl didn't look like anybody, except maybe my Grammy Ann. But Andy was the spitting image of me.

"I'd get to playing around with him in his playpen when I got home from work. He'd grab only my finger and smile and gurgle. Nine weeks old and the kid was grinning up at his old dad. You believe that?

"Then one night, here I am coming out of a drugstore with a mobile to hang over the kid's crib. Me! Kids don't appreciate presents until they're old enough to say thank you, that was always my motto. But there I was, buying him silly crap and all at once I realize I love him the most of all. I had another job by then, a pretty good one, selling drill bits for Cluett and Sons. I did real well, and when Andy was one, we moved to Waterbury. The old place had too many bad memories.

"And too many closets.

"That next year was the best one for us. I'd give every finger on my right hand to have it back again. Oh, the war in Vietnam was still going on, and the hippies were still running around with no clothes on, and the niggers were yelling a lot, but none of that touched us. We were on a quiet street with nice neighbors. We were happy," he summed up simply. "I asked Rita once if she wasn't worried. You know, bad luck comes in three and all that. She said not for us. She said Andy was special. She said God had drawn a ring around him."

Billings looked morbidly at the ceiling.

"Last year wasn't so good. Something about the house changed. I started keeping my boots in the hall because I didn't like to open the closet door anymore. I kept thinking: Well, what if it's in there? All crouched down and ready to spring the second I open the door? And I'd started thinking I could hear squishy noises, as if something black and green and wet was moving around in there just a little.

"Rita asked me if I was working too hard, and I started to snap at her, just like the old days. I got sick to my stomach leaving them alone to go to work, but I was glad to get out. God help me, I was glad to get out. I started to think, see, that it lost us for a while when we moved. It had to hunt around, slinking through the streets at night and maybe creeping in the sewers. Smelling for us. It took a year, but it found us. It's back. It wants Andy and it wants me. I started to think, maybe if you think of a thing long enough, and believe in it, it gets real. Maybe all the monsters we were scared of when we were kids, Frankenstein and Wolfman and Mummy, maybe they were real. Real enough to kill the kids that were supposed to have fallen into gravel pits or drowned in lakes or were just never found. Maybe . . ."

"Are you backing away from something, Mr. Billings?"

Billings was silent for a long time—two minutes clicked off the digital clock. Then he said abruptly; "Andy died in February. Rita wasn't there. She got a call from her father. Her mother had been in a car crash the day after New Year's and wasn't expected to live. She took a bus back that night.

"Her mother didn't die, but she was on the critical list for a long time—two months. I had a very good woman who stayed with Andy days. We kept house nights. And closet doors kept coming open."

Billings licked his lips. "The kid was sleeping in the room with me. It's funny, too. Rita asked me once when

he was two if I wanted to move him into another room.
Spock or one of those other quacks claims it's bad for
kids to sleep with their parents, see? Supposed to give
them traumas about sex and all that. But we never did it
unless the kid was asleep. And I didn't want to move
him. I was afraid to, after Denny and Shirl."

"But you did move him, didn't you?" Dr. Harper
asked.

"Yeah," Billings said. He smiled a sick, yellow smile.
"I did."

Silence again. Billings wrestled with it.

"I had to!" he barked finally. "I had to! It was all right
when Rita was there, but when she was gone, it started
to get bolder. It started . . ." He rolled his eyes at
Harper and bared his teeth in a savage grin. "Oh, you
won't believe it. I know what you think, just another
goofy for your casebook, I know that, but you weren't
there, you lousy smug head-peeper.

"One night every door in the house blew wide open.
One morning I got up and found a trail of mud and filth
across the hall between the coat closet and the front
door. Was it going out? Coming in? I don't know! Before Jesus, I just don't know! Records all scratched up
and covered with slime, mirrors broken . . . and the
sounds . . . the sounds . . ."

He ran a hand through his hair. "You'd wake up at
three in the morning and look into the dark and at first
you'd say, 'It's only the clock.' But underneath it you
could hear something moving in a stealthy way. But not
too stealthy, because it wanted you to hear it. A slimy
sliding sound like something from the kitchen drain. Or a
clicking sound, like claws being dragged lightly over the
staircase banister. And you'd close your eyes, knowing
that hearing it was bad, but if you *saw* it . . .

"And always you'd be afraid that the noises might stop
for a little while, and then there would be a laugh right
over your face and a breath of air like stale cabbage on
your face, and then hands on your throat."

Billings was pallid and trembling.

"So I moved him. I knew it would go for him, see.
Because he was weaker. And it did. That very first night
he screamed in the middle of the night and finally, when
I got up the cojones to go in, he was standing up in bed

and screaming, 'The boogeyman, Daddy . . . boogeyman
. . . wanna go wif Daddy, go wif Daddy.' " Billings'
voice had become a high treble, like a child's. His eyes
seemed to fill his entire face; he almost seemed to shrink
on the couch.

"But I couldn't," the childish breaking treble continued, "I couldn't. And an hour later there was a scream.
An awful, gurgling scream. And I knew how much I
loved him because I ran in, I didn't even turn on the
light, I ran, ran, *ran*, oh, Jesus God Mary, it had him; it
was shaking him, shaking him just like a terrier shakes a
piece of cloth and I could see something with awful
slumped shoulders and a scarecrow head and I could
smell something like a dead mouse in a pop bottle and I
heard . . ." He trailed off, and then his voice clicked
back into an adult range. "I heard it when Andy's neck
broke." Billings' voice was cool and dead. "It made a
sound like ice cracking when you're skating on a country
pond in winter."

"Then what happened?"

"Oh, I ran," Billings said in the same cool, dead voice.
"I went to an all-night diner. How's that for complete
cowardice? Ran to an all-night diner and drank six cups
of coffee. Then I went home. It was already dawn. I
called the police even before I went upstairs. He was
lying on the floor and staring at me. Accusing me. A tiny
bit of blood had run out of one ear. Only a drop, really.
And the closet door was open—but just a crack."

The voice stopped. Harper looked at the digital clock.
Fifty minutes had passed.

"Make an appointment with the nurse," he said. "In
fact, several of them. Tuesdays and Thursdays?"

"I only came to tell my story," Billings said. "To get it
off my chest. I lied to the police, see? Told them the kid
must have tried to get out of his crib in the night and . . .
they swallowed it. Course they did. That's just what it
looked like. Accidental, like the others. But Rita knew.
Rita . . . finally . . . knew . . ."

He covered his eyes with his right arm and began to
weep.

"Mr. Billings, there is a great deal to talk about," Dr.
Harper said after a pause. "I believe we can remove

some of the guilt you've been carrying, but first you have to want to get rid of it."

"Don't you believe I *do?*" Billings cried, removing his arm from his eyes. They were red, raw, wounded.

"Not yet," Harper said quietly. "Tuesday and Thursdays?"

After a long silence, Billings muttered, "Goddamn shrink. All right. All right."

"Make an appointment with the nurse, Mr. Billings. And have a good day."

Billings laughed emptily and walked out of the office quickly, without looking back.

The nurse's station was empty. A small sign on the desk blotter said: "Back in a Minute."

Billings turned and went back into the office. "Doctor, your nurse is—"

The room was empty.

But the closet door was open. Just a crack.

"So nice," the voice from the closet said. "So nice." The words sounded as if they might have come through a mouthful of rotted seaweed.

Billings stood rooted to the spot as the closet door swung open. He dimly felt warmth at his crotch as he wet himself.

"So nice," the boogeyman said as it shambled out.

It still held its Dr. Harper mask in one rotted, spade-claw hand.

WILLIAM F. NOLAN

Dark Winner

NOTE: The following is an edited transcript of a taped conversation between Mrs. Franklin Evans, resident of Woodland Hills, California, and Lt. Harry W. Lyle of the Kansas City Police Department.
Transcript is dated 12 July 1984. K.C. Missouri.

LYLE: . . . and if you want us to help you we'll have to know everything. When did you arrive here, Mrs. Evans?

MRS. EVANS: We just got in this morning. A stopover on our trip from New York back to California. We were at the airport when Frank suddenly got this idea about his past.

LYLE: What idea?

MRS. E: About visiting his old neighborhood . . . the school he went to . . . the house where he grew up . . . He hadn't been back here in twenty-five years.

LYLE: So you and your husband planned this . . . nostalgic tour?

MRS. E: Not *planned*. It was very abrupt . . . Frank seemed . . . suddenly . . . *possessed* by the idea.

LYLE: So what happened?

MRS. E: We took a cab out to Flora Avenue . . . to 31st . . . and we visited his old grade school. St. Vincent's Academy. The neighborhood is . . . well, I guess you know it's a slum area now . . . and the school is closed down, locked. But Frank found an open window . . . climbed inside . . .

LYLE: While you waited?

MRS. E: Yes—in the cab. When Frank came out he was all . . . upset . . . Said that he . . . Well, this sounds. . .

LYLE: Go on, please.

MRS. E: He said he felt . . . very *close* to his childhood while he was in there. He was ashen-faced . . . his hands were trembling.

LYLE: What did you do then?

MRS. E: We had the cab take us up 31st to the Isis Theatre. The movie house at 31st and Troost where Frank used to attend those Saturday horror shows they had for kids. Each week a new one . . . Frankenstein . . . Dracula . . . you know the kind I mean.

LYLE: I know.

MRS. E: It's a porno place now . . . but Frank bought a ticket anyway . . . went inside alone. Said he wanted to go into the balcony, find his old seat . . . see if things had changed . . .

LYLE: And?

MRS. E: He came out looking very shaken . . . saying it had happened again.

LYLE: *What* had happened again?

MRS. E: The feeling about being close to his past . . . to his childhood . . . As if he could—

LYLE: Could what, Mrs. Evans?

MRS. E: . . . step over the line dividing past and present . . . step back into his childhood. That's the feeling he said he had.

LYLE: Where did you go from the Isis?

MRS. E: Frank paid the cab . . . said he wanted to walk to his old block . . . the one he grew up on . . . 33rd and Forest. So we walked down Troost to 33rd . . . past strip joints and hamburger stands . . . I was nervous . . . we didn't . . . belong here . . . Anyway, we got to 33rd and walked down the hill from Troost to Forest . . . and on the way Frank told me how much he'd hated being small, being a child . . . that he could hardly wait to grow up . . . that to him childhood was a nightmare . . .

LYLE: Then why all the nostalgia?

MRS. E: It wasn't that . . . it was . . . like an *exorcism* . . . Frank said he'd been haunted by his childhood all the years we'd lived in California . . . This was an attempt to get rid of it . . . by facing it . . . seeing that it was really gone . . . that it no longer had any reality . . .

LYLE: What happened on Forest?

MRS. E: We walked down the street to his old address . . . which was just past the middle of the block . . . 3337 it was . . . a small, sagging wooden house . . . in terrible condition . . . but then, *all* the houses were . . . their screens full of holes . . . windows broken, trash in the yards . . . Frank stood in front of his house staring at it for a long time . . . and then he began repeating something . . . over and over.

LYLE: And what was that?

MRS. E: He said it . . . like a litany . . . over and over . . . "I hate you! . . . I hate you!"

LYLE: You mean, he was saying that to *you*?

MRS. E: Oh, no. Not to *me* . . . I asked him what he meant . . . and . . . he said he hated the child he once was, the child who had lived in that house.

LYLE: I see. Go on, Mrs. Evans.

MRS. E: Then he said he was going inside . . . that he *had* to go inside the house . . . but that he was afraid.

LYLE: Of what?

MRS. E: He didn't say of what. He just told me to wait out there on the walk. Then he went up on to the small wooden porch . . . knocked on the door. No one answered. Then Frank tried the knob . . . The door was unlocked . . .

LYLE: House was deserted?

MRS. E: That's right. I guess no one had lived there for a long while . . . All the windows were boarded up . . . and the driveway was filled with weeds . . . I started to move toward the porch, but Frank waved me back. Then he kicked the door all the way open with his foot, took a half-step inside, turned . . . and looked around at me . . . There was . . . a terrible fear in his eyes. I got a cold, chilled feeling all through my body—and I started toward him again . . . but he suddenly turned his back and went inside . . . the door closed.

LYLE: What then?

MRS. E: Then I waited. For fifteen . . . twenty minutes . . . a half hour . . . Frank didn't come out. So I went up to the porch and opened the door . . . . called to him. . .

LYLE: Any answer?

MRS. E: No. The house was like . . . a hollow cave . . . there were echoes . . . but no answer . . . I went inside . . . walked all through the place . . . into every room . . . but he wasn't there . . . Frank was gone.

LYLE: Out the back, maybe.

MRS. E: No. the back door was nailed shut. Rusted. It hadn't been opened for years.

LYLE: A window then.

MRS. E: They were all boarded over. With thick dust on the sills.

LYLE: Did you check the basement?

MRS. E: Yes, I checked the basement door leading down. It was locked, and the dust hadn't been disturbed around it.

LYLE: Then . . . just where the hell did he *go*?

MRS. E: I don't *know*, Lieutenant! . . . That's why I called you . . . why I came here . . . You've got to find Frank!

NOTE: Lt. Lyle did not find Franklin Evans. The case was turned over to Missing Persons—and, a week later, Mrs. Evans returned to her home in California. The first night back she had a dream, a nightmare. It disturbed her severely. She could not eat, could not sleep properly; her nerves were shattered. Mrs. Evans then sought psychiatric help. What follows is an excerpt from a taped session with Dr. Lawrence Redding, a licensed psychiatrist with offices in Beverly Hills, California.

Transcript is dated 3 August 1984. Beverly Hills.

REDDING: And where were you. . . ? In the dream, I mean.

MRS. E.: My bedroom. In bed, at home. It was as if I'd just been awakened . . . I looked around me—and everything was normal . . . the room exactly as it always is . . . Except for *him* . . . the boy standing next to me.

REDDING: Did you recognize this boy?

MRS. E: No.

REDDING: Describe him to me.

MRS. E: He was . . . nine or ten . . . a *horrible* child . . . with a cold hate in his face, in his eyes. He had on a black sweater with holes in each elbow. And knickers

. . . the kind that boys used to wear . . . and he had on black tennis shoes . . .

REDDING: Did he speak to you?

MRS. E: Not at first. He just . . . smiled at me . . . and that smile was so . . . so *evil*! . . . And then he said . . . that he wanted me to know he'd won at last . . .

REDDING: Won what?

MRS. E: That's what I asked him . . . calmly, in the dream . . . I asked him what he'd won. And he said . . . oh, My God . . . he said . . .

REDDING: Go on, Mrs. Evans.

MRS. E: . . . that he'd won Frank! . . . that my husband would *never* be coming back . . . that he, the boy, had him now . . . forever! . . . I screamed—and woke up. And, instantly, I remembered something.

REDDING: What did you remember?

MRS. E: Before she died . . . Frank's mother . . . sent us an album she'd saved . . . of his childhood . . . photos . . . and report cards . . . He never wanted to look at it, stuck the album away in a closet . . . After the dream, I got it out, looked through it until I found . . .

REDDING: Yes . . . ?

MRS. E: A photo I'd remembered. Of Frank . . . at the age of ten . . . standing in the front yard on Forest . . . He was smiling . . . that same, awful smile . . . and . . . he wore a dark sweater with holes in each elbow . . . and knickers . . . black tennis shoes. It was . . . the *same* boy exactly—the younger self Frank had always hated . . . I *know* what happened in that house now.

REDDING: Then tell me.

MRS. E: The boy was . . . waiting there . . . inside that awful, rotting dead house . . . waiting for Frank to come back . . . all those years . . . waiting there to claim him—because . . . *he* hated the man that Frank had become as much as Frank hated the child he'd once been . . . and the boy was *right*.

REDDING: Right about what, Mrs. Evans?

MRS. E: About winning. He took all those years, but . . . He won . . . and . . . Frank lost.

JACK L. CHALKER

No Hiding Place

It was a sleepy little river town, sitting on the silt bed beside the mighty Mississippi. The town of Newtownards, Louisiana, was a waystop for the steamers and barges that plowed the mighty river; it had been a refueling and rest stop on the waterway to New Orleans or up toward Vicksburg since 1850. It was a very small place, and the town hadn't changed much in the century-plus since the first river steamer piled on wood for the long journey north.

The people were a quiet sort, with little ambition and with that sense of peace and tranquillity that only an isolated community atmosphere can give. This isolation gave security of sorts as well, for the town had not been settled by the almost legendary Bayou folk of the surrounding lush, tropical swamplands, but by hardy capitalists who picked their location on the river for profit.

The Bayou people had become more legend than real by the twentieth century. No one alive could remember seeing any of the quiet, backward swamp folk for a long, long time, and even those who claimed experience with the mysterious backwater people were only half believed. Certainly the Bayou's secretive inhabitants were no longer any threat to the community welfare and, at best, were merely the poor people out in the sticks.

A town like Newtownards was a difficult place to keep a secret. The art of gossip had fallen into disuse simply because there was nothing the locals could whisper to each other that wasn't already common knowledge. Crime, too, was a rarity, and the town kept only two local policemen, two old war veterans whose major duty was checking the more deserted areas for hoboes and other itinerants who might be drifting through and looking for a free place to sleep. For anything more serious, a state police barracks ten miles to the south kept watch on several small towns in the swamp, which was a favorite hiding place for escaped fugitives. But since Newtownards had little to offer men on the run, being the most public of places, the only troopers who had visited the place officially came for ceremonial functions.

The town, as did all small communities, had its history, and it was especially colorful. Rackland's Maurauders had ridden through, back when the country was split and Grant was mapping his strategy, and had set up an observation post in the town's one mansion—deserted Hankin House, empty since the founder of the town and builder of his castle had fled, insane. Colonel Rackland's valiant party used the hilltop to look for any signs of Farragut's ships heading up the river toward Vicksburg, and for any signs of Yankee soldiers lurking in the swamps to the west. There, too, they had met the fate that had haunted Hankin House since 1850, when, after only three months in his new home, Josiah Hankin had suddenly gone mad and attempted to kill everyone nearby, while babbling of a horror in the house.

The old juju woman had come after that. She had originally warned Hankin not to build on the knoll, for, she said, a demon lived within the hill and would take all who disturbed its rest. She had not seen the thing, of course. But her grandmother's people, in 1808, had declared the hill a sacred place of worship, where weird, bacchanalian rites had been carried out by ex-slaves who lived in the Bayou. Now, the juju woman had warned, Josiah had paid the price, and so would all others who disturbed the demon who lived in the hill.

Yes, Hankin House was the town's true pride. In an open society, people, being human, still must talk of something, and the locals had talked about the old house for better than a century. The townspeople didn't really *believe* in *Obi* and voodoo demons living in hills, but they remembered, too, that Josiah had been the first, not the last, to meet a strange end.

Colonel Rackland and two of his men had died by fire

in that house, without a single part of the house itself being even singed. The lone survivor of his command had come down the hill a white-haired, raving maniac. Fearful townspeople had investigated, but found nothing but three bodies and a still, ever so still, empty house.

The house was vacant, then, when Farragut finally *did* move his force up the Mississippi. It had remained a still, silent, yet expectant spectator while the town wept at the news that at a place called Appomattox the world had ended. The house had slept while pioneers traveled the mighty river in large steamboats, moving beneath the hill on which the house stood.

Then in March of 1872, on that very same day that U.S. Grant was taking the oath of office for his second and tragic presidential term, Philip Cannon bought the house. Cannon had profited from the war, and even more from its aftermath. But his shady past seemed to be so very close behind him that he was always running, running from his past, his shadow, and himself.

He was running west when the ship he was on docked for fuel in Newtownards, and he had seen the mansion sitting majestically above the town. "Fit for a king," Phil Cannon thought, and despite the anxiety of the townspeople, he located the last Hankin relative, paid her off, and the house was his.

Cannon spent lavishly, building up, refurbishing, until the twenty-two-year-old house looked as if it had been built the day before, a shining monument to Josiah's taste for Gothic architecture and to Phil Cannon's desire to feel like a king.

And Cannon loved it. He became, by virtue of the smell of money, a very big man in Newtownards, and no one asked about his past. People with noble pasts seldom go to live and work in a tiny town in the midst of a swamp.

Then, one day, almost exactly two years after Cannon had moved in, the big man failed to put in an expected appearance with his usual pomp, strutting as he always did with his little saloon-girl on his arm.

It was not just the townspeople's dislike of the unexpected, nor their concern for the legends, that made them immediately investigate. Many had shady dealings with Cannon and they grew panicky at an unscheduled disappearance. So, a group of businessmen walked up the road to Hankin House and knocked. When they received no answer, they tried the door and found it unlocked.

The crystal chandelier Phil Cannon had imported from Spain tinkled as the hot wind blew off the river and through the open door into the main dining room.

They found *her* head, eventually, taken off her slender shoulders as if by a giant razor. They never did find Phil Cannon's.

As was the case when Josiah went mad, the servants were nowhere to be found. There was speculation that the juju people had a firm hold on those servants and that they might have done away with Cannon and his mistress as revenge for some of Cannon's shady dealings with the swamp folk. But no one ever found the servants, and the cleavage was too clean to have been the work of any sword or knife.

And so it was that Hankin House was closed again, and more generations passed as the silent old house looked on. The original panic and talk of a juju hex had caused some townspeople to cry out that the building be razed to the ground. But since Cannon's will left the old place to his local business syndicate, such talk was quickly suppressed. Besides, by the time talk became action everybody was convinced that the servants and the Bayou people had done the deed.

Hadn't they?

In 1898 the battleship *Maine* sank in Havana harbor, and America for the first time since the War of 1812 went to war a sovereign nation. One of the eager volunteers had been Robert Hornig, a youthful captain with the Fifth Cavalry Brigade. He had fought in Cuba, was wounded, and then returned. He chose as his point of disembarkation both from the war and the military the port of New Orleans, for he was a man with no family save the army. Now that he no longer had even the army, he was a man without a direction—only a discharge and a limp.

When he stopped off on the river trail westward at Newtownards he was immediately struck by the charm and simplicity of the town. He was also fascinated by the old deserted house atop the hill, and this fascination

grew when inquiries to the locals brought forth blood-
curdling stories.

The house cost him a bit more than he actually had, as
all important acquisitions do, but it was worth every
penny to Captain Hornig. A lonely man, he loved the old
place as a man would love his bride.

After a while, he was no longer alone. An orderly
named Murray, who had also faced the test of battle in
Cuba, passed through, as much a drifter as the captain
had been. Here was the man, thought Hornig, who would
at least temper the loneliness and who might also aid in
financing the renovation of the house. Although the captain was a crusty sort, the young orderly liked both the
man and the town, and assented.

They found Hornig at the bottom of the grand stairway, his body sprawled out on a rug in the entrance hall.
Murray's body was in the dining room; he had been shot
through the heart with a pistol, a pistol never found. The
coroner's verdict of a murder-suicide did not fit all the
facts, of course. But what alternatives were there? At
least, this time, both victims still retained their heads.

Again the house was shut up and remained so until
1929, when Roger Meredith moved into the house with
his wife and daughter. A heavy stock-market investor, he
had selected Newtownards and the house carefully as a
quiet and peaceful place in which to bring up his child
and to escape the hustle and bustle of Wall Street, where
his services were no longer required. He was quite a
comfortable millionaire and originally a Louisiana boy as
well, and so the townspeople offered little protest at his
arrival.

When little Carol Meredith was observed—bloody and
hysterical, crawling up Main Street not seven weeks after
the family had moved in, her face full of buckshot—they
said it was another murder-suicide, the last act of a man
driven mad by the collapse of the stock market. As
usual, the coroner's jury did not bother with details.
How could a small man like Meredith ever throw his wife
out of the west window? How did he, himself, inflict the
merciless blow to the head the doctor stated had killed
him? And what of the little girl, lying in the arms of
storekeeper Tom Moore, life oozing out of her, who

turned her face to his and, with a queer, maniacal smile, whispered as she died: "Daddy shot it!"

World War II came, and passed, and the house remained empty. No longer did fancy riverboats ply the Mississippi at the foot of the hill, but the town remained. Freight traffic had increased, and those ships still needed fuel.

Wars, hot and cold, passed, and generations came and went. The old house sat silently, as always, its mysterious demon undisturbed. Until one day . . .

August was a bad month for Newtownards. It was horribly hot and as humid as the air and the laws of physics would allow. Most people at midday would close their stores and stretch out for a nap while the intolerable heat of the day dissipated. But in the schoolyard, under the shade of a tall, old tree, there was activity.

"I am not yella!" the red-haired, stocky boy of about fourteen yelled to the tall, angular leader of the group of boys, "but nobody's stupid enough to commit suicide, Buzz Murdock!"

The tall, blond-haired teenager towered over the object of derision. "Ya must be, ya half-Yankee!" Buzz Murdock replied haughtily, and not without a deliberate sneer. He was playing to his audience now, the group of young teenage boys who formed the Swamp Rats, a *very* exclusive little club.

Ricky Adherne, the redhead, bristled, his face becoming so red and contorted with anger and rage that his freckles almost faded to invisibility. The "half-Yankee" tag had always stung him. Could he help it if his no-account pa had been from New York?

"Lissen," said Murdock, "we don't allow no chickens in the Rats." The other boys made clucking sounds, like those of a chicken, in support of their leader. "If'n ya caint prove t'us that ya ain't no stupid chicken, ya bettah git along home riaot now!" continued the leader.

"Lissen yuhself!" Adherne snapped back. "I don't mind no test o' bravery, but jumpin' inna rivah with a sacka liam is a shoah way ta diah quick!"

Murdock put on his best sneer. "Hah! Weall wouldn't be so afeared. We's Swamp Rats and ya ain't ouah type. Git along home, kid, afore we beat on ya!"

Adherne saw his opening, and he dived in. "Hah! Big ol' Swamp Rats! If ya *really* wanted a test o' bravery—why, you'n me, Murdock, we'd go upta ol' Hankin House at midniat and sit 'till morn!"

Murdock was in a bind and he knew it. He'd have to go through with this or he would lose face before his followers—*that*, he was smart enough to figure out. But, damn it all, why'd this little punk have to pick Hankin House?

It was 11:22 P.M. when town policemen Charles "Scully" Wills and Johnny Schmidt got into their patrol car—actually a loaned state police car with a radio connection to the Hawkinston barracks in case of emergencies—to make the rounds for the first time that night. As they drove toward their last checkpoint, Hankin House, Schmidt thought he spied a bluish gleam moving about in one of the old structure's upper windows. But when he blinked and looked again the light was gone. He mentioned his suspicions to his partner, but the older cop had seen nothing; and, when the light failed to reappear, Schmidt told himself he was just tired and seeing things in the night.

The two men made an extra check of the seals on the doors and windows of the old house, though, just to be on the safe side. Nothing human could get by those seals without breaking at least one of them, this they knew.

When all the seals proved to be intact, they left the old, dark place for town and coffee. They'd make their rounds again in about three hours. Both men settled back to another dull, routine night.

It would not be dull or routine.

There was a sound like a hoot-owl, and Ricky Adherne advanced on the little party of boys waiting in the gully near the roadside. Hankin House looked down, grim and foreboding, in the distance.

Murdock was scared, but he dared not show it. Adherne, too, was scared, the sight of the old house by moonlight being even more frightening to him than was his previous all-consuming fear that his mother would check his room and discover he wasn't there. Throughout the evening he had mentally cursed himself for suggesting this stupid expedition, and he'd convinced himself that the Swamp Rats weren't worth the risk. But he still had to go, he knew. His personal honor was at stake. Newtownards was an open town, and he had to live in it, and with himself as well.

The chirping of a cricket chorus and the incessant hum of june bugs flying to and fro in the hot night air were the only sounds as the small party of boys, Murdock and Adherne in the lead, walked up the road to the old manor house. Suddenly they saw headlights turn onto the road and barely jumped into the tall grass by the roadside in time to miss the gaze of Scully and Schmidt as they rode up to the old house. Minutes passed like hours, but no boy made a move. Finally, after an eternity, the car returned and sped back down the hill.

"Man! That was *real* close!" Adherne exclaimed in an excited whisper.

"Shaddup, punk!" called Murdock, who felt like running himself but who, also, had to live in Newtownards.

The old house sat dark and silent as the group reached the tall front steps.

"Now how d'we git in, smaht guy?" Murdock demanded, believing he had discovered a way out of this mess. But Adherne, now pressed on by Murdock's sarcasm and the will to get an unpleasant thing over and done with, was already up on the porch.

"If'n we kin jest git this here crossboahd off'n the doah, we kin git in thisaway," he whispered, not quite understanding why he spoke so low.

Together the frightened boys pried off the wooden crossbar whose nails had been rusted and weakened by weather for better than thirty years. After much tugging the board gave, and one Swamp Rat fell backward, board in hand, with a yelp.

A blue flickering light shone in an upstairs window. Suddenly it froze.

"It's open," one boy whispered huskily.

Murdock swallowed hard and drew up all the courage he could muster. He suddenly pushed ahead of the redhaired boy, who stood statuelike, peering into the black gloom. "Me first, punk," he snapped, but the tall leader wondered why his voice sounded so strange in his ears.

First Murdock, then Adherne, entered the blackness.

The blue light in the upstairs window, unseen by any of the waiting boys encamped below, moved away from the window. And the climax to a strange quest, spanning not one century but more than a score, was close at hand.

2

As the small scoutship lifted from the landing grid and rose into the sky above the peculiar red-green surface of the planet men called Conolt IV, a signal flashed in a larger, more formidable, and very alien vessel hiding in the darkness of space. As the tiny Terran scout pulled free of the planet's thick atmosphere, the alien ship's commander gave a crisp order and set out after his prey.

The scoutship pilot, a giant Irishman named Feeny, spotted the dark raider just after leaving radio range of Conolt IV's spaceport. He punched a button on the ship's instrument panel, where myriad dials and switches lay before him.

"Doctor, I'm afraid we've been had," he said, his voice calm and smooth. Intelligence men did not break under pressure and survive.

In the aft compartment, Alei Mofad, a cherubic, balding man in his late sixties who was known as *the* scientific genius of his age, jerked up with a start.

"How far, Feeny?" he asked in a level voice.

"About twelve thousand, Doctor, and closing fast. Too damned fast."

Mofad turned and examined the small cabinet which, aside from the bunk and his own person, was the only other thing in the compartment.

"Feeny, how much time have we got?"

"Ten, twelve minutes at the most. Sorry, Doc. Somebody made one *hell* a slip here."

"Yes, yes, I know, but no use crying over bad security now. I shall require at least fifteen. Can you give that much to me?"

"I can try," the pilot replied dryly, and he began to do more than try. As Mofad worked feverishly to connect his equipment to the ship's power supply, Feeny began trying every maneuver in the book.

The alien spacecraft swung around out of the planetary

shadow and shot a tractor beam, its purple glow slicing through the icy darkness of space. Feeny saw the beam only a fraction of a second before it was upon him, and his split-second reflexes urged the tiny scoutship upward, evading the powerful magnetic beam by inches.

The enemy craft swung around again, and for the second time shot out a purple ray from its bow tubes. Again Feeny dodged by inches, banking left and downward as if the two ships were master fencers, with one swordsman now disarmed but yet agile enough and determined enough to avoid his deadly opponent's thrusts.

Feeny knew he could not keep up the game indefinitely, but he was determined to give his illustrious charge as much time as was required. He dodged, banked, dropped up and down, all the time playing for Mofad's precious, essential seconds, while at the same time sending out a distress signal to the cruiser that should have been waiting nearby to pick them up, but was actually a hulk of twisted metal, the loser of an earlier duel with the enemy craft. Twelve minutes passed . . . thirteen . . . fifteen . . . and then the goal was passed.

Eighteen minutes after the game had begun, it ended, when Feeny's lightning reflexes were no longer quite quick enough, and he began to tire. A tractor beam lashed out, enveloping the scoutship in a purple glow, pulling the tiny craft slowly toward the greater ship in the grip of the magnetic field.

"Doctor, they've got us," Feeny called into the ship's intercom. "Are you ready?"

"Yes, Feeny, I'm leaving now," came the physicist's reply, a tinge of sadness in his voice as he thought of the fate to which the faithful pilot had to be abandoned. "Do you want me to do anything, Doc?" Feeny called back.

"You've done enough, but yet you must destroy this machine. You know the detonator." Then, more softly, "Good-bye, Feeny."

Alei Mofad reached up on top of the plasticine cabinet and removed a small box. He stepped into the cabinet then, and vanished.

The two ships collided with a *thunk* which reverberated down the corridor of the smaller ship. Feeny rose from his pilot's chair and began the walk back to the aft compartment, struggling under the excessive gravity taken

on when the two ships had linked and began to roll. But
he was too slow. The midsection airlock blew open before him, separating him from the precious cargo in the
aft compartment. He stopped and stood straight, erect.
After all, one died with dignity.

A creature entered the ship, a weird giant thing that
could never have been spawned on earth. Humanoid was
the closest to Terran that you could get, descriptively, for
it stood erect, towering a full seven feet, on two thick,
stiff legs. But it wore a chitinous exoskeleton that, as
natural body armor, was as strong as sheet metal, yet
half-transparent, so that the viewer could get a glimpse
of veins, muscle tissue, and even the creature's brain.
The two very long arms differed from one another. The
right one, which ended in a five-digit hand whose fingers
were extremely long and triple-jointed, bore a pistol,
aimed at Feeny's head. The left arm, however, ended in
a massive set of razor-sharp pincers—the Sirian ceremonial claw, used as a two-fingered hand or used in many
Sirian rituals, including the mating ceremony of the species.

Colonel Rifixl Treeg, Hereditary Colonel of Empire
Intelligence, fixed one of his stalk-like eyes on Feeny,
the other on the door to the aft compartment. There
could be no outward expression intelligible to a Terran in
that face that resembled the head of a lobster, nor any
sound, for the Sirians communicated—it was believed—
telepathically. The alien colonel motioned with his pistol
for Feeny to move back into the pilot's cabin.

Feeny complied, staring in fascination at his first Sirian.
Only a few Terrans, such as those in the original discovery expeditions like Mofad, had *ever* seen them. The
Sirians ruled a great stellar empire of allied and vastly
different races. They did not fight wars; they directed
them.

Feeny decided on a desperate gamble. If he could
surprise the Sirian, at least long enough to run to the far
wall and throw the generator-feed switches, it was possible that he might be able to blow up the ship.

Treeg watched the Terran captive almost halfheartedly;
this was not the prize he was after. As he stepped backward, another member of the Sirian crew entered, partially blocking the colonel's view of Feeny. Feeny saw his
chance and dived for the switches. The Sirian who had

just entered swung around and fired his pistol at the advancing Feeny. The Terran lurched back with a cry and was instantly consumed by the white-hot pistol fire. Only a burning heap on the control-room floor betrayed the fact that anyone named Feeny had ever existed.

Treeg was annoyed at the killing; he preferred his prisoners alive for interrogation, as his orders specified. There had been talk of late that the old colonel was getting too old for his duties, and this slip would not help his position with the High Command. Still, he was more than annoyed at what he found in the aft compartment—or, rather, what he did not find.

There was a bunk and a plasticine cabinet of dubious purpose. Nothing else. Alei Mofad was not on the ship. Treeg went over to the cabinet and examined it with both eyes. Apparently the only moving part was a small relay on the side which flipped up and down, up and down. Atop the cabinet were two small boxes, each without any writing—just thin little boxes with two buttons, one red and one green: purpose, also unknown.

The law of the survival of the fittest breeds certain characteristics common to all races who struggle to the top, and Treeg exercised one of those characteristics—he beat his fist in frustration against the compartment wall. He then turned and stormed out.

In every age there is a special one, a genius who can see beyond the horizon—Copernicus, Edison, Einstein, and the like being prime examples.

And Alei Mofad.

An explorer and trader in his youth, as he approached middle age, a wealthy and industrious man still full of life, he had built a great laboratory on the quiet Federation to experiment. His findings became the cornerstone in the later fight between his own people, the Trans-Terran Federation, and the other giant stellar empire he had aided in discovering, the Sirian League. The Terran-Sirian War of the Empires was a bitter, no-quarter clash between two equally ruthless and ambitious centers of power, born out of jealousy and greed and fed on misunderstanding and hate—too much alike in the way they thought to ever get along.

And in the midst of the conflict, Alei Mofad broke the fabric of time itself.

His original machine was still in his laboratory on Conolt IV, along with his notes and specifications. His newer, larger, model which Terran Command insisted be brought to Terra itself for its first public demonstration had been loaded secretly on a small scout. Then the doctor and one intelligence man had attempted to sneak off planet without arousing any curiosity, to link up with a cruiser off the sixth planet in the system. But Sirian allies could pass for Terrans, and their spies on Conolt had blocked the attempt. So Terran Control Center was left with just one clue, one hope of obtaining the crucial formulae that would make the Mofad computations on Conolt IV make sense. Mofad had that in his brain—but he had stated that, if he could escape, he would somehow place the location at the Terran test site, Code Louesse 155. They would use the original machine to retrieve it—and, hopefully, Mofad. But, the formulae were hidden in time itself. They knew where, but not *when*.

For the machines were still imperfect. The day would come when whole armies would be transported across space and time to the enemy's heartland in the remote past, then brought up to the present, an indetectable army of occupation.

Rifixl Treeg, too, had a time machine and the controls to make use of it. But he knew neither where nor when.

"The physics is quite beyond me," said the Empire's top physicist. "Mofad is someone centuries ahead of us all. However, the Terran pilot's failure to destroy the cabinet after Mofad escaped in it gives us more information than you might suspect, my dear Colonel."

"Terran intelligence knows what's happened, too, by now, and they have a head start," Treeg replied. "What can we do? You've already told me you can't duplicate the thing without Mofad's basic formula, and we can't get the formula without Mofad. It seems that he's beaten us."

"Pessimism simply will not do in an intelligence officer, Colonel Treeg. I merely told you that we could not duplicate the thing; I never said we could not *run* it."

"Ah!" exclaimed the colonel, and then he suddenly drooped again. "But we still don't know where or when.

Terran intelligence at least knows *where*, although, as you tell me, the thing's too unpredictable for them to know *when*."

"Where is not a problem," replied the physicist. "Obviously the *where* requires a setting. Since Mofad wasn't there to unset it, the machine will transport you to the right place, never fear. Your own intelligence reports show the original test site to be in the northern and western hemisphere of Terra herself. Since I credit the doctor with foresight, that's where anyone using the machine will go. At this point we are even with Terran intelligence. But now we go ahead of them."

Treeg suddenly stood extremely erect, the equivalent of a start in a race that could not physically sit down.

"You see," the scientist continued, "Mofad also had the time *period* set. The machine will follow through there, as well, but not exactly."

Treeg slumped. "Why not exactly, if—"

"Because," the scientist went on in the manner of a professor lecturing a schoolboy, "the machine is imperfect. It will transmit within, roughly, two centuries, I'd say. The disguised control panel here," he said, pointing to a spot on the machine, "is elementary. We can regulate the time sequence much better than could old Mofad, who had to go blind into a two-century span. We could make short jumps in time, with our agent searching the immediate vicinity for traces of Mofad. Since an agent, friend or foe, could appear only minutes after Mofad—even if that agent left days later by our standards—he would have to hide the thing fast. Was there any sort of transcribing equipment missing from the scoutship?"

"Yes," replied Treeg, "a minirecorder. You mean—"

"Precisely. That recorder is somewhere very near the point of emergence, and it contains what we must have. Terran intelligence does not have our present dials, so it will have hundreds of centuries to search. We may yet beat them. Who will you send?"

Treeg was still smarting from the lashing given him by the High Command for allowing Mofad to escape. There had been thoughts all around of retirement.

"Me," he said.

*   *   *

The two Sirians stood by the machine. The physicist began: "The device is based on a geographic point of reference. Mofad in his haste left the two portable units behind, an inexcusable blunder, but one very fortunate from our viewpoint." He handed Treeg a small box that was surprisingly heavy for its three-by-five-inch size and that only contained the red and green buttons which had interested Treeg when he had discovered them.

"This is the portable triggering device. When you want to go, we set the machine, and you step inside. Then you press the green button all the way down, and the machine transforms you into some sort of energy form we don't yet understand and resolidifies you on a preset point determined by the cabinet setting. When you wish to return, you need only return to your exact point of emergence into the other time and place and press the red button down all the way. This will reverse the process. I don't pretend to understand it—this is what we need in the way of Mofad's formulae, that mathematics which will tell us the how of the thing. Let's say that the machine somehow rips the fabric of time and place, which are linked, and that the tear is mended when you reactivate the device, thereby restoring you to your point of origin.

"I advise you to mark your point of emergence on Terra carefully, though. You must return to it exactly or you will remain where and when you are. Are you ready?"

Treeg nodded, and with an effort squeezed his rigid body into the upright cabinet. The scientist examined the control panel. "I have preset it—I think—for the earliest possible time. I will count down. When I say *Now!* you are to press the green button. All right. Five . . . four . . . three . . . two . . . one. . . . *Now!*"

Treeg pressed the button.

The first thought he had was that there had been no sensation whatever. It bothered him; this tampering with time should not be so quiet nor so sudden. But—one moment he was squeezed uncomfortably in that cabinet on Sirius; the next moment he was atop a lonely hillside surrounded by lush, green swamp. Below the hill a large river, glittering in the sunset, flowed its way past the spot. The time was 1808, forty-one years before a man named Josiah Hankin would found a town on the flats below, a town he would name after the Belfast street on which he had been born—Newtownards.

Treeg was overcome by the wildness of the place and by the idea that he was the first of his race to travel in time. The air, he noted, was sweet and moist, and it was almost as hot here as his own native world. He stood there on the hilltop, a grotesque statue silhouetted in the setting sun, and thought. He had all the time in the world. . .

He heard a rustling in the undergrowth.

Four men crept through the dense marsh grass, looking not at the hill and its weird occupant but out at the river. Two were old-time pirates who had fought with Laffite years before and had then changed occupations to become Bayou smugglers, finding the new line of work just as profitable but less risky.

The other two were renegade slaves, who joined the Bayou settlement as a sanctuary where they could relax, free from the fear of the law in a society where it was not race, but brains and muscle, that made a man a man. All four of them loved the art of smuggling, taking pride in it in the same way as a jeweler would pride himself in his skillful work.

Treeg had no ears with which to hear the men, and so, oblivious to the danger below, he began walking down the slope toward the base of the hill. He had decided that Mofad would surely have made traces in the virgin land if this was indeed the correct time, but he had a duty to perform, and all the time he would ever need. So he decided to check all the same. In the military caste society of his birth the first rule taught every youngling was "Never underestimate your enemy."

"Damn and double that stinkin' Joe Walsh," growled Ned Harrell as his eyes strained to catch a glimpse of a flatboat on the great expanse of the river. "If that pig's double-crossed me I'll—Hey! Did you hear that?" A crash and crackle of underbrush sounded nearby.

Carl, a giant black with a fugitive's reflexes, had already jumped around. Then he screamed. They were looking at a giant demon out of hell come down from his high hill, a demon with the face of a monster and the look of the swamp.

Harrell instinctively grabbed his rifle and shot at the thing in one motion. The bullet struck the Sirian's midsection, a strong point in his body armor, and bounced harmlessly off; but the force of the blast knocked Treeg back, and he grabbed a long vine to keep from crashing to the ground. The initial surprise of the attack wore off almost immediately, and Treeg saw the situation for what it was—he was faced with a bunch of primitives, and scared ones at that. Treeg, a born killer trained in his art, charged. Three of the men drew back, but Carl stood his ground. Stopping a few feet away, the Sirian surveyed the Terran who was as big as he.

The big black man charged, and Treeg stepped aside, letting his adversary sail past. The Sirian had spotted Harrell furiously reloading his rifle and wanted to eliminate the threat. Drawing his pistol, Treeg fired. Harrell went up in smoke and flame. The two others ran off, the short black man known as Eliot shouting: *"Juju! Juju! Oh, God, we done raised a juju!"* as he stormed through the brush.

Carl had recovered from his missed lunge and, rising to his feet, charged at the back of the monster. He knew he was facing a demon, but he also knew that demons could be wrestled into submission—and Carl was the best wrestler of them all.

The Sirian went down, caught completely off guard. He had forgotten his initial and greatest threat while shooting at the others. Carl pounced on top of him and for a few seconds the two wrestled, the big black man not being able to do much damage to the hard-shelled creature, while Treeg found himself pinned in a viselike grip, not being able to free either claw or hand. They were still in a test of brute strength, a frozen tableau as Carl sat atop the giant creature and strained to keep those arms pinned.

Treeg was virtually helpless if downed, and he had to be able to roll over in order to bring up his claw. He heaved with all his might, at the same time marveling at the strength of this soft Terran ape, as he thought of all Earthmen.

Foam poured from the mouth of the frenzied Carl as he struggled against the giant creature's strength in that death grip. Finally, after a few seconds that seemed to both to pass like hours, Treeg felt a slight slackening as the man tired, and he kicked over to one side. Carl went sprawling over, and Treeg rolled to his right, at the stunned man, claw raised.

Rifixl Treeg had a terrible time bringing himself to his feet again. Rigid, unbending legs propped out, he used his long arms to lift his body semiupright, then grabbed an overhanging vine and pulled himself erect. He then looked down at the cut and bleeding body of Carl, a Terran. He had been more impressed with the courage and skill of this one creature than with any he had encountered before. The primitive should have run away with the rest of his group, yet he had chosen to stay and fight. He had been closer to winning than he knew, for Treeg had been tiring as well, and a mighty blow into the pulpy Sirian face would have penetrated into his brain, bringing instant death.

Treeg resolved not to underestimate these Terrans again. He had often wondered why such seeming weaklings were any threat to the Empire. Then a saying one of his early tutors had drummed into him suddenly came back as he stood there: *Ignorance is not a synonym for stupidity, nor savagery for fear.*

Treeg cast one eye in each direction, looking for a sign of the return of the natives in force. He did not want to be caught off guard again. But he found no signs of any life save the crawling insects and flying birds; so, keeping a watchful eye, the Sirian decapitated the Negro, using the ceremonial claw, in the age-old gesture of respect for the dead of war. He then made his way around the hill, searching for the signs of a more civilized man's presence. He found none and, regretfully, walked back up the hill, back to where a stone marked his point of departure.

From back in the swampy glades, a group of cautious Bayou men and women, attracted by the sounds of a struggle, watched in awe and fear as a great demon stood atop the hill, visible as a fearsome specter in the last fleeting rays of the sun.

And suddenly vanished.

Treeg tumbled out of the time cabinet and onto the floor, unconscious. It was only a split second since he had vanished from the laboratory, but it was plain to the Sirian physicist that the colonel had been through an ordeal. The red blood almost completely covering the claw proved it, and Treeg was carried to the hospital, where Carl's blood was washed off and he was left alone to sleep off his exhaustion.

3

Less than two days later, Treeg was ready and able to try again. He had learned a lot about his enemy in his first try. This time, unhampered by the apprehension of transition, the passage to Terra was even easier to take. Yet this time, too, it held a surprise.

Treeg stood in a primitive dwelling made of wood. The size of the room was very large, and it was lavishly furnished. A great, long table divided the room almost into two parts, with chairs stretching endlessly down each side. At the head of the table was a great, padded chair where the master of the house would sit. A long mirror hung on one wall and, overhead, suspended directly above the center of the table, was a massive iron chandelier.

Treeg's first thought was that there had been some sort of mistake. The jump was not more than forty years, he thought, and those primitives of the swamp were surely incapable of making such a dwelling as this. But, of course, forty years brings inevitable change, external as well. The dwelling and the small town below were products of outsiders, who had used the time to carve a slice of civilization from the swamp.

In that time that shrewd old trader Josiah Hankin had built a town and a mansion. He had also been warned not to build on that hill. An old juju woman had prattled about a demon, one her grandmother saw, who lived in the hill and could disappear at a will. But Josiah was a hardheaded man, and he laughed.

It was almost midnight. The servants had retired, the slaves had been locked in their houses. Josiah sat in his study studiously examining the previous month's account books. But as far as Treeg was concerned, the dark house was empty.

The Sirian took a small tube off his wide utility belt, the only clothing he wore. The tube snapped to life, its brilliant blue-white glow illuminating even the darkest corners of the large room. Treeg narrowed the beam after an initial visual scan of the place, and he began his search. Although not conscious of sound himself or capable of fully grasping what it was, he still moved softly and carefully, knowing that the Terrans possessed a certain sense that he did not.

Then, in the most comic of ways, Rifixl Treeg tripped on the edge of the lush Persian carpet at the doorway and hit the floor with a crash, the blue torch flying against a wall.

Josiah jumped at the sound. He had never been quite comfortable in the wilds and was always a little jittery after dark. Cautiously, the old man tiptoed out onto the landing above the grand stairway and looked down into the dark entrance hall. He heard the sound of movement as Treeg dizzily and with great effort hoisted himself back to his feet. Feeling certain that a burglar was in the house, Hankin went back and got out his old flintlock pistol.

In the meantime Treeg, oblivious of discovery, had started his methodical search of the dining-room area, looking for spaces likely to hide a small recorder. He felt certain that the recorder was hidden in an obvious place—a place somewhere in the house, and one where a Terran searcher would be likely to look, since, were it hidden too well, Mofad's own kind would miss the object of their search.

Josiah crept softly down the stairs, loaded gun in hand. The sounds of movement in the dining room continued. Raising his pistol, the old man stepped across the threshold of the room, now lit by a strange blue glow.

Treeg, very near the door, chose that moment to turn around. As he did so, his right arm swung around and hit Hankin hard, sending the old man reeling back into the hallway. The gun fired on contact, but the ball missed its mark and lodged instead in the far wall.

The Sirian walked toward the old man, who was just getting to his feet. The fellow looked up and into the pulpy, grotesque face, screamed, and ran for the front door. Treeg, being slower, did not give chase as the old man sped out the door and down toward the slaves' house, screaming hideously.

Treeg quickly resumed his search. He was certain that he was still too early in time, and so, with only a few more seconds to survey the downstairs layout—and with pursuit probably imminent—he stepped back to the point just behind the great chair that sat at the head of the long table and pressed the button.

Josiah Hankin, driven mad by the horror that had touched him and pursued him, saw monsters in place of bewildered slaves. He grabbed a heavy stick off the ground and started after one of the men, a field hand. The others finally subdued him.

Hankin would live out his life in a New Orleans sanitarium, always babbling a description of the truth that men of 1850 could only accept as the ravings of a maniac.

Private Fetters jumped nervously as Colonel Rackland entered the house. Rackland grinned. A tall, gaunt man with a now-famous blond goatee, he delighted in scaring his men. It kept them on their toes.

"Well, Private," he drawled, "have you seen any signs of those wicked old Yankees yet?"

Fetters relaxed. "No, suh, but ah'm keepin' a shahp lookout, suh."

Rackland smiled again, and went over to the old padded chair that they had uncovered and put back where it rightfully belonged—at the head of the dining room table. The table was ideal for maps and conferences, and the east windows of the room gave an excellent view of the broad expanse of the Mississippi.

Two more men came in—the rest of the observation-post team, one of several Rackland had set up along the riverbank. Rackland walked over to the windows to confer with the new arrivals, and Fetters asked if he could be relieved. This granted, he walked over to the big chair. That saved his life.

Rifixl Treeg appeared between Fetters and the men at the windows, so close to the private that poor Fetters was knocked down. Treeg wanted no surprises and acted by reflex this time, drawing his pistol and firing point-blank at the men at the window.

The wide beam caught all three at once, and each man screamed once, then died from the intense heat. Fetters was only singed slightly, and he saw the creature in the room. One look was enough. Fetters managed to leap up and jump out one of the windows, then ran off, screaming and yelling for help as he raced down the hill toward the town below.

Treeg cursed himself for allowing one to get away, reflecting sourly that that seemed to be all he was doing of late. He made as quick a search as he could, but decided that if this place was being used by these men—seemingly soldiers—Mofad's presence would be marked in some way. Still, he made the rounds of the usual hiding places and then looked over the other downstairs rooms as well. His duty done, Treeg walked back over to the focal point just behind the great chair and pressed the red stud.

She took one look at the creature and fainted, something which puzzled Treeg, who was ever ready to kill but was unused to potential victims dropping unconscious without pain as a precipitant. He decided to kill her while she was out in order to save problems later. Then, despite the fact that head-taking was usually a ceremony of honor, he sliced off the woman's head simply because it seemed the easiest way of killing her.

For once, Treeg allowed himself every luxury of time. He had no reason to believe that anyone else was about, but he kept one eye on the main hall anyway. Lucky for him he did.

Phil Cannon bounced down the stairs, gun in hand. He had watched as the weird creature severed Mary's head cleanly with that claw, but the vision had not driven him mad. Cannon had lived too long and done too much to be scared of any monster that simply was more foul than he. He had accepted Treeg as a reality, probably some sort of unknown animal from the swamps, and he had reached for his .44.

He felt no emotion at Mary's passing. People were things to Phil Cannon; they could be replaced. What mattered was killing the thing in the dining room before it killed him.

Treeg saw movement out of the corner of his eye, drew his pistol, turned, and pulled the trigger. The shot was wide and on a thin beam as well and it missed Cannon, who darted to cover behind the wall partition, completely. Cocking his pistol, Cannon dropped low to the floor, then darted out, firing a volley at Treeg. One shot struck, and though it did Treeg no harm, it had the force to make him drop his searpistol.

Treeg realized that he had no cover and no weapon, and decided immediately that he had to rush the man. He bounded across the dining room and reached out, but Cannon was too fast.

"Com'on, you brute," Phil Cannon whispered, "com'on out where I can get a clear shot with this thing."

Treeg decided to oblige, chancing that the Terran would aim for his midsection. It was a risk, but there was nothing else to do. He charged, and guessed correctly. Cannon fired into the Sirian's chest, to no effect; but Treeg, ready for the blow of the bullet, was able to keep up his charge. Hand and claw reached out for Cannon, picked him up and threw him into the dining room, where the con man landed with a *snap*.

Treeg made certain that the man was dead by severing his head, but as he started to move the body, part of which was on the focal point, he saw people running for the house, attracted by the shots. Treeg decided that this time period was without doubt still much too early for Mofad anyway, and he pressed the stud.

When he arrived back in the Sirian laboratory, he discovered that Phil Cannon's severed head had come along as well.

Cannon's servants, running in the front door in response to the shots, stopped short at the gruesome sight in the dining room. Crossing himself, the butler said: "We'd all bettah git out of heah fast. They's gonna think *we* done it."

So it was that the town investigating committee found two bodies, one head, and were able to place the blame on the servants.

Murray was in the dining room when Treeg appeared. Stunned for a moment by the creature's sudden appearance, he recovered before Treeg could effectively act and ran to a wall, on which a prized pistol sat, ever loaded, the captain's symbol of his life.

Treeg advanced on him, and Murray fired once, the

bullet glancing off Treeg and putting yet another hole in the old house's wall.

The Sirian reached out and grabbed for the young ex-orderly, but missed and fell to the floor. Murray, in dodging, was thrown off balance and fell, too, but he retained a grip on his pistol.

Treeg saw the pistol and lashed out his hand, catching the man's arm in an iron grip. They struggled, rolling along the floor, each trying for possession of the pistol. The gun suddenly reversed under Treeg's mighty pressure, and fired. Murray jerked, then was still. Treeg had killed him by forcing the muzzle of his own gun to his side.

Rising, he went immediately to the dining-room doorway, not taking any chances on another Phil Cannon coming down the stairs.

The captain was standing at the head of the stairs. At the sound of the struggle he had painfully gotten up from his bed, where he had been for several days, fighting an old leg wound that had flared anew. At the sight of Treeg he drew back. His bad leg gave out from under him, and he fell headfirst down the grand stairway. When he hit bottom, he lay still, his neck broken in the fall.

Treeg looked down at the body, which was undeniably dead, a bit stunned at this death. It was, at least, the easiest of the lot, and Treeg was glad of that after his tussle with Murray.

This time the search was not interrupted, and Treeg explored the upstairs as well.

The little girl was playing with her doll in a corner of the dining room. She didn't see Treeg, who stood for a second pondering what to do. Younglings meant adults nearby.

Treeg was correct. Meredith walked down the stairs, spotted Treeg, and grabbed his shotgun, which was in the hall in preparation for a day of hunting. He stormed into the room and fired point-blank at Treeg before the slower-moving Sirian could react. The buckshot spread across the room, parts of the shot striking Treeg in the face; others, deflected, hit the little girl in the face as she watched in horror. Treeg blundered about in pain and in rage and lashed out in all directions. Roger Meredith

froze as he caught sight of his daughter, bleeding and in
shock, inching along the wall. He was thinking only of
her when one of Treeg's blows smashed into his head,
killing him instantly.

Mrs. Meredith came running in, and all but bumped
into Treeg. He grabbed her and threw her hard away
from him, doing so with such power that the unfortunate
woman was thrown out of the east window to her death.

Treeg didn't see the child, could think only of getting
back. The pain bit at him, driving him almost into a
frenzy. This allowed little Carol Meredith to back out the
dining-room door, out of the house, and to make it to
town, where she would bleed to death in a merchant's
arms.

Treeg stabbed at the button on the time-distorter unit,
but nothing happened. Suddenly, drawing in great gasps
of air, racked by nearly intolerable pain, he realized that
he was not precisely over the focal point. With effort he
stumbled to the place behind the big padded chair and
pressed the stud again. Again nothing happened. He
panicked. He pressed, and pressed, and pressed. Finally
he pushed the red button instead of the green.

It took two weeks in a Sirian hospital to heal the
wounds sufficiently for Treeg to continue. Command had
all but ordered him to get another man, but Treeg knew
that if he chose another in his place, he would be
finished—a final failure. The finding of Mofad was no
longer a mission with Rifixl Treeg, it was an obsession.
To a born warrior retirement would be a living hell—he
would commit suicide first.

This time he was very cautious. As soon as he emerged
in the darkened house he drew his pistol, prepared to fire
on sight. But the dining room was empty, the furniture
piled on one corner. Everything was covered with white
sheets, and a thick carpet of dust and cobwebs was everywhere. Treeg glanced around in relief. The house was
unlived in at this time.

First he checked the traditional spots, and then the rest
of the lower floor. For the first time he was completely
uninterrupted, but he never let down his guard. Slight
pains in his face reminded him to keep vigilant. His pale
blue torch flickered as Treeg mounted the grand stairway
with effort.

He found a body at the top of the stairs—a fresh one. Treeg, to whom all Terran apes looked alike, knew this one on sight, every feature from the tiny mustache to the potbelly burned indelibly into his brain.

Alei Mofad, in the initial stages of rigor mortis, lay on the landing, dead neither by murder nor suicide, but from a weak heart deprived of its medicine.

Treeg felt a queer thrill run through him. This was it! Even on this mad planet, Terra, he felt, he was still in command of himself.

Mofad had been upstairs, obviously. But had he been going up, or coming down? Coming down, Treeg decided from the angle of the body. Treeg stepped over the body of the scientist, dead in a remote area, remote in time and space—dead many centuries before he would be born. He walked down the second-story corridor.

The master bedroom, in the same dusty condition as the dining room, nonetheless had the look of being used. A big old stuffed chair, the same one that had been in the dining room through many reupholsterings, stood in the middle of the room, a stool resting in front of it. Clearly Mofad had spent his time here, awaiting Terran security, fearful that he would be overlooked and stranded. As Treeg searched the darkened room, his eyes caught the glare of headlights outside.

The police car pulled up and two men stepped out. They checked the front and back doors, and then went back to their car, got in . . . and drove off. Treeg waited a few seconds to make certain of their departure, then resumed his search. It would be midnight shortly, and the moon shone brightly in the window.

Suddenly Treeg glanced out the window again, nervously checking to see if the car would return. After a moment he made out a small group of figures creeping up on the house. Youngling Terrans, he decided. He watched as they moved closer, then up and out of sight underneath him.

Treeg crept out of the bedroom and back over to the stairwell. He watched the front door. After a while, it started to move. This time Rifixl Treeg would not be caught off guard! He switched off his light and melted into the shadows, still watching.

Two young Terrans entered cautiously, even fearfully,

each one seeming to urge the other on. They stood for a moment in the hallway, then went into the dining room, where moonlight flooded the interior. They pulled two chairs off the heap, very carefully, and sat down, backs to the wall. In silence, their eyes wide, apprehensive, they gazed at the open door.

Treeg decided that, with the others outside who might run for help, he could wait them out. He relaxed a bit, and leaned against a wall to wait, one eye fixed on the front doorway and the other on the entranceway to the dining room. He wasn't about to run and give the prize away. It was too close!

Hours passed, and Treeg fumed with impatience to get on with his search. But it was evident that for some reason—perhaps religious—those boys, scared as they obviously were, were going to stay the night.

Johnny Schmidt and Scully Wills drove back up to Hankin House. They had gotten bored as usual and decided to give the route a fast, clean check before turning in.

As their headlights reflected against the dark shingle of the house, Schmidt caught sight of a small figure running around the side of the place—a figure he knew.

"Hold up there, Tommy Samuels!" he cried, and the boy, who was more scared of the night than of the police, stopped, turned, and obediently came back to the front. Slowly the other Swamp Rats appeared as well. The game was up, and Tommy was known to be a blabber-mouth anyway.

"Now, just what the *hell* are you kids doing up here at this time of night?" the irate officer demanded, and in confused snatches the entire story was told.

"Well," said Schmidt disgustedly to his partner, "we'll have to go in and get them. Let's get it over with." With that the two men mounted the steps and threw open the door.

At that instant a bored and impatient Treeg, curious as to the meaning of the flashes of light outside, chose to risk a peek from his hiding place. So his face was fully outlined in Schmidt's casually aimed flashlight beam.

"*Oh, my God!*" yelled the police officer, who dropped

and drew his pistol. Treeg jerked back, but not without sound.

"Did you see what I saw?" Scully whispered huskily.

"I hope not," replied Schmidt, and then a thought struck him. "*The kids!*"

"Buzz Murdock! Ricky Adherne! You two get outa there fast, on the run, when I give the word," Scully shouted. "Then run like hell for town and tell 'em to bring help. We got *something* cornered upstairs."

The two boys ran out, joined their frightened compatriots, and ran down the hill as fast as their legs could carry them. None of them would give a warning! They hadn't seen anything.

"Scully, get out to the car and call the state troopers. Tell 'em we don't know what it is but to get some heavy stuff up here and *fast!*" Scully crept back out the door and ran for the car. There was noise on the second floor, as Treeg retreated to the master bedroom. He knew from the way they reacted that these men were armed professionals, and he wanted a good place both for a stand and for a view of the road.

He set the pistol charge to high intensity and aimed for the patrol car below at which the unfortunate Scully was standing, giving his call for aid to the state-trooper barracks. The beam lashed out from the upper window, exploding the car with a blinding glare and shock wave that was seen and heard in town. People awoke, looked out, and saw a burning heap in front of Hankin House.

Schmidt was knocked flat by the blast, but quickly picked himself up and stationed himself behind an overturned hall table near the stairs. Whatever was up there he was determined to *keep* up there until reinforcements arrived.

Treeg knew that with only one man downstairs he could get away, but he would return a failure, return to death. Better to make a stand here, he decided, and at least *find* the recorder, if only to destroy it. If the Sirian Empire didn't have it, then at least it would not be used against them.

A small group of villagers ran up the hill. Treeg saw them coming and aimed a shot that exploded the earth just in front of them. Men started screaming. Those unharmed ran back toward town.

Lights went on all over town, including those in the house of National Guard Major Robert Kelsoe, who had two advantages. He had a full view of the old mansion form his bedroom window, and he lived next door to the Guard armory.

Treeg fired a third shot, on wide beam, that cooked swamp grass and vegetation in a five-foot path down the hillside. He did not know where the other Terran man was lurking, but felt that he wouldn't charge without help. And the hilltop shots would discourage anyone coming to help. He continued his search.

Schmidt heard the thing moving furniture around upstairs. He tried to imagine what it was and what it was doing up there, failing on both counts. But he was Newtownards born and bred, and he knew the legends. He knew that he had just seen the demon of Hankin House and that no matter what it was, it was solid.

Major Kelsoe wasted no time in opening the armory. He didn't know what was going on, but he had seen the beams from the house and knew that some sort of power was loose up there. Three of his Guard unit were awaiting him at the armory, and they discussed what they had seen and heard as they broke out submachine guns.

It was eight and a half minutes since Scully had called the state police. Two cars roared into town, having done eighty along the narrow road. They matched Scully's incredible radio report, cut off in midsentence, with what the Guardsmen had seen. The state police corporal looked over at a far rack. "*Hey!*" he exclaimed, "Are those bazookas?"

A few minutes later a cautious group of men, three of them armed with bazookas, crept up the side of the hill to Hankin House.

When they reached the summit and were standing in front of the house, across from the crater left where the patrol car had exploded, Corporal James Watson found his voice and yelled: "*Wills! Schmidt!*"

Schmidt heard the yell and called back, "This is Schmidt in here! Wills was caught in the blast. This thing is unbelievable! It's upstairs moving stuff around at a fearful rate. Come in slowly, and watch it!"

As if on a commando raid, the men zigzagged across the road and up onto the porch, seconds apart.

"Thank God," Schmidt sighed when he saw them. He spotted the bazookas and said, "Get those things ready. The thing's sort of like a big crawfish, I think, and that body armor will be awfully thick on a baby his size. The thing's got to come down this way—maybe we can give it a bellyful."

Treeg was thoroughly frustrated. Not being able to hear anything at all, and not having seen the band of men creep up and into the house, he fancied himself still with only the problem of the lone sentinel below.

Mofad must have hidden the recorder downstairs after all, he thought disgustedly. He'd have to get rid of that pest down there and then have another look.

Quickly Treeg stepped out onto the landing, over Mofad's still body, and started down the stairs, slowly, pistol in hand.

The bazooka shell, designed to penetrate the toughest tank armor, sliced through his body like a hot knife through butter. The great, alien body toppled headfirst down the stairs and landed with a crash at the feet of the men below, almost exactly where Captain Hornig had lain after his fall.

Colonel Rifixl Treeg, Hereditary Colonel of Empire Intelligence, was dead.

The newsmen had left; the police and Guard had finished their examinations of the building, and the alien body, or what was left of it, had been carted off to Washington, where baffled biologists would almost be driven mad in their unsuccessful attempt to identify the thing. The physicists regretted that the bazooka shell had passed through the curious beltlike container the creature had worn, destroying forever the new science in the ray-pistol power pack and the portable time link.

The excitement was all over, and Hankin House was again boarded up. There was talk of finally tearing the old place down, but in the end the house gave the economy of the tiny town a much-needed boost. The only tourist attraction in the state that drew more year-round visitors was the Latin Quarter of New Orleans.

4

A man, Terran, materialized in the hallway, almost on the spot where Rifixl Treeg's body had fallen. He removed a sheet of paperlike material, upon which was written the location of the agreed-upon rendezvous Mofad had established before he had ever left Conolt IV. The slip stated: "LOUESSE 155—EMERGENCY LOCATION IN CASE OF ENEMY ACTION. POINT OF REFERENCE 221."

The agent mounted the stairway, turned at the landing where Mofad's body had lain—he who now was at rest as a John Doe in the potter's field—and went directly into the master bedroom.

The place was a shambles. Treeg had moved everything around, torn down cabinets, mantels, and other such hiding places.

"Now, where the devil would I hide a minirecorder in here if I wanted a place another Terran would probably find but a Sirian probably would not?" That was the problem.

Where?

After some exasperating searches the agent crossed his arms, stumped, and surveyed the room. Dammit, Point of Reference 221 in this house was the master bedroom!

The agent suddenly felt tired—he had had a day that spanned twelve centuries. He decided to sit down and think the problem out. Grabbing the overturned master's chair that had once sat at the head of the dining-room table and had, indeed, been Mofad's only comfort, he turned it over and sank down.

Click. "The frequency modulation of point seven two betas— "

The man jumped up out of the chair as if he had been shot. But then he smiled, and then he laughed. And then he couldn't stop laughing.

Where was a good place for a Terran to look but a Sirian to overlook? What might a tired Terran do when he reached here: chair and stool set up, inviting . . . but *when you're guarding against a race that was incapable of sitting down!* A simple matter for a genius like Mofad to rig the recorder. Treeg could have torn the chair apart without noticing the tiny minirecorder—but he would never have pressed hard on the seat!

Mofad's voice droned on, telling those precious formulae and figures that would win Terra the war. The Terran agent, still laughing, slit open the seat of the chair and dug into the wooden frame structure which Mofad had built as his recorder's final resting place. Only heavy pressure on the center of the seat would have made it begin playing.

The agent removed the recorder and shut it off. He then walked out of the bedroom, down the stairs, and into the main hallway. He took from his pocket a small control box, on which were two buttons. Pressing the red one, he disappeared.

And the last ghost of Hankin House vanished into time.

EDWARD BRYANT

Teeth Marks

My favorite vantage has always been the circular window at the end of the playroom. It is cut from the old-fashioned glass installed by Frank Alessi's father. As a young man, he built this house with his own hands. The slight distortions in the pane create a rainbow sheen when the light is proper. I enjoy the view so much more than those seen through the standard rectangular windows on the other floors, the panes regularly smashed by the enthusiasms of the young Alessis through the years and duly replaced. The circular window is set halfway between the hardwood floor and the peak of the gabled ceiling, low enough that I can watch the outside world from a chair.

Watching window scenes with slight distortions and enhanced colors satisfies my need for stimulation, since I don't read, nor go out to films, nor do I ever turn on the cold television console in the study. Sometimes I see jays quarreling with magpies, robins descending for meals on the unkempt lawn, ducks in the autumn and spring. I see the clouds form and roil through a series of shapes. The scene is hardly static, though it might seem such to a less patient observer. Patience must be my most obvious virtue, fixed here as I am on this eternal cutting edge of the present.

I possess my minor powers, but complete foreknowledge is not numbered among them. Long since taking up residence here, I've explored the dimensions of the house. Now I spend the bulk of my time in what I consider the

270

most comfortable room in the house. I haunt the old-fashioned circular window, and I wait.

Frank Alessi took a certain bitter pleasure in driving his own car. All the years he'd had a staff and driver, he had forgotten the autonomous freedoms of the road. The feel of the wheel in his hands was a little heady. Any time he wanted, any time at all, he could twist the steering wheel a few degrees and direct the Ford into the path of a Trailways bus or a logging truck. It was his decision, reaffirmed from minute to minute on the winding mountain highway, his alone. He glanced at the girl beside him, not hearing what she was saying. She wouldn't be smiling so animatedly if she knew he was chilling his mind with an image of impalement on a bridge railing.

Her name was Sally Lakey, and he couldn't help thinking of her as a girl even though she'd told him at least three times that she had celebrated her twentieth birthday the week before.

". . . *that* Alessi?" she said.

He nodded and half smiled.

"Yeah, really?" She cocked her head like some tropical bird and stared from large dark eyes.

Alessi nodded again and didn't smile.

"That's really something. Yeah, I recognize you from the papers now. You're you." She giggled. "I even saw you last spring. In the campaign."

"The campaign," he repeated.

Lakey said apologetically, "Well, actually I didn't watch you much. What it comes down to is that I'm pretty apolitical, you know?"

Alessi forced another half-smile. "I could have used your vote."

"I wasn't registered."

Alessi shrugged mentally and returned his attention to the awesome drop-offs that tugged at the car on Lakey's side. Gravel and raw rock gave way to forest and then to valley floor. Much of the valley was cleared and quilted with irrigated squares. It's a much tamer country than when I left, Alessi thought.

"I'm really sorry I didn't vote."

"What?" Distracted, Alessi swerved slightly to avoid

two fist-sized rocks that had rolled onto the right-hand lane probably during the night.

"I think you're a nice man. I said I'm sorry I didn't vote."

"It's a little late for that." Alessi envenomed the words. He heard the tone of pettiness, recognized it, said the words anyway.

"Don't blame me, Mr. Alessi," she said. "Really, I'm not stupid. You can't blame me for losing . . . Senator."

I'm being reproached, he thought, by a drop-out, wet-behind-the-ears girl. Me, a fifty-seven-year-old man. A fifty-seven-year-old unemployable. God damn it! The rage he thought he'd exorcised in San Francisco rose up again. He thought the rim of the steering wheel would shatter under his fingers into jagged, slashing shards.

Lakey must have seen something in his eyes. She moved back across the front seat and wedged herself uneasily into the juncture of bench seat and door. "You, uh, all right?"

"Yes," said Alessi. He willed the muscles cording his neck to relax, with little effect. "I am very sorry I snapped at you, Sally."

"It's okay." But she looked dubious of the sincerity of his apology.

They rode in silence for another few miles. She'll talk, thought Alessi. Sooner or later.

Sooner. "How soon?"

"Before we get to the house? Not long. The turnoff's another few miles." And what the hell, he asked himself, are you doing taking a kid little better than a third your age to the half-remembered refuge where you're going to whimper, crawl in and pull the hole in after you? It's perhaps the worst time in your life and you're acting the part of a horny old man. You've known her a grand total of eight hours. No, he answered himself. More than that. She reminds me— He tensed. She asked me if she could come along. Remember? She asked me.

I see the dark-blue sedan turn into the semicircular driveway and slide between the pines toward the house. Tires crunch on drifted cones and dead leaves; the crisp sound rises toward me. I stretch to watch as the auto nears the porch and passes below the angle of my sight.

The engine dies. I hear a car door slam. Another one. For some reason it had not occurred to me that Frank might bring another person.

The equations of the house must be altered.

They stood silently for a while, looking up at the house. It was a large house, set in scale by the towering mountains beyond. Wind hissed in the pine needles; otherwise the only sound was the broken buzz of a logging truck down-shifting far below on the highway.

"It's lovely," Lakey said.

"That's the original building," Alessi pointed. "My father put it together in the years before the First World War. The additions were constructed over a period of decades."

"It must have twenty rooms."

"Ought to have been a hotel," said Alessi. "Never was. Dad liked baronial space. Some of the rooms are sealed off, never used."

"What's that?" Lakey stabbed a finger at the third floor. "The thing that looks like a porthole."

"Old glass, my favorite window when I was a kid, Behind it is a room that's been used variously as a nursery, playroom and guest room."

Lakey stared at the glass. "I thought I saw something move."

"Probably a tree shadow, or maybe a squirrel's gotten in. It wasn't the caretaker—I phoned ahead last night; he's in bed with his arthritis. Nobody else has been in the house in close to twenty years."

"I did see something," she said stubbornly.

"It isn't haunted."

She looked at him with a serious face. "How do you know?"

"No one ever died in there."

Lakey shivered. "I'm cold."

"We're at seven thousand feet." He took a key from an inside pocket of his coat. "Come in and I'll make a fire."

"Will you check the house first?"

"Better than that," he said, "*we* will check the house."

*   *   *

The buzz of voices drifts to the window. I am loath to leave my position behind the glass. Steps, one set heavier, one lighter, sound on the front walk. Time seems suspended as I wait for the sound of a key inserted into the latch. I anticipate the door opening. Not wanting to surprise the pair, I settle back.

Though they explored the old house together, Lakey kept forging ahead as though to assert her courage. Fine, thought Alessi. If there is something lurking in a closet, let it jump out and get *her*. The thought was only whimsical; he was a rational man.

Something did jump out of the closet at her—or at least it seemed to. Lakey opened the door at the far end of a second-floor bedroom and recoiled. A stack of photographs, loose and in albums displaced from precarious balance on the top shelf, cascaded to her feet. A plume of fine dust rose.

"There's always avalanche danger in the mountains," said Alessi.

She stopped coughing. "Very funny." Lakey knelt and picked up a sheaf of pictures. "Your family?"

Alessi studied the photographs over her shoulder. "Family, friends, holidays, vacation shots. Everyone in the family had a camera."

"You too?"

He took the corner of a glossy landscape between thumb and forefinger. "At one time I wanted to be a Stieglitz or a Cartier-Bresson, or even a Mathew Brady. Do you see the fuzz of smoke?"

She examined the photograph closely. "No."

"That's supposed to be a forest fire. I was not a good photographer. Photographs capture the present, and that in turn immediately becomes the past. My father insistently directed me to the future."

Lakey riffled through the pictures and stopped at one portrait. Except for his dress, the man might have doubled for Alessi. His gray hair was cut somewhat more severely than the Senator's. He sat stiffly upright behind a wooden desk, staring directly at the camera.

Alessi answered the unspoken question. "My father."

"He looks very distinguished," said Lakey. Her gaze flickered up to meet his. "So do you."

"He wanted something more of a dynasty than what he

got. But he tried to mold one; he really did. Every inch a mover and shaker," Alessi said sardonically. "He stayed here in the mountains and raped a fortune."

"Raped?" she said.

"Reaped. Raped. No difference. The timber went for progress and, at the time, nobody objected. My father taught me about power and I learned the lessons well. When he deemed me prepared, he sent me out to amass my own fortune in power—political, not oil or uranium. I went to the legislature and then to Washington. Now I'm home again."

"Home," she said, softening his word. "I think maybe you're leaving out some things." He didn't answer. She stopped at another picture. "Is this your mother?"

"No." He stared at the sharp features for several seconds. "That is Mrs. Norrinssen, an ironbound, more-Swedish-than-thou, pagan lady who came out here from someplace in the Dakotas. My father hired her to—take care of me in lieu of my mother."

Lakey registered his hesitation, then said uncertainly, "What happened to your mother?"

Alessi silently sorted through the remainder of the photographs. Toward the bottom of the stack, he found what he was looking for and extracted it. A slender woman, short-haired and of extraordinary beauty, stared past the camera; or perhaps *through* the camera. Her eyes had a distant, unfocused quality. She stood in a stand of dark spruce, her hands folded.

"It's such a moody picture," said Lakey.

The pines loomed above Alessi's mother, conical bodies appearing to converge in the upper portion of the grainy print. "I took that," said Alessi. "She didn't know. It was the last picture anyone took of her."

"She . . . died?"

"Not exactly. I suppose so. No one knows."

"I don't understand," said Lakey.

"She was a brilliant, lonely, unhappy lady," said Alessi. "My father brought her out here from Florida. She hated it. The mountains oppressed her; the winters depressed her. Every year she retreated farther into herself. My father tried to bring her out of it, but he treated her like a child. She resisted his pressures. Nothing seemed to work." He lapsed again into silence.

Finally Lakey said, "What happened to her?"

"It was after Mrs. Norrinssen had been here for two years. My mother's emotional state had been steadily deteriorating. Mrs. Norrinssen was the only one who could talk with her, or perhaps the only one with whom my mother would talk. One autumn day—it was in October. My mother got up before everyone else and walked out into the woods. That was that."

"That can't be all," said Lakey. "Didn't anyone look?"

"Of course we looked. My father hired trackers and dogs and the sheriff brought in his searchers. They trailed her deep into the pine forest and then lost her. They spent weeks. Then the snows increased and they gave up. There's a stone out behind the house in a grove, but no one's buried under it."

"Jesus," Lakey said softly. She put her arms around Alessi and gave him a slow, warm hug. The rest of the photographs fluttered to the hardwood floor.

I wait. I wait. I see no necessity of movement, not for now. I am patient. No longer do I go to the round window. My vigil is being rewarded. There is no reason to watch the unknowing birds, the forest, the road. The clouds have no message for me today.

I hear footsteps on the stair, and that is message enough.

"Most of the attic," said Alessi, "was converted into a nursery for me. My father always looked forward. He believed in constant renovation. As I became older, the nursery evolved to a playroom, though it was still the room where I slept. After my father died, I moved back here with my family for a few years. This was Connie's room."

"Your wife or your—"

"Daughter. For whatever reason, she preferred this to all the other rooms."

They stood just inside the doorway. The playroom extended most of the length of the house. Alessi imagined he could see the straight, carefully crafted lines of construction curving toward one another in perspective. Three dormer windows were spaced evenly along the eastern pitch of the ceiling. The round window allowed light to enter at the far end.

"It's huge," said Lakey.

"It outscales children. It was an adventure to live here. Sometimes it was very easy for me to imagine I was playing in a jungle or on a sea, or across a trackless Arctic waste."

"Wasn't it scary?"

"My father didn't allow that," said Alessi. Nor did I later on, he thought.

Lakey marveled. "The furnishings are incredible." The canopied bed, the dressers and vanity, the shelves and chairs, all were obviously products of the finest wood-craft. "Not a piece of plastic in all this." She laughed. "I love it." In her denim jeans and Pendleton shirt, she pirouetted. She stopped in front of a set of walnut shelves. "Are these dolls your daughter's?"

Alessi nodded. "My father was not what you would call a liberated man. Connie collected them all during her childhood." He carefully picked up a figure with a silk nineteenth-century dress and china head.

Lakey eagerly moved from object to object like a butterfly sampling flowers. "That horse! I always wanted one."

"My father made it for me. It's probably the most exactingly carpentered hobbyhorse made."

Lakey gingerly seated herself on the horse. Her feet barely touched the floor. "It's so big." She rocked back and forth, leaning against the leather reins. Not a joint squeaked.

Alessi said, "He scaled it so it would be a child's horse, not a pony. You might call these training toys for small adults."

The woman let the horse rock to a stop. She dismounted and slowly approached a tubular steel construction. A six-foot horizontal ladder connected the top rungs of two vertical four-foot ladders. "What on earth is this?"

Alessi was silent for a few seconds. "That is a climbing toy for three-and four-year-olds."

"But it's too big," said Lakey. "Too high."

"Not," said Alessi, "with your toes on one rung and your fingers on the next—just barely."

"It's impossible."

"Alessi shook his head. "Not quite; just terrifying."

"But why?" she said. "Did you do this for fun?"

"Dad told me to. When I balked, he struck me. When

he had to, my father never discounted the effect of force."

Lakey looked disconcerted. She turned away from the skeletal bridge toward a low table shoved back against the wall.

"Once there was a huge map of fairyland on the wall above the table," said Alessi. "Mrs. Norrinssen gave it to me. I can remember the illustrations, the ogres and frost giants and fairy castles. In a rage one night, my father ripped it to pieces."

Lakey knelt before the table so she could look on a level with the stuffed animals. "It's a whole zoo!" She reached out to touch the plush hides.

"More than a zoo," said Alessi. "A complete bestiary. Some of these critters don't exist. See the unicorn on the end?"

Lakey's attention was elsewhere. "The bear," she said, greedily reaching like a small child. "He's beautiful. I had one like him when I was little." She gathered the stuffed bear into her arms and hugged it. The creature was almost half her size. "What's his name? I called mine Bear. Is he yours?"

Alessi nodded. "And my daughter's. His name is Bear too. Mrs. Norrinssen made him."

She traced her finger along the bear's head, over his ears, down across the snout. Bear's hide was virtually seamless, sewn out of some rich pile fabric. After all the years, Bear's eyes were still black and shiny.

"The eyes came from the same glazier who cut the round window. Good nineteenth-century glass."

"This is wild," said Lakey. She touched the teeth.

"I don't really know whether it was Mrs. Norrinssen's idea or my father's," said Alessi. "A hunter supplied them. They're real. Mrs. Norrinssen drilled small holes toward the back of each tooth; they're secured inside the lining." Bear's mouth was lined with black leather, pliable to Lakey's questing finger. "Don't let him bite you."

"Most bears' mouths are closed," said Lakey.

"Yes."

"It didn't stop my Bear from talking to me."

"Mine didn't have to overcome that barrier." Alessi suddenly listened to what he was saying. Fifty-seven years old. He smiled self-consciously.

They stood silently for a few seconds; Lakey continued to hug the bear. "It's getting dark," she said. The sun had set while they explored the house. The outlines of solid shapes in the playroom had begun to blur with twilight. Doll faces shone almost luminously in the dusk.

"We'll get the luggage out of the car," said Alessi.

"Could I stay up here?"

"You mean tonight?" She nodded. "I see no reason why not," he said. He thought, did I really plan this?

Lakey stepped closer. "What about you?"

I watch them both. Frank Alessi very much resembles his father: distinguished. He looks harried, worn, but that is understandable. Some information I comprehend without knowing why. Some perceptions I don't have to puzzle over. I know what I see.

The woman is in her early twenties. She has mobile features, a smiling, open face. She is quick to react. Her eyes are as dark as her black hair. They dart back and forth in their sockets, her gaze lighting upon nearly everything in the room but rarely dwelling. Her speech is rapid with a hint of eastern nasality. Except for her manner of speaking, she reminds me of a dear memory.

For a moment I see four people standing in the playroom. Two are reflections in the broad, hand-silvered mirror above the vanity across the room. Two people are real. They hesitantly approach each other, a step at a time. Their arms extend, hands touch, fingers plait. Certainly at this time, in this place, they have found each other. The mirror images are inexact, but I think only I see that. The couple in the mirror seems to belong to another time. And, of course, I am there in the mirror too—though no one notices me.

"That's, uh, very gratifying to my ego," said Alessi. "But do you know how old I am?"

Lakey nodded. The semidarkness deepened. "I have some idea."

"I'm old enough to—"

"—be my father. I know." She said lightly, "So?"

"So . . ." He took his hands from hers. In the early night dolls seemed to watch them. The shiny button eyes

of Bear and the other animals appeared turned toward
the human pair.

"Yes," she said. "I think it's a good idea." She took
his hand again. "Come on, we'll get the stuff out of the
car. It's been a long day."

Day, Alessi thought. Long week, long month, longer
campaign. A lifetime. The headlines flashed in his mind,
television commentaries replayed. It all stung like acid
corroding what had been cold, shining and clean. Old,
old, old, like soldiers and gunfighters. How had he missed
being cleanly shot? Enough had seemed to want that. To
fade . . . "I *am* a little bushed," he said. He followed
Lakey out toward the stairs.

Frank Alessi's father was forceful in his ideal. That lent
the foundation to that time and this place. Strength was
virtue. "Fair is fair," he would say, but the fairness was
all his. Such power takes time to dissipate. Mrs. Norrinssen
stood up to that force; everyone else eventually fled.

"Witchy bitch!" he would storm. She only stared back
at him from calm, glacial eyes until he sputtered and
snorted and came to rest like a great, sulky, but now
gentled beast. Mrs. Norrinssen was a woman of extraordinary powers and she tapped ancient reserves.

Structure persists. I am part of it. That is my purpose
and I cannot turn aside. Now I wait in the newly inhabited house. Again I hear the positive, metallic sounds of
automobile doors and a trunk lid opening and closing. I
hear the voices and the footsteps and appreciate the
human touch they lend.

She stretched slowly. "What time is it?"

"Almost ten," said Alessi.

"I saw you check your watch. I thought you'd be
asleep. Not enough exercise?"

She giggled and Alessi was surprised to find the sound
did not offend him as it had earlier in the day. He rolled
back toward her and lightly kissed her lips. "Plenty of
exercise."

"You were really nice."

Fingertips touched his face, exploring cheekbones,
mouth corners, the stubble on the jowl line. That made
him slightly nervous; his body was still tight. Tennis,
handball, swimming, it all helped. Reasonably tight. Only

slight concessions to slackness. But after all, he *was*—
Shut up, he told himself.

"I feel very comfortable with you," she said.

Don't talk, he thought. Don't spoil it.

Lakey pressed close. "Say something."

No.

"Are you nervous?"

"No," Alessi said. "Of course not."

"I guess I did read about the divorce," said Lakey. "It
was in a picture magazine in my gynecologist's office."

"There isn't much to say. Marge couldn't take the
heat. She got out, I can't blame her." But silently he
denied that. The Watergate people—*their* wives stood
by. All the accumulated years . . . Betrayal is so goddamned nasty. Wish her well in Santa Fe?

"Tell me about your daughter," said Lakey.

"Connie—why her?"

"You've talked about everyone else. You haven't said
a thing about Connie except to say she slept in this
room." She paused. "In this bed?"

"We both did," said Alessi, "at different times."

"The stuff about the divorce didn't really mention her,
at least not that I remember. Where is she?"

"I truly don't know."

Lakey's voice sounded peculiar. "She disappeared, uh,
just like—"

"No. She left." Silently: she left me. Just like—

"You haven't heard from her? Nothing?"

"Not in several years. It was her choice; we didn't set
detectives on her. The last we heard, she was living in
the street in some backwater college town in Colorado."

"I mean, you didn't try—"

"It was her choice." She always said I didn't *allow* her
any choice, he thought. Maybe. But I tried to handle her
as my father handled me. And *I* turned out—

"What was she like?"

Alessi caressed her long smooth hair; static electricity
snapped and flashed. "Independent, intelligent, lovely. I
suppose fathers tend to be biased."

"How old is she?"

"Connie was about your age when she left." He realized he had answered the question in the past tense.

"You're not so old yourself," said Lakey, touching him strategically. "Not old at all."

Moonlight floods through the dormer panes; beyond the round window I see starlight fleck the sky. I am very quiet, though I need not be. The couple under the quilted coverlet are enthralled in their passion. I cannot question their motives yet. Love? I doubt it. Affection? I would approve of that. Physical attraction, craving for bodily contact, psychic tension?

I move to my window in the end of the playroom, leaving the love-making behind. The aesthetics of the bed are not as pleasing as the placid starfield. It may be that I am accustomed to somewhat more stately cycles and pulsings.

Perhaps it is the crowding of the house, the apprehension that more than one human body dwells within it, that causes me now to feel a loneliness. I wonder where Mrs. Norrinssen settled after the untimely death of her employer. "A bad bargain," he said somberly time after time. "Very bad indeed." And she only smiled back, never maliciously or with humor, but patiently. She had given him what he wanted. "But still a bargain," she said.

I am aware of the sounds subsiding from the canopied bed. I wonder if both now will abandon themselves to dreams and to sleep. A shadow dips silently past the window, a night-hawk. Faintly I hear the cries of hunting birds.

He came awake suddenly with teeth worrying his guilty soul. Connie glared at him from dark eyes swollen from crying and fury. She shook long black hair back from her shoulders. ". . . drove her through the one breakdown and into another." He dimly heard the words. "She's out of it, and good for her. No more campaigns. You won't do the same to me, you son of a bitch." Bitter smile. "Or I should say, you son of a bastard."

"I can't change these things. I'm just trying—" Alessi realized he was shaking in the darkness.

"What's wrong, now what's wrong?" said Connie.

Alessi cried out once, low.

"Baby, what is it?"

He saw Lakey's face in the pooled moonlight. "You." He reached out to touch her cheek and grazed her nose.

"Me," she said. "Who else?"

"Jesus," Alessi said. "Oh God."

"Bad dream?"

Orientation slowly settled in. "A nightmare." He shook his head violently.

"Tell me about it."

"I can't remember."

"So don't tell me if you don't want to." She gathered him close, blotting the sweat on his sternum with the sheet.

He said dreamily, "You always plan to make it up, but after a while it's too late."

"What's too late?"

Alessi didn't answer. He lay rigid beside her.

I see them in the gilt-framed mirror and I see them in bed. I feel both a terrible sympathy for her and a terrible love for him. For as long as I can recall, I've husbanded proprietary feelings about this house and those in it.

Frank Alessi makes me understand. I remember the woman's touch and cherish that feeling, though I simultaneously realize her touch was yet another's. I also remember Frank's embrace. I have touched all of them.

I love all these people. That terrifies me.

I want to tell him, you *can* change things, Frank.

Sometime after midnight he awoke again. The night had encroached; moonlight now filled less than a quarter of the playroom. Alessi lay still, staring at shadow patterns. He heard Lakey's soft, regular breathing beside him.

He lay without moving for what seemed to be hours. When he checked his watch only minutes had passed. Recumbent, he waited, assuming that for which he waited was sleep.

Sleep had started to settle about Alessi when he thought he detected a movement across the room. Part vague movement, part snatch of sound, it was *something*. Switching on the bedtable lamp, Alessi saw nothing. He held his breath for long seconds and listened. Still nothing. The room held only its usual complement of inhabitants:

dolls, toys, stuffed creatures. Bear stared back at him. The furniture was all familiar. Everything was in its place, natural. He felt his pulse speeding. He turned off the light and settled back against the pillow.

It's one o'clock in the soul, he thought. Not quite Fitzgerald, but it will do. He remembered Lakey in the car that afternoon asking why he had cut and run. That wasn't the exact phraseology, but it was close enough. So what if he had been forced out of office? He still could have found some kind of political employment. Alessi had not told her about all the records unsubpoenaed as well as subpoenaed—at first. Then, perversely, he had started to catalog the sordid details the investigating committees had decided not to use. After a while she had turned her head back toward the clean mountain scenery. He continued the list. Finally she had told him to shut up. She turned back toward him gravely, had told him it was all right—she had forgiven him. It had been simple and sincere.

I don't need easy forgiveness, he thought. Nor would *I* forgive. That afternoon he had lashed out at her. "Damn it, what do you know about these things—about responsibility and power? You're a hippie or whatever hippies are called now. Did you ever make a single solitary decision that put you on the line? Made you a target for second-guessing, carping analysis, sniping, unabashed viciousness?" The over-taut spring wound down.

Lakey visibly winced; muscles tightened around her mouth. "Yes," she said.

"So tell me."

She stared back at him like a small surprised animal. "I've been traveling a long time. Before I left, I was pregnant." Her voice flattened; Alessi strained to hear the words. "They told me it should have been a daughter."

He focused his attention back on the road. There was nothing to say. He knew about exigencies. He could approve.

"None of them wanted me to do it. They made it more than it really was. When I left, my parents told me they would never speak to me again. They haven't."

Alessi frowned.

"I loved them."

Alessi heard her mumble, make tiny incoherent sounds.

She shifted in her sleep in a series of irregular movements. Her voice raised slightly in volume. The words still were unintelligible. Alessi recognized the tenor; she was dreaming of fearful things. He stared intently; his vision blurred.

Gently he gathered Connie into his arms and stroked her hair. "I will make it right for you. I know, I know . . . I can."

"No," she said, the word sliding into a moan. Sharply, "No."

"I am your father."

But she ignored him.

I hear more than I can see. I hear the woman come fully awake, her moans sliding raggedly up the register to screams; pain—not love; shock—not passion. I would rather not listen, but I have no choice. So I hear the desperation of a body whose limbs are trapped between strangling linens and savage lover. I hear the endless, pounding slap of flesh against meat. Finally I hear the words, the words, the cruel words and the ineffectual. Worst of all, I hear the cries. I hear them in sadness.

Earlier I could not object. But now he couples with her not out of love, not from affection, but to force her. No desire, no lust, no desperate pleasure save inarticulate power.

Finally she somehow frees herself and scrambles off the bed. She stumbles through the unfamiliar room and slams against the wall beside the door. Only her head intrudes into the moonlight, her mouth is set in a rigid, silent oval. The wet blackness around her eyes is more than shadow. She says nothing. She fumbles for the door, claws the knob, is gone. He does not pursue her.

I hear the sound of the woman's stumbling steps. I hear her pound on the doors of the car Alessi habitually locks. The sounds of her flight diminish in the night. She will be safer with the beasts of the mountain.

Alessi endlessly slammed his fist into the bloody pillow. His body shook until the inarticulate rage began to burn away. Then he got up from the bed and crossed the playroom to the great baroque mirror.

"This time could have been different," he said. "I wanted it to be."

His eyes adjusted to the darkness. A thin sliver of moonlight striped the ceiling. Alessi confronted the creature in the mirror. He raised his hands in fists and battered them against unyielding glass, smashed them against the mirror until the surface fragmented into glittering shards. He presented his wrists, repeating in endless rote, "Different, this time, different . . ."

Then he sensed what lay behind him in the dark. Alessi swung around, blood arcing. Time overcame him. The warm, coppery smell rose up in the room.

Perhaps the house now is haunted; that I cannot say. My own role is ended. Again I am alone; and now lonely. This morning I have not looked through the round window. The carrion crows are inside my mind picking at the bones of memories.

I watch Frank Alessi across the stained floor of the playroom.

The house is quiet; I'm sure that will not continue. The woman will have reached the highway and surely has been found by now. She will tell her story and then the people will come.

For a time the house will be inhabited by many voices and many bodies. the people will look at Frank Alessi and his wrists and his blood. They will remark upon the shattered mirror. They may even note the toys, note me; wonder at the degree of the past preserved here in the house. I doubt they can detect the pain in my old-fashioned eyes.

They will search for answers.

But they can only question why Frank came here, and why he did what he did. They cannot see the marks left by the teeth of the past. Only the blood.

MICHAEL REAVES

The Tearing of Greymare House

When he had first seen the old house, Lamar Warren had thought, I can make a pile of money off this job. His next thought had been, Ain't it a goddamn shame.

He had not wanted to take the job, despite the money to be made. But these were not good times for the wrecking business. The bank had him good, and their grip kept getting tighter. With the economy the way it was, few new buildings were being built, and so few old ones were being wrecked. The Warren Wrecking Company nearly folded this year. It didn't seem fair, Lamar had told his wife dryly, for the country to be falling apart without his even getting to swing a ball at it.

And so he had taken the Greymare job, despite his feelings about it. The contractor was a firm in Philadelphia, and they had not even taken bids—they had simply called and offered him a price he could not refuse. With that, and the salvage that was his, he stood to make a good profit. He tried to feel enthusiastic about that.

The truck lurched as one of the outside tires ground gravel on the narrow road's edge. George Colby cursed and wrestled with the wheel. "These damn roads ain't graded worth a damn," he said. "And there's another goddamn bridge up ahead," as the fifth in a series of narrow wooden creek crossings came into view. The wide GMC dump trailer barely squeezed through, and the old planks creaked ominously. Lamar watched in the side mirror as the crane truck and the rest of the caravan followed. They had a couple of irritated motorists behind the procession, he noticed. Well, that could not be helped.

The last truck rumbled over the bridge. "Our luck ain't gonna hold out forever," George said.

"That's why I brought a light crane."

"Yeah, it ain't but three times as heavy as these bridges were built to take." George spat out the window. "I got a bad sense about this job, Lamar."

Lamar looked out the window. He had watched the wide rolling fields slowly give way to swampy land, shaded by cypress and filled with tiger lilies and palmetto ferns. He had never liked the lowland country. It was getting toward noon, and hot, the drowsy, humid warmth of early summer. It had been over an hour's drive to Blessed Shoals, the Shadman County seat, and it was nearly another hour from there to the job. Lamar grimaced. Four hours of travel time out of every day. He mopped his bald, sweating head with a blue handkerchief. It would be worth it, he told himself. Even with the overtime, the gas and hauling expenses, it would be worth it.

Still, he wished he hadn't had to take the job.

It was not because of Greymare's reputation. That did not bother him. But when the contractor had offered him the job he had driven out and looked at the place, peered in the windows and walked around the grounds. Greymare was a magnificent house still, despite its dilapidated condition. It did not deserve to be destroyed. Lamar loved well-built structures, no matter what the style or period. He had no difficulty in reconciling that love with his work. Demolishing old buildings was a necessary part of raising new ones. He saw his work at times as granting a quick death to buildings that had grown old in service and deserved to die honorably beneath the crushing blow of the ball, rather than degenerate into ruin. The wife said he was crazy, but he didn't mind being a little crazy. Being a little crazy was the only way to stay sane in this world.

But this house was not ready to go. Despite its weathered exterior and broken windows, it was still in good shape; restored, it could easily last another century.

No, it did not deserve to be destroyed. But, he reminded himself, he did not deserve to go broke either. It was him or the house, and he did not intend to be the one brought down.

Because of the winding road and the trees, they were

upon the plantation before they saw it. It was on higher land, surrounded by what had been rice and cotton fields and were now overgrown with witch grass and thistles. Greymare had once been the largest plantation in the state, before the Civil War. Lamar could see the overgrown clumps that had been the barn and outdoor kitchen and slaves' huts; rebuilt, he had been told, several times in an attempt to restore Greymare to the status of a landmark, but always abandoned and left to rot again. Nothing worth salvaging there; a single run with a dozer would bring them down.

The house, however, still stood, old but unyielding. It would take all that they had to knock it down.

That's an odd way to look at it, he thought.

The truck's wide tires rolled across the overgrown lawn and stopped. Lamar climbed down from the cab stiffly, putting both hands over his kidneys and leaning backward to stretch. He watched the rest of the equipment arrive: the other dump trailer, the crane and forklifts. Following them were five old Ford Econolines carrying the crew, and a flatbed truck with the portable heads. Clouds of diesel smoke drifted low over the grass as the engines shut down. The crew disembarked, cursing tiredly about the long ride, a few finishing jokes and stories. All of them gradually became silent as they turned to stare at the mansion.

Lamar looked at them looking at the house. Some of the crew were new, for he had hired several men for loading and cleanup in Blessed Shoals. One of these, a young fellow named Jim Driffs, crossed himself as he looked at the house. Lamar looked at his own crew, most of whom had been with him for years. George Colby had helped him start the company nine years previously; the tall black man was one of his closest friends. He stood now beside the dump trailer, fingers hooked in suspenders, staring at the mansion.

Beside him was Alice, the crane operator, tucking her hair under her hard hat. Alice was the only woman in the crew; as far as he knew, she was the only woman in any wrecking crew in the state. She was forty-seven, a stocky, solid woman, not beautiful at all until one got to know her. She had lost a husband in Korea and a son in Viet

Nam, and was possibly the best crane operator Lamar had ever seen.

Those two had been with him the longest. The others had joined as the firm grew—Freddie and Larry Tom, the drivers, Dawson, Pettus and the other loaders, and the trimmers and bar men. And there was Randy Warren, the latest addition to the crew. He was twenty years old, the youngest on the crew. He looked uneasy and out-of-place, too soft for the hard hat and coveralls he wore. Lamar frowned, wondering if he should have brought his nephew along. This was only summer work for Randy, before he went back to college. Lamar did not want any valuable scrap damaged due to inexperience. He shrugged. The boy deserved a chance.

The crew's silence he took to be what he felt: appreciation, even awe, for the majestic old house. Lamar walked through the tall grass, waving absently at the clouds of midges, and stopped at the steps leading to the wide, porticoed entrance. Leaning back, he admired the house. The style was mixed: classic pilasters were combined with Gothic gables, lancet windows and Tudor half-timbered walls. But the effect was unifying and impressive. Though it had stood vacant for almost five years and the storms and seasons had weathered it sadly, still it was imposing. It was three stories tall, wide and sprawling. To keep most of the salvage it would have to be handtorn, and that would take a month or more. Lamar sighed. It was a crime to do it—more than a crime, almost a sin, almost as if he were destroying a life. . . .

"Lamar?" George had approached him and now tapped him on the shoulder. Lamar turned quickly, startled, and George retreated a step. "We'd better get started," he said quietly. "It's noon already."

". . . Sure. Just daydreaming, I reckon. Let's get on it."

He glanced toward Randy and noticed the boy sitting in the shade of one of the vans. That annoyed him slightly—he hoped Randy didn't think he could slough off just because he was family. He did not know the boy all that well; Grace, Lamar's sister, lived in Atlanta, which was a considerable trip. Well, now he would see what Randy was like.

"Randy! Come on, we're gonna open it up. Get your

boots and gloves—no telling what varmints have moved in." Randy looked up, then grinned reluctantly. Lamar nodded; the boy at least could make the best of a situation.

He named several others to accompany his nephew. To his surprise, not only Randy looked reluctant—they all did. It must be the heat, he thought. No one wants to work. Well, neither did he, but that was the way it was.

They approached the door, a large, carved oaken panel secured by a rusted padlock and hasp. There was no result from Lamar's key; he tugged at the lock, then took an adze from one of the men, lifted the heavy wrecking tool and brought the blunt end down on the lock. The sound of metal against metal was very loud. It took three blows to shatter it, and then the door swung open. It did not creak, as Lamar had expected; instead, it opened silently and slowly, revealing the shadowed foyer.

Lamar looked inside, then back at the men on the porch. They stood in a tight, silent group. "So what the hell is wrong with everyone?" he asked. "I've seen mules in quicksand move faster!" He looked at his nephew. "You planning on working like this all summer long?"

Randy looked back at him intently. "Don't you feel it?"

"Feel what? And what the hell are you whispering for?"

"This house."

"What about it?"

Randy glanced at the rest of the crew, then shrugged and said, "Well, this may sound silly, Uncle Lamar, but I don't think this house wants us here."

Lamar looked from Randy to the rest of them, all poised in uncomfortable stances, hands shoved into back pockets, heavy boots shuffling. But no one said anything further, and at last he had to ask, "What in hell does *that* mean?"

It was Jim Driffs, one of the hired loaders from Blessed Shoals, who answered nervously. "Well, Mr. Warren, there's been an awful lot of stories about this place." He swigged down the last bottle of warm Pepsi. "Lot of people lived here and died here, and there's those that say none of them people ever really left. That there's something in this house that keeps them here. Something evil. And if you tear the place down—it might not like it."

"You didn't seem too worried about all this when I hired you," Lamar said.

Jim Driffs shrugged. "I needed the money. And Greymare was a good forty miles away. Now I'm standing on the front porch, and I wonder how bad I need that money." He looked about at the others, somewhat embarrassed at his speech, and seemed relieved when it was obvious that many of them felt the same way.

Lamar almost made the mistake of laughing—but then he looked closer at each of them, and realized that the house really did scare them, all of them. Even George Colby, who usually had a head as level as a bulldozed lot, seemed nervous.

"Y'all wait here," he said, and walked back to the trucks. Stepping out into the sunlight, he blinked at the sudden heat and light. He hadn't realized just how cool it had been on the porch.

He got several six-battery flashlights, and when he approached the porch again it was with an odd reluctance, considering how hot the sun was. He handed the flashlights to Randy, George and the others. "Let's go," he said cheerfully, and stepped across the threshold.

The cool air inside raised gooseflesh on his arms. He wrinkled his nose at the musty odor, the smells of dead insects and rotting fabric. The foyer opened into a huge main room, of which shuttered windows and heavy curtains made a vast, dim cavern. Lamar flicked on his light, and the powerful beam cut the darkness. There was no furniture left, which made the room seem even more gigantic. A huge, cut-crystal chandelier hung from the ceiling. Lamar turned the light into corners and along the walls, checking to make sure no vagrant lay asleep in a pile of rags. He could hear the squeak and scurry of rats, and he suppressed a shudder. Dealing with vermin was part of the wrecking business, but still he hated rats. He remembered once demolishing an entire block of tenements; as each building came down, the rats had fled to the next, until at last they were all hiding in the last structure to be blasted. The old brick walls had fairly hummed with the sound of hundreds of thousands of panicked rodents. He had had to go in to plant the charges . . .

He gulped a sour taste and let the light ripple up a wide, balustraded staircase that led to the second floor. "Gonna flake that whole thing loose, if we have the time," he said, and the echoes of his voice made Randy and the others start. They had followed him in, as he knew they would—he was a good man to work for, and he inspired loyalty in his crew. They would not let him go in here alone. Lamar smiled as he looked at the hardwood floor, which had ornamental borders of teak. Against the far wall was a carved mahogany mantel framing a fireplace large enough to stand upright in, with a cast iron fireback. The house was a palace, no doubt of it. There was plenty of money in this room alone, and eighteen other rooms awaited his inspection.

He flashed the light back at Jim Driffs, who ducked as though struck at. "Some of you open these windows, let a little light and air in here! That should chase the spooks away!" He was immediately sorry he had added that—it sounded too contemptuous. Then he became angry at his regret as he watched them move reluctantly into the darkness, their flashlight beams shimmering off curtains of cobwebs. Was he going to have to mollycoddle the whole crew through this job?

He speared Randy and George with his light. "Come on, you two! Let's give this place the once-over."

To the left, a huge, linteled archway opened into the dining room. The dark walls gave off no reflection. From the ceiling hung an anachronism: a 1920's style ceiling fan with wooden blades, which the movers had somehow overlooked. Lamar trod on something that cracked; his light revealed the shed skin of a rattlesnake. "Watch your step," he said, and heard Randy gulp.

They continued into the kitchen, which had been a later addition to the mansion, replacing the outdoor kitchen of plantation days. A windowed rear door provided faint light. The gritty smell of decomposition came from a bloated dead rat under the double-basin sink. Lamar turned away to a door by the recessed pantry. As he reached for the glass knob, Randy said abruptly, "Don't open it!"

Lamar paused with his hand on the knob. "And why not?"

Randy looked sickly pale in the reflected brilliance of the flashlights. "It's probably . . ."

"Probably the cellar," George said. "Lots of rats, most likely."

Lamar glared at both of them. "I've about near had it with all of you," he said. "This ain't nothing more than an old house! Now we got to check out the cellar, same as everyplace else." He realized he was raising his voice because he was nervous himself; the feeling puzzled and angered him. There was nothing to be frightened of in Greymare House. Outside of the rats . . .

He released the knob. "All right. It don't matter what order we go through the place. Randy, you and I will try that staircase," and he pointed toward another half-open door, with a flight of steps leading upward. "George, get outside and set the trimming crew to marking the place."

"You don't have to tell me twice." George started out of the kitchen, then looked over his shoulder at them. "Be careful up there," he said, and left.

The steep, narrow staircase was most likely the slaves' route to the upper quarters of the house, Lamar thought. It was dusty and close, and once a rat skittered down the steps causing them both to jump. It opened onto a vast hallway on the second floor, one side of which had windows looking down on what had been an orchard. On the other side were four bedroom doors. Lamar stepped forward, then stopped in surprise.

"What is it?" Randy was still on the stairs.

"Chilly here," Lamar said. He waved one hand in the air as he advanced. After five steps, the feeling of cold air surrounding him lessened, and the humid summer warmth returned. He walked down to the other end of the hallway, but there was no further change in temperature. Then he turned and looked at Randy, who still stood on the last step, staring at him with wide eyes.

"Well, come on," Lamar said. "You scared of catching a cold now?"

Randy stepped into the hallway, then stopped. His eyes grew even wider, and he wrapped his arms about himself.

"It's not *that* cold," Lamar said impatiently.

"Yes, it is!"

Lamar could hear his nephew's teeth chattering. He stepped again into the chill area, which did not seem nearly as cold to him as it evidently did to Randy, took his nephew's arm and pulled the young man forward. "See? Nothing to be afraid of. Just a little draft. Hot as a turkey in the oven here, ain't it?"

Randy looked over his shoulder. "I'll be—" he did not finish the sentence. "It's a genuine cold spot."

"I don't need to be told it was cold."

"I mean it's a classic psychic phenomenon." Randy started to extend his hand into it, but did not. "I've read about them—they're a common occurrence in haunted houses."

Lamar sighed. "I can't believe that you, a college-educated boy, believes in ghosts." He was disappointed; he had admired Randy at least for his book learning.

"I didn't say I believe in ghosts, if you mean dead folks' spirits. But there's something wrong with this mansion, Uncle—and a lot of college-educated people would agree with me. I've talked to scientists at the university who say that ghosts are as good an explanation for the way the world works as anything else." Randy looked around him and shivered, though he was no longer in the cold spot.

"What, *scientists* believing in *spooks*?"

"Physicists," Randy said. "You'd be surprised at some of the things they believe in. Listen—let's go downstairs. We don't need to go through the rest of Greymare House, do we?"

"If you're doing a job," Lamar said, "you got to do it all the way, even if no one knows it but you. Come on, now." He started down the hall, and to his satisfaction saw Randy take a deep breath and follow him.

He entered the first bedroom, dimly lit by the hall windows. It was empty of furniture; Lamar looked with satisfaction at the ornate wainscoting and parquet floor pattern. In the second bedroom the walls were covered with peeling, patterned wallpaper. He glanced behind the door perfunctorily and almost missed the mirror. He swung the door almost shut and looked at it. It was full-length, the glass acid-etched with tracery, the frame brass, with finials and candlestick holders. It was a beau-

tiful piece of work, and it was all his. He looked at his
reflection in the gloom: a short, solid man with a fringe
of gray hair and lines, broken veins in the nose. Despite
the belly pushing over the belt, he felt he could say he
was still in good shape.

He frowned and looked closer at his reflection. There
was something slightly odd . . . perhaps it was just the
lack of light. The reflection of the room looked different.
Lamar squinted. There was nothing in the room, nothing
in the reflection, and yet. . . .

The walls, that was it. The wallpaper was not faded
and peeling, and cobwebs did not hang in the corners.
Just the darkness? No, for he could see the pattern very
clearly where the light from the door struck it.

Something moved in the shadows of the mirror.

He wheeled about, and at the same time he heard the
scream. He aimed his flashlight as he would a gun, illuminating nothing but cobwebs; at the same time he pulled
the door open and ran into the hallway, in time to see
Randy staggering back from the open door of the last
bedroom. The boy's face was plaster white, and one
hand was out in front of him. He turned and stumbled
into Lamar, who took him by the shoulders and held him
up. Lamar's heart was pounding. "What? What was it?"
he demanded.

"The—the bed . . . blood. . . ."

Lamar released him and started toward the last bedroom.

It took considerable effort on his part to do so. Randy's
constant prattling about Greymare being haunted was
obviously beginning to affect him. He could have sworn
he saw something large and dark come toward him in the
mirror. . . .

He took a deep breath and stepped into the room.

It was empty, save for a large brass-framed double
bed. It had evidently been standing there for years; it
was still covered with a patchwork quilt, dusty and faded
now. But there was nothing unusual about it, except
that, like the mirror, it should not be there. He could
understand the movers overlooking the mirror, but how
could they have passed over such a large piece of furniture?

Whatever the reason, it was his now. He walked around
it, admiring the brass frame. There was no trace of

blood, on the quilt or on the floor. A floorboard creaking behind him brought him around quickly. Randy stood there, staring at the bed.

"Well?" Lamar asked quietly.

"I—I don't—" he exhaled hard and tried again. "The floor was covered with blood. The bed was soaked in it. I never knew there could be so much blood. It was pouring off the quilt. . . ."

"I don't see any blood."

"Neither do I—now."

Lamar turned away from him in disgust. This had gone too far. He had tried to be patient, but by God, enough was enough! He pointed his finger at his nephew. "If I hear one more word about this place being haunted—"

There was the sound of heavy footsteps running up the front stairs.

In spite of himself, Lamar jumped. Randy turned around with a gasp. Then George Colby came into the room, breathing hard and obviously frightened. "Thought I heard someone holler," he said.

Randy stood quite still. "You didn't," Lamar replied, and saw his nephew relax slightly. "Just a squeaking hinge. How are things downstairs?"

George looked uncomfortable. "Goin' slow, frankly. Things keep happening."

"Such as?"

"Such as a casement window banging shut on Frank Scully's head. Or Pettus burning his hands."

"How did *that* happen?"

George shuddered. "He went into the fireplace to see how the back was mounted. Minute he touched it, he came out yellin' his hands were burned."

"That's impossible," Lamar said.

George shrugged again.

Lamar looked back at Randy. His nephew's face was expressionless. "Randy, go on back downstairs and see if you can help. George and I will go on up here."

He saw the relief in Randy's eyes, balanced by the reluctance in George's. Then Randy was out of the room and down the stairs, the echoes of his retreat fading slowly in the thick warm air.

"I'm tired of wetnursing him," Lamar said. "All the time talking about ghosts, seeing things. I know you

won't panic, even if this place does get on your nerves."
He saw George's jaw tighten, and knew the man would
not back down now.

The inspection of the rest of the floor went by without
incident. They hurried through the rooms, saying little,
and Lamar had to admit that even he was beginning to
be bothered by Greymare House. He did not let any of
this be noticed by George, however, who finally said, "I
got to admire you, Lamar. I confess this place has me as
nervous as a cat in a roomful of rocking chairs. But you
don't feel it, do you?"

"I never was one to let my imagination run away with
me," Lamar replied. "Never was scared of the dark
when I was a kid— never understood why other kids
were. My Grandpa used to tell us kids ghost stories, and
my brothers and sisters would tie themselves into knots."
He paused. "Just seemed silly to me. There's so much on
this old world that can hurt you—why make up more
things?"

"Knew a fella like that once," George said. "He'd spit
in the Devil's eye on Halloween. He was like those folk
what can't tell about music, what's the word?"

"Tone deaf?"

"Right, like that—'cept he was tone deaf to the
supernatural."

"That's me, too." But Lamar did not feel comfortable
saying it. For the first time in his life, he was feeling
uneasy without knowing the cause of it. The creaks and
groans of the old house as they walked through it made
him nervous and jumpy. And, though he would not
admit it, he was glad to have George with him.

"Ain't nothing left to check 'cept that attic," George
said finally. Lamar nodded, believing it for a moment,
and then realized that George was wrong. There was still
the cellar to be investigated.

His stomach tightened at the thought. It's the rats, he
told himself. Only the rats.

The door to the attic was squat and wide, set at an
incline against the stairs. It took both of their shoulders
against it to open it.

Lamar was thinking about something Randy had said.
He had an uneasy respect for science that he did not
have for the supernatural. If scientists now believed in

ghosts—well, that was very disturbing. After all, scientists had put men on the moon, you couldn't deny that, unless you were like old Abe Jeffries who still insisted it was all a hoax. But when you got right right down to it, what was more incredible—men walking on the moon or ghosts walking the halls of Greymare?

It was not quite dark in the attic; some light and air came through the venting eaves and the shuttered windows. But it was dark enough. The attic was L-shaped, bending about the inclined doorway. Lamar flashed his light toward the large side of the room. He saw nothing except dust and webs, some scraps of cloth and paper. A hornets' nest hung near the ladder to the cupola. Lamar heard the whispering movements of the rats. It sounded, he suddenly thought, almost like someone or something chuckling.

It was then that George said in a careful calm voice, "Randy ain't the only one who's seeing things, Lamar."

Lamar turned and looked at him. George was staring at one of the rafters near the bend in the room. He was standing quite still, save that his hands were trembling.

Lamar saw nothing. "What is it, George?"

"You mean to say you don't see it?"

"Not a thing." And that was true. But he *felt* something; it was as though the nervousness he was feeling somehow seeped out of him and poisoned the air about him. It was a heavy, close sensation, and he felt his muscles tightening in response, his breathing growing more rapid. The scurrying of the rats increased, and the sound seemed more and more like dry, whispery laughter, the laughter of something old and evil.

"Describe it to me, George."

George said slowly, "I see a body hanging from that there beam, by a hemp rope. It's the body of a Confederate soldier, looking like it was hung yesterday. And underneath that, there's a Union soldier, lying in his blood. I swear I see those things as plain as I see you."

Lamar went forward and stopped beneath the beam. His heart was beating fast enough to make him dizzy, but he was determined to show none of his fear. "Here?" he asked. He flashed his light up at the rafter, saw nothing but wood.

"You—you're right beside 'em. Lamar. You're stand-

ing in that Yankee's blood. Please—don't go no closer.
I'm awful scared that they're gonna move. . . ."

Lamar still could not see anything, but now he most
definitely felt something. His heart was pounding like a
jackhammer, and the hair on his arms was standing up.
The air seemed charged with electricity. He forced himself to breathe slowly.

He stepped around the corner to see what lay beyond
it.

As he did, he felt as though he broke through a wall of
spiderwebs—that insubstantial, yet at the same time very
strong. The feeling of electricity in the air vanished.
Behind him, he heard George say in amazement and
relief, "They're gone! Just like soap bubbles!"

Lamar put a hand against the wall to keep himself
upright. The release of tension left him feeling weak.
"Well, then," he said, "come on and see what they were
hiding."

George approached and looked around the corner. He
still looked calm, but there was a jerkiness to his movements and a bright sheen of sweat on his brown temples.

Before them was a small rolltop desk.

"Do you suppose they were hiding it?" George whispered.

"I don't know what to think," Lamar replied, "except
that we've been finding more booty in this house than in
Cap'n Kidd's cave." He examined the lock on the desk.
It was locked, and he had no intention of forcing it open.
"We'll figure a way into it later, maybe," he said. "Let's
get it out of here."

It was not heavy. They carried it down to the second
floor hallway. Lamar mopped his face with his handkerchief. "We'll leave it here for the crew to take out. Let's
get downstairs. We got work to do."

It took all his willpower to walk slowly down the wide,
curving staircase.

Most of the crew had assembled outside. There was
little talk among them, Lamar noticed. Other items had
been found, and assembled on the overgrown lawn: a
wingback chair, a dry sink, a gate-leg table. Lamar looked
at them in satisfaction. There were antique dealers who
would pay a great deal for treasures like these. Outside
the house, in the bright warm sun, he realized how

foolish he had been to let the others' fears get to him. It was unfortunate about the bruise on Scully's head—unfortunate, but hardly the work of ghosts. The old counterweight ropes in the window had no doubt broken, that was all. As for Pettus' hands, that would be a bit harder to explain, but he was sure there was a reason. Fire ants, possibly.

"Well, time's wasting," he said. "Let's get started. We'll break down the attic first—"

He stopped abruptly, for he had once again remembered the cellar. He had not looked down there, nor had anyone else. Let it go, he told himself. After all, the tearing started at the top; it would be weeks before they had to concern themselves with the cellar. Let it go, or send someone else down. But as he looked at the faces of his crew, watching him, he knew none of them would do it. Could he ask one of them to go where he was reluctant to go?

His words to Randy came back to him: You got to do a job all the way, even if no one knows it but you.

This is foolish, he told himself angrily. It's only a cellar. There's nothing down there except a few old boxes, possibly some old furniture. . . .

And the rats.

The thought made Lamar ill. Nevertheless, his voice was steady as he continued, "Start trimming down the attic, while I check out the cellar." He turned back toward the house, feeling some small amusement at the surprised and worried looks his announced intention had caused.

As he stepped back onto the porch, Randy called, "Uncle Lamar—!" and stopped, as though unable to finish.

Lamar looked back at him and said, "George'll get you started on a job." He looked at George, who was staring at him in disbelief and worry, and said with as much cheeriness as he could, "Be back in a minute." Then he was inside the house again, listening to his footsteps echo as he walked toward the kitchen.

When he opened the cellar door, he could not help recoiling a step from the sheer intensity of the darkness—it was like a black curtain. There was also the damp, earthy smell of mold and rat dung. Lamar started down the steps, holding the flashlight out before him. The beam, more than enough for the darkness upstairs, seemed almost absorbed by the close cellar night.

There was nothing to be afraid of, he told himself. All right, so maybe there was something wrong with Greymare House—maybe it *was* haunted. Just because he had never seen a ghost did not mean there wasn't something to the idea. but he had heard somewhere that there was no record of ghosts having hurt people—the most they could do was appear and frighten. And perhaps they could not even do that to him, for he had not even seen what Randy and George saw—

The risers under the last step were loose—he tripped and almost fell on the slippery stone floor. One hand, flailing to regain his balance, ripped through the sticky gauze of a spider web above him. He ducked, feeling the back of his neck prickle with the expectation of something loathsome dropping down his shirt. He almost turned and bolted back up the stairs. Calm *down!* he told himself fiercely. He struck out with the flashlight beam against the darkness. He had never been afraid of the dark before in his life, but this darkness was different—he could almost feel it, wrapping about him, seeking to smother him.

He flashed the light around the cellar.

It was very large—much larger than he had expected. As the light swung about, he heard the scrabbling sound of rats running, could see the green gleam of their eyes. The smell of them, mixed with the other smells of decay and dampness, made him feel ill. It was not cool in the cellar, not even as cool as it had been on the porch. Instead, it was oddly warm, a humid, jungle warmth.

He could see the chewed remnants of cardboard boxes and old newspapers, shredded by rat teeth and claws to make nests. There were a lot of nests. Somehow, he could never manage to catch the rats in the light longer than momentarily. But he could see enough to know that they were big.

Lamar walked out into the cellar, turned and shone the light under the steps. Nothing there but webs; he saw one huge black widow spider frozen by the beam, the hourglass like a drop of blood. He backed away, his back still hunched, though the joists were far over his head.

He turned around again, panning the light, causing the rats to jump and burrow into their nests in an attempt to escape it. God, he thought, how the scratch and patter of all those claws did sound like dry, sinister laughter.

He turned back toward the stairs. There was nothing down here worth having. But, as much as he wanted to leave the cellar, he hesitated. There was something about the floor. . . .

Lamar shone the beam over the floor again. The pool of light stopped on a large square that was a different shade of black. It was a trap door, old and moldy, with a ring handle near one end. Greymare House had a sub-cellar.

Lamar stared at it, not breathing, thinking: I've got to check it out, too.

He shook his head, feeling gooseflesh alive all over him. I can always say I didn't see it, he told himself. But instead of retreating, he approached the trapdoor with stiff, numb legs until he stood over it, looking down at it, the moldy wood shining in the light.

The rats were quiet now, he realized. As though they were waiting. Not one moved, but he could still hear the laughter, papery and evil and coming closer . . .

The trap door moved.

He screamed, and suddenly the cellar was alive with rats, rushing everywhere, startled by his scream; he kicked them and trod upon them as he ran toward the stairs. He tripped on the loose step, falling; the flashlight slipped from his fingers; hit the floor and the darkness was complete about him, suffocating him as he went up the steps on his hands and knees, feeling rats running over him, the sound of them deafening. He crawled for a lifetime, driving splinters into his fingers and knees, until suddenly he was lying on the tiled kitchen floor and kicking shut the cellar door.

He lay there for a moment, sobbing and shuddering. Then he stood, leaning against the wooden counter until his breathing returned to normal. Then he yanked open the back door and walked out into the hot afternoon sunlight.

He stood near the rusting husk of a bell that had once been used to summon slaves from the fields, and looked at the house. It looked no less stately and solid from the back. Lamar looked at it, let his eyes travel up to the dormered attic windows and the cupola. He could hear faint sounds from within as the crew went about stripping the walls of paneling.

For the first time in his life, he had been terrified by his own imagination. It could not be anything else, he told himself. There could not possibly be anything alive in that subcellar.

Nevertheless, he swore he would not see that cellar again until the house above had been ripped away and the sun allowed to burn out the filth and mold.

He stared at the house, feeling none of the admiration and regret he had when he first saw it. All that had changed now. He was going to enjoy this job.

"I'm gonna bring you down," he said to Greymare House.

The trimming crew stood on the attic and second floor, and soon the sultry afternoon air was full of the sounds of nails shrieking loose from wood and chisels stabbing into plaster. Lamar looked in satisfaction at the amount of salvage that began to come out of the house. Greymare was a treasure trove of woodwork alone: the carved walnut window casings, the redwood ceiling beams and corbels, the mahogany railings . . . all this would resale at a fine price. He had to make a good profit at this job, he thought grimly; otherwise, the Warren Wrecking Company would not last much longer. He could not afford for things to go wrong.

But things did go wrong.

One of the first jobs was flaking loose the cupola from the roof and lowering it with the crane. This was Alice's job. She sat in the worn green leather chair in the open cab, her grinning face protected by a visored helmet, and worked the hoist and swing levers with a delicate touch. The heavy ball and hook at the end of the cable came within reach of the crew men on the roof, and was secured to the ropes woven around the cupola. Lamar listened to the heavy chugging of the diesel engine as the cupola lifted free of the roof, hovered a moment and then swung slowly away from the roof as the crane house turned. He watched Alice fondly. He had often claimed she could lift a baby from a carriage without waking it.

Which is why he was so shocked to see the boom suddenly jerk slightly, and the dangling cupola suddenly snap free of its ropes and plummet downward. It was a large cupola, almost big enough for a man to stand upright in, with an iron wethervane tipped with an arrow. The men in the flatbed truck beneath it, who had been waiting to guide the cupola to its resting place on sawhorses, stood frozen in disbelief; then they leaped over the sides of the truck as the cupola crashed into it, shattering a chair and table set that had already been roped into place.

Lamar and the rest of the crew ran to the truck. The cupola and the majority of the furniture on the truck had been smashed to kindling, though thankfully no one had been hurt. Lamar felt a hand on his shoulder and turned to see Alice, her square face pale with shock and disbelief.

"I swear I don't know how it happened, Lamar."

"It's okay," he said. She was blinking back tears; he held her wide shoulders soothingly, attempting to calm her. "It's okay. You've gone for nine years without an accident—you're still 'way ahead of the game." She looked at him gratefully. He turned back to look at the damage done and saw George Colby standing nearby, looking at him. The tall man's face was noncommittal, but for some reason Lamar felt quick rage rise up within him. "What the hell you staring at, George? Ain't we lost enough time and money? C'mon, let's get back to work!"

George merely nodded without comment, and turned and walked briskly back toward the house. But Lamar could see him slow for a moment as he crossed the threshold, as though reluctant to enter.

He turned away from the others, who were looking at him in surprise at his outburst. It was unlike him, he knew. Well, Christ, if Alice was allowed an accident, he was certainly allowed to get upset over it.

He looked back at the house, and muttered a curse.

The work continued. Shingles fell from the roof like dirty brown leaves. Tied wood joints were cut, and the bargeboard came down. By the time the long slow summer evening was complete, a large hole in the roof had been opened and the attic stripped bare. One man had been wasp-stung from the nest there, and another had cut his arm on the flange of a metal vent, but such minor injuries accompanied every job. There was nothing, really, to indicate anything out of the ordinary was going on, Lamar told everyone repeatedly. Yet, as the sun sank behind the trees and dark, knifelike shadows slid over the grounds, the crew made haste to vacate Greymare House. They assembled around the trucks, silent and pensive for the most part. A few among them professed to sense nothing wrong with the house, but they did not voice their opinions very loudly.

Lamar did not know what he could say to the crew to cheer them up. For the first time since he had started this company, he felt unable to talk to his employees. It was all foolishness, he told himself irritably; and the worst of it was, he was being affected by it. He flushed at the thought of his behavior in the cellar, though no one knew about it but him. There could not be anything down there. This house was simply a job, like any other.

Still, as the truck pulled away from the grounds and he looked back at the house, limned in the red sunset, he could not help shuddering. If ever a house should be haunted, Lamar thought, Greymare House was it.

They arrived early the next morning, and the work continued. Forklifts carried wood and debris to the loaders, wrenches loosened bolts, screwdrivers removed screws and hinge pins. While work proceeded on the main house, Lamar instructed Bill Antoine to dozer down the mounds of rooting wood and kudzu that had once been the rebuilt slaves' cabins.

The yellow scoop dozer rolled down toward the old buildings, its wide tires crushing elephant's-ear plants and Judas vine, the engine firing slowly, sending puffs of blue smoke from the upright exhaust. Antoine lowered the blade, and the wide curved wall of metal hit the gray wood, pushed it forward with hardly a change in the engine's sound, grinding it into the red dirt like a lawnmower running over an ant hill. Lamar, watching, could smell the strong sweet smell of crushed plants mingling with diesel smoke. He felt a fierce satisfaction as the first building collapsed. See that, house? he thought, amused at his feelings but nevertheless enjoying them. See that? You're next.

The dozer struck the second building. A yellow explosion of sunflower birds scattered from beneath the eaves as their home was destroyed. Lamar turned away toward the house, intending to go inside and get out of the heat. He stopped at the sight of Randy standing near a skiploader with Jim Driffs and several other men. Randy was talking; the other were listening and nodding.

Lamar started toward them; at that moment, nephew or not, he was ready to fire Randy. Why prolong a bad situation? The boy was obviously not taking his work seriously. Let him go back to college and his crazy professors.

But he had not taken three steps when he heard a scream from behind him, coming just after the crash of the dozer into another building. Lamar spun around, shocked, and saw Antoine leap down from the dozer, tearing his helmet off, to stand staring in horror at the structure he had just brought down.

Lamar ran back to him, puffing in the humid heat. He reached into the open cab of the dozer and shut off the motor. In the loud, throbbing silence that followed, he could hear Antoine's rasping breaths; verging on sobs, as he stood there with his face hidden in his hands. "What is it, Bill?" he asked. "What's happened?"

Antoine's voice was muffled behind his hands; his fingers were digging into his forehead, the nails drawing blood. His body rocked as the words came out. "I didn't know anybody was in there, Lamar, honest to God I didn't—oh, God. I'm sorry, I'm sorry, that poor little girl. . . ."

Lamar looked down at the crushed and oozing tangle of plants and wood. There was no sign of a body in the wreckage. A shadow fell across the scene, and he looked up to see George. Remembering what had happened in the attic, he pointed to the ground beneath the blade and asked, "See anything?" dreading the answer.

George shook his head.

Lamar sighed in relief. "It's okay. Bill." He tried gently to pull the man's hands from his face.

"No—don't make me—I don't want to see her—"

"Ain't nothing to see. Look."

Antoine's hands crept slowly down his face. He looked, and blood followed the lines on his forehead as his eyes went wide. "Oh, thank the Lord!"

"Tell me what you saw."

"It was a young black girl—no more'n a child—the—" he shuddered. "—the blade had took off the top of her head—her eyes still open—" he covered his own eyes again.

Lamar looked down at the crushed cabin again. Then he said to George, "Take care of him," turned and walked away. The members of the crew that had gathered parted to let him through. "Keep working," he said in a low voice, and slowly, reluctantly, they returned to their jobs.

During the rest of the day minor accidents plagued them. A loader, his arms full of paneling, tripped over a bootscraper outside the back door and cut his shin. The engines on the machinery would sputter and die for no reason. A trimmer was bitten by a rat and had to be rushed to the Blessed Shoals Hospital.

Lamar told himself that such misfortunes could happen on any job. But he could not explain the hallucinations more and more members of his crew were having, or the feeling of tension in the air. A worker would rip a section of wainscoting from a wall and suddenly stop in a cold sweat and stare over his shoulder. Lights were strung everywhere, banishing the darkness, and by unspoken agreement no one went into any of the rooms alone.

Riding back along the winding, twisted roads, hemmed in by darkness, Lamar stared at the black and white glare of the headlights on the road. Only the second day, he thought, and already they were behind schedule.

There were more ways than one to demolish a house. He remembered the tenement building, and the living carpet of rats he had crossed to plant the dynamite that had brought the building down. He looked out the side window, into the darkness, and saw the brief glimmer of foxfire in the swamp. He shivered.

The next day, most of the loaders Lamar had hired locally did not return. "There ain't much we can do about it," George told him. "We won't be able to get anybody from that town to help tear this place now."

"We'll have to just get on as best we can," Lamar said. The walkout had come as a shock to him. But they had to keep going; the company's future depended on their completing this job.

This day went no better. One of the small bobcat dozers punctured a dump loader's tire with the corner of its sharp blade as the driver was swinging around. A large section of masonry simply fell from one of the gables, narrowly missing several men. The crew worked with the grim, leaden determination of convicts on a road gang.

At noon, Lamar was sitting under a large catfaced pine, eating a bologna sandwich. He sat alone. He noticed Randy and Jim Driffs—who, oddly, had not quit with the others—bending over the rolltop desk in the back of the flatbed. Lamar stood and walked quickly to the truck. He had spoken little to his nephew since the episode in the bedroom, but he had not been happy with Randy. The boy had refused to enter the house again, working instead outside on the cleanup crew. He had continued to talk to others, asking them what they thought of the house and of the strange things that had happened. Lamar felt he had bent over backward to give Randy a chance to come around. He could not continue to let the boy stir up more anxiety; this job was causing him too much trouble as it was.

He also did not want him damaging the few pieces of furniture left intact, and so he leaned over the side of the truck. He saw Jim Driffs probing the desk's lock with a wire; before he could say anything there was a *click!* and Jim slid the top up. Lamar swung himself up into the truck with a grunt. Randy and Jim looked up in surprise, but Lamar's curiosity had made him forget his anger. They investigated the contents of the desk together.

The many shelves and drawers were crammed with the usual heterogenous collection that accumulates in desks: a brass candlestick with the melted remnant of a candle in it; a plate with a blue Currier and Ives design; several soiled and faded antimacassars. There were also a great many yellowed papers and envelopes—and a diary.

All three of them reached for it—Randy seized it and opened it. Lamar covered the pages with his hand. "I'll read it," he said, surprised by the surliness in his voice.

Randy looked at him levelly for a moment, then handed the diary to him without comment. Lamar glared at the

pages in confusion for a moment before he realized what
was wrong. He felt heat creep up the back of his neck.

"What is it?" he growled.

"French."

Lamar gave the book back to him. Randy looked at
the first page.

"It belonged to a woman named Danielle Avinaign
. . . the first entry is dated October 15th, 1975. She must
have been the last tenant . . . 'How happy Arnaud and I
shall be here! This is a house much like the ones of which
my mother told me; solid and spacious, with a depth and
charm we could find nowhere in New Orleans' highly
touted architecture. The movers have finally finished,
and we are starting now to make sense of the great chaos
they have left us. Arnaud says we will have to make do
by ourselves for a time until proper servants can be
found; this area is, after all, hardly the height of civilization! Nevertheless, it is what we have chosen for our
remaining years; a simple and, God provide, peaceful
existence—' " Randy frowned. "The page is torn slightly
here, and inkstained—I think something startled her and
she slashed the paper with the pen . . . uh-huh, listen: 'I
must tell Arnaud to purchase some traps immediately.
There are rats here.' " He stopped.

"That all?" Jim Driffs asked.

"All for that day." Randy turned over several pages.

"Sounds like she's trying to make the best of a bad
situation," Lamar said, interested enough to forget his
anger.

Randy glanced at him, then at the house behind them.
"Doesn't it." He began to read again.

"The local inhabitants—in particular, one Eudora Hines,
a local termagant with seemingly not a good word to say
for anyone—have gone to great effort to acquaint me with
the sordid history of Greymare. I have learned much that
Arnaud did not tell me, though my sources can hardly be
called reliable. If they are to be believed, Greymare is
a veritable House of Usher. Since its antibellum origins, it
has evidently been the site of constant murder and rap-
ine. A few of the less disgusting events, as recounted to
me by the salacious Madame Hines:

'The house was built by Claiborne Greymare in the
late 1700's as a retreat for his ailing wife. She complained

constantly of being cold, even in the summer, and she hated the house. Evidently she went quite mad, for she at last immolated herself in the downstairs fireplace. Greymare sold the house to William Jared, a cotton baron and from all accounts a devil in human form. He beat and tortured his slaves; Eudora has described how a slave was tied to what she terms "That catfaced pine out front," and whipped until he chewed the bark away in his pain. They say it has never grown back. This continued, until the Civil War, whereupon the slaves rose up in revolt and literally hacked Jared to pieces while he slept, soaking his bed in blood—' " Randy stopped with a sudden gasp. "The bed!"

Lamar knew what he meant. "Now wait," he began. "That couldn't be the same bed—"

"Why couldn't it? I saw the blood, Uncle Lamar!"

"I don't think you better read any more." Lamar reached for the diary. Randy backed out of reach and continued reading rapidly.

" '—Evidently Greymore drew crimes of passion to it. During the war a young man in the Confederate Army stalked his brother, a Union soldier, through the house, killed him and then hanged himself—' "

"George Colby saw them in the attic!" Jim Driffs shouted.

Lamar was aware of others in the crew gathering around and listening to Randy's rising voice. He felt panic beginning within him—this could cause them all to walk out. "I said give me that!" he snapped, grabbing the diary from Randy's hands. Randy stumbled backward, sprawled over the desk and into a clutter of furniture and lumber.

The silence that followed was quite intense. Lamar and Randy looked at each other in shock. Finally, "I'm sorry, Randy," Lamar said. He leaned forward, offering a hand to his nephew. "This job's been considerable strain to me—"

Randy ignored Lamar's hand as he got to his feet. "Uncle," he said quietly, "What's a catfaced tree?"

Lamar did not answer him. He did not seem to be able to organize his thoughts.

Jim said slowly, "It's what they call a scar on a tree that's healed around. Like that pine yonder," and he pointed to the tree under which Lamar had been sitting.

"That's a big tree," Randy said. "It's probably over a hundred years old."

He and Jim looked at each other. Then they both leaped from the truck bed and ran toward the tree, followed by several others who had been listening.

Lamar watched them helplessly. If only he knew the right things to say, he thought; the words that would bring them all to their senses, that would stop this increasing madness. . . .

"There!" Randy shouted, pointing at a spot on the tree trunk. "There it is!"

Lamar stared with the rest of them. He could see it quite clearly across the hot green distance: a white wound on the dark body of the tree, glistening with fresh sap.

The next day, half of the crew did not show up for work. George Colby arrived quite late. When Lamar saw him, he began to shout. "Goddamn them! They know this is a make-or-break job for us! How could they—"

"They could real easy," George said. "It ain't that easy for me, Lamar—but I got to do it anyway. I just come to tell you I won't be on this job no more."

Lamar stared at George. It was late afternoon, and they stood by Alice's crane, watching the few crew members left go about the day's work. "George," Lamar said slowly, "You're my right-hand man. You're co-owner of this here company. You—you were never one to lose your common sense, George. You've always had nerve. Remember that burnt job we had over in Beatriceville? We were in there with the scoop when half that burnt-out roof started falling."

"I remember."

"You never turned a hair," Lamar went on, his voice quietly desperate. "You just raised that blade over us like an umbrella. You saved both of us. Now you want to ruin me, George?"

"It won't work, Lamar," George said. "You got to remember—you don't feel what most of us feel in this house. Eveything a man puts a bar to it, seems like it cries out in pain—pain and hatred. You can't feel that. But those men that quit felt it. And I feel it. We stayed as long as we did because of you. But we can't stay no longer. Don't try to make us. Please. You don't know how it feels."

Lamar thought of the cellar; the thick warm darkness, and the cold gleam of the rats' eyes. The hell I don't feel it, he thought angrily. I'm as scared as you all are. But I've got a job to do. Aloud he said, "Go on then, if that's all the spine you have. But we ain't no union company. Don't think you can get your jobs back."

George looked at him with great sadness. "This ain't at all like you, Lamar. I don't know why you're being this way—but it don't change anything. We can't stay here! I'm telling you that house is *alive*, and it's fighting for its life! I'm telling the crew to pull out!"

"You'll put this company underground if you do!" Lamar grabbed George by his shoulders. "You're going to ruin us!"

"If I don't," George said, "Greymare House will!" He pulled free and started toward the house.

Lamar looked after him, seeing through a red filter of fury. They *had* to finish tearing this house! He could not let anything stop him—not the house, not the rats, and not George.

He started to run after him, but at that moment he heard a car pull onto the grounds behind him. He turned to see Randy's Volkswagen come to a stop. His nephew got out and ran toward him, the diary clutched in one hand. His face was quite pale, but full of determination.

"I read it," he said. "The whole thing, last night." He opened the book. "Listen to this: 'I am now convinced that Greymare House is the haven of some hostile, preternatural force, a malignancy that brings out and thrives upon the worst in people. It dwells within the cellar, or in the ground beneath Greymare and drives people to their deaths. But then—ultimate horror!—*it does not let them die*. Their spirits remain, tied to the halls and rooms of Greymare. I know this is true. I have seen in the empty cabins slaves William Jared tortured, such as the truncated specter of a little girl. I have seen his bloodied bed. In the mirror on my bedroom wall I have seen reflected things of which I cannot write.' " Randy turned the pages. "This is the last entry: 'It has taken Arnaud; driven him mad with horror. He has gone to it. The house will not let us leave. The doors close and lock themselves; the shutters cannot be forced. As I write this, the sun is setting. So far I have been able to keep my sanity, but its power is greater at night.

'The sun is almost down. I write this in the attic, as far away from the evil locus as possible. I can hear Arnaud's mad laughter far below. I can see the slain forms of the brothers, one lying in his blood, the other twisting slowly above him. And now the rats are appearing in the dusk . . . they seem quite fearless. . . ."

Randy shut the diary with a snap. "That's all. Don't you see, Uncle? That spirit, or force, or whatever it is, is still there!"

Lamar looked at Randy, but could not see him clearly; there seemed to be a roaring in his ears, a soundless pounding that made his head ache. "It's impossible," he said slowly. "You're making it up. Can't nobody here but you read it—"

Before Randy could reply, they heard shouting from within Greymare House.

Lamar turned and ran toward the house. Randy hesitated a moment, then followed. Lamar pounded up the steps colliding with men on their way out, running, clawing, fighting with each other to get through the door. Lamar pushed and shoved against them, at last tumbling into the dark interior.

Randy followed him in. George Colby was the only one still there. He stood staring into the fireplace. Lamar looked; at first he saw nothing. He stared, shaking with intensity, feeling it somehow very important that he see what they had seen.

Gradually, the room seemed to fill with flickering orange light. The huge stone fireplace became ablaze with flame; he could hear the crackling of pine knots and smell the smoke. And in the midst of the flames stood a woman. She had evidently just stepped into the fire, for her nightgown was still burning, her hair just beginning to ignite. As Lamar watched, rooted with horror, he saw her turn and stare at him; her blue eyes, at first filled with the calm of madness, suddenly widened as the agony brought realization. She threw back her head and screamed, as her skin began to blacken and shrivel. . . .

And then the scene seemed to waver, to ripple like

disturbed water, and was gone. The fireplace stood empty and cold.

George turned to Lamar. "You saw that," he said quite calmly.

Lamar slowly nodded.

George turned and walked out the door. Outside was the sound of engines turning over. The men had piled into the old Ford vans and the flatbed. Through the front door he could see them driving away at breakneck speed.

Randy grabbed his arm. "Uncle, we've got to get out of here!"

Lamar blinked. There were quite a few rats in the shadows he noticed—all still, all watching. He shook Randy's hand away and turned to face him. "This is your fault," he said thickly. "All of it. You turned my crew against me. . . ." He swung the back of his fist at Randy, felt his knuckles strike the boy's cheekbone, splitting the skin. Randy fell away from him and sprawled on the floor. He scrambled to his knees and ran, away from Lamar and the front door, toward the arch that led to the dining room.

Lamar looked blankly at his smarting hand, then after his nephew. The blow he had struck Randy seemed to have struck him as well, shocking him out of his rage. "Randy," he shouted. "Are you all right?" He ran after him.

He came through the archway and stopped. Randy stood in the middle of the dark, empty room, eyes wide and face bloodless, staring at the floor in front of him. Lamar heard the dry, sinister rattle even before he saw the snake. It was a huge diamondback, coiled a foot from Randy. Randy stood very still.

"Easy," Lamar whispered. "Take it easy," as he looked about for something to use as a weapon. There was nothing. Then, suddenly, his eyes caught a flicker of motion in the darkness above Randy. Lamar stared upward, unable to believe what he saw.

The ceiling fan was beginning to turn.

There as no electricity to power it, yet the fan was spinning; slowly at first, then faster. Randy looked up as the musty air breathed over him. The fan was spinning quite fast now, faster than it had been designed for. Lamar could feel the floor beginning to vibrate, could hear the high, keen whine of the wooden blades cutting the air. The fan was beginning to shake, but still it spun faster and faster, producing a propwash that tore at their hair and clothes. Randy stood beneath it, staring alternately at it and the coiled rattlesnake. He closed his eyes and began to sob. A fine powder of ceiling plaster frosted the air. . . .

"*No!*" Lamar screamed, as the fan tore loose from the ceiling and hurtled downward. He hid his face behind his arms, but could not avoid hearing Randy's scream, or the hideous sound that cut it off. He felt a wet mist on his arms as he hurled himself backward, running across the floor under the watchful gaze of the rats.

He burst from the house and ran toward the abandoned heavy equipment. He sagged to his knees against the dump loader and was sick.

Then he stood, slowly, and stared back at Greymare House.

It stood, quiet, substantial and ominous against the afternoon sun. Most of the roof was gone, and part of the upper walls, but it had not been defeated. Lamar stared at it for a long time, feeling his horror and sorrow subside slowly, leaving nothing but icy determination.

He was alone. They crew had left, and Randy . . . Randy was dead. It was him against the house, now.

He would have to bring it down alone.

Lamar turned and climbed into one of the transport trucks. From a locked cabinet he brought forth an extra heavy pair of coveralls, gloves and a face visor. Then he lifted out a stout wooden box, and a wooden chisel and mallet. He stood the box on one end, and carefully tapped the cover loose. Within were the long, brick-red cylinders, packed in sawdust. He had packed the box two days before, telling no one. I could have lost my license for improper transportation of explosives, he thought, and let go a single note of dry laughter.

He worked slowly and carefully, refusing to let himself think about anything but the job. He snapped blasting caps onto each stick of dynamite, attached the black and red wires to each cap. He wired them in parallel, five to a set, and each set to a small radio receiver unit. Then he donned the coveralls, gloves and visor, gathered up the dynamite and turned toward the house again.

The sun was near the horizon, but it had not yet set. The diary had said Greymare's power was weaker by day. And perhaps it would be weaker still after the effort it had just expended. In any event, he would have to take the chance.

Lamar took a deep breath, and walked toward the house.

The door had swung shut, and would not open until he used a crowbar on it. He went inside.

It was as he had feared: the rats were there, everywhere, covering the floor in a dirty flood, the sound of their restless prowling filling the room, sounding so much like laughter. . . .

Lamar swallowed bile and forced himself across the floor toward the fireplace, one of the structural strong points of the house. The rats tore at his heavy boots, scrabbled up his legs, slashing at his two pairs of coveralls with teeth and claws. He clubbed them off with the crowbar. He put one of the sets of dynamite on the mantel, where the rats could not reach it, then turned and fought his way toward the kitchen, not looking at Randy's body in the dining room. He left another of the sets on the counter. As he did, a creaking sound swung him around, and what he saw tore a scream from his throat. He turned and clawed his way up the back stairs against the tide of rats. The cellar door was opening. . . .

He ran, planting the rest of the dynamite against the supporting walls upstairs. The rooms and corridors were like a maze; they seemed to twist and turn back on themselves, nightmarishly, as he searched for the front staircase. And everywhere were the rats, tearing at him, biting and clawing. But even that was not the worst of it, for through the sound of the rats he could hear laughter, coming closer, and he knew that something was following him, something that had come from the cellar to drag him back to it, something dark in the darkness of the corridors, grinning, and gaining on him.

Lamar's clothes and gloves were ripped to shreds now, and he had lost his visor. A rat leaped at him, sinking its teeth into his arm—he staggered back, and suddenly there was the staircase. He fell down it, dropping the crowbar, the bodies of rats cushioning his fall. He managed somehow to get to his feet. As he ran across the

floor he glimpsed the huge chandelier above him swaying—
he dodged to one side as it fell, crashing to the floor and
spraying him with crystalline fragments. The front door
was closing; Lamar hurled himself forward, twisting
through the narrow opening. Then he was outside, stumbling across the grass in the bloody evening light.

Behind him, he heard the door open again.

Lamar did not look back. He ran toward the truck
where he had left the detonator. Behind him something
was coming, something even more horrible than the formless terror his mind pictured. It was close upon him, he
knew, perhaps already reaching for him as he seized the
detonator and, knowing he was still too close to the
house, jammed both thumbs onto the button.

Then a huge, slamming sound, more felt than heard
lifted and hurled him. Lamar felt himself turn completely
over once. He did not feel himself hit, or hear the echoes
of the explosion rumble away into the pattering rain of
debris, and finally into absolute silence.

The last thing Lamar heard as he lost consciousness
was the laughter.

When Lamar woke, it was night.

His awakening took a long time. He was semiconscious
several times, feeling dimly the night breeze on his face
and body, before sinking once more into blackness. At
last he became fully conscious. One of the first things he
noticed was the acrid smell of cordite. He tried to open
his eyes, could only open one—the other seemed crusted
over. He looked at a strange, upside-down scene: the
blasted ruins of Greymare House.

The moon, just past full, illuminated everything in
stark black and white. He had placed the charges well,
Lamar thought, feeling absurdly proud of himself. Most
of the house had been blown apart. The fireplace and
chimney, the spine of the structure, had been broken,
and the other blasts had disintegrated the already-
weakened upstairs. One wall had collapsed completely,
and only fragments of the other three stood. The first
floor had caved in. Everywhere were scorched and twisted
pieces of wood and metal, fragmented beams, shattered
glass and tile. The front window had been blown out on

one of the trucks, but he could see no other damage to the equipment.

Lamar was lying upside down in the bank of kudzu where he had been thrown by the explosion. Surprisingly, he did not feel much pain—not until he moved. Then a burst of agony from his left arm told him that it was probably broken. He was bleeding from cuts caused by the blast and the crashing chandelier, but none of them seemed too serious. All in all, he realized, he had been extraordinarily lucky. The plant wall had cushioned his fall and saved him from major injuries.

His movement, slight as it was, overbalanced him, and he slid slowly downward and toppled over, clenching his teeth against the pain as his arm was twisted. He grabbed a broken balustrade from the staircase that lay nearby and used it as a cane to pull himself to his feet. He put his hand to his eye to explore the damage, and took it away again quickly; most of the eye seemed to be gone. He felt faint and sick from his injuries, and he did not know how far he could walk. But he was alive. He was alive, and Greymare House was dead.

The night was very quiet, he thought. Then he realized that he had been deafened by the explosion. He looked up at the stars—his neck crackled painfully, but he kept his head up. I did it, he thought. I brought Greymare down.

He looked at the ruins again, and saw the rats.

There were not merely as many as there had been. They were crawling about the ruins, and paid no attention to him as he limped painfully toward the truck. They were not interested in him, now that Greymare and its evil had been destroyed.

It would not be a comfortable ride back to Blessed Shoals—he did not know how he would shift gears with a broken arm. But he would manage somehow. He had already been through the worst, he told himself, as he made his slow way past Alice's crane.

The crane moved.

Lamar stopped, turned his head and stared at the crane. No, he said to himself. No. Please, no.

But as he watched, it moved again.

There was no mistaking it; the housing moved slightly,

left, then right, like an animal sniffing. The boom lowered slightly, and the steel cables tightened.

Then it began to roll toward him.

Lamar backed up slowly, not thinking at all, simply watching. He could see the crane quite clearly in the moonlight, could see the deep, scarlike paths the treads were leaving in the ground, could see the empty cab, where none was riding, no one pulling the hoist lever back. And yet the drum was slowly turning, the cable winding, and the clam shell bucket that had been used to pick up salvage was slowly rising, and opening.

The silence was the worst part of it. His deafness prevented him from hearing the creakings of the boom and cables, the clacking roll of the treads. But he knew that the engine was not running—he might not have heard the starter engine crank, but the heavy pounding of the diesel was a subsonic, gutwrenching sound that shook the ground. No, the motor was off—but the crane was moving.

It's not fair, he thought.

He stepped backward again and stumbled, then slid down an embankment of loose earth, tumbling, crying out in agony.

He opened his one eye and realized he was in the cellar.

It had survived the dynamite quite well. Over half of the floor sagged, making a brooding cave. The rest was bathed in moonlight, the jointed stone a cold silver over which rats flickered like shadows. Lamar stood, staring at the center of the floor.

The trap door was open.

Of course, he thought quite calmly. It's stronger at night.

A movement overhead made him look up. The crane boom was swinging over him—and the bucket was dropping!

Lamar scrabbled to one side, feeling the vibration as the heavy steel bucket slammed into the stone beside him. He stared at it as it rose again, the welded bolts covered with dirt, the cables drawing open the serrated halves like giant jaws.

He half-ran, half-limped into the darkness beneath the first floor. A moment later the broken floor beams shook as the bucket dropped on top of them. Lamar hid under his good arm as small pieces of wood and plaster rained down on him.

The bucket struck again. The floor sagged. It was coming apart. He knew he could not remain under it.

He ran out, holding his broken arm in his good hand, trying to use his feeble momentum to carry him up the embankment. It was useless; he slid back down.

The bucket hit the stone beside him again. Lamar backed away, felt nothing under one foot—and then he was falling. . . .

He did not fall far. The impact knocked him breathless nonetheless. He tried to stand and could not.

He was in darkness, lying on a damp dirt floor. He looked up—the trap door was well out of reach.

He thought longingly of how the eventual sunrise would burn out the evil that had dwelt so long beneath Greymare. But it would not come in time for him.

Though he was deaf, he could still somehow hear the dry, crackling laughter—or was it the scrabbling of the rats? Something touched his ankle, began to creep up his leg.

Oh please, he thought; please—let it be a rat.

CHARLES L. GRANT

The Children,
They Laugh So Sweetly

The rain stopped falling after midnight had passed, and it hangs now in the black, a fog newly formed; the street-lamps grow diffused, the branches grow facets, and puddles on the sidewalk reflect nothing but the night until, an hour later, they glaze over with ice. The lawn shades to white. The leaves stiffen. A twig snaps. On the corner a cat puffs its tail and hisses when the first of the day's winds begins to rattle the trees.

The house, not a large one, sits back from the hedge like an old man in the park—somewhat hunched, grayed by weather, its unlatched storm door flapping unevenly like a hand jumping in fitful sleep. Years past its prime, it watches and welcomes the birds that use it for warmth, and when a light is switched on in a room above the porch, an eye snapping open to stare dimly at the lawn, it seems to shift as if startled by the voices it hears.

Peter lowered his hand from the lamp's switch and put a finger to his lips to prevent Esther from questioning the look on his face. After a moment he sat up and cocked his head, turned it, and listened, and heard only the wind and the drip of a faucet.

"Are you all right?" she whispered.

He rubbed his eyes with a knuckle, scratched his chest, and blinked. "Dreaming, I think." The tone said he wasn't sure. He listened again and tossed the blanket aside. "You didn't turn the water off."

"Hey, not me, I wasn't the last to use it," she said through a yawn.

He didn't argue; it wasn't worth it. He got out of bed

and held his breath against the cold, then hurried into the bathroom to turn both handles as far around as they would go. The dripping stopped, and he leaned against the sink for a moment before feeling his way back into the wide hall. Squinting against the bedroom light, he looked left into the spare room and saw nothing but dim furniture shapes and the glowing outlines of windows; to his right was the staircase and another, smaller room whose door was kept closed, the radiator turned off. He had taken a half step toward it when he heard it, when he heard what had broken into his dreams.

Children's laughter, muffled behind a hand; small children enjoying a game and giggling, trying and failing to keep silent as they played.

"Peter!" Esther called, whispering again.

"Shhhh!" as he ducked back into the room and switched off the light.

Softly, and sweetly.

Through the narrow side window, he could see their lawn and hedge, and the distant trees and grass on the other side of a tall fence that wasn't theirs. All of it was empty, and bristling with frost. A glimmer from a shard of glass or a prowling cat's eyes, but nothing moving that he could see, out there in the dark.

He started when he heard Esther leave the bed, and joined her at the front, the two of them looking over the sloping porch roof to the grass, hedge, road, houses as dark as theirs should have been this time of the morning when, he thought, dreams were the strongest.

"Boy," she said quietly, took his hand, and drew him into the hall to the stairs and down to the landing, left down into the foyer where the streetlight barely reached, where the dry cold gathered.

He opened the front door and checked the porch as he pulled the storm door and locked it, clenching his teeth against the cold and feeling his muscles tighten. Then he followed his wife's explorations through the double parlor, the dining room, back into the kitchen.

"Nothing," he said, and staggered with a moan against the refrigerator when she switched on the light. "God, you could at least warn a guy, huh?"

"So what are you, a vampire or something?" She wore only a yellow T-shirt that reached halfway to her knees, and most of her dark hair was atumble over her face. She was smiling. "Well?"

"Well what?" He picked his feet up gingerly. "Christ, it's cold! I gotta do something about that damned furnace before we freeze to death come December."

"Well, how'd you do it?"

"Do what? And please, have a heart and turn off the damned light."

She did with a laugh, and settled against his hip when he put his arm around her. "You know . . . the kids."

"Me? I didn't do it. That's what woke me up."

A gust punched at the narrow window over the sink and rattled the back door.

"There," she said, nodding decisively toward the wind as they returned to the stairs. "That's what it was."

"I heard kids. You heard kids."

"At three o'clock in the morning? C'mon, Peter. It's an old house. It makes noises."

He didn't care if it made symphonies or Sousa as long as it didn't do it while he was trying to sleep. It was bad enough the place wasn't as perfect as they had thought when they bought it. Since moving in the June before, they had discovered a hundred hidden defects, each more expensive to repair than the last, each inevitably postponing the new car, the vacation, the interior renovations they had wanted to make to bring the century-old Victorian in line with its elegant neighbors.

"Hey," she said gently in the dark of the bedroom, "don't worry about it, O.K.? I think it's neat."

He nodded as he fell asleep wondering what the hell was so great about someone else's children, was awake and eating breakfast before he remembered. Esther was already gone, off to find draperies for the six-foot windows, and, with a bit of luck, locate an inexpensive shop for wallpaper to cover the faded vines and blossoms that made all the rooms seem too old. He cleaned the dishes, put them away, and walked slowly through the first floor, listening to the floorboards, pressing a palm against doorframes, finally pulling on a sweater and going out to the front yard.

A knowing grin then when he realized as he walked over the browning grass that he was searching for footprints, broken branches, betrayals of the kids who had played there the night before. And of course there was nothing he could not blame on the squirrels.

The grin faded, and he stopped at the hedge wall on the property's north side and peered through it. On the other side was the chain-link fence that canted away from him at the top and was strung with barbed wire; beyond the reach of the Memorial Park itself, though the first of the headstones was almost a hundred yards away.

Jesus, he thought with a sharp shake of his head; the sun is out, the sky is blue, and you're walking around hunting for bloody ghosts, for God's sake.

Feeling suddenly exposed and foolish, he returned to the porch steps and thrust his hands in his pockets, looking left down the street. The trees here were nearly as tall as the house and, despite the bright sunlight, somewhat gloomy without their leaves. There was no activity in any of the yards—the kids were in school, the adults off to work. As far as he could tell, he was the only man on the block who didn't have a job.

Esther did by the end of the day, however, and they celebrated that night by ripping a hole in their budget to buy steak and champagne. A miracle, he said; luck, she corrected. She had stopped in at the library to see what they had, and started talking with a woman whose husband turned out to be the editor of the local paper. Who was also, it turned out, looking for a secretary to start in two weeks when his old one left to join the ranks of new mothers.

"A miracle, like I said," Peter told her with a laugh.

"Luck," she insisted. "If I'd gone to the store like I should have, I never would have met the woman. I was in the right place at the right time." She emptied her glass and poured herself another. "It has to be luck, Peter, because that would mean ours is finally changing."

His smile was the best he could give her, while he couldn't help wondering if that was a crack about his status.

Never mind, he decided when he finally staggered off to bed; and never mind the next day when he worked in the yard, raking leaves into the gutters and cutting back the hedge. When Esther returned from the paint-and-paper store, he strode into the kitchen feeling damned good.

She was at the sink, the water running, no dishes to clean.

The line of her back told him there was trouble.

"Why did you tell me you'd gone to the school board?" she asked as she turned to watch him warm his hands with dry scrubbing.

He licked his lips and almost said that he had, but the dark expression on her face killed the lie in his throat. "I didn't want you to worry."

"Worry!" Her right hand became a fist that pushed her hair back. "Worry? Jesus Christ, Peter, what the hell were you thinking of?"

A shrug, and he walked slowly into the living room to flop onto the couch.

"And don't pull that Hamlet act on me, you hear? It doesn't work anymore." She stood in the doorway, trembling. "I saw that Mrs. Player on Center Street, the woman from the school board you called that time. She asked me when you were going to submit your application. They need substitutes badly, she said. And I could only stand there like a jackass because you told me you'd already done it!"

"I—"

"No!" she said, chopping the air with one hand. "Don't you dare give me that crap about not wanting to teach anymore. I don't want to hear a thing about being burned out and fed up and not caring anymore." She took a step into the room, and he flinched. "We are almost broke, Pete, do you understand that? The money is almost gone. If you don't—"

He waited for the threat, then looked up. She was gone, and there was no sense going after her. Nor was there any sense in feeling sorry for himself. He had played every game in the book, most of them more than once, and his luck had run out.

His legs stretched out under the coffee table; his arms extended along the back of the couch.

It wasn't true that he didn't like teaching anymore; it was everything that had gone with it that had finally worn him down—the students were undisciplined, but the administration seldom backed him; the administration was too busy figuring budgets and manpower to give a damn about education, decent or otherwise; and education became a conveyor belt on which students rode, the teacher machines stamped "passed" on their foreheads, a word half the kids couldn't read.

In the beginning, shortly after they married, Esther had agreed with him, and wasn't dismayed when they moved to Oxrun Station after his last position had been eliminated because of a cut in school funds. There was, after all, a reasonable amount left from his parents' estate, and they had used it to purchase the house on Northland Avenue—investing in their future instead of losing it on rent. But she had also counted on his finding a job to supplement her own, up-until-now temporary income; she had not counted on him being apparently untrained and unfit for anything but standing in front of a class.

He was afraid he would lose her, so he'd lied about his efforts.

"Dumb," he said to the fireplace and hearth. "Really and truly dumb, Peter Hughes."

That night he slept alone, though she was in bed beside him.

The following day he worked in the yard while Esther went to the *Herald* to see what she'd be doing. And when she returned she ignored him, though he could see she had recently been crying.

Dumb, he thought as he raked the leaves hard across the grass; dumb, stupid, idiot, jackass.

And that night he was awakened by an elbow in his side. He pushed at it; it returned; and it was several seconds before he realized she was trying to get him up. He nearly asked her why, until he heard it downstairs— the sweet quiet laughter, the ripple of giggles.

And something else a moment later—the tread of someone small slowly coming up the stairs.

A look at the windows filled with moonlight, a look at the clock on the nightstand. Then he swung his legs over and crept cautiously around the bed, realizing as he reached the door that he didn't have a weapon. He hesitated while Esther watched him, then decided he would simply have to rely on surprise—he could stand against the wall and kick the intruder when he reached the top step.

He moved, then, and he waited, and saw his skin turn to marble in the light of the moon.

But when he finally poked his head around the corner, the stairwell was empty, and the laughter had stopped a long while ago. He considered returning to bed and laughing it off, changed his mind and went downstairs, just in case. The rooms were all empty, doors and windows locked from the inside. The kitchen clock marked four in the morning, but the night felt closer to dawn.

She was asleep by the time he returned, and he wished a silent curse at the sheet now icy cold, lay staring at the ceiling, wondering about the house and the noises it made.

"The pipes," she said at breakfast. "Air in them, the cold—the wood contracts and expands when the heat escapes at night."

"All figured out, huh?" he said lightly, pleased she was at least speaking to him again.

"Nothing to it."

"No ghosts?"

She gave him a smile and a lift of an eyebrow. "I'd like that, actually, wouldn't you? Some kids maybe murdered here a hundred years ago, trying to find their way back to . . . I don't know . . . wherever kid ghosts are supposed to go."

"Sounds good," he said, "but as I recall, no kids ever lived here. And no one ever died here."

"Jesus, you are no fun, Peter, you know that? You aren't any fun at all anymore." Her coat was on, a woolen cap and mittens. "What are you doing today?"

He shrugged, and she left without giving him a kiss; he sat there for an hour, then dressed in a good suit, and, with a nod to the guilt that filled his stomach with acid, he walked to the board of education office, where he filled out an application for substitute teaching, and on impulse walked the two miles out to Hawksted College and did the same.

The day was cold, staining his cheeks and forehead an angry red, but he didn't mind it once he fell into stride. The snap of the wind, the swift gray of the clouds, the feel and sound of his heels on the pavement forced him to think for the first time without self-pity what it was that had failed him in the classroom, what it was that had made him reach out to the kids, and pull back when he thought he couldn't take it anymore.

He had deserted them, no question about it; he had deserted them and run away.

Not bad, he thought; it might even be true.

Afterward he wandered into the park and stood at the edge of the playing field, watching a gang of youngsters from the grammar school across the street having races with another class. They shrieked, they cheated, they wrestled, they laughed, and he couldn't help noticing how miserable their teachers looked, how they seemed to wish a miracle truck would appear and mow their classes down.

He shuddered and turned away, disgusted at the idea, sickened by the notion he must have looked like that, too, toward the end, before he quit.

When Esther finally returned from the *Herald*, dinner was ready. "I still haven't forgiven you," she said when he told her about his day, about everything but the park. "But thanks for doing the cooking."

"You ought to be getting paid, y'know?" he said. "All the time you're spending at the paper before you're supposed to start working, I mean."

"But they're nice," she told him, helping him clear the table and wash the dishes. "They really care about you, they want to make you feel right at home."

"It's a small town."

The telephone rang before he could answer, and when he returned to help put away the plates, he was grinning.

"What?" she said suspiciously. "You win the lottery or something?"

"Not quite as good; not so bad, either. A second-grade teacher's been in a car accident over in Harley. Nothing serious, she's O.K.," he said hastily to Esther's concern. "A bump on the head and a couple of cuts, but she's taking the rest of the week off. I get to cover."

"Oh, God," she said, and embraced him warmly. "God, Peter, I'm so glad I could bust!"

"Yeah," he said, frowning into her hair. "Yeah, me, too."

"You know, if you impress them," she said hesitantly, "you might be able to find yourself with a permanent job there, not just substituting."

"It crossed my mind," he lied, and was relieved when at last she lifted her face to kiss him. One crisis over; now all he had to do was figure out what to do with the rest of his life.

He was still thinking about it after they'd watched some television, taken a communal and long shower, and she fell asleep before he could reach for her, to cuddle.

There's always the local supermarket, he thought. Unload a few trucks, work the register, maybe even get to be manager of the produce section. It ain't rich, but it's a living. Or a shoe store. The bookstore. With the two of them working, they might even be comfortable.

And when he felt himself scowling at every suggestion made, he couldn't believe he'd jeopardize both his and Esther's future just because of damned pride. Jesus, he was going back to work tomorrow, at what he was trained to do. Why the hell couldn't he see it as a sign or something? Why the goddamned hell couldn't he be as happy as his wife?

He dozed, half-dreaming and not remembering a thing.

He woke to soft silence, turned his head, and saw the snow—large flakes clinging like white spiders to the panes, drifting past the streetlamps to bury the lawn, turn the hedge to a wall, make the black behind it deeper, colder.

And the laughter, just as soft, down in the foyer.

"You hear it?" Esther whispered, nearly frightening him to death. When he nodded and made to rise, she put a firm hand on his shoulder. "My turn. I've always wanted to see what a ghost looked like."

Still, drowsy, and angry at himself, he grunted and watched her shadow leave the room, heard the steps creak under her weight, and heard the laughing continue.

Suddenly the room chilled, and he jumped from the bed and ran out to the hall.

"Esther!"

Giggling behind a hand, from downstairs, from behind him, from the attic above.

"Esther, you see anything?"

The distant rumble of the furnace, and the radiators popping, clanking, hissing their steam.

He was halfway down the steps when the furnace clicked

off, and the silence that replaced it made him hold his breath and pause.

"Hey, Esther, knock it off, huh?"

The streetlight from the front was too dim for details, strong enough for shadows, and he waited until his eyes adjusted before moving down to the landing and scanning the foyer.

He wanted to call his wife's name again, but he listened instead.

To the silence.

To the snow.

To the fill of his lungs as he took the last steps and took hold of the doorknob. It was locked, from the inside.

The parlors were empty, the dining room, the kitchen.

It was a trick. It was long past midnight, and she was playing goddamned tricks when she knew damned well he had to get up in the morning and go stand in front of a bunch of empty-brained, unfeeling, goddamned spoiled little brats.

She knew that! Goddamnit, she knew that and she—

Oh, hell, he thought.

"Esther, c'mon, the fun's over."

He hesitated at the cellar door, then flung it open and went down, slapping at the light switch and cursing when it failed. Before he took another step, he grabbed a flashlight from a drawer, tried the lights in all the rooms, and damned the damn fuses.

The fuses were fine.

He couldn't think of anything else then but someone, maybe two or three, throwing a blanket over her head and dragging her from the house. He raced back to the bedroom and dressed as warmly as he could, picked up the telephone to call the police, and stared at the receiver when the dial tone failed.

"Esther!"

All the windows and doors were locked as before—from the inside, never opened.

He searched the closets, the pantry, looked under the couch and chairs, moved standing lamps and hassocks, kicked the rugs and checked the attic. When his voice grew hoarse from calling, he leaned against the kitchen door and looked out at the yard, blinking, nearly weeping, at the snow an inch deep and as smooth as the moonlight that had been there before.

He looked out every window, went out to the porch, and stood at the railing to stare at the street.

Nothing but the snow, falling silently white.

And when his teeth began to chatter, he returned inside, went up the steps to the bedroom, and dropped the flashlight on the floor. Then he sat on the bed and stared out the window. Sooner or later she would tire of the game and come back to him, kid him a little about the neat hiding place she'd found, then listen when he told her how often he had lied. It wasn't, he would say, the system, or the administration, or the parents, or even the lousy pay. It was the kids. It was always the kids—somewhere in there he had started to hate them.

And tomorrow he was going to hate them again.

He waited until he felt the cold enter the house, until the snow thickened, the silence deepened, and he knew without reason he wouldn't see her again.

Then he heard the laughter, soft and sweet, filling the house downstairs.

They know, he thought; they know the way kids do, and they don't want me back.

Giggling; quiet running.

"Esther?" he whispered, crushing a pillow to his chest.

They weren't ghosts at all.

They were only his nightmares.

Soft.

And sweet.

And coming up the stairs.

DAW

SPECIAL FOR HORROR FANS

THE YEAR'S BEST HORROR STORIES: VIII
Karl Edward Wagner, editor   (UE2158—$2.95)

THE YEAR'S BEST HORROR STORIES: IX
Karl Edward Wagner, editor   (UE2159—$2.95)

THE YEAR'S BEST HORROR STORIES: X
Karl Edward Wagner, editor   (UE2160—$2.95)

THE YEAR'S BEST HORROR STORIES: XI
Karl Edward Wagner, editor   (UE2161—$2.95)

THE YEAR'S BEST HORROR STORIES: XII
Karl Edward Wagner, editor   (UE1975—$2.95)

THE YEAR'S BEST HORROR STORIES: XIII
Karl Edward Wagner, editor   (UE2086—$2.95)

THE YEAR'S BEST HORROR STORIES: XIV
Karl Edward Wagner, editor   (UE2156—$3.50)

VAMPS
Heart-freezing tales of those deadly ladies of the night—
vampires. Martin H. Greenberg & Charles G. Waugh,
editors   (UE2190—$3.50)

DAW

Don't Miss These Exciting DAW Anthologies

ANNUAL WORLD'S BEST SF
Donald A. Wollheim, editor

- ☐ 1986 Annual   UE2136—$3.50
- ☐ 1987 Annual   UE2203—$3.95

ISAAC ASIMOV PRESENTS THE GREAT SF STORIES
Isaac Asimov & Martin H. Greenberg, editors

- ☐ Series 13 (1951)   UE2058—$3.50
- ☐ Series 14 (1952)   UE2106—$3.50
- ☐ Series 15 (1953)   UE2171—$3.50
- ☐ Series 16 (1954)   UE2200—$3.50

SWORD AND SORCERESS
Marion Zimmer Bradley, editor

- ☐ Book I   UE1928—$2.95
- ☐ Book II   UE2041—$2.95
- ☐ Book III   UE2141—$3.50
- ☐ Book IV   UE2210—$3.50

THE YEAR'S BEST FANTASY STORIES
Arthur W. Saha, editor

- ☐ Series 10   UE1963—$2.75
- ☐ Series 11   UE2097—$2.95
- ☐ Series 12   UE2163—$2.95

Write for free DAW catalog of hundreds of other titles.
(Prices slightly higher in Canada.)

NEW AMERICAN LIBRARY
P.O. Box 999, Bergenfield, New Jersey 07621

Please send me the DAW BOOKS I have checked above. I am enclosing $_____
(check or money order—no currency or C.O.D.'s). Please include the list price plus
$1.00 per order to cover handling costs. Prices and numbers are subject to change
without notice.

Name _____

Address _____

City _____ State _____ Zip _____
Please allow 4-6 weeks for delivery.

DAW

TANITH LEE

"Princess Royal of Heroic Fantasy"—The Village Voice

THE FLAT EARTH SERIES
- ☐ NIGHT'S MASTER   (UE2131—$3.50)
- ☐ DEATH'S MASTER   (UE2132—$3.50)
- ☐ DELUSION'S MASTER   (UE1932—$2.50)
- ☐ DELIRIUM'S MISTRESS   (UE2135—$3.95)
- ☐ NIGHT'S SORCERIES   (UE2194—$3.50)

THE BIRTHGRAVE TRILOGY
- ☐ THE BIRTHGRAVE   (UE2127—$3.95)
- ☐ VAZKOR, SON OF VAZKOR   (UE1972—$2.95)
- ☐ QUEST FOR THE WHITE WITCH (UE2167—$3.50)

OTHER TITLES
- ☐ DAYS OF GRASS   (UE2094—$3.50)
- ☐ DARK CASTLE, WHITE HORSE   (UE2113—$3.50)
- ☐ THE STORM LORD   (UE1867—$2.95)

ANTHOLOGIES
- ☐ RED AS BLOOD   (UE1790—$2.50)
- ☐ THE GORGON—AND OTHER BEASTLY TALES
                                      (UE2003—$2.95)

TRADE PAPERBACK EDITION
- ☐ THE SILVER METAL LOVER
    0-8099-5000-6
                                              ($7.95)

NEW AMERICAN LIBRARY
P.O. Box 999, Bergenfield, New Jersey 07621

Please send me the DAW BOOKS I have checked above. I am enclosing $_____
(check or money order—no currency or C.O.D.'s). Please include the list price plus
$1.00 per order to cover handling costs. Prices and numbers are subject to change
without notice.

Name _____

Address _____

City _____ State _____ Zip _____
Please allow 4-6 weeks for delivery.

DAW

MAGIC TALES FROM THE MASTERS OF FANTASY